"SF infused with a cosmopolitan and literary sensibility... accomplished and affecting."
Paul J. McAuley

"*Helix* is equal parts adventure, drama and wonder. Sometimes they work alone, providing a raw dose of science fiction. Other times, Brown uses them in concert to spin an irresistible blend that pulls the narrative along almost faster than you can keep up. However it's served, *Helix* is a delightful read and is an excellent reminder of why we read science fiction: it's fun!"
SF Signal

"Classic science-fiction components and a general reverence for science make this tale of intergalactic travel a worthy, occasionally awe-inspiring read... Brown's spectacular creativity creates a constantly compelling read... a memorable addition to the genre."
Kirkus Reviews

"*Helix* is essentially a romp—a gloriously old-fashioned slice of science fiction... What gives the novel a unique spin is its intertwining parallel plots. It's smart, fun, page-turning stuff, with an engaging cast and plenty of twists... A hugely entertaining read."
SFX Magazine

"The parallel plotting lends the novel much of its energy with Brown alternating his focus from one chapter to the next and often leaving each thread on a cliff-hanger. The other thing that Brown does

well is balance the big concepts with the character drama... Brown's prose is very readable... You'll have a good time with it."
Deathray Magazine

"Brown concentrates on stunning landscapes and in the way he conveys the conflicting points of view between races... No matter how familiar each character becomes, they continue to appear completely alien when viewed through the opposing set of eyes. Brown has a casual and unpretentious style and... the accessibility, the tenderness between characters and more importantly the scale of wonder involved are what makes this highly enjoyable escapism."
Interzone

"Eric Brown is a masterful storyteller. *Helix* is put together extraordinarily well, jumping between the POVs of Hendry and Ehrin, holding back on key bits of information and delaying inevitable moments with leaps of perspective timed precisely to make us want to read to the end. It's a fun read... the action is all worked through with great finesse... All the elements are here for something great: a massive construct, first contact with an alien species, an autocratic government... Eric Brown is often lauded as the next big thing in science fiction and you can see why..."
Strange Horizons

ALSO BY ERIC BROWN

XENOPATH

A BENGAL STATION NOVEL

ERIC BROWN

SOLARIS

First published 2009 by Solaris
an imprint of BL Publishing
Games Workshop Ltd
Willow Road
Nottingham
NG7 2WS
UK

www.solarisbooks.com

ISBN-13: 978 1 84416 743 2
ISBN-10: 1 84416 743 7

Designed & typeset by BL Publishing

Printed and bound in the US.

This novel is for Julian Flynn, Michael Harrington and John Moran.

ONE

MIND NOISE

Vaughan was refuelling *The Pride of Calcutta*, just in from Ganymede, when the call came through.

He crouched beneath the freighter's bulging belly, jacking fuel leads into the main tank. The stench of high-grade octane made him dizzy and the warm wind blowing in across the spaceport did nothing to stir the air beneath the ship.

It was six, and his shift was almost over for another day. He'd grab a beer or two at Nazruddin's before heading home.

When his handset chimed he assumed it was Sukara, wanting to know what time he'd be back. He smiled as he accessed the call. He never thought he'd be a slave to domestic bliss. Hell, how things had changed in just two years.

The face that stared out from the tiny screen on his wrist was not Sukara's. The woman was white, with a thin face, a peroxide blonde crew cut, and feral suspicion in her squinting gaze.

"Jeez, Vaughan. How long's it been?"

He recognised the high Sydney whine a fraction of a second before he put a name to the face.

"Kapinsky?" Reception was bad. He crouch-walked from under the belly of the ship and eased himself upright, his legs aching from the effort. The running lights of the *Calcutta* threw his shadow ahead of him as he walked across the deck towards the perimeter fence.

"Back from the dead, pal," Lin quipped. "How's yourself?"

"I'm okay. Fine. Never better."

"Christ, you know something? You sound as though you mean it. Am I talking to Jeff Vaughan here, Mr Cynical himself?"

"It's been four years, Kapinsky."

"But you're still at the 'port, still reading heads. So what's changed?"

He hesitated, wondering how much to tell her, and curious about why she'd called. He stared through the diamond mesh fencing, down to the moonlit scales on the Bay of Bengal a kilometre below, then looked back at Kapinsky's mug shot on his wrist-screen. "I'm still at the 'port, but I'm no longer reading."

She squinted out at him. "Come again? No longer reading? What, you trashed your pin?"

"It's a long story, Kapinsky."

"You sound as if you don't want to tell me."

"That's right." He had no desire to share his story—his new-found happiness—with someone as jaded as Lin Kapinsky.

"Okay, but listen. Reason I called. I need to see you."

"Ah... I'm busy right now."

"Listen, Pal. I'd be doing you a favour."

He almost said that that'd be a first: Kapinsky, doing someone a favour?

"Like what?"

"Like, I can offer you a job." She went on before he could register surprise, "So you no longer read. You got promoted upstairs, right? Admin. You pulling in, what? Five thousand baht a month?"

She had it so wrong. Two years ago, after he married Sukara and settled down, he'd needed a steady job for a while, something to tide him over for a few months. So he'd applied for menial work at his old employers, the spaceport authority, and found himself injecting octane into old class III interplanetary tubs. A few months had lasted over two years.

Five thousand baht a month? He was on less than half that, which hardly paid the rent on the coffin that passed for a two-person apartment on Level Ten.

Despite himself, his curiosity was piqued. "What job?" How was it that Kapinsky, wasted, washed-up, chora-addicted Lin Kapinsky, was in any position to offer him work?

"Not over the air, Vaughan. Can you skip work and meet me at seven?"

He was tempted to end the conversation there, but something stopped him. If Kapinsky thought he was holding down an admin job at five thou a month, and she could offer him more...

He nodded. "I might be able to do that."

"Good man. Look, I have an office on Level Two, outer edge."

He whistled. "You on the outer? What happened?"

"Later," she said. Her smile was monomolecular thin. "I'm in Myrabad district. Unit Seven on Gandhi Mall." She cut the connection.

He was left gripping the fence, staring at the blank screen and wondering if he'd dreamed the dialogue.

He returned to the *Calcutta*, finished the refuelling and drove his truck back to the garage, beetling between the big voidliners just in from the colony worlds.

He made a quick change from his grease-stained overalls and walked from the spaceport. The streets around the 'port were tributaries flowing with an ebb tide of humanity. Restaurant lights branded the tropical darkness. The scent of cooking spices, wafted on the warm night air, reminded him he hadn't eaten since noon. Half a kilometre ahead, Nazruddin's faulty, flickering neon promised ice-cold Blue Mountain beer. He was tempted, but he knew that one beer would turn in to three, and he'd be late meeting Kapinsky, and then late home... And Sukara, in her present condition, wasn't likely to be too forgiving.

He caught a dropchute to Level Two, crammed into the cage with a gaggle of near-naked, ash-coated sadhu mendicants. At times like this, he was grateful he no longer possessed tele-ability. He'd used an augmentation pin when reading, but even without it the background mind-mush of the press around him would have been an intolerable white noise.

Now he enjoyed absolute mind-silence. His thoughts were his own. The noise—the audible sound—of the creaking cage, the chanting mendicants, and giggling schoolchildren, he could ignore.

The cage opened and he spilled out onto a wide mall packed with citizens. Strip lighting illuminated the tunnel and Hindi holo-movie music blared from speakers placed strategically to leave no area unaffected.

His handset chimed again. This time it was Sukara. Her broad Thai face filled the screen, bisected by the knife wound that served only to make the two halves all the more beautiful.

"Jeff," she said.

"Su, you okay?"

"Just wanted to see your face." She looked glum. "Baby blues again."

Vaughan smiled. "I'll be home soon."

"When?" She sounded petulant. "I want you now."

He laughed. "Su, I'll be late. Another hour, say."

She scowled out at him. "Jeff... I've been alone all day, and now you—"

He hadn't planned to tell her about the job offer, but her tone prompted him. "Look, Su. Something's come up. You know you're always telling me to get a new job?"

She brightened. "You looking?"

"An old colleague contacted me today. There might be something. I'm meeting her now."

"What kind of job?"

"I'll tell you all about it when I get back, okay?"

She beamed. "Good luck, Jeff!"

He told her he loved her and cut the connection, then headed west towards the outer edge of Level Two.

He'd known Lin Kapinsky for a few years way back, when he'd worked as a telepath for 'port security. She'd been in his team for a year, reading the passengers on colony ships newly arrived on Earth. A model officer, she'd discharged her duty with efficiency, but Vaughan had never really warmed to her. Telepaths, as a breed, tended not to be the most rosily optimistic of people—but Kapinsky had turned cynicism into an art form. She had no friends, even among the usually close-knit coterie of fellow teleheads, and she'd gone through lovers as if trying to set a world record.

Misery loves company, was the old adage, and while Vaughan back then had been a miserable son of a bitch, he found Kapinsky's existential despair too familiar a reminder of his own cares and concerns.

He'd worked with her when he had to, and avoided her the rest of the time.

A couple of years before he quit 'port security, Kapinsky's addiction had got the better of her. All telepaths used chora—the drug kept the mind-noise tolerable—but Kapinsky had snorted the alien dust in brain-burning quantities. One shift she'd gone schizo aboard a ship, punching a VIP from Rigel II, and a few weeks later she tried to hang herself from one of the 'port loading gantries. An act of macabre symbolism, Vaughan had thought. Someone had cut her down, saved her life, and the last he'd heard she'd been committed to the state psychiatric ward on Level Fifteen.

And now here she was, arisen like a phoenix, and was offering him a job.

He found Gandhi Mall and paused outside the sliding steel door of Unit Seven.

He touched the broad lapel of his leather jacket, felt the reassuring bulge of the mind-shield where he'd stitched it years ago. The last thing he wanted was some snooping telepath rummaging around in his head.

The door slid aside without Vaughan's announcing himself.

He stepped into a bright reception area, equipped with a host of alien flora and a secretary in a sharp suit.

The man looked up from his screen. "You have an appointment with Ms Kapinsky?"

"Vaughan. I'm due to see Lin at seven."

"Right on through there," the man said.

Vaughan stepped through a second sliding door and found himself in a big office. More than just the acreage of floor-space indicated that Kapinsky had come up—in all senses of the word—in the world. Modern carvings, in real wood, adorned the corners of the room, and a vast floor-to-ceiling viewscreen looked out over the neon-lit waters of the Bay.

Vaughan tried not to appear impressed.

"Jeff, you look well."

Lin Kapinsky sat behind a vast desk. She, too, looked healthier than Vaughan recalled. He remembered her as being pale and anorexic, her expression forever haunted.

Now she was tanned and smiling, sporting a fashionable crew cut and outfitted in a smart cream suit. Her face was as sharp as ever, though, her steel-grey eyes almost silver, like eucalyptus leaves.

"Some place you have here," he said.

"Sit down. Still drink coffee as if it's going out of fashion?"

"Could do with a cup," he said, sitting in a swivel chair across the desk from her.

She was smiling at him, and he found that disconcerting. Lin had never smiled. She poured him a big cup of something that smelled authentically Brazilian and pushed it across the desk to him.

He sipped. Dammit, the stuff was authentic. He smiled, this time unable to hide the fact that he was impressed.

Lin leaned back in her chair, her thin lips pulled into a smile.

He looked around. "This place must set you back... what? Five grand a month?"

"This is Myrabad, Jeff. Select district. Try ten a month."

He nodded, staring through the viewscreen at a voidship coming in low over the sea. "So... what the hell are you doing that allows you to pay rent like that?"

"What I always did, Jeff. What I was good at."

"Reading?"

"What else?"

He shrugged. "When I heard about what happened after you left the 'port, the psych ward and all that... I assumed you'd had your implant removed."

Her cold grey eyes regarded him. "I did."

He nodded. "So you got rid of your implant, got sane... and then had it put back?"

If that was the case, then it didn't make much sense to Vaughan.

She stood and walked out from behind the desk. She was small, barely five foot tall, approaching fifty, but her new-found wealth had bought her the latest in body-couture and face-sculpting.

Vaughan contrasted Kapinsky's vanity with Sukara's refusal to waste money on having her scarred face fixed.

She stood with her back to him, staring through the viewscreen.

"Why do you think I asked you here?" she said.

He sipped his coffee. "I seem to recall something about a job."

She nodded, turned on a stiletto heel that endangered the thick pile carpet, and stared at him. He was profoundly grateful that he was carrying a mind-shield, then, as her gaze raked his crumpled trousers, scuffed leather jacket, and unshaven jawline.

She said, "I was always impressed with you, Jeff. You got the job done, and done well. You were accurate. You didn't moan like some whinging teleheads, but the pain was always in your eyes."

She moved to the corner of the desk, hitched herself onto it side-saddle and regarded him. "Then I heard about what happened a couple of years ago. You were involved in something big, some scam the then spaceport director was running. You got wise to it and blew the thing sky high."

Her précis was vague, suggesting that she didn't really know what had gone down back then. He intended to keep it that way.

"I did some investigating," Kapinsky went on, "found out you quit the 'port, nearly got yourself zeroed by a serial killer. But some Thai street-kid saved your skin and, happy ever after like in some fairy story, you married her."

He nodded. "Sounds something like what happened," he said, not liking the sneer in her tone.

"Tell me, Jeff. Why did you stop reading? It got too much, right?"

"I didn't intend to stop reading. I could live with it. I didn't like it, but I reckoned I'd done it for so long, why stop?"

"What happened?"

"The killer who nearly did for me... he ripped out my implant so he could read my suffering as I died. Only the street-kid, as you called her, Sukara, she shot him and got me to hospital."

Kapinsky narrowed her eyes. "And you elected not to have the implant replaced?"

Vaughan nodded. "When I came round, I experienced mind-silence. Absolute calm, serenity. No voices, no subliminal mind-noise. Bliss. How could I go back to reading, after that?" He shook his head and stared at her. "But you must've known what it was like, when you had your implant removed?"

She nodded. "Oh, I knew. And you're right. It was bliss."

"Yet you had it put back. You chose to return to what drove you mad?"

She was watching him, and he didn't like something in her expression, something calculating.

"Six months ago I opened an investigative agency," she said. "I started small, just me and a secretary, working from the seventh level. I did okay, kept in work. Then I hit lucky. I was hired to find the killer of the holo-star, Ravi Begum."

"I heard about it."

"His wife wasn't happy with how the police were handling the case. She hired me. Anyway, to cut a long story short, I got the killer way ahead of the cops."

"Good for you."

"Too right, Jeff. The Police Commissioner was impressed. On the strength of my work on the Begum case, he said he'd put work my way. And he has—so much work I can't handle it all myself."

Vaughan didn't care for the way this was heading. He smiled; spread his hands. "I drive a fuel tanker," he said. "Detective work isn't my line."

"No? Not even for a flat seven thousand baht a month, and a ten per cent bonus on every successful case?"

"You forget one thing, Lin—" he tapped the back of his head. "I'm no longer implanted."

She had the peculiar ability of flashing an ironic smile from nowhere, like a flick-knife. "And you've no desire to be, ever again?"

He pointed at her. "You've got it in one."

She sighed theatrically. "I was like that, Jeff, back when I was in the Level Fifteen bin. I had mindsilence, no more chattering voices, and I loved it."

"And?"

"And I met this guy, a friend of a friend. He worked for the United India Corporation. He was a telepath; only he wasn't equipped with the second-rate implants and augmentation-pins 'port security palmed off on us. He had the latest neo-cortical rig, just in from Rio."

Vaughan shrugged. "How did it differ from what we used?"

"In a few ways," Kapinsky said. "Like, it was more powerful. Amplified thoughts approximately fifty per cent more efficiently than our implants."

Vaughan winced. "I don't like the idea of that. So okay, you might be able to read more effectively—but what about when you take the pin out?"

"You don't. The pin is integral to the implant."

"But the mind-noise!" he protested.

That blade-thin smile again, laughing at him. "There's no mind-noise, Jeff. No subliminal white noise, no background hum to drive you schizo."

"How?"

She raised a forearm, indicating the handset that encompassed her wrist like a splint. She tapped a key on the set. "When I want to read, I simply turn the implant on from here. There. I'm reading." She cocked her head. "I'm picking up Lazlo's thoughts out there. The bastard's wondering if he stands a chance with me. Thinks I'm not bad, for a geriatric. You... you're shielded."

She stabbed the button, silencing her secretary's fantasies. "Enough of that."

Vaughan stared at her. "And now you're getting no mind-noise? Not the slightest hum?"

"Nothing. Nada. Silence." She slipped from the edge of the desk and reseated herself in the swivel chair, staring at him over laced fingers. "So once I read up about the latest implants, I decided I wanted one. I mean, the only line of work I knew was security, and who'd employ an ex-telehead? A deadhead?"

"Tell me about it."

"The Rio implants don't come cheap, Jeff. I had to pay nearly fifty thousand dollars for this gadget... but it allowed me to set up the agency, got me where I am today."

He watched her.

She said, "You know what I'm asking?"

He nodded. His gaze slid through the viewscreen. He watched the passing underbelly of a void-freighter rumble overhead, perhaps a hundred metres from the edge of the Station.

"And?" she pressed.

He made a decision. "I'm not interested, Lin. Thanks, but I can't do it."

"No mind-noise," she said. "You finish reading, turn off the implant, and silence."

He shook his head. "It's not that... I just don't want to read again, period. I don't want to get into heads I'd rather have nothing to do with."

"You'd rather bury your head in the sand, Jeff?"

"If that's what you want to call it."

"Know what I think?"

"What do you think?"

"I think," she said, "that you're so wrapped up in marital harmony, so in love, so happy with the tiny life you've managed to eke out with your cute Thai ex-call-girl, that you're frightened of reading again."

"Bullshit!"

"You're frightened of all the uncertainty out there. Frightened that it might make you question the certainty of everything you've got."

He was shaking his head in denial, but Kapinsky was clever.

Lately, he'd looked at his life, his happiness, circumscribed by so little—a woman he loved, the prospect of the baby—and he'd experienced an obscure feeling of guilt. He was so damned happy, and the world out there was such a cesspool, but he'd turned his back on it and satisfied himself with his small, personal world, Sukara and a few friends,

holo-movies and the occasional restaurant meal...
and thoughts of his unborn daughter.

Maybe Kapinsky was right.

The fact remained, he'd turned his back on the
old life, and he was happy. There was no way he
was going to sacrifice that.

Kapinsky said, "Seven thousand baht a month,
guaranteed, Jeff. Know what that'd get you? A two-
room apartment on the outer edge, Level Two, with a
couple of kay left over for bills and a good lifestyle."
She accosted him with her flick-knife smile. "Where
you living now, Jeff?"

He held her gaze. "Trat, Level Ten."

"Ten? Jesus Christ, Jeff. Level Ten? Come on, pal,
that's the pits. Don't tell me, Harijan beggars and
Tata factory workers, no?"

"I'm happy."

She let the silence stretch, watching him. "Something I haven't told you, Jeff. Think about this.
That seven thousand, that's basic. You know what
the cops are paying me, per successful case?"

"Surprise me."

"Twenty thousand baht. I get roughly six jobs a
month from the department, and my success rate is
running at five out of six right now. We'd work
cases together, and you'd get ten per cent of all
solved crimes. Work it out."

He nodded. "Some carrot. Ten thousand baht a
month?" His pulse, despite himself, quickened at
the thought.

"Ten kay on top of your seven basic. You could
live like a Brahmin, Jeff."

He was pulling in two thousand baht a month at the
moment, working long shifts refuelling at the 'port.

"One question," he said

"Sure. Fire away."

"Why me?"

"Because, Jeff, I know you. I know you're good. Dependable. And it looks to me, pal, like you could use the break."

"Lin Kapinsky, the altruist? Why does that sound phoney?"

She shrugged. "I'm no altruist. I work hard for number one. I get what I want. You'd be an asset to the agency." She stopped, regarding him. "Look, I've made my offer. Go home, to your tenth level dive among all the Indian dregs, talk it over with wifey, and see what she says to an upper level suite, okay?"

Vaughan stood and moved to the door. "Thanks for calling me, Lin. Sorry to have wasted your time."

Her ironic smile was out again, sharpening itself on his denial, as he stepped through the door with a feeling of relief.

He walked the relatively uncongested corridors to the nearest dropchute station, then descended to Level Ten. He caught a shuttle into the very heart of the Station, the train passing street after street thronged with a continually moving press of humanity. Twenty-five million citizens lived on Bengal Station, more than a million to a level, swarming like ants in a formicary.

The shuttle was packed with factory workers, tiny Indians rocking with the motion of the carriage, tired after a long day's shift. Vaughan thought of the mind-noise he'd be picking up from them, if he were still implanted.

But an implant that could be switched off, together with an opportunity to earn seventeen thousand baht a month?

His apartment was situated down a dark corridor patrolled by beggars and the halt and lame waiting to be admitted to the nearby hospital. Vaughan ran the gauntlet of proffered hands—and a few ill-carpentered stumps—before making it home.

Home... The amazing thing was that, over the year they'd lived here, they had made it home, or rather Sukara had. She'd bought gaily coloured Thai wall hangings and, in pride of place on the far wall, a massive holo-scene. It showed a Thai beach: a stretch of sand and a lapis lazuli lagoon, with people strolling along the sands. The holo was randomly programmed with near infinite variation. It gave the cubby-hole the illusion of space; he felt he could step through the wall and onto the sun-drenched island.

Sukara was in the kitchen, fixing coffee, when he slipped in and embraced her, his hands finding the prominent bulge of her belly. As if in response, his daughter-to-be turned, sending a ripple across the distended skin.

Sukara laughed and turned to kiss him.

"Love you," he whispered into her hair. "Done much?"

"Paid bills. Seen my health worker. Everything A-okay, Jeff."

She carried two mugs of South Indian coffee into the cramped lounge and sat beside him on the settee. She lodged her bare feet on his thighs and sipped her coffee, staring at him with her massive eyes over the rim.

He could sense the unspoken question on her hidden lips.

He looked around the room. It was grim. Despite Su's best efforts—or perhaps because of them—the basic run-down state of the place was apparent: cracks in the plastic walls, a fungal stain on the ceiling. Every time the shuttle drew into the station a hundred metres away, the room rattled like the command module of a phasing voidship. Between times, the Choudris next door kept up a running commentary on the state of their disintegrating marriage.

Sukara said, "You?"

"Highlight of the day was filling a ship in from Vega," he smiled.

"So... nothing came of the job offer?"

He hesitated. She'd understand, if he explained to her. She wasn't materialistic. She was stoic, and never complained. She had him, and the baby, which was more than she'd ever had before.

But, he told himself, she could have a hell of a lot more.

"Su, I've been offered a job bringing in around seventeen thousand a month. It's mine if I say yes."

She watched him, silent, blowing on her coffee. At last she said, "But you don't want the job, right?"

"Hell... It'd mean being implanted, Su. I'd be reading again, working for an investigative agency."

She lowered her cup. "I don't want you to live with all that noise," she said, "not even for seventeen thousand a month."

"That's just it," he said. "There'd be no mind-noise." He told her about the latest Rio implants.

A long silence stretched when he'd finished speaking. Sukara was nodding slowly, saying nothing. He felt a sudden, almost overwhelming surge of love for her, this woman who loved him, who put no pressure on him to do what he didn't want to do. She would reconcile herself to an existence of near poverty, shut out thoughts of a life topside, all for him.

How could he deny her a little luxury, merely because he feared reading corrupt and jaded minds again?

He said, "So, there'd be no mind-noise. Hey presto, I'd just switch off the implant, come home, forget the case I'm working on."

She was staring at him, hardly daring to smile. "You mean you're going to...?"

"What do you think?"

"Jeff!" She put her coffee aside and pressed her palms to her cheeks. "Seventeen thousand baht a month?"

"We'd get a place on Level One or Two. You'd be able to take Li for walks in Himachal Park."

"We'd be able to leave this place!"

He smiled at her glee. "So... should I go for it?"

She stared at him. "Jeff, can you take all that pain again, reading all those minds?"

He smiled. "Sure I can."

She looked at him, wide-eyed.

He hugged her. "Get changed," he said. "Let's go out for a meal. Somewhere exclusive and expensive where we haven't been before."

She clapped her hands. "Ruen Thai, Level One?"

"Why not?" He watched her dance from the lounge and into the bedroom, and smiled as she began singing a Thai folk song.

He lifted his handset and traced Kapinsky's code from her call to him earlier that day.

Seconds later her thin face peered out. "Jeff? Been thinking things over?"

He nodded. "Long and hard." He considered explaining himself, telling her that he was doing it for Su, as if to excuse his climb-down. But he couldn't bring himself to do that. He was big enough to let Kapinsky make her own guesses about his motivations.

"When do I start?" he said.

"Good man," Kapinsky said, and the weapon of her smile hit him, and twisted.

TWO

GOODBYE LEVEL TWENTY

Pham had two burning ambitions. The first was to have a proper family—to have a loving mother and father, and maybe even a brother or sister. The second was to see real daylight for the first time in her life.

Well, her first ambition was more of a dream. She knew she'd never have a real family ever again. She was a seven-year-old girl with no money and no education, so who would want her? Her second ambition, to see the genuine light of day, was not that difficult to achieve.

In fact, she was setting out today on a big adventure to see the sun and the upper levels and all the marvellous things she'd heard about up there.

She sat on her bunk and sorted through her few possessions. She had a plastic comic book, a map-book of Bengal Station, a blanket, a carved wooden Buddha, a comb, a new tablet of soap in a plastic box, a change of clothes, and a creased pix of her mum and dad.

Her most treasured possession was a teddy bear backpack, into which she placed all her belongings one by one. When she got to the pix, she held it in her hand and looked down at the strangers who stared out at her. She could recall very little of them, her mother holding her after a fall, her father drinking beer and shouting at the holo-screen in their Eighteenth level apartment. Pham had been four when they died in a dropchute accident. She didn't like to think of that day, when a cop explained to her what had happened, and she had thought of her mother and father, falling and falling and knowing that they were going to die...

She had lived on the streets for a month before meeting a bunch of kids who said they had good jobs working in a factory on Level Twenty, and that the factory owner was always looking for more workers.

Pham didn't like the sound of a factory on the bottom level, but she was hungry. She'd eaten only a stale chapatti and a rotten apple in two days.

So she had found herself being led into a big, steamy room full of clanking machinery and sweating boys and girls in underpants and nothing else.

A fat man called R.J. Prakesh sat behind his desk and questioned her, and then with a smile asked her if she would like to work for him.

Pham had said yes, if he would feed her.

Laughing, he had shown her to her very own bunk, and then the machine press she would be working on with two other kids, taking eight hour shifts around the clock. After that she'd eaten a big meal of dhal and rice, then slept in her bunk, and started work on the big machine at midnight.

Pham had been in the factory on Level Twenty for three years now, and today was her very last day.

In some ways she would be sorry to be leaving the factory. Mr Prakesh was a good man who looked after all his kids and fed them well, and she had made some good friends here. But she'd seen holo-movies about the Station, the upper deck with all the open spaces and big buildings and air-cars and everything else. She had saved a few baht over the years—enough to buy food for a week or so, until she found work on the top level—and she was getting sick of the hard work and the constant hacking cough which her friends told her was because they were inhaling tiny bits of plastic which floated in the air of the factory.

She wanted to get out, experience the world, and have an adventure.

She looked at the poster of Petra Shelenkov, her favourite skyball player, and wondered whether to take it. There would be other posters she could buy when she reached the top: her friends could have this one, when they realised that she wasn't coming back.

She looked around the quiet dormitory, at the bundled, sleeping figures of the other kids in their bunks, and found it hard to believe that she was leaving.

From the pocket of her shorts she pulled a note she'd painstakingly written earlier, and left it on her pillow for Mr Prakesh.

Then she stood up, slung her backpack over her shoulder, crept through the dorm and pulled open the big door.

The corridor was quiet. She moved to the exit of the factory, tapped in the exit code and slipped through the door, emerging into a crowded corridor as wide as a city street and just as busy with rickshaws and crowds of people and shambling cows.

It was strange, but because she was leaving all this for ever, it was as if she were experiencing it for the first time. The press of people, the constant bustling movement, the noise—music and cries and rickshaw bells and the growl of electric motors that illegally lighted some of the makeshift food-stalls along the street.

She pushed into the crowd, her tiny size giving her the right to push and elbow her way through the press of bodies, earning not reprimands for her audacity but smiles.

Pham had never been higher than Level Eighteen, and that had been as crowded as down here. She had seen the sky and open spaces on holo-movies, but she wondered what it would be like in real life. What would it be like to look up and see nothing but never-ending blue sky? What would it be like to be able to run across a park without bumping into people? She couldn't imagine it. It couldn't be real. The thought that soon she would be experiencing all this filled her with excitement.

She came to the 'chute station and barged her way inside. The cage door clanked shut and she found herself standing in a forest of bare brown legs, the silk of baggy kameez, flowing saris, and the occasional business suit. The cage rose with a jolt, and an indicator beside the door flashed the levels as they arrived at them. A few people pushed their way out on Level Nineteen, and their places were taken by even more people squeezing into the cage. They ascended. Level Eighteen came and went, and

Pham found herself rising into new and alien territory. Every time the cage door slid open, she peered out, eager to see new sights, hear new sounds. Each level above Eighteen seemed bigger and brighter and less impoverished than those she knew.

The 'chute terminated at Level Fifteen. She was forced to get out, consult her map-book, and make her way to another 'chute station a kilometre away. Like this, in a series of steps, she made her way up the Station and eventually, two hours after setting out, she was riding in a cage towards the top level. She was surrounded by rich people in smart new clothes, businesswomen, and handsome men talking into handsets.

Excitement fluttered like something living in her chest.

Ten minutes later she stepped from the upchute cage into the amazingly fresh air and bright sunlight of the upper deck.

She stood rooted to the spot. She could only stare about her in awe. She felt tears stinging her eyes. She was buffeted from behind by the passengers leaving the upchute cage. She pushed her way through the crowd and hurried along the sidewalk until she came to...

Well, she knew what it was because she'd seen it—or one like it—on holo-vision. It was called a park, and the green stuff was grass, and it was alive, like some of the plants she'd seen down below.

And amazingly, the open space was not crowded. People walked across the park, and rich kids played with toys she'd never seen before, but every metre of the grass wasn't crowded with noisy citizens.

Her chest felt as if it were filled with bubbles like a bottle of pop. She stepped off the sidewalk and trod on the grass. Beneath her thongs, the grass was soft, spongy. She kicked off her right thong and, warily, placed her foot on the grass—then withdrew it quickly. The grass tickled her!

She replaced her thong and looked around. Not far away, on the edge of the grass, was a bench. She hurried across to it and sat down, amazed that she had the seat to herself. On Level Twenty, she would have been crushed by other people, until she submitted and gave up her seat.

She stared about her, open-mouthed. Far, far away was a line of buildings, great towering needles. She turned. They were all around, filling the horizon with long, piled up houses where people lived and worked.

Then, remembering, she looked up, and gasped with wonder.

The sky was blue and it was hard to tell where it began and where it ended. It seemed to go on forever. The only things in the sky were clouds—and it was hard to tell how big they were: were they the size of a feather, close to her, or great white sheets, far away?—and air-cars zooming along red and blue lanes that criss-crossed the sky like a child's crazy pattern.

Pham knew, suddenly, that she had done the right thing.

Confident, full of hope for her new future, she left the park bench to explore the upper deck.

"You're new here."

Pham turned quickly. She had been staring into the window of Patel's Sweet Centre, at the trays piled with pyramids of gulab jamons, idli, and a hundred other sweets, wondering whether to treat herself, when the voice sounded loud in her ear.

The boy was taller than her, perhaps ten years old. He was a Muslim with a white lace skullcap and only one arm. The stump of his left arm poked from his T-shirt like a nub of dough.

She was immediately defensive. "So?"

"So... it isn't often we see new kids up here." He spoke Hindi with bits of Thai here and there. He squinted at her. "Where you from?"

She stared back. "Where are you from?"

"I asked first."

"If I tell you where I'm from, you tell me where you're from, okay?"

He nodded. "Ah-cha."

"I'm from Level Twenty," Pham told him with something like pride in her voice. "It's my first time on the upper deck."

The boy stared at her. "Level Twenty?" he gasped. "And you've never been up here before?" He seemed to find that hard to believe.

Pham nodded. "I came all the way up on my own. I'd had enough of life down there."

The boy was shaking his head. "All the way by yourself. What did you do on Level Twenty? You were a beggar, right?"

She pulled a disgusted face. "A beggar? Do I look like beggar? I worked in a factory, operating a Siemman's Nylon Extrusion Press."

"You had a job, and you left it to come up here?" He obviously thought her mad.

"I wanted to see the world," she told him. "Anyway, I've told you where I came from. Where are you from?"

He puffed his skinny chest. "I live on a spaceship between Levels Eleven and Twelve."

Pham wished that she hadn't told the boy the truth about herself, because he was obviously lying to her.

"A spaceship?" she scoffed. "I might be from Level Twenty, but I wasn't born yesterday."

The boy laughed. "No, really. Many years ago, when Level Eleven was the upper deck, this spaceship crash-landed, ah-cha? Rather than move it, they built around it. And it's still there, owned by Dr Rao."

The way he said the doctor's name made Pham think that she should have heard of him. "Who's Dr Rao?" she asked.

"Don't you know anything? Dr Rao is a very famous man on Bengal Station. He is a doctor with a Big Heart. I work for him."

Pham cocked her head and regarded the boy dubiously. His lies were getting bigger and bigger. "So what are you," she asked, "a junior doctor?"

He didn't understand her humour. "Why do you think I'm a doctor?"

"Forget it. So, what do you do?"

He grinned. "I beg. This is my patch, all the way from Nazruddin's to Patel's. I give half the money I make to Dr Rao."

She said, "Haven't you ever had a proper job?"

He shook his head, matter-of-factly. "Who needs a proper job when I can beg?"

She wanted to ask him what he would do when he grew up. Would he still beg on the streets then?

He was watching her closely. "How long are you staying up here?"

She shrugged, casual. "Oh, forever, I think. I like it better than down there. More space, more to see. I'll get a job, rent an apartment, go up in the world."

He was trying not to laugh. "But you're only... what? Six?"

"I'm seven," she said.

"So you're seven. And you think you'll get work, just like that? And an apartment?"

"Why not? I can work hard and save money."

He was shaking his head. "Things are hard up here," he said. "It isn't like in the movies. Kids can't get good jobs, only begging." He paused, thinking, then said, "Where will you sleep tonight?"

She'd already decided that rather than spend money on a hotel room, she would sleep in a park on Level Two. "Ketsuwan Park," she told him.

He was shaking his head like a wise old man. "Dangerous. Bad men go to the parks, looking for kids."

She peered at him through her fringe. "They do?"

"Murder them for baht, sometimes do other things. Look," he went on, "why don't you come with me? I'll show you the ship, introduce you to Dr Rao. He'll let you stay for a couple of nights."

"He won't try to make me beg for him?" she asked.

The boy looked away, shrugging. "Well, he might ask. But you can always say you've got a job."

"I don't know..."

"So come with me and look at the ship, ah-cha? It really is amazing."

She still didn't believe him, but she nodded anyway.

"Great!" He held out his right hand. "I'm Abdul."

"Pham," she told him, shaking his hand very formally and laughing. Abdul might be a big liar, but there was something about him which she liked.

"Follow me! We'll cut across the upper deck and I'll show you a few things on the way!"

He scooted into the crowd, pushing aside bodies, and Pham gave chase.

They crossed the crowded street and came to a crossroads, and Pham found herself holding Abdul's hand, frightened of losing him in the crush.

"Tell you what," he shouted in her ear as an air-car screamed low overhead. "We'll go to Kandalay by train. We'll see the spaceport then. You ever seen the spaceport?"

"No." She shook her head. "Only on holo-vision. Where's Kandalay?"

"Central Station. There's a big amusement park there, only it's closed down now. From Kandalay we'll take a ladder right down to the spaceship."

The spaceship, again. He really was trying to make her believe that he lived in a crash-landed spaceship!

He dragged her across the street towards the Chandi Road railway station and bought two tickets at the kiosk. A minute later Pham found herself sucked aboard a carriage with what seemed like a million other citizens.

Abdul pulled her along the corridor to a window. They pressed their faces against the glass and stared out as the train pulled from the station.

The sun was going down, making a big red sky in the west. "Look!" Abdul cried with excitement.

Pham gasped. A massive voidliner was coming in over the sea, a dark shape against the sunset, its lighted viewscreens showing the crew going about their business inside. Pham wondered what it must be like to be a spacer, to see all the wonderful alien worlds out there.

The train rattled past the spaceport, and Pham stared down across the apron at the dozens of ships lined up in neat rows. They were all shapes and sizes and colours, and Pham decided that when she earned her first wage on the upper level she would find a shop that sold model spaceships and buy one.

The train pulled away from the spaceport and passed a massive park, with acres and acres of grass and big trees, and families walking back and forth in the twilight. Pham saw a girl of about her age, holding hands with her mother and father, and she felt a moment of sadness and a swift stab of jealousy.

"Himachal Park," Abdul was saying. "It's the biggest park on the Station. Two square kilometres!"

Pham just nodded.

"Are you okay?" Abdul looked at her, concerned.

"I'm fine. Do you really live on a spaceship?"

Abdul slapped his cheek. "I swear, Pham! You'll see... Okay, we get off at the next stop."

They squirmed their way through the packed bodies as the train slowed at Kandalay. Abdul took her hand again, and Pham felt pleased and safe as he tugged her off the train, along the platform and out into a noisy street.

It was dark now, and the street was alight with a thousand signs advertising shops and restaurants.

The sidewalk was crowded with food-stalls. Pham saw one selling idli. She bought two big sticky lattices and passed one to Abdul, earning a big grin of thanks.

The only trouble now was that Abdul didn't have a free hand to hold on to Pham, so she had to be extra careful as she followed him across the busy street and down a dark alleyway.

They came to a high tattered polycarbon wall, covered with peeling posters of holo-movie stars and skyball players.

Abdul ducked through a loose flap in the wall, and Pham bent down and pushed her way through after him, then stood up and stared about her in wonder.

She had never seen anything like it in her life, not even in the holo-movies.

She was surrounded by a hundred rides and stalls and things that she couldn't even describe—massive wheels with seats all around them, slides with rocket ships ready for take-off, oval shapes like little fliers hanging by wires from tall frames. Okay, so some of the attractions were old and faded, and some had been ripped apart—and none were working—but, even so, Pham could imagine how wonderful it must have been, and walking through the amusement park even now was a magical experience.

"My favourite is the ghost train," Abdul said. "Have you ever seen one?"

She shook her head. "A train that's really a ghost?" she asked, confused.

Abdul laughed. "No! Come on, I'll show you. The cars don't work anymore, but we can still walk through it."

He'd finished his idli now, and he grabbed her hand with sticky fingers and dragged her through the faded glory of the park.

Five minutes later they came to an open area surrounded by tumbledown food kiosks, with the ghost train at one end and a starship ride at the other.

They hurried across the concourse and stared up at the façade of the ghost train. It was the shape of a castle, covered with paintings of ghosts and ghouls, vampire bats and zombies. There were two openings, where the little cars went in and came out, and these openings were the mouths of screaming banshees.

Abdul ran up a short flight of steps, pulling Pham after him. She dragged him back as he made to enter the first screaming mouth. It was dark in there, and she could see something green and luminous and scary lurking just inside.

"I'm not sure..."

He turned and stared at her. "Are you scared?"

"No. It's just that... I thought you were taking me to see the starship?"

"You *are* scared! Look, there's nothing to be frightened about. They're just mechanical monsters. And you'll be with me. I won't let anything hurt you."

That persuaded her. She felt comfortable with Abdul. Nothing would go wrong while she was with him. All this was his world, the upper deck, and if she stuck close to him she would be fine.

But even so, as she timorously stepped into the dark maw of the ghoul's slavering mouth, she felt her tummy flutter with fear. She grabbed Abdul's hand with both of hers and squeezed.

Something green was dangling from the ceiling: it was a hanged man, who'd been there too long. His flesh was rotten and his eyeballs had fallen out.

"Yech!" Pham said, shivering and pressing close to Abdul.

They hurried past the hanged man. They were walking between two rails where the car would have run, years ago. It took them further into the make-believe castle, leaving behind the little light that spilled through the mouth-shaped entrance. Pham could feel the hairs on the back of her neck bristling in fear, and she wanted to scream out loud and run back the way she had come.

She did scream when something leapt out of the darkness and yelled in her face. It was a disembodied head, blood spilling from its open mouth.

She yelled at the top of her lungs and almost jumped into Abdul's arms.

"It's okay!" he laughed. "It's only a hologram."

She knew that, but somehow it didn't make the experience any the less frightening.

Next, a ghostly laugh crept up on them and Pham felt fingers brush the back of her head. She turned, but couldn't see anything. When she faced forward again, a vampire bat was flying straight at them. This time, even Abdul yelled out and ducked.

For what seemed like an hour, though it was probably only minutes, Pham gripped Abdul's hand, squeezed her eyes tight shut and hurried around the rest of the castle. She heard all kinds of horrible noises, and felt bony hands plucking at her clothing, but at least she couldn't see anything now.

"There," Abdul said. "What did you think of that?"

She opened her eyes. They were standing just inside the exit. Outside was the familiar, reassuring park. Pham wanted nothing more than to leave the ghost train and continue their journey to the starship—if it existed.

In a small voice, she said, "I didn't like it."

Abdul smiled at her, and she liked him for what he said then. "It is scary, isn't it? Even though you know it's all machinery, it's still frightening."

He was about to duck out of the open mouth when he stopped suddenly and pulled back into the shadows.

"What?" Pham said, her heart beating fast with new alarm.

"Shhh. There's someone out there."

Pham peered past him. At first she didn't see anyone. Then, on the other side of the concourse, she saw a man in a black suit walk straight towards the ghost train.

They ducked and drew back. "Maybe it's the owner of the park," Pham whispered.

Abdul was silent. He found Pham's hand and squeezed.

The man paced across to the ghost train, then stopped and turned. He glanced at his watch, then looked around the concourse.

Pham felt relieved. He hadn't seen them. He hadn't come to arrest them for trespassing.

The man walked back and forth, away from the ghost train, then towards it, then away again.

Abdul leaned towards Pham and whispered into her ear, "When he turns and walks away again, follow me, ah-cha? Down the side alley there's a toilet block. In the floor is a hatch—it leads to the level below this one."

"Ah-cha," Pham replied, her eyes on the man. He was walking towards them. She felt Abdul tense beside her as the man arrived at the ghost train, paused and turned.

Quickly, so quick that Pham was left behind, Abdul ran from the mouth of the ghost train, jumped down the steps and turned left and out of sight. Startled, Pham made to follow him—then stopped.

The man hadn't walked as far away this time. He turned and walked back towards where Pham was cowering. Okay, so when he turned away again, then she would jump down and follow her new friend.

Except, this time when the man arrived at the ghost train, he turned and stood right at the bottom of the steps, so that there was no way for Pham to get past him.

Surely he wouldn't stand there forever?

From time to time he looked at his watch. Maybe he was meeting someone, and when they arrived they would leave and let Pham escape.

A minute later the man looked up, across the concourse, and started walking away from the ghost train. Perhaps he'd seen the person he was due to meet?

What happened next was so sudden and horrific that Pham didn't have time to scream. It was so much more frightening than anything she had experienced in the ghost train that it made her blood turn cold and sent her rigid with shock.

A blinding blue light shot across the concourse and hit the man in the chest. The light wavered a little, which was enough for it to carve its way through the man's torso, cutting off his arms and his head. He seemed to fall apart in slow motion as Pham watched, and then something happened which she could not explain at the time, and which changed her life forever.

A fraction of a second after the laser sliced the man into pieces, a white light seemed to bounce from his head and streak towards Pham. Before she could move, it hit her full in the face, knocking her backwards. She cried out and scrambled to her feet, feeling her face with her fingers. She expected to touch burned flesh, but oddly her face seemed okay.

Had the laser bounced off the man and hit her, weakened, so that it hadn't sliced her up?

She realised then that there was a killer out there, and she knew she had to get away. She quickly jumped from the open mouth, tapped down the steps, and raced along the alley between the attractions. Ahead she saw the toilet block that Abdul had told her about. She hauled open the door and dived inside. Thankfully Abdul had left the hatch in the floor propped open. She was about to squirm through it, hopefully into Abdul's arms, when something exploded behind her and a laser shafted through the door above her head and drilled a neat hole through the far wall.

So the killer had seen her escaping, and was chasing her...

She dived through the hatch and hauled it shut after her. She found herself in a narrow shaft and scrambled down the rungs of a ladder.

Seconds later she emerged onto a lighted catwalk high above a busy tunnel on the second level. Above her, she heard the hatch scrape open, then the sound of boots on metal rungs.

She fled. Further along the catwalk was a ladder that descended to the corridor. She reached it in seconds, slid down the ladder and slipped into the crowd. She squirmed through the bodies, pausing only once to look over her shoulder at the catwalk. She made out the bulky figure of man in a technician's overalls drop onto the catwalk and look up and down the length of the tunnel.

Then she was on her way again, turning down corridor after corridor on a crazy zigzag course across Level Two. She wished that Abdul was with her, but at the same time she was proud that she had managed to escape all by herself.

Perhaps half an hour later she came to a big park surrounded by tall trees. She looked at her mapbook and found to her delight and surprise that this was Ketsuwan Park.

She bought a plate of masala and pakora from a kiosk just inside the western gate of the park, then found a bench and sat down and ate. She was famished, and minutes later she had wolfed down the meal and was considering what had happened in the amusement park.

She hugged her bare legs and stared across the grass. The lighting was low here, to simulate the darkness outside. She could see street-kids huddling in the bushes all around, and sleeping on the park benches.

She pulled her blanket from her backpack and arranged it on the bench, then lay down and stared up into the amazingly complex arrangement of a tree's branches high overhead.

She had seen someone murdered. One second they had been alive, and the next someone had killed him. Then the killer must have seen her jump down and run, and maybe the killer thought that she'd seen him, and decided that she must die too.

But the white light that had hit her in the face?

She fingered her snub nose and high cheekbones and her forehead under her fringe. They felt fine, no burns or cuts or anything.

She had a headache, but that might have been from all the excitement of the past hour.

She snuggled down into the blanket and closed her eyes. She thought about Abdul, and wished he was still with her.

Minutes later she heard a voice in her head.

Pham, it said, *do not be frightened. I can help you.*

THREE

THE CUT

Vaughan awoke to dazzling sunlight and sat up, hospital linen cool to his touch. The last time he'd come awake to the warmth of the rising sun... It'd been two years ago, again in hospital, just after Osborne had tried to kill him and Sukara had saved his life.

Only then did he open his eyes fully and make out Sukara, sitting beside the bed, her outline dark against the sun's glare. She was gripping his hand.

"Su," he whispered.

"How do you feel?"

"Great. Tired." He'd had the operation, then? To say he'd undergone intrusive brain surgery, he felt well. Not even a headache. He reached up, felt around the base of his skull. He could feel the bulge of the implant beneath his skin.

He was implanted. He was telepathic again. But the world was mind-silent.

Sukara leaned forward and kissed him.

He lost consciousness and slept.

The next time he woke, a doctor or technician was tinkering with his handset, presumably reprogramming it in order to control the function of his occipital implant.

He closed his eyes and dozed.

Then Kapinsky was in the room with him. This time, the tiredness had gone; he felt bright, alert. He sat up.

"How long—?"

"You had the cut yesterday," Kapinsky said. "Everything went well. I had techs check the implant—it's doing fine. Your handset's been boosted." She laid a pin in a case on his bedside table. "This'll fill you in on your handset's new functions."

He raised a hand to his head and felt stubble, then recalled that he'd been shaved before the cut.

Kapinsky was standing beside the window, looking out over a sloping greensward. She turned and said, "You're going home today. I'll be in contact in the morning, fill you in on the cases we'll be working on."

He nodded. "Great."

She smiled. "It's good to have you on board, Jeff."

"Thanks." He tried to work out how he felt about the new life that awaited him. He concentrated on how Su's life would be changed for the better, and tried to disregard the thought of mind-reading again.

Later that afternoon, Su waddled in, holding her bump and smiling. He was up and dressed and ready to leave.

"Guess what, Jeff?" Her eyes were dancing with the delight of good news.

"Surprise me."

"I've been doing some apartment hunting while you've been recovering. I've been given tours of some real palaces. You wouldn't believe it."

"Found anything?" He packed his bag, watching her. She was dressed in baggy maternity trousers and one of his old shirts.

She beamed. "Two places lined up. Both west side, with sea views. One on Level Three, in Song Mah. Four rooms, five kay a month."

"Expensive." He whistled. "But exclusive."

"The other's on Level Two, Chittapuram."

"Which do you like better?"

She rocked her head, lips pursed. "Maybe the Level Two. It's cheaper, just four kay a month. Three big rooms like you wouldn't believe. I mean, the kitchen alone is bigger than our old place."

"Lead the way," he said.

They left the hospital and dropped to Level Two, then took a short walk through wide, airy corridors towards Chittapuram. Sukara's delightful excitement at their relocation dispelled his apprehension. She gripped his hand and chattered like a child.

Five minutes later they reached the apartment.

She proudly swiped the lock and swung open the door, almost dragging him inside. "Well, what do you think, Jeff?"

The first thing that struck him was the cascade of sunlight that slanted in through the west-facing wall-to-ceiling viewscreen. He gazed around the lounge, open-mouthed. It was vast, perhaps ten metres long by five, plush cream carpet, sunken sofas, a holo-unit in the corner. The sheer view over the sea increased the apparent area of the room to agoraphobic-inducing proportions.

She took his hand and tugged him into a bedroom perhaps half the size, and then a small bedroom. Both had en suite bathrooms. "This one is for Li," Sukara pronounced.

Finally she showed him the kitchen. "I'll be able to create feasts here, Jeff. Just look at all the space!"

They returned to the lounge. "What do you think?"

"This is the one. I don't even want to see the other." He held her. "Well done."

She lodged her hands on the jut of her belly. "We'll be happy here, won't we?" she said, tears in her eyes.

He kissed her forehead, where the scar began. "We'll be ecstatic," he said.

For the next hour Su was on her handset, arranging the lease of the apartment and hiring a company to move their possessions from Level Ten. She had packed their few belongings yesterday, and they would be delivered first thing in the morning.

Vaughan sat in a sunken sofa, staring out through the viewscreen. They were not far from the 'port here—and close to Kapinsky's office, too—and he found the sight of the voidships, coming and going like so many bees at a hive, reassuring. Below, a variety of boats from lowly fishing dhows to ocean-going hydrofoils cut feathered wakes across the blue expanse of the sea.

While Sukara was still busy on her handset, he slipped a penknife from the pocket of his jacket, laid the jacket over his knees, and sliced at the lapel.

He withdrew the silver oval of the mind-shield, turning it in his palm.

Sukara finished and joined him.

"What's that?"

"A present, from me to you." He handed her the shield.

"Great. It's what I've always wanted. But what is it?"

He told her.

She stuck out her bottom lip and nodded, staring at the silver oval in her hand.

After due consideration, she passed it back to him. "I don't need it, Jeff. I've got no secrets from you. When I married you, I told you everything. The good and the bad. Everything. If you read my mind, then that's fine by me."

He smiled at her, wondering if she were offended.

He had never read Sukara, even when he had tele-ability two years ago. He'd picked up, when not scanning, the background miasma of her thoughts, and he knew from these that she was a good person.

But the notion of invading her private thoughts now disturbed him. For all she said that she had no secrets, what she could not apprehend was that everyone, often unbeknown to themselves, har-boured subconscious desires and longings, prejudices and petty jealousies, that no one should pry upon, not even loving husbands.

His relationship with Sukara was damned near perfect. He feared reading things deep in her mind that might spoil that.

He passed the shield back to her. "Su, the chances are that I'll never read you—I can switch the implant off—but other telepaths might. For security reasons, you'd better keep it. If I told you about a case, and a rival telepath scanned you... See what I mean?"

She nodded, then slipped the shield into her shirt pocket and looked around the lounge like a child on Christmas day.

As the sun set over distant India in a blazing panoply of saffron banners, Sukara said she'd treat him to a takeaway. She'd scouted out a couple of interesting Rajastani restaurants in the area. She left the apartment promising to return with a feast.

Vaughan sat in the silence of the lounge, watching the sun go down, then stood and approached the viewscreen.

A narrow balcony ran the length of the apartment, which he had failed to notice earlier. It was accessible from the kitchen. He slid aside the glass partition and stepped out.

The breeze was warm, spice laden. He stood and gripped the rail, listening to the muted roar of the arriving voidliners, the distant drift of sitar music.

He examined his handset, then looked along the length of the balcony. He was perhaps ten metres from the neighbouring apartments—sufficiently distant not to pick up the thoughts of their inhabitants, if he were to activate his implant.

He wondered what the background mind-noise might be like, when the implant was in operation.

Tentatively, fearing the consequences but knowing that he would have to take the plunge sooner or later, he entered the start-up code.

A familiar warmth surged through his head, followed by the even more familiar medley of a million minds. Familiar, he realised, but different, muted.

Whereas his old implant would have amplified the emanations of surrounding minds to a clamouring white noise, this rig kept the noise at a manageable level, a background hum that he could tolerate.

He experimented, probed. Two years ago, he had needed a drug called chora to make this mind-noise manageable at all times; now, even in scan mode, he could live with it.

He concentrated, and it was as if the miasma of anonymous feelings and emotions that swirled around him was a piece of music, a symphony in which various individual thoughts were the instruments, each one different, unique, some blaring, a surge of anger here, jealousy there; some understated, a strand of contentment from someone strolling in the park overhead, a feeling of love emanating from the corridor.

Then someone, obviously in the neighbouring apartment, came within scan range, and their thoughts cried out at him.

They were clearer than he had ever before experienced: crystal sharp. He read, first, a swirling undercurrent of emotion, almost like some expressionist daub of colour on a canvas—a wave of elation, of triumph. Then he read specific thoughts: >>>*Done it! Yes...* (Non-specific feelings of victory, of having bested a business rival.) >>>*That will show the extortionist—*!

Vaughan fumbled with his handset and killed the program, and instantly the balm of mind-silence replaced the noise in his head. He felt obscurely guilty for eavesdropping on his neighbour's thoughts, but more than that a familiar, painful reminder of other people's shallow hopes and desires, preferences and prejudices. Life with Sukara had made him even less materialistic than of old, and the reminder that for so many citizens what mattered was the pursuit of wealth and possessions he found dispiriting.

He smiled as he stepped from the balcony and shut the sliding glass door behind him. He'd just accepted an extravagantly paid job and taken the lease on a luxurious new apartment. He wondered if he was as shallow as those around him.

He found the answer later that evening, when he and Sukara had eaten a sublime dhal and aloo masala. They were sitting at the table before the viewscreen, moonlight catching the cusps and curlicues of the distant waves. Sukara was telling him about what the midwife had said at her last appointment a couple of days ago, and Vaughan realised that the only thing that mattered in his life, now, was the happiness of this blithe and innocent woman, who loved him.

The following morning, as they had breakfast at the bar in the kitchen, his handset chimed.

It was Kapinsky.

"Change of schedule, Jeff. We're dropping all the cases on file and concentrating on a laser killing that happened late last night. Meet you outside the gates of Himachal Park at ten, okay?"

And without waiting for his response, she signed off.

After breakfast, which he finished in silence, he hugged Sukara to him and set off for the park, managing to hide his apprehension for as long as it took him to quit the apartment.

He hurried through the crowded corridors, then took an upchute to Level One, arriving at the park fifteen minutes later.

Kapinsky was waiting for him in the passenger seat of an over-engineered Russian air-taxi. She signalled him and he slipped into the rear of the vehicle as it lunged into the air with a whine of labouring turbos.

She passed him a holstered weapon. "Keep this on you. You don't know when you might need it."

He took the pistol and strapped the holster under his jacket.

"What's happening?" he asked, as the taxi inserted itself into the flow of air traffic following colour-coded lanes high above the Station.

"Big commission," she said over her shoulder. "Biggest I've handled to date. Homicide is stretched as it is, and then this comes in. Guy got himself sliced up in the derelict amusement park in Kandalay. The commissioner got a Scene of Crime team in before realising they didn't have enough detectives for the follow-up investigation." She grunted. "Lucky us. It means all the groundwork will've been done by the time we get there. We just take the SoC's collated information and do the footwork."

"Who's the guy?"

She shrugged. "That we'll find out when we get there. All I know is what the Commissioner told me—a laser slaying in the park, and it's a messy one. Hope you didn't have a late breakfast."

He stared through the side window as the air-taxi whined in a tight arc, coming in low over the skeleton of an ancient big dipper and tumbledown amusement arcades.

The taxi settled on a concrete apron between a broken-down starship simulation and the shell of a bankrupt McDonald's franchise. Vaughan stepped out, staring across the apron to where a knot of SoC officers were kneeling beside a body in front of an old ghost train ride.

Kapinsky introduced herself and Vaughan to the officer in charge, a big Sikh called K.J. Kulpa. As the SoC team wrapped up their work, dismantling cameras and laser-measuring apparatus, Kulpa gave Kapinsky the lowdown and Vaughan stared, despite himself, at the murder victim.

The guy was Caucasian, in his fifties, dark haired and pale skinned. He wore a neat business suit and had died, Vaughan hoped, instantly. It was hard to tell, though. The killer had taken no chances, scoring a big X through the guy's chest, joined at the top so that the loop had effectively decapitated his victim and dismembered the arms.

Vaughan had seen the work of a laser before. A single, fraction of a second blast at long range was enough to halt a charging rhino: this gory elaboration was either the work of a sadist or someone who was taking no chances that his victim might survive.

The SoC team boarded a police flier, leaving Kulpa and a corpse crew to mop up when the preliminary investigation was through.

Kulpa handed Kapinsky a pin. "That should contain everything we have on the case, Linda. Call me if you need anything. Good luck." He nodded to Vaughan and climbed into a private flier.

Only the corpse team remained, kicking their heels while Kapinsky knelt and examined the body.

Still crouching, she tossed Vaughan the pin and said, "Access that. The usual questions."

He slipped the pin into his handset and spoke into the mouthpiece. "Victim?"

The program's voice, female and Indian, answered, "*Robert Kormier, fifty-eight, male, South African. Victim employed by the Scheering-Lassiter Colonial Corporation. Position: Executive xeno-zoologist.*"

"Estimated time of death?" Vaughan said.

"*Midnight, plus or minus twelve minutes.*"

"Means of death?" It was always worth asking the seemingly obvious question in case the laser wounds were intended to cover the real cause of death, strangulation or some such.

"*Instantaneous laser laceration of right pulmonary ventricle.*"

"Weapon used?"

"*Kulatov MkII blaser, set at maximum burn.*"

"Estimated range of laser when fired?"

"*Between fifteen and twenty metres.*"

Vaughan looked around at the eerily deserted amusement park. "Witnesses?"

"*None.*"

Kapinsky stood. "Ask who discovered the body."

Vaughan relayed the question and the program responded with, "*Night-watchman employed by Raja Amusements PLC. Alibi corroborated: at midnight he was in visi-contact with superior at Kandalay Security.*"

Vaughan said, "Dependants, next of kin?"

"*Victim's marital status: Married, no children. Spouse: Hermione Kormier.*"

"Address?"

"*Two Gulshan Villas, Allabad, Level One.*"

He looked at Kapinsky. "Anything else?"

"Ask about his last job posting, when he arrived on Earth, things like that. It's a long-shot, but you never know."

"Victim's last professional posting?"

"*Information unavailable.*"

"Arrival on Earth?"

Again the information was unavailable. Kapinsky shrugged. "We'll get all that when we question his boss at Scheering-Lassiter."

She nodded to the corpse boys. "Okay, we're through here."

They moved in, and Vaughan turned away—but not fast enough. With the dispassion of their calling they lifted the corpse onto the waiting stretcher, torso and legs first, leaving behind the head and arms like pieces of a jigsaw puzzle.

Vaughan looked around at the rusted stanchions. He shook his head and said to Kapinsky, "We're out of luck if we thought a security cam might've caught the killing."

"None installed?"

"Once upon a time." He gestured to the vandalised remains of surveillance cams.

He turned and stared across the park, wondering if a cam surveying the streets beyond the park might have caught something. It was a long shot, but one worth checking out later.

He copied the information to his handset's memory, ejected the pin and handed it to Kapinsky.

He watched the corpse-wagon rise into the air and bank low over the decrepit panelling of the amusement park, leaving silence in its wake. Gaudy advertisements for unlimited family fun hit the eye from every direction, contrasting with the forlorn ghost-town aspect of the abandoned park. Vaughan thought it a ghoulishly apposite setting for a laser slaying.

"Two things, Lin," he said. "What was Kormier doing here anyway, and why at midnight?"

"Meeting someone?" She shrugged. "Okay, looks to me like we have two obvious lines of enquiry. His employers—the Scheering-Lassiter outfit—and his widow." She went on before Vaughan could state a preference, "I'll take his bosses. You talk to his widow, find out if—"

"Lin, I know what to do, okay?"

She flicked him a smile. "Two years out of practice, driving a tanker..."

"Fuck you, Kapinsky." He strode towards the waiting Russian flier. "I'll take the taxi, okay?"

"You're such a gentleman, Vaughan."

He slumped into the padded rear seat and said, "Gulshan Villas, Allabad."

He stared out as they rose. Far below, Kapinsky was a tiny figure dwarfed by looming epitaphs to a happier time.

He watched the streets flicker past, then turned his thoughts to Sukara, and their daughter, and wondered what his wife was doing now.

FOUR

VOICE

"Pham…"

A voice nearby, and a hand on her shoulder, waking her up. She opened her eyes and blinked up at a small brown face. She recognised the young boy, then remembered his name.

"Abdul?" She sat up. "How did you find me?"

He grinned. "You told me you'd spend the night here, remember?"

She did, and she remembered everything else, too. The ghost train, the laser killing, the white light that had smashed into her face.

Then the voice in her head.

She had been so sleepy that she had thought it might have been a dream. The voice had said nothing more, just told her not to be frightened, that it could help her.

Then silence, and she had slept all night.

Abdul was kneeling before her, staring into her face as she rubbed her eyes with both fists. "What happened, Pham? When I got away I waited for you in the Level Two tunnel. You were ages, and when you did appear you just ran off before I could catch you."

Pham smiled. "The murderer. The man with the laser. He came after me, tried to kill me."

Abdul's eyes were massive. "Did he see your face?"

"I don't know. I don't think so. He just saw me. He fired at me. I had to run, Abdul."

He reached out and squeezed her fingers. He looked around. "You're not safe here. If the killer's still after you, the parks are the first place he'll look. It's where most of the homeless street-kids live."

Pham grinned at him. "So you're going to take me to see this make-believe spaceship of yours?"

"You still don't believe me, do you? Like to bet on it?"

He looked serious. Perhaps there was a crashed spaceship, after all. And perhaps she would be safer there than out here.

"I don't have enough money to gamble," she said, "and anyway, I think I believe you."

He grinned. "Come on then," he said, holding out his hand.

She wadded her blanket and stuffed it into her teddy-bear backpack, took Abdul's hand and hurried from the park.

He took her along a wide corridor bustling with well-dressed people. Big shops lined the way, with windows as wide as holo-movie screens. Pham had never seen so many things on sale before. There were no big shops on Level Twenty, just stalls and kiosks selling essentials.

She wanted to stop and look into the shop windows at all the new clothes and jewellery, but Abdul was hurrying her along as if the killer were still chasing her.

They turned down a narrower tunnel, this one not so busy. Abdul stopped at the foot of a metal ladder welded to the wall. "Follow me."

For a boy with only one hand, he climbed the ladder with amazing speed, pulling himself up with a series of one-handed grabs at the next rung. Pham followed, going more slowly, careful to reach for the next run only when she had a good grip on the one below.

She came to a catwalk, which ran the length of the tunnel. Abdul tugged her towards another ladder and they climbed again. This time they climbed through a small trapdoor and Pham found herself in a dark crawlspace.

"We're in the maintenance space between Levels One and Two," Abdul informed her self-importantly.

"I thought your spaceship was on Level Twelve, Abdul?"

"Twelve-b, but this is the quickest way to get to it from here."

On hands and knees he crawled away from her, and Pham gave chase. A minute later he stopped. He was pulling something open in front of him, a big square door set into a thick metal column.

He slipped through the door feet first, and peered out at her. "And now we climb all the way down to Level Twelve-b."

She climbed in after him and peered down past Abdul. Occasional dim lighting in the thick column showed that the ladder dropped for ever, vanishing to a tiny point far below. Pham gripped the rungs in fear. If she slipped and fell now, she'd hit Abdul and send them both crashing down until they hit the bottom... wherever that might be—Level Twenty, she thought. She smiled at that as she began the long climb down. If she lost her grip, she would end up where she started, only then she would be dead.

The descent seemed to last for ever, Pham became tired and slowed, then called down to Abdul to stop and wait for her while she rested. He grinned up at her, his single arm hooked around the rung as he took a breather too.

They began again, and Pham called down, "How long have you been living on the spaceship, Abdul?"

"Oh... since I was four or five, I think.

"What happened to your parents?"

"I don't know. I can't remember ever having any. I lived with a stallholder on Level Fifteen when I was three. He might have been my uncle. One day he took me to Dr Rao and I've lived in the ship ever since."

Pham thought about life on a spaceship, begging every day and giving half the money to Dr Rao. "Does Dr Rao give you food?" she asked.

"Food and a bed and blankets and clothes. Dr Rao provides everything for his children."

Perhaps it might be a good life, living on the spaceship with Dr Rao and the other kids... but she didn't like the idea of begging. Perhaps, if she could find a proper job, she could live on the ship and pay Dr Rao some rent money... if she liked it down there, of course.

"Abdul, what happened to your arm?"

A silence from below, and then, "I don't know. I think it happened when I was two or three. Maybe a wild animal bit it off!"

"On Bengal Station?"

"Or maybe it got pulled off in a sugar-cane press!"

She said, "Maybe it got stuck in a 'chute cage door!"

"Or maybe I was so hungry I ate it for breakfast!"

"Or perhaps," she laughed, "it decided it didn't like you, and one morning decided to go its own way and see something of the world."

"I'll keep a look out for it, then," Abdul said.

Thirty minutes later he called out, "Pham, we're nearly there."

"Thought we were never going to stop! My hands ache so much!"

She heard a sound below, the creak of hinges. When she looked down, Abdul was slipping through an open hatch. Pham climbed down and squirmed through the opening, then stood and looked around her.

She was in a vast, dark space, lighted with a few dim tubes in the distance. The floor was metal, and hundreds of columns filed away into the distance, holding up the deck above.

"Where are we?" she asked.

This is the level between Eleven and Twelve," he explained. "Many years ago it was the upper level, then the starship crashed. Later the bosses decided to build even more levels, so they just left the ship where it was, for safety reasons, and built around it."

It was an amazing story. Pham said, "I really don't know whether to believe you, Abdul!"

He laughed. "Come on, then, I'll show you."

He grabbed her hand and they set off, stepping over the seams and joins in the floor where years ago walls had stood. They passed great hanks of wires and bulky, throbbing machinery, and two minutes later Abdul opened a trapdoor in the floor and climbed down. Pham followed, pulling the hatch shut after her.

They were in a brighter area now, and when the ladder ended Pham turned and found herself on a catwalk overlooking a vast chamber.

She stared, gasping. Abdul was smiling at her reaction.

She moved to the edge of the catwalk, gripped the rail and stared.

She turned to Abdul. "You were telling the truth," she whispered in amazement.

Down below, fixed into place amid a great web-work of girders, was the silver shape of a starship, like a great teardrop with fins. As her eyes adjusted to the sight, she made out many viewscreens along its length, with people moving about inside.

All around the chamber, strange plants grew in the artificial light, big flowers and vines hanging from the girders. Abdul explained that when the ship had crashed it had been carrying a cargo of seed from a colony world, which had escaped and grown into this crazy jungle.

"Welcome to my home," Abdul said, leading her from the catwalk along a narrow bridge strung from the edge of the chamber to the entry ramp of the spaceship.

He ran ahead, hardly touching the rail with his one hand. Pham followed, gripping both rails as the bridge swayed from side to side.

At last they came to the ramp and climbed into the starship.

He led her through a wide corridor to a place he said was the bridge, or control room, a big room shaped like an amphitheatre surrounded by screens and control panels.

The first thing she noticed was that it was full of children. There were hundreds of them, of all shapes and sizes, Indians and Thais and Burmese and Chinese, and even a few white kids in among. They were sitting around, eating or playing or just chatting.

The second thing she noticed was that every child she could see was injured in some way. Some had arms missing, some legs; others were blind.

She turned to Abdul and said, "Is this a hospital?"

He shook his head, not meeting her gaze.

"But all the kids, they're..."

"Look," Abdul said, pointing. "There's Dr Rao. Do you want to meet him?"

Pham stared across the bridge to where an elderly Indian man was moving among the groups of children with the aid of a cane. He stopped to chat with the kids, smiling and laughing.

Despite having a strange feeling about the place, she nodded. It would be rude to have come so far with Abdul and refuse to meet the Doctor.

He took her hand and led her down a slope into the bridge, and they weaved their way among the children. Pham felt self-conscious as some kids stopped what they were doing and looked up at her.

Dr Rao saw Abdul and beamed. He looked, Pham thought, like a toothless turtle with old-fashioned spectacles.

"Abdul! And your little friend?"

"Pham," Abdul said, and he sounded proud. "I said I'd show Pham were I live. She doesn't have a home. She ran away from a factory on Level Twenty."

Dr Rao turned his wizened, leathery face to Pham. "Is that so? You ran away? A girl with daring and spirit, no? Now, would you care to live here, with Abdul and the other children?"

Pham looked around, wordless. She wanted to ask the doctor why all the kids were maimed in some way.

In a tiny voice, she asked, "What do I have to do?"

Rao grinned. "We shall talk over specifics once Abdul has shown you more of the ship, shall we? But first—Abdul, would you be so kind as to fetch me a glass of chai? There's a good boy."

"Be back in a minute," Abdul whispered to Pham, and scooted off back up the ramp and disappeared along a corridor. Dr Rao shuffled off, inspecting his charges. From time to time, Pham saw him bend to inspect more closely the stumps of arms and legs recently amputated.

Pham stood alone, frozen to the spot. For all she liked Abdul, she hated this place. There was something about it that made her very uneasy, something about all the injured children...

As she looked around her, a voice in her head whispered, *Get out of here. Go the way you came. You will be fine, believe me.*

The voice startled her. So she hadn't been dreaming, last night. At the same time, there was something soothing in the words, in the *feel* of the voice in her head.

She knew that the advice was right. She should get out of here.

She wished she could say goodbye to Abdul, but she felt that he might be upset if she told him that she didn't like where he lived.

She hurried up the ramp and into the corridor, then followed the way she had come to the exit. She looked behind her. There was no sign of Dr Rao, chasing after her to drag her back.

She hurried down the ramp and across the swaying footbridge. When she reached the gallery, she looked back one last time. The ship was a magnificent sight, but she shivered when she thought about what it contained. She quickly climbed the ladder, opened the hatch and pulled herself through.

She was in the space between the decks now, and she wondered if she would be able to find her way back.

It was as if something were telling her to look down, and when she did so she saw a series of footprints scuffed into the dust of the deck.

She followed them to the column and dragged open the hatch. Then, she climbed towards Level Two and safety.

On the way she tried to talk to the voice in her head.

"Voice?" she asked. "Are you still there, Voice?"

But the voice in her head was silent.

FIVE

LIES

Vaughan paid off the taxi and hunched his shoulders against the hot down-draught as it rose and sped off across the Station. The vision of the dead man would not erase itself from his memory, and the thought of intruding on his wife's grief, of having to read her mind, did not appeal.

Gulshan Villas was a strip of exclusive residences on the north side of the Station, each one custom built by an architect famed for innovation. The Kormier residence was an elegant silver arrowhead arranged with its point facing the quiet boulevard; behind it, a long greensward fell towards the edge of the Station. On the lawn Vaughan made out a series of domes arranged so that they rode each other piggyback style, like an agglomeration of soap bubbles.

His handset chimed. Kapinsky stared out at him. "I've drawn a blank at the Scheering-Lassiter HQ," she said. "I'll tell you about it later. I'm going over to the police records office now, checking other laser killings. Thing is, the place is sealed, so you won't be able to get through, okay? If you need me, leave a message."

"I'll do that."

"Catch you later, Vaughan."

He cut the connection and approached the house. There was no reply at the front entrance. He walked along the arrowhead's angled wall and tapped the implant's code into his handset. Briefly he felt a belt of raw emotion—grief and anger—emanate from the domes on the lawn.

He killed his implant and headed across the grass to the domes, his apprehension increased by the power of the woman's grieving.

An airlock gave access to the massed bubbles. He stepped through, moving from a hot, humid summer's day to an atmosphere even more humid: it was like a sauna, and his every breath was more a draught of liquid than air.

He was surrounded by a thousand varieties of flower, a polychromatic panoply of colour. He suspected that many of the blooms were alien—not only by the fact that they looked elegantly tortured and unearthly, but because most of them were thriving in alien atmospheres within their own mini-domes.

He followed a gridded metal walkway around the display and into a second, much larger dome. Here, alien shrubs of every conceivable hue gave the impression that he had left Earth and stepped onto the surface of some far-flung colony world.

He headed towards where he judged Hermione Kormier to be—in a smaller, adjacent dome—and paused on the open threshold.

He decided to question her first, unaided by his tele-ability. Only later, briefly, would he access her thoughts and feelings.

She was tending a cactus with a spray-gun, half-turned away from him. She was perhaps fifty, silver-grey hair cut short, dressed in a kaftan as colourful as her horticultural collection.

He cleared his throat. "Excuse me. I'm sorry. There was no reply from the house."

She turned, startled, a hand moving involuntarily to the wrinkled skin of her throat. "Oh, that was a shock. I'm sorry—I usually leave a note on the door. You've caught me unprepared."

He smiled, reassuring, and showed his identity card. "I'm Jeff Vaughan. I work for a private investigative agency commissioned by the Station police to investigate your husband's case." He immediately regretted the euphemism: it sounded even more crass than "your husband's death".

Hermione Kormier smiled. She had blue eyes emphasised by a sun-seared face, and something about her no-nonsense outdoors appearance warmed Vaughan to her. He would not have labelled her as someone grieving the death of a loved one, but he knew that appearances were often deceptive.

"Ah, I was expecting someone, sooner or later." She gestured at the surrounding cacti. "Through here, if you'll follow me, Mr Vaughan, are my pride and joy: these are moonblooms from Iachimo, Rigel II. They flower only in the dead of night, once a month. They are notoriously difficult to transplant."

The blooms, in a specially filtered half-light, were tiny and delicate and a thousand shades of silver.

They gave off a subtle scent that hit the nose in a wave, and then subsided, leaving him wondering if he'd imagined the fragrance, until the next wave.

He followed her through to another dome.

"All these are examples of Dendri polycarpus, from the uncolonised world of Aldebaran IV. They are really two plants in one."

Vaughan stared around at the rude bursts of colour. He could only make out a single scarlet bloom in each pot, but beside each one was a withered stem.

Kormier said, "They exist in a unique symbiotic relationship, Mr Vaughan. Each cannot live without the other, but often their existence appears mutually destructive. One will feed off the other for a time, gaining sustenance, and then the roles will reverse. We have been studying the species for years, but we still don't fully understand the process."

She reached out and laid a sun-tanned hand on the apex of a dome. "I often think that their life cycles are analogous to the human institution of marriage, Mr Vaughan. Would you agree?"

He opened his mouth to reply, but allowed a few seconds to elapse before saying, "Could I interpret that as a comment on how you viewed your own marriage?"

She looked away, feigning interest in a vulgar, liverish bloom like a lolling ox tongue.

"Come, I'll show you to the house. One can become intoxicated by the atmosphere in here after a while. Coffee?"

Taken aback by her matter-of-factness, Vaughan followed her.

They left the domes, crossed the lawns and entered the arrowhead dwelling through a sliding rear door. She escorted him up a wide helical staircase and into an open-plan study overlooking the greensward and the glittering sea.

She told him to make himself comfortable and left to fetch coffee. He moved around the room, glancing at the ranked books—academic treatises on horticultural subjects—and holograms of riotous blooms.

He stopped to examine a shelf of holo-cubes. Each one showed a man and a woman against an alien backdrop. The woman was Hermione Kormier, at various ages from perhaps thirty to the present. The man was her husband, handsome and smiling in every cube, his arms around his wife, staring out in blithe ignorance of what the future held in store.

Vaughan felt something catch in his throat and turned away.

"Are you married, Mr Vaughan?"

She was standing in the doorway, carrying a tray. Evidently she had been watching him.

He was still at that stage of his marriage where he felt compelled to tell people about it. "Nearly two years now, to Sukara. We're expecting our first child in three months."

"Are you happy?"

He smiled, looking away from the woman and staring out to sea. "I would never have thought that I could be so happy, before meeting her. I worked as a telepath for years before that. It made me cynical."

"As it must, I imagine, reading the minds of the criminal and corrupt."

"Of course, our happiness is conditional on personal experience."

She looked across at him. "Are you still a telepath?"

He nodded. "But I haven't been for two years—"

"As long as you've been married?"

He smiled. "That's right."

"The cynic in me would say that either the resumption of your telepathic duties, or a few years of marriage, might blunt your happiness."

He had seen so many relationships founder that he felt fear for his own marriage and, at the same time, guilt at his happiness.

Hermione Kormier crossed the room and laid the tray on a coffee table before the window. She indicated a wickerwork settee and sat down opposite.

Vaughan picked up a holo-cube and joined her. The cube was recent, he guessed. He held it up. "You look happy in this one. It can't have been taken that long ago?"

"Oh, I don't deny that I was intermittently happy. Robert was a wonderful man. I was in love with him until the very end. But I also hated him, just as passionately, from time to time."

"Can you tell me why?"

She sipped her coffee, then said, "You aren't reading me?"

"Not yet."

She inclined her head. "Robert could be very self-centred. Driven. Ambitious. I've no doubt that he loved me—but, you see, I've no doubt also that my love for him was stronger. He could do things which I interpreted as neglectful, unloving, things which I would never dream of doing to him. He wouldn't think twice about going away on a field trip for months on end, without me."

"What exactly was his job?"

"He was a xeno-zoologist, latterly for the Scheering-Lassiter Corporation."

"He studied alien wildlife?"

"That's right. He was well respected in his field. We met on Cavafy, Vega VI—the planet of a million moons. You can't get much more romantic than that!"

"How long ago was that?"

"Twenty years ago. We were married the same year. We managed to mesh our working lives pretty well, arranging it so that our field trips coincided. We saw a lot of the inhabited worlds together." For the first time, Vaughan detected a haze of sadness in her eyes.

He took a mouthful of coffee, too on edge to fully appreciate its excellence. "Are you aware of anything that might explain why someone wanted your husband dead, Mrs Kormier?"

She stared into her coffee. In a small voice, she said, "Robert was a good man, a respected academic. He never made an enemy in his life."

But, he thought, she was holding something back. He knew it from some almost subliminal reading of her facial mannerisms, a slight tightening of her lips, a sidewise shift of her eyes away from him as she spoke.

He said, gently, "What is it?"

She looked up, surprised. "I thought you weren't reading me?"

"I'm not. That is, I'm not reading your thoughts." He shrugged. "Telepaths become very aware of moods and nuances." He hesitated, then said, "Maybe later, if it's okay?"

She nodded, a slight frown pulling at her lips.

He went on, "Something is worrying you, though. Something about your husband. You didn't want to mention it, but…"

She manufactured a brave smile, even a laugh, almost of relief. "You're very astute, Mr Vaughan. Yes, there was something. I don't know if it's in any way connected with what happened—"

"Let me be the judge of that," he said.

"Very well." She laid her cup aside and stared at her hands, as if wondering where to begin. She looked up. "Earlier this year Robert was posted to the colony world of Mallory, Eta Ophiuchi VII. It's a Scheering-Lassiter world. They wanted him to look at some aspect of population control of a native herbivore: he was commissioned to produce an extensive bio-ecological report on local conditions."

"And?"

She looked at him, silent for a second. "When Robert returned from Mallory, he'd changed. Something had happened out there—" She stopped abruptly and made a production of pouring more coffee so as to hide her distress.

Vaughan waited, then said, "He didn't tell you what happened, though?"

She shook her head. "It was obvious that something was wrong. He was quiet, withdrawn. Irritable. Usually, he discussed every aspect of his work with me—as I did my own work with him. But he said nothing and wouldn't be drawn, even when I asked him about the report he was working on. He denied that anything was wrong, Mr Vaughan. He was... he seemed a different person."

"You've no suspicions what might have happened, nothing at all?"

She forced a laugh. "Of course I had—I *have*—my suspicions. It occurred to me that he'd discovered something on Mallory so... I don't know... so dreadful that he couldn't even share it with me. But," she went on, "I also suspected something far more prosaic, but perhaps more hurtful to me."

He knew what was coming, and she obliged him by saying, "I suspect that he met someone out there, Mr Vaughan. He was having an affair."

Vaughan nodded, feeling for the widow who might never know, for certain, if her husband had been unfaithful. "If you don't mind me asking, what made you suspect this?"

She sighed. She was close to tears. "Twice during the last couple of months he went out late, without explanation, and came back in the early hours. He refused to speak to me about where he'd been. We were not sleeping together at this point, Mr Vaughan. We were leading separate lives."

"And of course you have no idea where he went."

"No," she said, then went on, "My husband kept an extensive diary. Handwritten. Had done so for almost twenty years."

"You have it?"

"It's in his study."

Vaughan lowered his cup. "And you haven't been able to bring yourself to read it, right?"

She almost laughed, then. "You understand, Mr Vaughan. I had hoped you would. You see... part of me wanted to know, but another part... I don't want to hate my husband, Mr Vaughan. I want to remember all our good times together."

"You don't mind if I take a look at the diary?"

"Of course not. I'll show you to his study." She led him from the room, across a gallery and into a study the mirror image of her own. The library appeared identical, as did the selection of holo-cubes on display.

A big timber desk sat beside the viewscreen.

Hermione Kormier stood at the door, as if reluctant to trespass on the territory of her murdered husband. She indicated the desk. "In the top drawer on the right. It's unlocked. I'll be in my study."

He watched her withdraw, then crossed to the desk and sat down in an old-fashioned timber chair, pulling open the drawer and lifting out a thick, old-fashioned ledger.

It was marked with the year's date. He turned the pages, admiring the dead man's meticulous script. He scanned a few entries from earlier in the year, before Kormier's posting to Mallory.

It was not what he was expecting, abstruse musings from a world-leading xeno-zoologist, but the endearing day-to-day observations and jottings of a man very much in love with his wife. Indeed, Kormier himself was less the subject of his entries than was Hermione.

17th January. Dined with Hermione after writing. Discussed the parallax theory I've been working on. H is so damned astute. It's been twenty years, and Christ I love the woman more and more every day...

Vaughan stopped reading, his throat constricted.

He flipped a sheaf of pages, arriving at more recent entries.

They were mere one-liners, and often cryptic. A week before his death: *Considering autumn, vague thoughts of home.*

Two days after that: *Sunsets on Mallory... will I ever see them again?*

He turned back to the dates that Kormier was on Mallory. There were entries for the first couple of weeks, then nothing for weeks. He read all the entries on Mallory, mainly technical reports he had no hope of understanding, with no hint of anything untoward.

The very last entry made on the colony world read: *Begin field trip tomorrow with Travers. Looking into his pachyderm hypothesis. Should be fascinating.*

Then nothing until two months later, two weeks ago, and his abstract jottings about Mallory and sunsets. There were three more entries made over the last fortnight. The first, ten days ago, reported: *Travers called yesterday. See him today.*

Three days later: *T—meet him tonight.*

Vaughan sat back. Travers. He had to find Travers. Could it be that Travers was the man he had arranged to meet at the amusement park?

There was no entry for the day after his meetings with Travers, however.

He closed the diary and examined the desk. Amid papers and com-pins, he noticed a metallic pass-card. He picked it up, smiling. The card showed a pix of Kormier, beneath the legend: Scheering-Lassiter Authorised Staff.

He slipped it into his pocket. Kapinsky would ball him out when he produced this little ace.

He lodged the diary under his arm and left the study, pausing on the gallery outside Hermione's room.

He hesitated, tempted to spare himself the torture of scanning the woman.

Before he could give in, he tapped in the access code and braced himself. He reached out for the wall, held on, as the full force of her emotions assailed him.

It was as if she were consumed by an interior whirlwind of grief, a vast swirling twister of guilt and regret and the raw emotion of knowing that her husband was dead, that she would never again share her life with him.

And caught in the typhoon, like debris sucked up and swirled, were fleeting verbalised thoughts: >>>*Miss him! The bastard! I love him... (His last seconds... Pain? Suffering... I should have been with him!)*

On another level, in the calm dead centre of the storm, Vaughan caught references to himself.

>>>*When will the ingratiating bastard leave me alone? Police fascist! Happy with his little Thai slut.* (Anger, jealousy...)

Deeper, he probed rooted memories of her life with Robert Kormier, was hit by images of them in bed, ecstatic in sexual abandon, and then arguing fiercely, hurling abuse.

He quickly killed his implant. What she had told him had been the truth. He had no desire to pry further.

He stepped into her study, telling himself that her mental anger at him was justifiable. He smiled and held out Robert Kormier's diary.

She stood, facing him, her tanned, lined face innocent of the emotions that swirled deep within her psyche.

He wanted to hug her, tell her that her husband loved her. Instead, he passed her the diary and said: "Read it. You have nothing to fear."

Her face, fleetingly, showed hope.

He said, "Your husband was meeting a fellow scientist called Travers. It's important that I trace him."

"Sam Travers? He was a colleague of Robert's. He lives on the southside, Lohng Kla, Level One. Seventeen Khaosan Road."

"Were they friends?"

"They'd known each other since university. But Sam was away so much of the time that Robert hardly saw him. They made sure they met at least once a year, though."

"Did Travers work for Scheering-Lassiter?"

"No, he was employed by the Station University."

"But Travers was working on Mallory earlier this year?"

"That's right. He was on research leave from his department."

"Did you know him?"

She shook her head. "I met him once or twice. He wasn't my type. Overambitious, overconfident. Full of himself. But he and Robert got on."

He hesitated, then said, "Your husband and Travers never had reason to disagree on anything, professional arguments?"

"Absolutely not. They shared many of the same views and ideals. They worked together on many conservation schemes."

Vaughan made to leave. "I'm sorry for intruding. I want to find who did this. I hope you understand?"

Wordlessly, she nodded. She hesitated, then said, "I thought you were going to read me, Mr Vaughan?"

He looked at her, then shook his head. "That won't be necessary," he lied. "I'll show myself out."

He hurried down the helical staircase and stepped out into the merciless afternoon sunlight.

SIX

TRAVERS

Lohng Kla was a prosperous district on the south side of the Station, away from the noise and bustle of the spaceport to the north-west. Parks and gardens alternated with neat suburbs, the residences of university workers and affluent students.

Khaosan Road paralleled the edge of the station, and a terrace of black polycarbon dwellings, like beetles on a starting line, overlooked the sea.

Vaughan found number seventeen, set back in a lawned garden. It was a surprisingly small dwelling for the area, just one storey high. He was about to push the doorbell when he noticed that the door was open an inch. He pushed it further open and called out, "Hello? Travers?"

There was no reply. Cautiously he stepped into a narrow hallway, relieved now that Kapinsky had insisted on his carrying a weapon.

He stopped, activated his implant and scanned.

Mind-noise rushed him from every direction. There were people in the houses to either side, and

on the level below. He caught stray strands of verbalised thought and heightened emotion.

Now he saw why the building appeared small
from the street: a staircase descended through the
deck. He followed the stairs, scanning as he went. It
was impossible to tell whether the mind-noise
below emanated from this dwelling or others
beyond. He deactivated his implant as he arrived at
the foot of the stairs, which opened out onto a
gallery overlooking a lounge with a vast viewscreen
giving onto the ocean.

He paused at the edge of the gallery, looking
down. He fingered the bulk of the pistol beneath his
jacket. Despite what Hermione Kormier thought,
he knew enough not to dismiss the possibility that
Travers had killed Kormier. They had met a couple
of times over the past two weeks, and had been
together on a field trip on Mallory. Vaughan was
willing to gamble that, if Travers was not directly
responsible for Kormier's death, then he had information that might help the investigation.

He thought about calling out again, but remained
silent. He slipped his hand beneath the flap of his
jacket and closed his fingers around the butt of the
pistol, pacing along the length of the gallery and
taking another flight of steps down into the vast
lounge. The viewscreen here was opaqued, giving
the long room the dim, still atmosphere of an
aquarium.

He looked around, his heartbeat loud. The place
was still silent. He accessed his implant again.
Three people were dining to his left, perhaps thirty
metres away in the neighbouring apartment. None
of them was Sam Travers. A sea of mind-noise

surged below him, from Level Three. This apartment seemed to be empty.

So was this neighbourhood so safe that Travers left his front door open when he went out?

Uneasy, Vaughan moved from the lounge. He checked the adjacent bedroom and bathroom but found nothing, then re-crossed the lounge to another room.

Sunlight falling through the un-opaqued viewscreen to his left dazzled him for a second, before his eyes adjusted and he made out what was obviously a study. Books lined three walls, and overspill piles tottered on the carpet, alternating with holo-cubes showing various specimens of alien fauna.

He stopped on the threshold, staring at the messy remains that filled the chair before the desk. He glanced at the coagulated blood that covered the carpet. Evidently Travers had been dead for hours.

He moved back into the lounge and got through Kapinsky's answering service, gave Travers's address and told her to get here fast. Then he called K.J. Kulpa and reported a second slaying.

He knew he had to go back into the study, but something stopped him. He lifted his handset again, and before he realised what he was doing he had tapped out Sukara's code.

Her smiling face filled the screen, dazzling him with relief. "Su, you don't know how good it is to see you."

"Jeff, you okay? You look white as a ghost!"

He smiled. "I'm fine. I thought I'd call, see how you are."

"Oh, I'm okay. Tired. You know. Oh—she just kicked!" She laughed, and her delight filled Vaughan with joy. "It's so strange, Jeff, having someone inside you."

"What have you got planned for this afternoon?"

She gave a guilty smile. "I'm meeting Lara for coffee. What have you been doing?"

"I'll tell you all about it tonight," he said. "I love you, Su."

"Love you, too," she echoed. He cut the connection and stood in silence, his heartbeat loud, wanting to be far away from this place, drinking coffee at some quiet, shaded café in the Park.

He moved to the study door and leaned against the woodwork. The killer must have stood right here, he judged, said something to attract Travers's attention: Travers swivels in his seat, and the killer fires his laser, sweeping it in his or her signature loop, causing maximum injury with minimum effort.

The result was that Travers's head and arms lay on the carpet. His torso sat on the charred swivel chair, feet planted incongruously on the floor.

Vaughan returned to the lounge. He de-opaqued the viewscreen and sat in the sunlight, dictating into his handset a report of that morning's interview with Hermione Kormier and the latest discovery.

Kapinsky arrived ten minutes later, closely followed by Kulpa and the SoC team.

He gave Kulpa the pin detailing his investigations, as protocol dictated, and waited until Kapinsky emerged from the study. She crossed the lounge as if breezing down a fashion catwalk and sprawled in a deep armchair across from him, arms and legs spread.

He told her about his meeting with Hermione Kormier.

She watched him, her expression blank.

"You've been busy for a new boy," she said when he'd finished. "Any thoughts?"

He stared at her. He could live with his new job, the intrusive mind-reading and butchered bodies, but it was hard to take the fact that he was employed by someone he didn't particularly like.

"Where to begin?" he said. "The common link is Mallory, of course. They came across something there, saw something, heard something... I don't know. Kormier's wife said he was a different person when he got back, a month ago. He had a couple of meetings with Travers, and they both end up dead."

Kulpa emerged from the study and tossed Kapinsky a pin. "That's all the information we've collated from this one. If you need anything more, shout."

While the SoC team packed up, and the corpse team moved in, Kapinsky inserted the pin into her handset. She spoke into her 'set, sounding bored.

"Estimated time of death?"

A neutral female voice replied, "*Two a.m., plus or minus ten minutes.*"

Vaughan said, "Couple of hours after the killer got Kormier."

Kapinsky grunted, "All in a night's work." To her handset she said, "Means of death?"

"*Instantaneous laser laceration of carotid artery.*"

"Weapon used?"

"*Kulatov MkII blaser, set at maximum burn.*"

"And estimated range of laser?"

"*Between two and three metres.*"

"Does the victim have dependants, next of kin?"

"*Victim's marital status: single, no known relations.*"

Kapinsky killed her 'set and looked across at Vaughan. "Let's presume, for the time being, that we're dealing with one killer here, okay?"

"Looks that way."

"So where were we?"

Vaughan said, "Mallory. The connection. Kormier and Travers found something there. You know anything about the planet?"

"Christ, Vaughan, there're so many colony worlds out there I've lost count. I'm an investigator, not an encyclopaedia."

"It was simply a question," he said, staring at her.

She shrugged. "I know fuck all about the place." She indicated her handset. "But I'll access the Station's database."

He nearly congratulated her, but held his tongue.

She tapped her handset's keypad and said, "Colony planet. Mallory. Information by specific question."

Vaughan glanced across the lounge. The corpse team was manhandling a white body bag through the door and up the narrow stairs, their task not made easy by the fact that the corpse was in four pieces. He looked away.

Seconds later a transistorised male voice issued from Kapinsky's handset. "*Connection established. Proceed.*"

She said, "Political situation, population, indigenous population?"

Ten minutes later they had a brief outline of the colony world of Mallory, Eta Ophiuchi. It was a class II Earth-norm world, land–sea ratio seventy–thirty, equable climate approximating to Earth sub-tropical, approximately the size of Luna. It was owned by the Scheering-Lassiter organisation, who governed by a democratically elected committee of twelve. The planet had no sentient native life forms, but a vast ecology ranging from bacteria up to arboreal primates. Its population was just 6.3 million, its main industries uranium and diamond mining and agriculture.

Vaughan said, "We really need to talk to someone at Scheering-Lassiter."

"So okay," Kapinsky said, "except the Scheering-Lassiter people aren't playing ball."

"What did they say?"

"I requested a meeting with some official in charge of colonial affairs. A stone-faced bitch said no-can-do. She told me they're detailing their own in-house team of investigators to look into the killing. Which, Vaughan, is entirely within their rights. We're private investigators—we've no jurisdiction. Can't make the bastards see us."

Vaughan almost mentioned the pass-card he'd palmed from Kormier's study, but something stopped him from showing his hand. Chances were if he told her about it, she'd commandeer the card and waltz into the Scheering-Lassiter headquarters all guns blazing.

He'd go there himself; make discreet enquiries.

He said, "I have contacts at the Station. I'll see what I can do, okay?"

"You get in there, you're a better man than me, Vaughan."

She stood up and moved to the viewscreen, leaned against it and said to him, "I went over to the police

HQ, accessed the files. I thought I'd check Kormier's death against any others over the past year or so."

"And?"

She shrugged. "I dunno. I might've found a match. It's a long shot. Nine months ago, a woman was found lasered in the arboretum on Level Two—in the same way, crossed loop, same weapon. It was in the dead case file."

"Who was she?"

"Dana Mulraney. An off-worlder, from Tourmaline. She'd been on the Station for six months. She was with a lover at the time. I did some checking. Her partner's still living here."

"You plan to question him?"

"I'm meeting *her* at four."

"I'll check out Scheering-Lassiter."

Kapinsky was shaking her head. "Let's do this together. I want to see you in action."

Uneasy, he nodded. "Fine by me."

They left the apartment and took an air-taxi north.

Five minutes later the taxi decelerated, banked tightly and came in to land outside the Bengal Tiger's skyball stadium. From the outside, the edifice looked like some corporeal HQ in downtown Manhattan. The imposing matt black polycarbon façade was inset with a thousand silver viewscreens, which reflected the late afternoon sun in a scintillating array, like so many holo-screens tuned to the same station.

Vaughan climbed out and stared up at the towering southside of the stadium. He glanced at Kapinsky. "She works here?"

"You could say that," she replied. "You heard of Petra Shelenkov?"

"Can't say I have."

"You not up on skyball?"

"Don't follow sport."

"Not even the Tigers?"

Vaughan sighed, eager to be out of the heat of the sun. "Didn't know it was compulsory," he said.

"Jeez, I thought every citizen on the Station was following them last season. They won the World Championship, you know? Famous last minute victory over Chicago?"

He shrugged. "So Shelenkov plays skyball."

"Star signing from Vladivostok Vampires a couple of seasons ago."

Vaughan looked at Kapinsky. "You follow the Tigers?"

"Me?" she wisecracked. "You're joking, right? It's a mug's game."

He stared at her as she set off across the parking lot and entered the dark shadow of the stadium, then followed.

They flashed their IDs at a security guard and stepped through a revolving door. Kapinsky led the way along a corridor until they came to a steep flight of concrete steps. They climbed, minutes later arriving at the first tier of banked seating.

Vaughan had never been inside a skyball stadium, and he was surprised at the size of the place. On all four sides, six tiers rose around the central playing area—a great box-like rectangle, demarcated by low-powered lasers, two hundred metres long, seventy wide, and fifty deep. He was reminded of an aquarium, and the way the skyball players darted through the air, like so many polychromatic tropical fish, heightened the effect.

Kapinsky edged along a row of seats and sat down.

Vaughan joined her and watched the players practise defensive manoeuvres. They wore power packs and jetted through the air in pursuit of an oval rubber disc, which they struck with shields towards a goal board at each end of the playing area.

He was surprised at how physical the game was, even in this workout. The players wore padding, but even so the way they rammed each other seemed sufficient to break bones. From time to time a collision resulted in a malfunctioning power pack, and the unfortunate players tumbled from the playing area and landed with a thump on a sprung rubber mat far below.

They'd been watching for about ten minutes when one of the attacking players, swaddled in a red padded jacket, swooped from the playing area and landed in the aisle a few metres below where they were sitting.

The woman climbed, unbuckling her helmet and wiping sweat from her face.

She was a big-boned Slav in her late twenties, blonde hair cropped spiky short, with muscles on her arms and legs like a cartoonist's caricature of a superhero on steroids.

She sidestepped along the row of seating below Vaughan and Kapinsky and sat down in front of them. She nodded at Vaughan suspiciously, smiled at Kapinsky. "You wanted to talk to me about Dana, no?"

Vaughan let Kapinsky do the talking.

"We think her death might be linked to a case we're investigating," she said. "We're just checking out a few leads."

Shelenkov shuttled an ice-blue glance between them. "So who's the sidekick?"

"Vaughan," he said, before Kapinsky could answer for him.

"You both telepaths, no?"

He nodded. Kapinsky said, "It's the best way to get results, darling."

"Listen, I don't want no man fucking with my head, okay?"

Vaughan held up both hands. "That's fine by me," he said, glancing at Kapinsky and killing the beginning of a smile.

"You don't mind if I...?" Kapinsky began, indicating her handset.

"If it's necessary for the investigation, then okay."

Kapinsky tapped her handset and smiled. "This won't take long. I just want to ask you a few questions."

Shelenkov nodded. "Just like the pricks who said they were investigating Dana's death, and then did fuck all?"

Kapinsky said, "The cops, they're stretched a lot of the time, yeah? Haven't always got time to follow things up. These days, a cop's lucky to have three days on a murder before it goes in the dead case file."

Shelenkov looked none too impressed. "That's what the bastards told me nine months ago," she said. "You know what? They asked me half a dozen questions—just six, yes?—then left and never got back to me. We're talking about a murdered woman, no? They treated her death like a fucking traffic violation."

Kapinsky closed her eyes, then opened them and looked at Vaughan. He could see that she'd read something.

Discreetly—not wanting to anger the skyball giant in the slightest—he pressed the start-up code into his implant and awaited the painful flare of an angry mind at close range.

It came, rocking him.

Shelenkov carried an image of her dead lover in her mind like an icon, to which she paid daily devotion: they had been together six years when Dana was murdered, the best six years of Shelenkov's life, and now—

Raging pain, a whirlwind of grief so powerful that Vaughan reached out to kill the link.

Then he read something that stayed his hand.

He sifted through images of the women together, recollections of conversation. They were in a park on Level One, and Dana was agitated, talking fast, looking around constantly to ensure they were not overheard.

Vaughan picked the meat of the conversation from Shelenkov's memory, and knew instantly that whoever had killed Kormier and Travers had also murdered Dana Mulraney.

"Something's happening on Mallory," Mulraney had told her lover. "Something big. Scheering-Lassiter are covering it up, but we're onto it."

The image fragmented; Shelenkov's memory of the day, the conversation, was imperfect. He scanned deeper, looking for any other recollections of Mulraney's mentioning Mallory or Scheering-Lassiter.

Then he had it: Mulraney had told Shelenkov the name of her contact on the colony world.

He deactivated his implant, and the sudden silence was bliss.

Kapinsky was following up what she'd read so far, attempting to jog Shelenkov's memory with careful questions. "Tell me about Dana's work? She was an environmentalist, wasn't she?"

"A xeno-environmentalist. She worked for Eco-Col, monitoring the effect of human habitation on the settled worlds."

"And she was posted to Mallory for a while?" Kapinsky asked.

She nodded, almost winced. "She went to Mallory. She was there just before she was killed. She told me that the government was involved in a cover-up. It had something to do with some animals on Mallory, yes? She was sure she was onto something. And then she was killed."

"You think there might have been a link?"

"You know something, I told the cop all about what Dana had said, and he told me he'd look into it. But he did nothing. A couple of days later, they said the case was closed. What was the phrase? Insufficient evidence?"

Kapinsky said, "You were questioned by a private investigator?"

Vaughan glanced at Kapinsky, trying not to be impressed. He hadn't scanned a hint of any private operative.

"Yes. She was working for someone—she wouldn't say who. I guessed Eco-Col." She shrugged. "But she was as useless as the cops. She worked on the case for a month, told me there wasn't a link to Mallory. You know what she said?"

Kapinsky nodded. "She told you that Dana was the victim of a motiveless murder."

Shelenkov smiled, tears in her eyes. "I don't know which would be the worse, do you? To have your lover killed for a reason, or for no reason."

Vaughan said, "What was the name of the private investigator?"

The skyball star pulled a face, recollecting, then said, "Something Javinder. Can't remember her first name." She looked from Vaughan to Kapinsky, then asked with a note of hope, "You said you were investigating another murder, that it might be linked with Dana's death?"

Kapinsky, showing a compassion which surprised Vaughan, reached out and laid fingers on Shelenkov's big hand. "This is off the record, and goes no further than us three, okay? It looks as if the killings are linked. Dana's case is reopened. We'll do our best to nail the killer."

Spring came to the tundra of Shelenkov's Siberian features. She smiled.

A minute later Kapinsky deactivated her implant. Vaughan noticed that she winced with relief.

Shelenkov stood and said goodbye. Her smile included Vaughan, this time.

He watched her elbow her power pack into ignition and rise into the playing area. As if invigorated, she attacked the defensive line-up with a war cry and drove home a goal from short range.

As they were leaving the stadium, Vaughan asked, "Did you get the name of Dana Mulraney's contact on Mallory?"

She looked at him sharply. "No. Nothing... You?"

"Jenna Larsen," Vaughan said, unable to suppress a satisfied smile as they left the stadium.

SEVEN

SOMETHING FROM A DREAM

Sukara paced from one end of the lounge to the other, avoiding the sunken sofa, her toes sinking into the plush carpet. Forty-five paces. Next she paced the width of the lounge, from the door to the floor-to-ceiling viewscreen. Twenty paces.

She stopped with her nose to the viewscreen and stared out at the ocean, glittering in the afternoon light. Then she turned and took in her new apartment, and still it didn't seem real.

Two years ago she had been a working girl in Bangkok, living in a tiny cubbyhole no bigger than the sunken sofa.

Now she was married to the finest man in the world and about to have his daughter—and then this. She smiled to herself, wiping tears from her eyes. Life on Level Ten had been good enough—even though the apartment had been tiny, and the neighbours loud—but this apartment and the life she would lead on Level Two was like something from a dream.

But best of all was the thought of the child growing inside her. She placed her hands on her swollen belly and felt for movement, something she did constantly now, reassured when she felt the pressure of her baby's head against the wall of her womb.

She still found it hard to imagine what it might be like to be a mother—still less that she was actually going to be one. It seemed a thing that happened to other women, not to her. The thought filled her with a happiness such as she'd never experienced before, and at the same time a terrible fear of all the many things that might go wrong. To have Jeff's child was so wonderful that she felt that such fortune could not be hers: at any moment, fate would take away everything it had given her.

She banished these depressing thoughts, found her jacket and left the apartment.

She took the 'chute to Level One and walked through Himachal Park to her favourite coffee shop overlooking the ocean.

She sat at a window table, sipped a strong Indian coffee and watched the voidships phase in over the ocean and bank towards the spaceport.

She fingered the cool silver oval in her pocket and thought about Jeff. She wondered if it was because she once had nothing, and now had everything, that she felt so guilty—or if it was because Jeff had agreed to do a job he didn't really want to do, so that she could have a big apartment and a rich lifestyle.

A combination of the two, she thought.

She hadn't mentioned it to Jeff last night, but she worried about his new job. Not only because he would be reading minds, which he'd hated doing in the past, but because the job might be dangerous. He would be investigating criminals, murderers, and Sukara didn't like the idea of that. And if he were doing it all for her...

She took the mind-shield from her pocket and stared at it.

What had he said yesterday, when he'd insisted on giving her the shield? That he didn't want to risk her thoughts being read by competing telepathic investigators?

Sukara smiled. She guessed that that wasn't the reason at all. He was afraid, perhaps, of reading her mind, sharing in her past in Bangkok and the life she had led there. Perhaps—and the thought occurred to her suddenly, shockingly—he was afraid of reading that she didn't love him.

Well, the only way to reassure him about that would be to get him to turn on his implant, and for her to toss aside the shield—then he would find out what she felt for him. But Jeff wouldn't agree to that, so she would simply continue to show him that she loved him in the only way she knew how, by being interested in him, in his life, his thoughts and opinions, by simply... *loving* him.

She slipped the shield into her pocket, next to her jutting stomach, and finished her coffee.

She left the coffee shop and made her way back through the park, strolling in the sunlight with all the other rich, well-dressed citizens of the upper levels. It was hard to think of herself as one of these people now—but she was, she told herself. She might feel they were looking at her, wondering what a Level Tenner was doing up here, but there was nothing to distinguish her from any of the other upper-class Thai and Indian women out for a stroll—some of them with babies—this afternoon. They might glance at the big scar that bisected her face, but Sukara had long ago ceased to be self-conscious about that—"long ago" being around the time that Jeff first said he loved her.

From a Thai market stall she bought some freshly ground spices, spring onions, mushrooms, and an aubergine, then made her way back home. She'd cook Jeff's favourite tonight—hot green Thai curry—to celebrate their first dinner in the new apartment.

She caught the downchute to Level Two and walked along the boulevard to Chittapuram, pausing at the observation areas to look out over the ocean. She was almost home when she saw a small Thai girl—nose pressed against the glass—in shorts and a white T-shirt. From behind, with her bare brown limbs and jet black pudding bowl hair style, the girl looked just like Sukara's sister, Tiger—and she felt a sudden painful kick of longing and grief.

Tiger had left Sukara and Thailand seven years ago, and Sukara had never again seen her little sister. Just over two years ago, on arriving at Bengal Station, Sukara had learned of Tiger's death—and learned also that Tiger had known a telepath called Jeff Vaughan.

It was through Tiger that Sukara first met Jeff, and became involved with the killer he'd been trying to trace at the time.

If not for Tiger's death, Sukara knew, she might never have met Jeff Vaughan, would not have everything she had now.

It was yet another reason to feel guilty.

She smiled and told herself to grow up, as the kid turned and skipped away from the viewscreen: seen front-on, the girl didn't look anything at all like Tiger.

Sukara hurried home, thrilled again as she opened the front door and stared around at the dimensions of the apartment. She thought of a child running around the vast lounge, and the image filled her with joy.

For the next hour she cooked the curry, with plenty of fresh galangal and juniper berries, then steamed a pan of sticky rice.

She was still in the kitchen, cleaning the workbench, when she realised that Jeff had snuck into the apartment and was watching her.

She turned and laughed. He was angled in the kitchen doorway, filling it, and smiling at her.

"How long have you been there?"

He grinned. "About an hour."

"Liar!" she cried, and ran to him.

He looked tired, in his scruffy leather jacket, with his jaw unshaven and the stubble on his head growing out after the operation.

He kissed her. "Mmm. Smells good."

"What? Me or the curry?"

"Both."

"You smell like a pig. Busy day?"

"Why do I expect compliments from my charming wife?"

They had been married two years, and it still thrilled her when he called her his wife.

She said, "You're the best pig on the Station, will that do?"

"I'm honoured. I'll get a shower and tell you all about it."

She watched him cross the lounge, sling his jacket over a chair, and begin undressing before he reached the bathroom. Singing to herself, she returned to the workbench and prepared the chilli sauce.

They ate in the kitchen, at the big table by the viewscreen, and Jeff told her all about the case he and Kapinsky were working on.

Sukara shook her head, fork stalled before her mouth. "Three murders in nine months... and you think they're linked?"

"The first two certainly, and maybe even the third." He was a big man, and his movements and speech were slow, deliberate.

"Jeff, the man who murdered these people—"

"Probably a hired assassin."

"An assassin? So if he knows you're onto him...?" Panic flared in her chest. She waved her fork. "What's to stop him going after you and Kapinsky?"

He chewed, finished his mouthful, and nodded. "One, he doesn't know we're investigating him. Two, even if he did, we're just a couple of small-time private eyes, not worth bothering about."

She stared at him. "I'm not that stupid, Jeff! You'd be worth bothering about if you were close to discovering who he was, yes?"

"Su—we're professional. We won't let the killer know we're on to him, okay?"

She bit her lip, nodding grudgingly. "It's just that I worry, Jeff. I love you and I'm frightened."

He reached across the table, gripped her fingers. "I don't want you to worry. I'm not some kid playing games, okay?"

She smiled. "What do you think of the curry, Jeff?"

He shook his head. "Words can't do it justice. You should open a restaurant."

That night, in bed, Sukara held Jeff and whispered, "You do know I love you, don't you?"

He traced the line of her cheek with the back of his hand. Moonlight cascaded through the open viewscreen, silvering his jaw. "Of course."

"Jeff…" she began, and fell silent.

"Mmm."

"Jeff, I wish you'd read my mind. I want you to read what I feel about you. I want to show you that I love you."

He pulled away and blinked at her. "I know you love me, Su."

"No, but I want you to see how much I love you!"

He laughed. "Su—do you believe me when I tell you I love you?"

"Of course!"

"But you can't read me, can you?"

"No."

"Then trust me when I say I believe you love me."

She lay in his arms, in the moonlight, thinking about that. She smiled. "Mmm… Okay, Jeff," she said.

Minutes later she was asleep.

EIGHT

MALLORY

Next morning Vaughan was awoken by the chime of his handset. He dragged it from the bedside cabinet and clamped it around his wrist. "Vaughan here."

Kapinsky was evidently an early riser. She was already in her office and it wasn't yet eight. "Vaughan, what are your plans for today?"

He rubbed his eyes and tried to order his thoughts. "This morning, going over to the Scheering-Lassiter HQ, see what I can dig up there."

Kapinsky shook her head. "I've tried it. No go. They don't like private investigators."

"I'll work out some way of getting in there."

"You're an optimist, Vaughan," she said. "What about this afternoon?"

"I'll check the surveillance cams in the area around the amusement park. You?"

"I'm spending the day on the Mulraney case, questioning a few people, seeing if I can dig up a witness or two. Meet you here first thing tomorrow to collate what we've got, okay?"

"See you then," he said, and cut the connection.

Beside him, Sukara stirred. She rolled onto her back and blinked up at the ceiling. Light—real *daylight*—slanted into the bedroom.

"Like it here, Jeff," she murmured.

He leaned over and kissed her. "I've got to be going. I'm late already."

"Jeff, I don't like what you told me about that killer last night." She gripped his hand. "Take care," she said, reluctant to let go of him.

"I'll do that," he whispered.

He showered, left the apartment, grabbed a couple of samosas from a kiosk beside the upchute, and rode to Level One with a cage full of businessmen and schoolchildren.

He took an air-taxi the three kilometres to the centre of the Station. He would normally have travelled by train, but as Kapinsky was picking up the expenses he could afford to travel in comfort.

The Scheering-Lassiter headquarters was situated in the high-rise business sector, a tapering obelisk like extruded glass, which, until last year and the construction of the central government tower, had been the tallest building on the Station.

It looked, Vaughan thought as he stood in the plaza outside the edifice, suitably phallic and thrusting for a company whose aim it was to seed the stars. He watched the comings and goings of business execs and company workers, fingering the pass in his pocket and hoping its validity had not been erased after its owner's death.

Everyone going into the building through the single, sliding entrance proffered a pass-card, which was scanned by an electronic eye. Security guards were on hand to turn away *personae non gratae*. A small proportion of the people entering the building made enquiries at reception; far more simply walked through the lobby and made for the elevators.

The thing to do was to go in exuding confidence, an air of belonging, and once inside take it from there. With luck he would get a bit further than Kapinsky had yesterday.

He walked towards the building and activated his implant. Instantly a hundred minds flared in close proximity—a cacophony of hope and desire, anger and joy—with a dull backing of the mind-noise of the rest of Levels One and Two.

He felt his pulse race as he approached the sliding glass door. As it opened to admit him and a couple of suited Thai women, a curious thing happened.

The mind-noise that was a constant background hum remained in his head, but the bright flares of individual minds cut out the instant he entered the building. He was so surprised that he almost forgot to show the staring camera eye his purloined pass. He fumbled with it, heart hammering, and passed into the lobby without being apprehended.

He bypassed reception and headed straight for the elevators, where a wall plaque described the departments on various floors.

He bought himself time by consulting the plaque, at the same time coming to terms with the fact that everyone in the building—everyone employed by Scheering-Lassiter—was mind-shielded.

There were exceptions: a cleaner scouring the marble tiles was without a shield, as were a couple of lowly office boys, along with casual visitors to the building—but Vaughan estimated that more than ninety per cent of everyone in the building was unreadable.

Which meant that he wouldn't learn as much as he'd hoped this morning—but the fact that the company kept its personnel shielded was interesting in itself.

The first floor was given over to individual offices and a list of executive's names. The second through tenth floors housed various departments, corporate strategy, research and development, and Terran administration among others.

On the fifteenth floor he found what he was looking for: colonial affairs. In offices one to five were housed the Mallory Department.

Vaughan entered the elevator and rose to the fifteenth floor.

He stepped out into a spacious area of wide corridors and open-plan offices, decorated with what he took to be specimens of Mallorian flora: blue shrubs and startled-looking blood-red cacti, alien to eyes accustomed to verdant Earthly horticulture. Men and women in smart business suits moved back and forth, barely giving him a second glance. They, too, were shielded. He killed his implant, and the distant mind-noise from the rest of the Station fell blissfully silent.

Across the wide corridor, facing the elevator, was a big head and shoulders photograph of Gustave Scheering, the head of the organisation. He appeared to be in his sixties, the beefy slab of his face staring out at the world with all the self-confidence of a self-made millionaire. Vaughan read a potted biography of the great man beside the photograph: born in New York, he'd risen from obscurity to the status of a major tycoon in his twenties, running a couple of Luna–Mars shipping Lines before starting up in the colony business with his business partner, Reb Lassiter. Scheering had assumed total control of the company after Lassiter's death five years ago.

To the left of the elevator was an exhibition area given over to educating the visitor on the positive aspects of Mallory's human colonisation.

Vaughan browsed the softscreens and holo-cubes, which gave condensed histories of the planet's discovery, exploration, and colonisation. Documentary footage was accompanied by a saccharine female voice-over, sotto voce corporate hard sell.

It was, he had to admit, a stunningly beautiful world.

Take Switzerland, expand it, add a North African climate and gravity a little less than Earth's, and the result was the exotic colony world of Mallory. The fact that the grass and most growing things were a shade of blue only added to the planet's allure.

There was very little on Mallory's native fauna, and nothing about Scheering-Lassiter's ecological policy. Not that he'd expected much in that department.

He read everything there was to read in the exhibit, listened to all the anodyne commentaries, and came away knowing he'd been fed the party line.

It was time to find someone who might be able to answer a question or two.

He bypassed the open-plan office area—the desks occupied by glorified secretaries—and made for an enclosed office at the far end of the chamber.

The door was marked: Gita Singh, Co-Director.

He knocked and opened the door without awaiting a reply.

A woman in her thirties, power-dressed in a severe black suit more like a uniform, looked up from a softscreen in surprise. "Can I help you?"

He'd decided to be direct, rather than try to catch her out with dissimulation. "I hope so. I'm Jeff Vaughan and I'm investigating the murder of one of your colleagues."

Singh was suspicious. "Have you cleared this with security?"

He flashed his identity-pass. "How do you think I got this far?" he smiled, disarmingly. "I know you won't be able to tell me anything linked directly to the case itself, but I'd appreciate some background information about the planet."

Singh's gaze was professionally neutral. "Mr Vaughan, I really am very busy this morning. By the elevator you will find an informative display, which should tell you all you need to know."

He shook his head, his smile sardonic now. "I think not. I've taken the tour, and in fact I think it told me nothing about what I really want to know about Mallory."

She held his gaze. "And what might that be?"

Vaughan was placatory. He spread his hands. "Look, I'm on your side. Someone sliced one of your colleagues to bits and I want to solve the case. I'm sure you appreciate my concern?"

"Of course, Mr Vaughan. But I cannot see how anything I might tell you about Mallory could have any bearing—"

"Perhaps I should be the judge of that, Ms Singh? To begin with, I'd like some information about Scheering-Lassiter's ecological policy regarding Mallory, its relations with Eco-Col, and the management of indigenous fauna."

Discreetly, but not so discreetly that Vaughan missed it, Singh slipped a hand beneath the desk and applied pressure.

The audience was over.

Vaughan sighed. "Well, I can see that I'm wasting my time here, Ms Singh. It's been pleasant chatting."

She watched him with an expression that indicated the sentiment was not mutual.

He rose and left the room, quickly, before security arrived and quizzed him about the pass-card. He took the elevator to the ground floor and stepped out into the punitive noon sunlight, happy with the morning's work. At least he'd got a lot further than Kapinsky, and he'd come away with one or two interesting pieces of information.

As the air-taxi powered down onto the landing shelf, Vaughan looked out at the sable edifice of the Law Enforcement headquarters, rising from the deck of the Station like an Aztec ziggurat. It brought back a slew of unpleasant memories.

Two years ago he'd found himself involved in an investigation with a cop called Jimmy Chandra. Their enquiries had taken them off-planet, to the colony world of Verkerk, where Chandra had died.

Chandra had been an optimist, his Hindu cheer a foil to Vaughan's then cynicism.

Vaughan had changed since then, however; now he could share Chandra's upbeat world-view. The world had not changed one bit—but Vaughan had.

He showed his ID at the entrance and dropped into the bowels of the building, making his way through the dimly lit corridors to the surveillance room.

It was a long, low chamber, badly lighted, and the ventilation system seemed to have given up trying to cool the place. It was like a sauna in there, made worse by three cops smoking cheap cigarettes as they stared at their screens.

Vaughan found a corner booth and powered up the com. It flared, showing a grid-map of Level One, beside a rank of numerals should he require views of other levels.

He found the amusement park, entered its reference number and the day and approximate time of the scene he wished to view, and waited.

As expected, there were no surveillance cams in operation in the park itself. He returned to the map, worked out where the killing took place, and entered the reference of the nearest street which might be covered by a cam.

This time he was in luck.

There were three cams covering the length of the deserted street, and one of them showed a section of the area where Kormier had died.

He magnified the view, enhanced the image: he made out the concourse between the ghost train and the empty McDonald's kiosk.

He ran the tape at three times the normal speed, and the only indication that time was elapsing was the flicking digital display at the top right of the screen: the scene itself remained static.

He glanced at the timer: 23.40. According to the SoC's report, the killing had taken place at some time twelve minutes either side of midnight.

He slowed the image to real-time and watched.

Two minutes later he saw movement.

He leaned forward, magnifying the image, and saw two small figures cross the concourse, climb the steps of the ghost train and enter it through the ghoul's open mouth. Children: a boy and a girl. From the way they were dressed, in ragged shorts and T-shirts, he guessed they were homeless street-kids taking refuge for the night in the park.

They appeared again, minutes later, emerging from the exit of the ghost train—another open mouth. Then they stopped suddenly, and one of them pointed across the concourse before ducking back inside the open mouth.

Vaughan made out what the boy had pointed at.

Another figure had appeared on the concourse.

Vaughan reached out and stilled the image, his pulse racing. He stared at the figure. It was a man, tall and dark, in his fifties: Robert Kormier.

He restarted the footage, playing it real-time now. He glanced at the digital display: it was nine minutes to midnight.

Kormier paced back and forth, between the ghost train and the fast-food kiosk. From time to time he glanced at his wristwatch. So he had clearly arrived at the amusement park to meet someone.

Seconds later, the boy jumped from the exit of the ghost train.

Vaughan stilled the image and examined the ghost's gaping rictus. The girl was still in the shadows, peeping out.

He restarted the image. Kormier paced. Each time he reached the ghost train and turned, Vaughan expected him to face his killer.

So far, however, there was no sign of the laser slayer.

Then, at a minute before midnight, Kormier came to a halt before the ghost train. He turned, lifted his cuff again to glance at his watch. He looked up, across the concourse, then lifted an arm as if in greeting.

It was the last living movement he was to make.

The dazzling laser vector lasted barely half a second. It lanced from off-screen, hit Kormier, then vanished. That was all it took: Kormier lay on the concrete, head, arms, and torso sliced into four neat sections.

Vaughan stilled the image, sat back in his seat. He realised that he was sweating and breathing hard. It was as if he had been there, had witnessed the slaying in the flesh.

For the next hour he accessed other cameras in the vicinity of the amusement park, attempting to get an image of the killer. Half a dozen other cameras gave partial views of the park, but none had captured the murderer. He'd been either very lucky, or had known the surveillance cams' blind spots and had planned accordingly.

Vaughan checked all the cams in the vicinity of the park for anyone entering through the boarded-up perimeter fence, but found nothing. The killer had arrived and departed without allowing himself to be caught by a single camera. Luck, it seemed, had had nothing to do with it. He was obviously dealing with someone professional and meticulous.

He returned to the original scene of the concourse. He viewed the killing again, and again, and then the minutes leading up to it, and after.

At least he had another valuable lead here: the girl cowering in the mouth of the ghost had seen the killing. It was also possible that she had caught sight of the killer.

He viewed the scene in the minutes after the killing. He watched the girl jump from the mouth of the ghost, turn, and run down a narrow alley between the ghost train and the neighbouring attraction.

He rewound the footage and looked for the best view of the girl. For the most part she had her back to the camera. Only when she was emerging from the ghost's mouth, preparatory to making her escape, did she present a frontal image.

He magnified the scene, homing in on the girl.

He computer-enhanced the picture, cleaning up the granular pixels and coming out with a sharp image of a young Thai girl, perhaps seven or eight, in dirty red shorts and a white T-shirt.

He printed the image and sat back with it in his hand, staring.

The legend across the front of the kid's shirt was: *Tigers*.

Years ago he had known Sukara's kid sister, Tiger, before she'd overdosed on a virulent off-world drug. Tiger, a big fan of the skyball team, had worn a T-shirt just like this kid's.

It was a day, he thought, haunted by spectres of the past.

He returned to the screen and re-ran the minutes either side of Kormier's killing, playing the images in slow motion to ensure he missed nothing.

The laser hit—in slow motion, he could make out the vector's minimal waver that created the grisly loop effect—and winked out of existence.

He played it again, and again, and only on the third time did he notice something.

He sat forward, wondering if the effect had been the result of tired eyes.

But there it was again.

In the split second after the laser's impact, a light seemed to rebound at right angles to Kormier and lance off towards where the kid crouched in the ghost's open mouth.

It hit her in the centre of her forehead, sending her reeling backwards.

Which, he told himself, was insane. Lasers didn't ricochet.

He replayed the image perhaps twenty times. The rebounding light was not blue, like the laser vector, but white. He wondered if it was some reflection of the laser on the screen of the surveillance cam. But that was ridiculous, and anyway the girl had clearly been affected, startled, by the rebound.

Affected, he thought, but evidently not harmed, as she had jumped from her place of concealment and made her getaway. He ran the tape and watched as she ran down the gap between the ghost train and another concession, entering what looked like a toilet block. Seconds later she was followed by a bright blue laser vector. It burned through the toilet door, but too high to have hit the kid—and when the door swung open it revealed an empty room.

Then Vaughan made out a dark figure sprint down the alley after the girl, enter the toilet block, and squirm down through a service hatch in the floor.

He magnified the image of the killer, but got nothing more than a vague, granular outline.

He sat back and considered his next move.

He made a dozen printouts of the kid, wallet sized, then killed the screen and left the ziggurat. He rode the elevator to the landing shelf and emerged into bright sunlight.

He sat on a bench, in the shade of a cedar tree, overlooking the sprawl of the station as noisy aircars came and went.

His next move was to locate the street-kid—if she had succeeded in evading the killer. She had seen the killing, maybe even the killer. If she were still alive, then he knew exactly who might be able to help him find her.

He tapped a code into his handset and hoped it was still in use. It was a long time since he'd contacted the doctor.

He smiled as the ancient face—looking more than ever like the wrinkled headpiece of a querulous turtle—peered out at him. Talk about ghosts from the past...

"Dr Rao," he said.

Rao blinked. "My word, my word indeed. If I'm not mistaken, if my eyes do not deceive, I do believe it is Mr Vaughan."

"Your eyes are working perfectly, Rao. How's things?"

"Mr Vaughan, what can I say? Life, as ever, is hard for the likes of me—a citizen who wants only to bring light into the dark lives of those more unfortunate than himself."

Vaughan tried to hide his smile. This was the Rao of old, as sanctimoniously self-serving as ever. To listen to him, you'd think Rao was a saint, not some Hindu Fagin out to line his own pocket.

Vaughan said, "I think you might be able to help me, Rao."

The old man's dull eyes took on a predatory gleam.

"Mr Vaughan, you know that I am ever available to aid those I deem worthy."

"I'm looking for a street-kid. I know nothing about her. I have a pix, that's all."

Rao gave a lipless smile, increasing his resemblance to a turtle. "I have been known to work miracles with less, for..." he went on, "shall we say, certain considerations?"

"We'll talk money when we meet, Rao. When can I see you?"

"Time presses, and is valuable. I will be available in two hours, for thirty minutes only, at four o'clock."

"Fine. I'll see you then. How about Nazruddin's?"

"You are a creature of habit, Mr Vaughan. Nazruddin's it is. Until then..." And Rao tipped his head graciously and cut the connection.

He had two hours to kill before meeting Rao. He hailed an air-taxi and told the pilot to take him to the amusement park, Kandalay.

NINE

THE GIRL

The abandoned park had the aspect of a ransacked city left to the elements.

Everywhere he looked his eye met with dilapidated façades and the skeletal remains of once exhilarating concessions. Mock voidships and aircars sat redundant, their once bright colours excoriated by the sun. An air of sadness, almost tragedy, hung over the place.

He crossed the concourse to where Kormier had died in front of the ghost train. Nothing remained to indicate his passing, not a trace of blood or laser scorch marks. Vaughan looked up at the garish façade of the ghost train, the leering ghosts, blood-soaked vampires, and the wailing ghoul like Munch's *Scream* where the boy and girl had hidden two nights ago.

He climbed the steps and peered into the ghost's mouth, then ducked inside. Shafts of bright sunlight fell through the cracked weatherboard roof, illuminating loose virtual relays, pneumatic stanchions, and the luminous remains of green monsters.

He examined the area where the kid had crouched, found nothing, as expected, and climbed down again.

He sighted along the trajectory of the laser vector and sourced it to a blocky powerhouse beside the starship ride. He crossed to it and pulled open the door. The powerhouse had been stripped of generators and controls. Only an oily shell remained, and a trapdoor in the centre of the floor.

He knelt, opened the heavy cover, and peered into the semi-lit dropshaft. It was a maintenance conduit, lined with wires and junction boxes, accessible by a welded ladder. Was this how the killer had entered the park?

He squeezed himself into the gap and climbed down, the confined area reeking of burnt electrics and rusting metal, the temperature a punishing hundred plus.

The Station was riddled with a maze of secret shafts, passageways, and tunnels used by engineers and mechanics in their bid to keep the place functioning. Vaughan had used the service shafts before—in fact two years ago, when being taken to Dr Rao's hidden lair between Levels Eleven and Twelve—and he was sure that many of them had been abandoned and forgotten decades ago.

Now, they were the haunt of opportunists like the laser killer, and the homeless street-kids who found refuge in the interstices between the populated levels.

He descended for two minutes before the dropshaft terminated. Before him was a small hatch, like the door in a submarine. He eased it open and found himself on a walkway high above a teeming corridor on Level Three.

Sensing another break, he looked around for a ubiquitous surveillance camera—and found one not three metres from the hatch, and pointing directly at it.

His joy was short-lived. The lens of the cam had been sprayed over with black paint.

He should have known that the killer would have covered this angle, too.

In hope, he moved along the walkway. Every cam covering the hatch to the service shaft had been disabled.

Not for the first time, Vaughan realised he was chasing a professional.

He retraced his steps, squeezed back through the hatch, and began the arduous climb up to the powerhouse.

Ten minutes later he was standing in the sunlight, breathing hard. He crossed the concourse to the ghost train and stepped down the narrow alley where the girl had vanished the other night. He approached the toilet block and made out the fist-sized entry hole punched through the plastic swing door.

He pushed through and entered the john, lifted the service hatch and peered down, part of him expecting to see the butchered remains of the kid at the foot of the shaft. He saw only a narrow ladder, welded to the wall.

He inserted himself into the narrow space, grunting with the unaccustomed effort. He climbed down, and minutes later found himself on a walkway above a busy thoroughfare. He looked right and left for surveillance cams... but he was out of luck, again. This stretch of corridor was without the luxury of watching cameras.

He turned to the shaft and climbed, wondering as he did so if the killer had managed to catch the kid somewhere in the corridors of Level Three. Or had she, with the cunning of her kind, managed to evade pursuit and lose herself in the crowds?

If the latter, then the killer would still no doubt be trying to trace her.

He emerged from the exit in the john, crossed the concourse, and called an air-taxi.

Five minutes later he ducked from the taxi and pushed his way through the crowds that thronged Chandi Road night and day. He ignored the importuning cries of maimed beggars, the incessant sleeve tugging of pleading street-kids, and eased himself into the air-conditioned calm of Nazruddin's.

He found an empty booth at the back of the restaurant, ordered a Blue Mountain beer and waited for Dr Rao.

He was on his second bottle, at the stroke of four, when the elderly doctor stepped through the entrance, paused to scan the seated diners, then lofted his walking stick in greeting.

He tottered towards Vaughan, his turtle lips stretched in a rictus approximating a smile.

"Mr Vaughan, Mr Vaughan! It is a delight to make your acquaintance after so long!" He seated himself and to a hovering waiter snapped an order for salted lassi.

Vaughan smiled. Rao, sitting bolt upright in his high-collared Nehru suit, arthritic fingers clutching the head of his stick, appeared the very epitome of patriarchal Brahmin probity. Vaughan marvelled at the contrast between the doctor's outward persona and the schemes he knew festered in the Indian's fertile mind.

Rao leaned forward. "And might I enquire as to the health of your young wife?"

"Sukara's doing fine, Rao."

"And if my information is not erroneous, the patter of tiny feet is imminent?"

Vaughan shook his head in amazement. "How on earth did you know that, Rao?"

The old man laughed. "Nothing is a secret from Dr Rao, Mr Vaughan! You should know that." His rheumy eyes became even more liquid. "Ah, children. They are truly one's hope for the future."

And your meal ticket in the here and now, Vaughan thought.

"I heard also, on the grapevine, shall we say, that you had your telepathic implant removed... in somewhat adverse circumstances."

Vaughan nodded. "Old news, Rao. That happened two years ago."

"And you have not had it replaced?"

He shook his head. "I elected for the quiet life," he said. Why alert Rao to the fact that the good doctor's lies could be seen through?

"I must admit that I never thought you the type of man to settle down," Rao went on.

"Life is full of surprises, Rao."

The doctor laughed. "You are so right, my friend. For instance, it was a surprise to hear from you, but a pleasant surprise, might I add? You mentioned something about trying to locate a certain child of the street?"

Vaughan nodded and pulled out his wallet. From it he drew the computer-enhanced pix of the Thai girl and slid it across the table to Rao.

Rao tapped the pix with a nicotine-stained fore-finger. A light appeared in his eye, and Vaughan guessed that Rao knew something about the kid.

He was tempted to activate his implant and read what Rao knew, but at the same time he was loath to immerse himself in Rao's self-serving righteous-ness, and whatever else he might come across in the doctor's scheming brain.

Rao sucked his lips, shaking his head. "Ah, Mr Vaughan. So many children have passed my gaze over the past week or so, so many tiny Thai girls with pudding-bowl haircuts and beseeching eyes. One, I must admit, looks very much like another."

"She was wearing a Tigers' T-shirt," Vaughan prompted.

"Do you know, I do think that I might have seen a child answering to her description—seen very briefly, I must add—"

"When?" Vaughan said.

Rao smiled. "I said I *might* have seen the girl, Mr Vaughan. Of course, I might have been mistaken. As I said, one child looks very much like another. However, if I were to bend my efforts in order to locate this child, it would be a costly procedure for me, I hope you understand." He looked up. "Might I ask why you wish to locate the girl?"

"She was witness to a murder," Vaughan said.

Rao nodded, assessing whether this information might conceivably be to his advantage. "Indeed," he said. "I see. Hmm... Now let me consider the various ins and outs of the situation as I see it, Mr

Vaughan." He took time to sip his lassi, then wipe the foamy moustache from his upper lip. "Mr Vaughan, information, as a commodity—as you well know—is valuable. What I mean to say is that I could put you into contact with someone who might know something about the child, but of course, as is the nature of things, I would have no option but to expect recompense for effecting such a service." The doctor beamed across the table with the innocence of a saint.

Vaughan sighed, trying not to smile. There was something almost entertaining in listening to Rao's self-justifying circumlocutions. "How much, Rao?"

"Now let me see. If the child was indeed witness to a murder, then this is very serious indeed, and my guess is that your need to locate her is corresponding-ly acute—which leads me to the inevitable conclusion that you would be willing to part with perhaps, let's say, in the region of five hundred baht for any information leading to your locating the girl..." Rao beamed like a guiltless babe, "...and a further five hundred if such information successful-ly leads to her apprehension?"

"I'll give you three hundred baht up front, if the information is solid. If I find her, you get the same again. Take it or leave it."

"Mr Vaughan, you drive a hard bargain. You fail to understand quite how financially draining it is to look after my flock."

"Three and three, Rao. My final offer."

Rao looked down at the pix of the Thai girl on the tabletop, considering. "I find myself beholden to accept your paltry offer, Mr Vaughan. One moment."

He turned and called a waiter, who hurried to the table. Rao fired off a volley of Hindi and the waiter nodded and made for the exit. Seconds later he returned, with a shaven-headed Thai boy, about eight years old, in tow.

Vaughan recognised the kid as one of a bunch of beggars who hung around outside Nazruddin's night and day. The boy's left arm had been removed, expertly, at the shoulder.

The boy stood meekly beside the table, like a pupil called to the headmaster's office for wrongdoing.

"Now Kam," Rao said, lifting the pix from the table and showing it to the boy, "I wish you to help me in a certain important matter." He switched to rapid-fire Thai, and Vaughan caught only the odd comprehensible phrase. "Thai girl... very serious crime... was Abdul with her that night?"

The boy responded in a whisper, eyes downcast. At last Rao said, in Thai, "Go, bring Abdul here to me!"

The boy hurried off and Rao beamed. "The first stage of the process of locating the girl is under way. You will have no regrets in coming to Dr Rao, my friend!"

Vaughan smiled. "You're one in a million, Rao."

Rao's pleased grin displayed an abundance of gold filling. "You should not have left it almost two years to reacquaint yourself with my efficacy, my good friend. Remember—Dr Rao is on hand to facilitate all manner of requirements!"

Vaughan nodded. "I'll bear that in mind."

He ordered a third beer and another lassi for Rao, and two minutes later Kam appeared at the door with a gangly Muslim ten-year-old.

Rao dismissed Kam and gestured Abdul to approach the table. The boy glanced from Rao to Vaughan with stark fear in his dark eyes.

Rao spoke to the boy, this time in Urdu, which Vaughan had no hope of following.

"Ah-cha," Rao said, nodding. "Ah-cha, very interesting."

He quizzed the boy again, and nodded at his reply. At last the boy fell silent and Rao smiled beatifically at Vaughan.

"It would seem, my friend, that Abdul made the acquaintance of the girl in question on the night before last. They met at perhaps nine o'clock, quite by chance, and fell into conversation."

Vaughan said, "Does he know her name?"

"Her first name only—Pham. I have elicited all the relevant details from the boy and they are as follows. Pham is seven, and hails from Level Twenty. She was indentured to a factory owner manufacturing plastics. She ran away from the factory and followed her ambition to travel to the upper level. You see, Mr Vaughan, Pham had never in her short life seen the light of the sun."

Vaughan said, "Two nights ago they entered Kandalay amusement park. I saw them on a surveillance cam. I know that Pham witnessed the murder. Will you ask Abdul if he saw anything?"

Rao turned to the boy and questioned him. The kid looked scared, shook his head, and replied in a murmur.

Rao said, "He saw a man in the amusement park. He thought it was a security guard, so he ran off. Pham was not so fast. Seconds later Abdul heard the sound of laser fire. He escaped down a service shaft to Level Three and did not go back."

Vaughan said, "And Pham? Does Abdul know what happened to her?"

Rao spoke to the boy, who answered in a monosyllable.

Rao reported to Vaughan, "No, he does not know what happened to the girl." He hesitated, then said, "He has not seen her since that night. He was too frightened to go back, after hearing the laser fire."

Vaughan sighed and leaned back in his chair, taking a long drink of beer and considering his next question. "Will you ask Abdul if Pham told him if she was going back to Level Twenty, or if she planned to stay topside?"

Seconds later Rao said, "Pham told him that she never wished to return to the factory. She said she would rather die than go back."

"Does he know the name of the factory owner?"

Rao asked. The boy replied, but Rao reported, "No, that he does not know."

Vaughan nodded, suspecting that the doctor was withholding the factory owner's name. "Ask Abdul if Pham told him where she intended to stay up here."

Rao asked the question and duly translated, "Abdul does not know. The girl said she would beg on the streets."

"She didn't ask to stay with you, Rao?"

"Mr Vaughan," Rao said disingenuously, "I would have told you if I had made the child's acquaintance!"

"Okay, Rao. Anything else? Is that all Abdul knows about her?"

The doctor jogged his head in an Indian affirmative. "That is all he knows." He paused, then went on, "However, I am certain that I could elicit certain answers—like the name of her employer, and where she planned to stay on Level One—from other sources. Of course, this would take time, and time—as I do not have to remind you—is money."

Vaughan had to admire the doctor's barefaced duplicity. "I'm happy with my three hundred's worth, Rao," he said.

Rao snapped something to Abdul, who was grateful for the opportunity to flee. Vaughan watched the boy leave the restaurant. He remained outside, talking to a group of street-kids.

Vaughan peeled half a dozen fifty baht notes from his wallet and dropped them in front of the Indian.

Rao smiled. "Mr Vaughan, you can rest assured that your kind donation will furnish the comfort of many a foundling street-child."

He looked at his watch. "My word, sir. My generosity knows no bounds. I granted you thirty minutes and lo, one hour has elapsed. By rights I should make a certain surcharge to recompense for time lost."

Vaughan laughed. "I'll pick up your tab, Rao. Be thankful for that."

Rao made a quick bow and said without irony, "Your munificence knows no bounds, Mr Vaughan. I will contact you if I should learn anything more about the girl." He stood and made to leave. "Namaste, my friend. May your God go with you."

"And the same to you, Rao."

He watched the elderly Brahmin shuffle through the exit, then finished his beer in a thoughtful mood. He waited until Rao had vanished into the crowd surging down Chandi Road, then paid his bill. He glanced through the window. Abdul was still there.

Vaughan left the restaurant, but not before activating his implant.

He winced as his head was assailed by a piercing shriek of mind-noise. The scrambled thoughts of a thousand passing minds jumped him like a sudden migraine. Almost staggering under the onslaught, he filtered out the extraneous mush—the tangled emotions of the diners and passers-by—and concentrated on the bright point of Abdul's mind as he pushed through the swing door.

He approached the timorous street-kid, who cowered back as Vaughan looked down at him.

He pulled a ten baht note from his wallet and passed it to Abdul, who took it with a muttered thanks.

Vaughan scanned, sank into the boy's memories of the night in the amusement park, the little Thai girl he'd befriended, and the fear of what had happened soon after.

He read two things that Rao, in a bid to extort more baht from him, had failed to reveal: the name of the girl's employer was Ranjit Prakesh, and Abdul had met Pham a day after the shooting, in Ketsuwan Park on Level Two.

Vaughan felt a stab of relief that the kid had survived.

He quickly deactivated his implant, breathing with relief at the instant cessation of mind-noise.

Smiling at the thought of Dr Rao's flagrant lies, and heartened by the turn of events, he pushed through the crowd and made his way to the nearest dropchute station.

TEN

KHAR

Pham spent the afternoon in Ketsuwan Park. She bought a big bottle of water and a plate of dhal and rice from a kiosk beside the eastern gate, then found her bench beneath the cedar tree and ate.

All in all, she had had an exciting time on the upper levels. She'd witnessed a murder, been chased by the killer, seen a crashed spaceship full of injured children... and then the voice. A voice had got into her head and spoken to her.

She had thought about the voice for a long time, even tried to speak to it again. She thought she knew what it was.

When people died, if they had been good in this life, then they were reincarnated as something better in the next. If they had been bad, then they came back as... rats or spiders or something horrid like that. But sometimes she knew if someone had been extra specially bad, then their souls were destined to haunt the earth in torment, until they were exorcised and could move on.

So, for some reason, the soul of the man lasered to death in the amusement park the other night had jumped into her head. Perhaps something to do with the laser had helped his soul to make the journey to Pham, the person closest to him when he died. That had to be the answer.

So… she had the soul of a bad person living in her head, and even though the voice had told her not to be frightened, that it could help her, she did not trust it. She would have to be careful.

"Voice," she said now, under her breath so that people didn't hear her and think she was mad. "I know you're in there, and I know what you are. You accidentally got into my head because you were killed by a laser. You were bad in your last life, but now you're with me you'll have to be good, ah-cha?"

Silence.

Only, she wondered, how long would the bad man's soul stay in her head? Would it stay with her until she died, or would it leave before then?

"Perhaps if you're good, and we pray to Buddha every day, then he'll let you out before I die, and you can be reborn as a better person than you were."

She smiled to herself. She liked the idea of that.

"Voice?"

It was stubborn. It spoke to her only when it wanted to, and never replied to her questions. She wanted to know more about it, see if it would agree to be good while it lived in her head.

She had a worrying thought. What if it wanted to be bad, put bad thoughts into her head, and made her do bad things?

But, she told herself, it had told her not to be frightened, that it would help her. And in the crashed spaceship, it had told her to get out...

She finished her dhal and took a long drink of water. She checked her money pouch and found that she had just fifty baht left, which was not a lot. It would buy her food for another three days, four if she had only one meal a day. The thing was, how did you find work on the upper levels? She hadn't seen any kids working anywhere up here, only boys and girls begging. What would she do when her money ran out? She didn't want to beg, and she didn't want to go back to Mr Prakesh's factory.

She thought of Abdul, who was nice. Perhaps her only option might be to live with him and the other kids on the starship?

The voice in her head said: *No*.

"Voice?" she said, sitting upright. "Are you there? Why don't you want me to go back to the ship?"

The silence stretched. Just when Pham thought Voice was not going to reply, it said: *It is not a good place for you*.

"But why?"

Silence.

"Voice, what are you?" she asked. "You're a bad soul, right? The man who was killed, you're his bad soul. But... but you won't make me bad, will you?"

Maddeningly, Voice did not respond.

"You can live in my head until you've earned the right to move on, ah-cha?"

This time, after a delay of a few seconds, Voice replied: *Do not be frightened. I am not a bad soul.*

I wish you no harm. In time I will move on. Before that, I will try to help you.

"You will? But how can you help me?"

Listen to me. From time to time I will speak. Then, do as I say. The rest of the time I will be silent.

Pham nodded. "Ah-cha," she whispered. "Voice," she said after a while, "what is your name?"

Voice said: *Call me Khar.*

She nodded. "Khar," she said. "Pleased to meet you. I'm Pham."

Khar was silent for five minutes, then said: *Would you like to see the zoo on Level Three?*

"I didn't even know there was a zoo."

I think you will like it there.

"I don't know the way—"

I do. Just get up and walk from the park, and I will show you...

She did as she was told, leaving the park by the western exit and boarding a shuttle train for the southern edge. The odd thing was, Khar never said a word to her after she left the park. It was as if she knew how to get to the zoo without being told. She wondered if Khar could put thoughts, information, into her head.

She wondered if she should be frightened, but another odd thing was that she didn't feel a bit scared. Perhaps Khar was controlling her fear, too?

If Khar wasn't a bad soul, she wondered as she jumped from the train and hurried out into the street, then what was it?

The zoo was a massive complex that ran for a kilometre along the southern edge of the Station, with great viewscreens that overlooked the ocean. Pham paid five baht for a ticket and received a brochure telling her all about the zoo.

She read that the animals didn't live in cages, but had whole compounds to themselves. And, she discovered, the zoo housed not only animals from Earth—like lions and tigers—but extraterrestrial animals from many of the colonies across the galaxy. They lived here for one year, and then they were returned to their planets and set free.

She wondered why Khar wanted to visit the zoo.

A wide boulevard ran between the vast viewscreens looking out over the ocean and the animals' compounds. Pham strolled along the boulevard, stopping from time to time to stare down at the strange beasts grazing on odd-looking grasses. Some of the compounds were sealed, because the atmosphere inside was not like Earth's, and these animals were even stranger than the others. She saw things like blue crabs the size of air-cars, and great orange creatures that rolled through a vast tank of blue water.

She walked on. She felt that Khar was moving her towards where it wanted to be.

At last she came to a compound that stretched back for what seemed like a kilometre, and was almost as wide. Tall blue grass glinted under the glare of an artificial sun, and the plain was dotted with twisted trees bearing big red flowers.

Then she saw the animals, and she had the strange feeling that she had seen them before somewhere. Which was impossible, because surely she would have remembered seeing creatures like these in books and on holo-vision.

Three big animals were grazing close to the glass canopy that arched over the compound. They had hides like elephants, but brown and wrinkled, and longer legs than elephants, and shorter, thicker trunks. Their eyes were big and blue, and set on either side of their big heads. From the sides of their mouths, several sharper tusks projected, and similar horns sprouted from above their eyes.

They looked fearsome, but at the same time friendly.

A recorded voice from a nearby speaker said that the animals were called Grayson's Pachyderms, and came from the colony planet of Mallory, Eta Ophiuchi.

As she watched, two of the pachyderms wandered off, but the third looked up and seemed to stare directly at her. Slowly, it approached the canopy and stood perhaps three metres from where Pham leaned against the padded rail, looking down with wonder at the strange beast.

She felt suddenly sleepy. "Khar," she said, "why did you want to…"

But she never finished the sentence. Her eyes fluttered shut, incredibly heavy, and though she fought against slipping into sleep, she felt herself going under.

Then she was awake, and amazingly she was still standing upright, and the pachyderm down below was moving off, its big feet plodding ponderously through the high blue grass.

"Khar?" she said. "What happened?"

Maddeningly, the thing in her head chose not to reply.

She watched the animals for a while longer, then wandered along the boulevard and stared in at the other alien exhibits.

The sun was going down over the ocean when she decided that she had seen enough for one day. She would return to the park, get something to eat and sleep on her bench—even though Abdul had said the park was not a safe place.

As she was leaving the zoo, Khar decided to speak to her.

Thank you, it said.

"Khar—what was so important about seeing those animals?"

It did not answer her question, but said instead: *You have little money for food and other things. Listen to me when I speak.*

It said no more. Pham boarded a train heading north for Ketsuwan, and ten minutes later alighted at the station beside the park.

Instead of entering the park—which is what she wanted to do—she found herself walking down a nearby street. Many stalls were set out here, selling food and trinkets and ornament for tourists. Pham elbowed her way through a crowd surrounding a small stall, and when she reached the front she saw a stick-thin Indian in a loincloth. He stood behind a small table, and had three cups placed upside-down before him. Under one of the cups was a small bronze model of Kali. He showed it to the audience, then clapped a cup over it and with lightning speed moved the cups around. Pham watched closely, sure that the figure of Kali was underneath the right-hand cup when the man finally brought them to rest.

A Thai boy beside Pham, who had laid a ten baht note on the table, now pointed at the right-hand cup.

Grinning and shrugging his shoulders as if in commiseration, the Indian lifted up the cup. Kali was not there. The Indian snatched the ten baht and lifted the cup on the left to reveal the bronze statuette.

The crowd laughed and the Thai boy skulked away.

The Indian beamed around at the watching crowd. "Ten baht—or even more! I'll match it if you guess where Kali's hiding! Come, do none of you trust your eyes?"

Khar said: *Take the fifty baht note from your pouch and put it on the table. Do as I say.*

Fifty baht, she thought.

Do it!

Hesitantly, wondering if she was acting wisely, she did as instructed. All around her the crowd laughed in derision.

The old Indian smiled. "Aha! The little girl is braver than the rest of you."

"Or more foolish!" someone called out.

The Indian winked at her. "Watch closely, little one. If you guess where Kali is hidden, I will match your fifty baht!"

He dropped the central cup over Kali, then shuffled them around, slowly at first, then a little faster. Pham watched closely, her heart beating fast. She followed the cup under which she knew the figure was hidden.

Suddenly, the old man's thin brown claws stopped their movement.

Pham smiled to herself. This was easy. The figure was under the cup to the left.

The Indian said, "Well, little one, are your young eyes faster than my old hands?"

She was about to point to the left-most cup—but Khar said: *No! The central cup. The figure is beneath the central cup, Pham.*

She hesitated, her finger reaching out. She was so sure that Kali was sitting under the cup to the left. The Indian smiled, his eyes twinkling with greed.

The central cup! Khar called in her head.

At the very last second, just as she was about to indicate the left-hand cup, she moved her finger and pointed to the cup in the middle.

The Indian's expression turned to barely suppressed rage.

The crowd roared. "Lift the cup! Lift the cup!"

Grudgingly, with bad grace, the Indian snatched away the cup to real the figure of Kali.

"Give her the money!" someone called out.

The Indian muttered something in Hindi.

A chorus went up, "Give the girl her money!"

At last, with bad grace, the Indian slapped a fifty baht note next to Pham's on the tabletop, and Pham, unable to meet his eyes, snatched the money and pushed her way back through the crowd amid much cheering.

She hurried towards Ketsuwan Park. "How did you know?" she asked Khar.

No response.

She tried again. "Khar, tell me. How did you know where Kali was? Did you read the Indian's mind?"

At last it said: *Do not worry yourself with that, Pham. Trust me. I will ensure that you come to no harm.*

She entered the park and hurried towards her bench. A young Indian girl was sitting there, shoving barfi into her mouth. She smiled at Pham when she approached.

"You're new here, aren't you?" the girl said. "I haven't seen you before."

Suddenly shy, Pham nodded. The Indian girl smiled. "Did you know that Raja, the stallholder by the eastern gate, gives away all the food he hasn't sold by eight o'clock? If you're quick, you'll be able to eat for free tonight."

"Ah-cha," Pham said. "Thank you."

She turned and hurried towards the eastern gate. She might have won fifty baht, but that didn't mean she must miss the opportunity of free food. She had to think of the future, when she might need the money in an emergency.

She found the stallholder, and sure enough he was handing out plastic plates of puri and deep-fried chillies. Pham lined up and received a big portion.

She sat down beside the stall and began eating. The puri dripped with oil and the chilli peppers were good and hot.

As she ate, she thought about what had happened to her since arriving on the upper decks, and something occurred to her.

"Khar," she said. "Why did the killer kill you?"

Because, Khar replied, *he thought he could kill me...*

Pham thought about that for a long time. It did make a kind of sense, she realised. The killer had killed the body of the man, but he hadn't killed the man's soul.

She wondered what would happen to her, if the killer succeeded in killing her. Where would her soul fly away to?

She tried to question Khar again, but he would not reply.

ELEVEN

LEVEL TWENTY

In the old days, even dosed up on chora, the din of mind-noise had been like an incessant migraine, and the thought of descending to levels where he would be surrounded on all sides by a clamorous press of humanity had not appealed.

Now Vaughan dropped through the levels with impunity, enveloped by total mind-silence. The knowledge that, at the tap of a few keys, he could access that mind-noise made the silence all the more wonderful.

From the dropchute station on Chandi Road he plummeted five levels, and then caught a crowded shuttle train west to the nearest dropchute station. It was impossible to drop from Level One right down to Level Twenty. For one thing, it had never been economically viable to build a 'chute accessing all levels, as few citizens had business on more than their immediate levels; for another, the Station had been built in stages, two or three levels at a time, and it had not always been expedient to extend existing 'chutes to the new levels. If citizens should wish to travel the Station from top to bottom, they had to do so in series of tortuous steps involving vertical dropchutes and horizontal shuttle trains.

Vaughan decided to check out the girl's old workplace on Level Twenty first, and later have a look around Ketsuwan Park. It would make sense to check the park when there was more chance of finding the kid settling down for the night.

All he had to go on were the pix in his wallet and the mental image of her he had gleaned from Abdul's mind. The latter, as it happened, was clearer than the pix. It was as if Vaughan had met her himself, seen her laughing and joking, climbing with the agility of a chimp through the abandoned rides of the amusement park. Abdul had been a little in awe of the precocious slave-kid from Level Twenty, not least because she had escaped her employer and set out on an adventure he would never have contemplated himself. Also, she had shown an intelligence, quick-wittedness, and confidence he had never come across before in a girl so young.

Vaughan felt as though he knew her already—and her resemblance in both character and appearance to Sukara's sister, Tiger, amazed him. Having her in his head like this—a vicarious recollection, as it were—brought back memories at once painful and wonderful, for had it not been for Tiger he would never have met Sukara.

He left the shuttle on Level Five and dropped to Level Ten, taking the same 'chute he had used every day on his way back from the spaceport. Strap-hanging in a press of tired Indian factory workers, he considered his apartment on Level Two, and Sukara's manifest joy at no longer being buried in the Level Ten coffin. The thought of bringing up a child down here had worried him for months: what had Rao said about Pham, that she had never in all of her seven years seen the light of day?

At least Li would have the opportunity of seeing the sun every day of her life.

At Level Ten, he made the short walk to the dropchute station and fell to Level Thirteen.

He had read that each level possessed its own unique character; its own identifiable atmosphere, much as land-based cities even within the same country varied in character and appearance. Certainly in his experience of the various levels he had visited and lived on, he knew this to be true. Levels One and Two were obviously affluent and, as a rule, less congested; Levels Three to Five were spacious but crowded, boasting parks and gardens created when the Station's architects had assumed that the levels would rise no further. All these levels had about them a liberal, cosmopolitan air, an atmosphere of privilege, which manifested itself in the confident demeanour of the residents.

From Levels Five to Ten, the standard of living corresponded to the appearance of the various areas. For one thing, the space between floor and ceiling was a mere six metres, far less than that of the levels higher up. The tunnels were narrower too, forever thronged with a noisy, elbowing press of humanity, and the individual buildings more cramped. The lighting this far down was poorer: although the halogen bulbs in the ceiling were spaced at the compulsory five-metre intervals, they radiated a paler light than those on the upper levels. Vaughan suspected that some cut-price company had greased palms for the commission to light the lower levels, and had done so with third-rate materials.

He could only assume that the levels below Ten were even more impoverished, even more at the mercy of unscrupulous councils and maintenance departments: the citizens down here were, after all, by definition poor and therefore lacking in political influence.

He squeezed from the cramped dropchute cage in a press of surging humanity, carried along involuntarily before elbowing his way free of the flow and gaining his bearings. The tunnels were amazingly confined down here—a mere four metres from wall to wall. The air of claustrophobia was not helped by stallholders who had set up shop along the length of the main thoroughfare to the next dropchute station. Vaughan passed a mixture of Thai and Indian entrepreneurs selling everything from miracle cures to outdated artificial limbs, their microprocessors long since worn out so that the limbs were no more useful than wooden legs or arms.

As if the physical press of humanity was not daunting enough, the noise and stench was overpowering. Every stallholder yelled in a bid to out-do his neighbour, and the sickly sweet miasma of incense and dhoop filled the air, masking other, more noisome aromas: the waft of human excrement, sweat, and the gagging reek of bad meat peddled by illicit market traders.

Vaughan made the dropchute station five minutes later and stepped into the cage with relief.

He descended to Level Twenty, wondering what horrors of human endurance might greet him there. The cage itself, if a microcosm of the degradation below, was bad enough. A woman and three near-naked children were squatting in the corner; she had set up a gas-stove and was cooking puri on a griddle. While good sense told him that the cage could not be her home, he feared otherwise. Fellow travellers in the cage included a gaggle of holy men in loincloths and group of mendicants missing various limbs, returning home from a day's begging on the rich upper levels.

The cage came to a sudden, jarring halt. The gate clanked open and the travellers poured out. Vaughan eased himself from the crush and stood to one side of the exit, staring about him in appalled fascination.

His initial impression was that he had strayed into the inspiration for a canvas by Bosch. Certainly the low, roseate lighting was appropriate—the furnaces of hell replaced here by the open fires of food-vendors and blacksmiths—as was the press of humanity going about their arcane and mysterious business; while tableaux of torture were absent, butchered beggars and citizens supported by crude crutches and wooden legs could easily have passed for models of the damned.

Vaughan was assailed by a dozen varied scents, from cooking food to woodsmoke, hair oil to joss sticks. If the tunnels down here were not congested enough, the congestion was not helped by the occasional meandering, khaki-coloured cow, holy and sacrosanct and thus given the freedom of the level—where in the upper levels their freedom had been proscribed long ago.

No sooner had he emerged from the dropchute station than he was jumped by half a dozen street-kids, tugging his sleeves and trousers and demanding either baksheesh or the right to furnish him with hotel rooms, drugs, or girls.

Vaughan selected a scrawny boy in shorts and a soiled vest and pointed at him. "You," he said in poor Hindi. "You others, *challo*. Go!"

The boy advanced, hissing at the other kids to retreat.

Vaughan said, "Can you take me to the Prakesh Quality Plastic Company?"

The boy rocked his head from side to side. "Ah-cha. No problem, Babu. You come this way. Follow me."

Without waiting for Vaughan to follow, the street-kid set off at a trot. Vaughan pushed his way through the crowd in pursuit, helped by his greater physical stature than those around him. It was, he thought, an alien world down here; culturally Indian, it had developed its own unique atmosphere away from the sunlight and open spaces of the sub-continent: poverty ruled, and fatalism prevailed, creating a jungle culture where the ethos of the survival of the fittest was a given.

He followed the boy through a maze of badly lit corridors. The odd thing was that, while Vaughan had expected the tunnels and thoroughfares down here to be even meaner and maze-like than those above, the reverse was true: the corridors were wide, even spacious. However, the enterprising mercantile mind of the Hindu had utilised the space to good effect: just as nature abhorred a vacuum, so businessmen down here abhorred the waste of valuable space. The margins of the byways were filled with the kiosks and stalls of food-vendors, restaurateurs, and even makeshift shacks housing destitute families, all piled two or three storeys high and accessed by precarious plastic ladders.

He caught up with the boy, who gestured him along.

At one point the kid saw Vaughan's expression, and guessed right. He grinned. "Much space down here, no? You see, this Level One. First level, yes? So the builders, many years ago, they need space to store all material, you see? All the things they use to build up, up!"

Ten minutes later they came to a polycarbon wall scabbed over with a rash of Hindi holo-movie posters. Among them, almost indiscernible amid the gallery of overweight action heroes, was the legend: R.J. Prakesh Quality Plastics Pty, Ltd— and below the ill-painted lettering a narrow doorway.

The boy was beaming up at Vaughan and holding out his hand. "Ten baht, friend!"

Vaughan slipped him a twenty baht note and the kid dashed off in delight.

A buzzer was set into the wall, above a speaker. Over the door, staring at him, was the lens of a security camera.

Vaughan thumbed the buzzer. Seconds later a querulous voice said, "Yes?"

He leaned towards the speaker. "Vaughan, Kapinsky Investigations. I want to see R.J. Prakesh." He hung his ID before the camera and waited.

The door clicked and he pushed it open.

He was hit by the adenoid-crunching stench of hot plastics and concentrated body odour. Gagging, he stepped inside, peering into the gloom.

He was in a narrow corridor lit by a flickering fluorescent above the door. At the far end of the corridor, a door opened and a skinny barefoot Indian in his twenties, wearing a dhoti and a vest, peered out at him. "Mr Prakesh, he very busy man," he said. "But he will see you. Come this way, please."

Vaughan followed him through the door, into a longer corridor just as badly lighted. The door at the end of this corridor, however, opened onto a factory floor packed with machinery—plastic extrusion devices, Vaughan guessed—worked by a sweating army of boys and girls. If the stench was bad back at the entrance, it was overbearing here, and made worse by the incredible heat of the place. Most of the kids worked in their underpants, their thin brown bodies slick with sweat. No wonder Pham had elected to escape this hell for the uncertainties of the upper decks.

The youth trotted between the hissing machines, zigzagging across the factory floor towards a raised, glassed-in gallery area. Metal steps climbed to the entrance, marked with the factory owner's self-important title: Ranjit Jamal Prakesh, Director, Manager.

His guide indicated the steps and departed.

Vaughan climbed, already sweating and exhausted by the intolerable heat. He knocked and opened the door without waiting to be invited in, the conditions on the factory floor imbuing him with indignation.

He expected the office to be air-conditioned, but only an ancient ceiling fan laboured vainly against the humidity.

A fat, moustachioed Indian in his fifties lolled in a swivel chair, his huge bare feet propped next to a flickering computer screen at least ten years out of date.

Vaughan sat down and showed his ID. "Prakesh? I'm Vaughan. Kapinsky Investigations. I'm working on a police case and I think you can help me."

Wide-eyed, Prakesh pulled his feet from the desk and sat up, buttoning his shirt, which had been open to reveal a bulging Buddha belly.

"Mr Vaughan. Of course, of course. You will find R.J. Prakesh always willing to aid the forces of law and order." He beamed betel-stained teeth and said, "How can I be of assistance, Mr Vaughan?"

Vaughan flipped a pix of Pham across the desk. "I'm trying to locate this kid. I know her first name. Pham. I understand she worked here?"

Prakesh studied the picture. Vaughan considered activating his implant and quickly reading what Prakesh knew about the kid, but held off. He'd see what he could get verbally, first.

Prakesh returned the pix. "Indeed, Mr Vaughan. Phamtrat Kuttrasan. She was one of my favourites, a very good worker. No trouble. Quiet and respectful. Very good girl."

"When did she go missing?"

"Three days ago, after a night shift. Very distressing, Mr Vaughan. I run a fair factory here. I treat my boys and girls well. Good pay and hours. I have many orphan children work for me, Mr Vaughan. Street-kids with no home and no prospects, other than R.J.

Prakesh. I give them shelter, work and food." He leaned forward. "Please tell me, she is in trouble?"

Vaughan shook his head. "She witnessed a crime. I need to question her about what she saw." He glanced at the pix of Pham before returning it to his wallet. "What can you tell me about Pham? Did she have a family, relatives?"

"Sad story, Mr Vaughan. Her mother and father, they were killed in dropchute accident three years ago, when Pham was four. Her uncle, he could not look after her, so she came here begging for work. Mr Vaughan, I'm a successful businessman, but I also have a heart. I am not an exploiting monster. I took her in, trained her how to use the Siemman's press. For three years she worked with no problem. Then—" Prakesh opened fat fingers in an exploding gesture. "Then *phooff*! She disappears."

"This uncle. Do you have his address?"

"I do not, Mr Vaughan. The truth to tell, I did not know that she had an uncle until yesterday."

Vaughan leaned forward. "Yesterday?"

"At noon yesterday, the uncle comes looking for Pham. He is most upset when I tell him that Pham left her dorm and has not come back."

Vaughan nodded, sensing that he was onto something. Pham had told Abdul that she had no family, had no one in the world. "Can you describe the man, Mr Prakesh?"

"Most certainly. It was strange you see, although he was a Thai, like Pham, he was not at all like a Thai, if you understand me."

"I'm not sure that I do."

"He was big, Mr Vaughan. Tall and broad, like a Westerner."

"What did he say?"

"Simply that he was looking for his niece, Phamtrat Kuttrasan. He too had a picture of her. He was most concerned about her safety."

"He didn't leave you an address, a contact number?"

Prakesh shook his head. "I suggested that he should do this, but he told me that he would be in touch if he needed to ask further questions. I must say, Mr Vaughan, that he struck me as very odd."

Vaughan recalled the surveillance cam above the door to the factory. "Do you still have yesterday's surveillance recording? I take it he entered the factory from the front?"

Prakesh said, "Indeed, Mr Vaughan. We keep recordings for a week." He propelled his bulk in the swivel chair across the room and accessed a comscreen.

Seconds later he had called up a grainy image of a tall, smooth-faced Thai.

"Can you print out a copy of the image of his face?" Vaughan asked.

"No sooner said than done!" Prakesh obliged.

If his suspicions were correct, and this Thai was indeed the killer of Robert Kormier, then how had he traced Pham to the factory?

Prakesh pulled a glossy pix of Pham's alleged uncle from the printer and passed it to Vaughan.

He stared at the image. There was indeed a disparity between the man's smooth Thai features, his angular cheekbones and merciless eyes, and his broad shoulders.

Prakesh was saying, "To aid your investigations, Mr Vaughan, would you care to inspect the dorm where Pham lived? I am very proud of the living conditions of my charges. I will give you a conducted tour."

He decided to accept the offer, if only to build a better picture in his mind of the girl he was seeking. "Lead the way."

As Prakesh hauled himself from his seat and waddled towards the door, Vaughan tapped the access code into his handset and winced as the full force of the businessman's mind hit him in a wave.

Contending with an overlaid set of memories and emotions, Vaughan stood and followed Prakesh from the office. As they wended their way between the crashing machines, he worked at filtering out the bright minds of the kids around him and concentrated on the Indian's fiery cerebral beacon.

The first thing that hit him was the realisation—surprising him—that Prakesh was a good man.

He had taken the Indian's high-flown sentiments about his charges, his altruism and concern for their welfare, as so much hot air. But R.J. Prakesh, Vaughan found, genuinely did care for the kids he employed in his factory. He ran a profitable business, yes, but he paid his children well, offered good holidays, and ensured that their working conditions were the best possible in the circumstances.

He slipped through Prakesh's recent memories, came upon his meeting with Pham's "uncle" yesterday.

It had taken place in the office, Prakesh seated in his swivel chair, the Thai in the seat Vaughan had occupied minutes ago.

Something about the man had profoundly unsettled R.J. Prakesh, and it was more than just the disparity between the Thai's features and his soma-type.

Vaughan had a better picture of the Thai now, a whole body image, an impression of how the man moved and gestured—and he knew that there was something very wrong in the man's demeanour. It was as if the Thai were an actor, playing a part, and playing it badly.

The man spoke Hindi fluently, without a trace of an accent—but his hand gestures were those of a Westerner mimicking a Thai.

Vaughan went through their dialogue, and again sensed something not quite right about the man.

Then he had it, and the realisation sickened him.

Again and again the man questioned Prakesh about the girl, Pham—where she might be now, had she mentioned leaving, where might she go if she were to venture topside?

And, again and again, the man anticipated Prakesh's replies—hardly giving him time to answer.

Suddenly, Vaughan knew why. It was a technique—barraging a subject with questions in order to guide the subject's mind—that he had used again and again when mind-reading criminals in his old job at the spaceport.

Pham's supposed uncle, the killer of Kormier and no doubt of Travers too, was a telepath.

Which would explain how he had traced Pham to the factory. While chasing her from the amusement park the other night, he had read her mind.

Sweating, he deactivated his implant and enjoyed the ensuing mind-silence.

They had reached the dorm without Vaughan being aware of the fact. Prakesh was saying, "As you will be aware, the rooms here are all fully air-conditioned. Cramped, yes—space is at a premium down here. But I like to think that my children can rest in comfort and security."

The rooms were spacious, and lined with caged bunk-beds three high. Some held sleeping children, and all were personalised with posters and possessions as varied as teddy bears, holo-units, toy guns...

Prakesh led the way to a bunk in the corner and indicated the lower berth.

The scant possessions were pitiful: a battered black doll with one eye missing, a battered holo-unit, and at the foot of the bed a pile of folded T-shirts and shorts. Vaughan smiled at the poster stuck to the wall: it was of the Bengal Tigers' star forward Petra Shelenko.

He noticed a corner of notepaper sticking out from beneath the pillow.

He pulled it out and read the childish Thai script: *Dear Mr Prakesh, Thank you, but I must go up to see the sky and the Tigers and everything else up there. I will be back one day when I am rich and happy. Don't worry, I will find a safe place to sleep.* Signed, *Pham.*

Vaughan stared at the note, then passed it to the businessman.

Only then did it hit him.

His pulse quickened and he cursed himself for being so slow.

Prakesh looked up. He thumbed something from his eyes. "The airborne pollutants down here are annoying, Mr Vaughan. I must attend to the filter system—Mr Vaughan?"

Vaughan reached out and took Prakesh's pudgy hand in a fierce shake. "You've helped considerably, Mr Prakesh. I'm sure I'll find Pham soon. I'll be in touch, okay?"

He hurried off, leaving the fat Indian staring after him as he made for the exit.

He had been a blind fool. As soon as he realised that the Thai was a telepath, he should have made the connection.

If the Thai had read Pham's mind as he chased her from the park, then he must have read her intention to spend the night in Ketsuwan Park.

Vaughan quit the factory and followed the signs to the nearest upchute station.

After the congested hell of the lower levels, Level Three seemed an oasis of space and calm. From the 'chute station he caught a southbound shuttle to Ketsuwan, an affluent residential area bordering the exclusive outer edge. The Park, a five hundred square metre area of lawns and gardens—like some vision of old England transplanted in space and time—was lighted by a series of mirrors and daylight halogens and gave the exhilarating impression of existing in the open air.

Couples and families strolled across the manicured lawns, street-kids played kabadi and soccer between the trees. Vaughan, aware of the bulk of the pistol under his jacket, made a quick circuit of the park, on the lookout both for the Thai telepath and for Pham. There were about ten entrances to the park, and he was unable to keep them all covered at the same time.

Lone men stood out among the couple and families. Vaughan stared at them, discounting them one by one. It was almost impossible to keep a watch on everyone entering the park, and on this occasion his tele-ability would be of no use, as telepaths wore mind-shields as a matter of course.

He stopped at a chai stall by a southern entrance to the park, bought a mug of spiced tea and a plate of mixed bhaji and pakora. Wolfing down his first meal since that morning, he eyed the kids begging food from the stallholder.

Discarding his mug and plate, he tapped the start-up code and his implant kicked into life.

He moved from the group, wincing, as the flares of a dozen minds cascaded into his consciousness. He worked at winnowing through the thoughts and emotions of the kids and the stallholder, accessing their short-term memories for an image of the skinny, Tiger T-shirted Pham.

He found nothing and moved off, making a circuit of the park, then crossing it, still scanning. He sorted through individual minds, one after the other, discarding hopes and dreams, fears and anguish, love and hate. He didn't allow himself to dwell long in any one mind: that way might lead to disorientation, to the sympathetic identification with individual psyches to the detriment of his own sense of self. He'd worked with teleheads in the past who'd suffered identity trauma from empathising too readily with subject personalities. Vaughan skipped, butterfly-like, hoping to come upon an image of Pham.

He stopped. Something connected in his head, the answer to his earlier inkling that his reasoning had been flawed. Impatiently he killed his implant. Basking in mind-silence, he concentrated on his own thoughts. His logic had been skewed by the natural assumption that the assassin wanted Pham dead because she had witnessed Kormier's killing.

He sat on the nearest bench and thought it through.

Why would the assassin want to eliminate Pham? There was no way that, from where she had been crouching in the mouth of the ghost train, she could have made out the assassin firing from over twenty metres away, on a dark night. She had seen Kormier killed—but would that have been enough to set the assassin on her trail?

Why would the assassin want to kill her? He had obviously read her mind immediately after the shooting, and then had elected to shoot her.

For some reason—that was the question at the heart of Vaughan's consideration.

If Pham had not seen the killer, then what had he to fear from her continued survival?

Perhaps it was not that she had witnessed the killing, but something that the assassin had read in her head which made it imperative he locate her?

Or, perhaps, he was wrong—the killer simply feared that Pham had seen him, feared she might be able to identify him, and had reasoned that she had to die.

Frustrated, both by inability to fathom the killer's motive, and the fact that he was getting nowhere in trying to find the kid, Vaughan activated his implant again and set off on another circuit of the park.

One hour later, he got the break he'd been looking for.

It was after nine, and the lights were dimming. The kids who had been playing among the trees had either drifted away or settled down in the bushes, their minds small points of fire in the gathering twilight.

Vaughan was considering whether to quit and go home, or contact Sukara and tell her he'd be an hour or so late, when he read something in the mind of a six-year-old Indian girl nesting in a stand of frangipani. She had spoken to Pham about fifteen minutes ago, told her that the stallholder by the eastern gate would soon be giving away leftover food.

Galvanised, Vaughan jogged across the grass, making for the dark shape of the eastern archway silhouetted against the lights of the level beyond.

He could see the stallholder, packing up his polycarbon cart. A couple of kids were standing close by, munching on puri and deep-fried chilli peppers.

One of the kids was Phamtrat Kuttrasan.

Her mind was ablaze. He caught only a second of it—a few memories of the factory, the adventure of rising through the levels, and then the frightening night in Kandalay amusement park—and then, as if sensing his presence in her mind, she looked up, across the intervening twenty metres, and saw him advancing. Her mind took fright.

She ran. She barged through the knot of kids by the gates, and Vaughan lost his grip on her cerebral signature. It became confused with the other minds in the vicinity.

He called out in bad Thai, "Pham, wait! I can help you!"

She darted through the gate, into a long boulevard that flanked the park, and he gave chase. He scanned ahead, attempting to read her intentions, but intervening minds scrambled her signal. He gave up scanning, concentrated on running after her instead.

She turned a corner, into a narrower corridor packed with late-night shoppers, a diminutive barefoot girl with the natural athleticism of her age.

He ran around the corner, scattering shoppers, provoking angry cries, and sprinted in pursuit. He could not see her now, obscured as she was by the milling citizens. Her fiery mind signature was drawing farther and farther away by the second, until it merged with the overriding mind-hum of the Station, and then was lost.

Vaughan came to a panting halt, braced his arms on his knees and breathed hard.

Not giving up yet, he continued along the corridor at walking pace, scanning minds, coming up with nothing. She might have darted down any one of a dozen tributary tunnels, might be a kilometre away by now.

He returned to the park, read the minds of the kids there, the girl who had spoken to Pham earlier—but they knew nothing of her intentions for the future. She was just another waif and stray, a playmate for the evening, soon absorbed into the mass of seething humanity on the Station.

Vaughan stilled his implant and enjoyed the respite. He might not have captured the kid, but at least he'd frightened her away from the park. With luck, she would have more sense than to return.

With luck, she might evade the assassin for a while yet.

He made for the nearest 'chute station and home.

TWELVE

REAL DANGER

It was late by the time Sukara cleared away the remains of the meal and Jeff suggested they take a bottle of wine onto the veranda and relax for a while.

Jeff sat with his outstretched legs propped on the rail. He looked exhausted. He'd eaten his meal quickly, as if he'd had nothing since breakfast, and told Sukara all about his investigations between mouthfuls.

A warm breeze wafted in, and soft music drifted down from the top level.

Sukara leaned against him, clutching his hand, and said, "This kid, Pham. She's in real danger, right?"

Jeff nodded. "For some reason the killer's trying to find her."

"Because she saw him in the amusement park."

He was silent for a while. "Maybe. Or maybe because of something he read in her mind. I don't know. The only clear-cut fact is that he's after her."

"But you scared her away from the park, right? So she won't go back there."

He tapped his head. "Let's hope she's as quick up here as she is at running away."

Sukara grinned and dug him in the ribs. "You're getting old, Jeff! You can't even catch a seven-year-old kid!"

"You should have seen her move!"

"Strange, isn't it? The other day I saw a girl. She reminded me of Tiger. Now you tell me about this kid. I can't get Tiger out of my mind."

Jeff smiled at her and stroked her hair. "I thought of Tiger earlier. Pham does look a lot like her."

Sukara was thoughtful. At last Jeff said, "What is it?"

"What?"

"Su, you're dwelling on something. What is it?"

"I was thinking... When all this is over. When the killer is caught and the case is closed. Maybe we could find Pham, help her out. You said she's a street-kid, right? An orphan?"

"Her parents were killed in a dropchute accident a few years ago. She had a decent job till she decided to see the world."

Sukara smiled. "She must be brave, Jeff. To give up a job, and a place to live, and just take off like that."

"Brave, foolish. Perhaps they're the same thing."

"Anyway, I'd like to help her. Maybe find her a job up here, give her some money."

Jeff hugged her. "We've got to find her first."

She looked up at him. "You'll try, won't you? You and Kapinsky?"

"Of course we'll try. The kid's vital to the case. Hell, I don't want the killer to get her."

She smiled and sipped her wine. Until she'd met Jeff, she'd never tasted wine, only beer. He'd introduced her to red wine, a good vintage from India, as well as many other things.

She looked up at him. "Jeff?"

"Mmm?"

"Are you okay? I mean, reading minds again? You told me what it was like, back then."

"That was different, Su. Then I couldn't turn the damned thing off. The mind-noise was always there, even when I was dosed up on chora. And the drug wasn't good for me."

When Sukara first met Jeff, over two years ago, he had looked pretty awful, thin and haunted, with an addict's frantic look in his eyes. He'd been a different person, then—depressed and cynical and without hope.

Then Osborne ripped Jeff's implant from his head, intending to kill him—and it had been the best thing that had ever happened to Jeff Vaughan. Far from killing him, it had renewed his life, given him mind-silence and allowed him to concentrate on small, day-to-day concerns... Like personal relationships. Sukara had sought him out, detecting something good behind the haunted eyes, and decided that he was the man for her.

And now he was reading again, all because of her, and Sukara felt more than a little apprehensive.

"So it's different, now that you can turn it off. But... but you're still reading minds, aren't you? All those evil, cynical minds you said drove you mad back then?"

He turned to her and stroked her cheek. "You know something? I can bear that, now that I know you. Back then I had no one. I knew Tiger, knew how good she was, but I wasn't this close to her."

"But you read her mind?"

"Su..."

"You knew her better than you know me?"

Jeff sighed. "Su, that's not true. I never read her. I just picked up her mind-noise, and I knew she was good. I didn't know her better than I know you. My God, we've been together two years now—that intimacy is how I know you're a good person."

She was quiet, choosing her words. "But you don't want to read me?"

He hung back his head and stared at the stars. "Su, Su... How to explain?"

"You said that I should use the mind-shield so that no other telepaths might read what you tell me." She paused, then went on, "But I think you just don't want to read my mind, my secrets." Something awful occurred to her. She stared at him, to observe his reaction. "You don't want to read me because you might find out that I'm not as good as my sister, right?"

He returned her stare, shaking his head. "That isn't the reason at all, Su."

"But you don't want to read something in here, do you? Is it my past? What I did in Bangkok? Is that it?"

He took her cheek in his hand, cupping it. "Su, what you did back then is what made you who you are today. It's not that I don't want to read it, it's just that... Look, some things should remain your own." He stopped and closed his eyes. She watched him. She'd seen him do this before, in apparent frustration at being unable to find the words to explain something to her. He opened her eyes and said, "Okay, so we have telepathy. Thanks to some neuroscientist working twenty years ago, some of us can have an operation to enable us to read the minds of others—"

"I don't see..." she began.

"What I'm trying to say is that it isn't natural. It wasn't meant to be. If everyone could read each other's minds, the world would be chaotic. It wouldn't function. You see, all of us have stray thoughts, desires, that are more fantasy than reality—it's the animal in us, playing something out on a primitive level. And it's these that shouldn't be read, especially by people who are close, who have something special." He shook his head. "I'm not explaining it very well, but all that matters to me, Su, is you, and your happiness—" he lay a hand on her stomach, "and little Li in there."

She said quietly, "So you don't want to read my mind because you don't want to find my secrets, my fantasies?"

"Something like that," he said.

She shook her head. "I have no secrets, Jeff. And my fantasies are all about you."

Gently, he kissed the top of her head.

"One day, Jeff, one day will you read me?"

After a short silence he nodded and said, "Okay, one day, Su, I promise I'll read you, if that'll make you happy."

She beamed. "More than anything," she said.

They finished the wine, and Jeff stood suddenly and scooped her up and carried her into the bedroom, and Sukara wondered whether anyone in the world was any happier than she was now.

Later, in the early hours, she lay awake and stared out at the gibbous moon and wondered about what she had told Jeff about her secret thoughts and fantasies. She was convinced she had no secrets from her husband, but perhaps Jeff wanted to save himself from reading all her petty irrationalities—her jealousy when they were in the company of other women, her hatred of smooth-talking men in business suits, her grief at what had happened to Tiger... She turned and hugged Jeff to her, and fell asleep thinking that perhaps he was right in not wanting to read her mind, after all.

She awoke in pain around six, and tried not to wake Jeff. She sat up, agony like stabbing daggers in her right calf. Jeff awoke, alarmed, and then relieved. "Thought you were in labour, Su," he said, digging his thumbs into her muscle, easing the cramp.

He was called away at eight by Kapinsky, just as Sukara was looking forward to a leisurely breakfast talking to him about nothing at all. She had breakfast alone, ate a grapefruit, and drank a glass of Vitamilk until it was time to go for her fortnightly appointment with her midwife. Later she was meeting Lara for coffee. She hadn't seen her friend from the Thai restaurant for a while, and she had so much to tell her.

The midwife enclosed Sukara's stomach in a scanner and she watched the image of her daughter appear on the screen, in full colour and astounding detail. Her baby had grown a lot since the last scan, three months ago. She could tell already that, six months on, their daughter had Jeff's long face and strong jaw—not Sukara's round Thai face. She stared at the curled, pink little girl in her womb and could not stop her tears of joy.

The midwife downloaded the images and Sukara copied them to her handset. She would show them to Jeff after dinner tonight, a special surprise.

She was well, and the baby was thriving, and Sukara left the clinic in a buoyant mood.

She made her way to the Himachal Park café to meet Lara, riding a crowded upchute from Level Three and then strolling through the relatively uncrowded lawns of the park.

It was as she passed a particularly beautiful flowerbed—a blaze of red azalea—that she was struck by a sudden wave of... she could only describe it as despair. She found a park bench and sat down quickly. It was more than despair, a feeling more definite. Almost a premonition. She was so happy now; life was going so well, that she knew, with a terrible certainty, that things could only get worse. She thought for a second that she was going to lose Jeff, but somehow knew that that was not the cause of her despair. It was something to do with her... or the baby. No, not the baby, *her*. She was convinced, then, that she was going to die.

She was so happy, and most people in the world were so sad, and she was going to pay for her happiness with an early death.

Then, suddenly and inexplicably, the feeling passed. She told herself that she was fine. She was fit and healthy and still only twenty-three; she had all her life ahead of her. Years with Jeff, watching their daughter grow...

It was her hormones, she knew: she was taking on the burden of the world's despair, feeling guilty for her own good fortune.

She stood up, suddenly optimistic again, and hurried through the park to the coffee shop.

THIRTEEN

THE END JUSTIFIES THE MEANS

"So, where do we stand?"

Kapinsky leaned against the floor-to-ceiling viewscreen, staring out over the ocean with her back to Vaughan.

He sprawled in a comfortable lounger and gave her a detailed account of everything he'd found out the day before: his infiltration into the Scheering-Lassiter HQ, and the fact that its employees were shielded to a person. He told her about his finding Pham on the surveillance cam, and his investigations which had led to the pix of the Thai assassin.

He voiced his concern over the assassin's motives in trying to locate Pham. "What I don't get," he said, "is why he's after her."

She turned and stared at him. "Vaughan, she saw the fucking shooting, for Chrissake."

He held her stare. "So?"

"So—she's a witness. He's an assassin. Therefore: he wants her dead. It looks pretty fucking simple to me."

"Well, it doesn't look all that damned clear-cut to me, Kapinsky. Listen. Okay, so she saw the killing. Saw Kormier sliced. But there was no way she could've seen the killer. He was twenty metres away. It was a dark night."

"So, the killer was taking no chances. He read her in the vicinity, and decided to eliminate her. I don't see your problem."

"Dammit, my problem is that he had no *reason* to kill her. He's a telepath—he knew she didn't see him."

"So, he's taking no chances. Listen, we aren't dealing with your regular Station citizen here. This guy kills for fun. 'So a street-kid might have seen my handiwork? Great, let's butcher her while I'm at it.'"

Vaughan was silent for a time. "I think it's more than that. I think it was something he read in her mind."

"Yeah, like she might've seen him."

"No, something else."

"Like what?"

"I don't know."

"You don't know? What kind of investigator are you, Vaughan?"

"Ease up, for Chrissake." He stared at her, then said, "So okay, what've you been doing?"

"Looking into the Mulraney killing. I've come up with something. She was lasered in a park on Level Two. I trawled through the surveillance cams around the place, came up with this."

She crossed to her desk and turned the com-screen to face him. She tapped the keypad and a second later the full-body image of a tall, dark-suited guy filled the screen. It was a distance shot, and indistinct. "Gimme that pix of the guy you brought in."

He took it from the lounger next to him and carried it across the room, sitting in a swivel chair and staring at the pix on the com.

Kapinsky held up the pix next to the screen, comparing.

The two images were similar—both guys were of the same height, the same build.

Kapinsky looked at him. "But you said there was something not quite right about this guy? Like, he was built like a Westerner but had Thai features?"

He thought she was going to get into another critical riff—say that there were such people as Eurasians who combined characteristics of both races. He got in first. "Not only his features. There was something wrong about... well, all of him. He didn't act right. He was a Westerner trying to act like a Thai." As he said it, he knew how dumb it sounded.

"But he had a Thai face?" Kapinsky said. Surprisingly, there was no sneer in her tone. "So," she went on, "look at this." She tapped the keys again.

The image bloomed, homed in on the guy's face.

Vaughan stared. "He isn't Thai."

The guy was Indian.

Vaughan looked at Kapinsky. "So Mulraney's killer wasn't the guy who killed Kormier and Travers?"

"What do you think?" she said. "Same height, build, but different faces—gotta be two guys, right?"

"Seems that way."

Kapinsky smiled for the first time that morning. "You ever heard of chus?"

He stared at her. "Shoes?"

"C-H-Us. Capillary-holo-units."

She opened a drawer of the desk and pulled out a small, flat case. She opened the lid, hinged it back and turned it to show Vaughan.

The thing inside, nestling in red velvet, resembled a silver face-stocking, connected to what might have been a control box.

"What is it?"

"A chu. Watch."

She pulled the device from its case and laid it on the desk, then tapped a code into the control box.

Instantly, the silver filaments changed colour. Vaughan made out flesh tones, a hank of what looked like fair hair.

Kapinsky held it up. It was as she were lofting a severed head for his inspection, or an empty face mask, its hollow cheeks and open mouth giving the face a ghoulish expression.

She slipped the mask over her head and adjusted the controls. The face changed, became that of a young woman in her twenties with long fair hair.

"What do you think, Vaughan?"

He resisted the urge to tell her it was a big improvement. "Impressive. Never even heard of these things before."

"No wonder," the blonde beauty said, "they're the latest hi-tech disguise out of Rio. Been available, at exorbitant prices, for about a year."

Vaughan nodded. "So... you think the killer has one of these things?"

"It makes sense. It'd explain how he looked like a Thai in the plastics factory when he posed as Pham's uncle, but had the body language of a Westerner." She pulled off the chu, its features distorting horribly.

She sat down facing Vaughan and said, "I've been thinking about what Shelenkov told us, and what you learned from Kormier's widow."

"And?"

"And one angle we have to consider is this: what if Scheering-Lassiter are behind the assassinations?"

He nodded. "Certainly Mulraney thought they were hiding something. And the fact that every last one of their employees is shielded..."

"Perhaps we should try looking a bit further into Scheering-Lassiter?"

"Easier said than done," Vaughan grunted. "Any ideas?"

"Two ways we could go about this, Vaughan. One of us goes to Mallory, does some rooting around there."

"And the other way?" he asked. He didn't much care for the idea of leaving Sukara, taking a voidship to a company-run planet.

"We read a Scheering-Lassiter high up, try to find out what's going on."

"Like I said, they're all shielded."

"I know they are. I've been doing a bit of my own nosing around the S-L empire. And they don't use just portable shields."

"Sub-cutes?"

She nodded. "They're implanted as part of the signing on deal when you become a S-L employee. They have fingers in a lot of pies—they don't want competitors reading their best personnel. It's established practice now among the big multicolonials."

"So how do we go about reading a Scheering-Lassiter executive if they're all shielded?"

"How else, Vaughan? We unshield the bastard."

Vaughan nodded. "You make it sound like stealing candy from a baby."

She regarded him. She had a sharp way of piercing him with her steel grey eyes, making him feel as if he'd said something stupid.

"Harder than that," Kapinsky allowed, "but not impossible."

"You've obviously been giving it a lot of thought."

"Been doing nothing but for most of yesterday. First consideration is, who to target?"

"Some exec in the Mallory department," Vaughan said. "I talked to a woman called Gita Singh."

Kapinsky nodded. "She's the Co-Director of the Mallory division." She paused, thinking about it. "Or we could go right to the top and get Scheering himself. He lives on the Station. He's a big celebrity, thick with all the politicians, greasing palms. Trouble is, he has more security guards around him than flies on a turd."

"So who, then?"

"The Director of the Mallory division is a guy called Anton Denning. He spends half his time on Mallory. At the moment he's on Earth. Specifically, on the Station."

"You think this is the guy we should target?" She was, he realised, serious about this.

"That's the guy, Vaughan. If anyone knows something about what Scheering's hiding on Mallory, and why he hired an assassin to take out Kormier and Travers, Denning's the guy."

"Okay, fine, so Denning it is. He's also the guy wearing a subcutaneous mind-shield."

Kapinsky sneered. "No probs, Vaughan. They're implanted here—" she tapped her chest just above her right breast. "A quick slice with a scalpel, a squeeze, and they slip out as easy as pie."

Vaughan massaged his eyes. "Can I ask a few questions, Kapinsky? Things you might have over- looked in you sudden enthusiasm to cut up a Station citizen?"

"I've gone over every angle. Fire away."

"First off, have you noticed that just about every square metre of the Station is covered by surveil- lance cams these days? So even if we did lure this Denning character to a blind spot, what're the chances we'd have avoided cams tracking us to wherever the blind spot is?"

Kapinsky was smiling, as if the word "smug" were her private property.

"What?" Vaughan asked.

"Like I said, I've got every angle covered. Den- ning goes into the S-L building around ten every morning. He employs a firm who supply chauffeur- driven air-cars. They pick him up at nine-forty-five on the dot."

Vaughan thought he saw what she was driving at. "And?"

"We hire a swish flier. I drive, get there two min- utes earlier, and we have our man."

Vaughan restrained his smile. "So, there we are, we've got our man in the back of the flier. What then?"

"Then I simply turn around before we set off and spray Denning with a face full of atomised sedative. I pick you up, you slice the guy and remove his shield—they're effective a metre away from the subject, so we stow it in the dash—then we read Denning's head and all the secrets he keeps there."

Vaughan spread his hands. "Then how do we explain what we've done to the cops when Denning files a kidnap and assault suit on us?"

"He doesn't. You see, he doesn't find out that his shield was removed. He doesn't even dream we read his head. When we've done, we substitute his shield with something the same size, just in case we need to read him in future. Then seal the wound with synthi-flesh and take his wallet to make the assault look like robbery."

"And how do we get away?"

"Simple. We ditch the flier, and Denning with it, in a blind spot and leave the area on foot—"

"Allowing all the surveillance cams in the vicinity to get a good long look at us."

Kapinsky smiled. "We'll be wearing chus, Vaughan. We'll lose ourselves in the crowds, run around a level or two, remove the chus and come up smelling of roses."

Vaughan nodded. "And if Denning knows anything about what Scheering is hiding on Mallory, we'll have it all in here." He tapped his head.

"That's about the size of it, Jeff." Kapinsky looked at him. "So... what do you think?"

He held up a hand. "Just give me time to think this through, okay? I mean, it isn't every day I'm asked to kidnap a company exec like this, slice him open, and read his mind."

Kapinsky said, "The end justifies the means, buddy. Now and again you gotta break the law to solve a crime."

He nodded. Two years ago he'd attacked the then head of the Law Enforcement agency and cut his shield from his chest. The circumstances had been different, then—he'd known the guy was corrupt. This time, he and Kapinsky merely suspected that Denning knew something.

"Well?" Kapinsky prompted.

"It might work, as a last resort."

"A last resort?" she sneered. "You got any brighter ideas?"

"How about we spend a couple more days tracking this assassin? If we find him, then we find out what all this is about."

"Always assuming we can trace the bastard," she said.

"Two days," Vaughan said. "After that, we seriously think about ambushing Denning. What do you say?"

Her reply was interrupted by her handset. "Kapinsky here."

Vaughan heard the tinny voice of her caller. Kapinsky stared at the screen of her handset. "No kidding? You sure about that?"

Her caller replied.

"Okay. We're on our way." She cut the connection and looked across at Vaughan. "That was Sergeant Kulpa. They've found the guy who killed Kormier and Travers. Officially the case is closed."

Vaughan stared at her. "Who is he?"

"Kulpa didn't say. But he did say the guy's dead."

Vaughan took this in. "Okay, but if he was a hired assassin, then his death doesn't close the case. We need to know who hired him."

She nodded. "Let's go take a look, Vaughan."

FOURTEEN

NECROPATH

They left the office and took an air-taxi east.

There were a lot of very expensive apartments on the sunrise side of the Station, as far down as Level Five. The outer pads on Level Two were usually rented by politicians and business tycoons, not assassins.

The unimaginatively named Sunrise Villas projected from the side of the Station in a series of steps, so that each four-bedroom apartment had long windows giving onto a garden area situated on top of the apartment below.

The flier came down over the lip of the Station and banked out over the ocean. A Scene of Crime team was at work on the patio of the uppermost villa. The flier eased to a gentle landing with a whine of turbos, and Vaughan climbed out.

The garden was the size of a skyball court, with a brilliant blue swimming pool, an ornamental garden, and half a dozen sun-loungers set out on a patio.

The SoC team was concentrating on a body on one of the loungers.

Kulpa indicated the corpse. The dead man was perhaps in his late thirties and European. "Sven Nordquist," Kulpa said. "A European national. He'd been on the Station a little over a year."

A neat hole—Vaughan was unable to tell whether it had been made by a bullet or a laser—marked the man's right temple. He lay in the lounger, arms dangling, mouth slightly open. But for the entry point, Nordquist might have been sleeping.

Then Vaughan saw the automatic pistol on the tiles, inches below the guy's dangling hand.

"Suicide?" Kapinsky said.

Kulpa nodded. "Around seven this morning. The shot was heard by the owner of the villa two below this one. She called the villas' private security team, who called us in."

"You're certain it was suicide?"

"The apartment door's locked from the inside. The apartment below this one is locked, so no one could have got in through there."

Kapinsky indicated the lip of the station, high above. "What about over there?"

"I've had a man check the security cams—not a thing. Forensic's certain the wound was self-inflicted."

Vaughan said, "What makes you think this is the guy we were looking for?"

Kulpa nodded. "Come this way," he said, indicating the sliding glass panel of the viewscreen.

They stepped inside. The room was vast and minimally furnished, a white mock-leather suite lost amid an expanse of cream floor tiles. There was no sign that Nordquist had stamped his personality on the place—either that, or his personality had been as bland as the décor.

Kapinsky said, "So who was Nordquist?"

"A small-time businessman, import–export from Europe to the Station. We have reason to believe that his business wasn't doing so well."

He led them over to a desk in the corner of the room. Its surface was scattered with printouts and a photograph showing three figures sitting at a restaurant table, smiling at the camera. One of the men was Nordquist.

Vaughan recognised the other two: Kormier and Travers.

"It was taken a month ago, on the occasion of their last meeting." Kulpa indicated a personal com-diary on the desk. "We've been through this. Kormier and Travers were lending Nordquist money to bale him out of a series of bad business deals he'd made a while back."

"How much?" Kapinsky asked.

"They each loaned him a quarter of a million."

"Baht?"

"Dollars."

Kapinsky whistled. "Some loan. And you think Nordquist killed the guys who were bailing him out?"

"An entry in the diary," Kulpa said, "about two weeks ago. Kormier and Travers were asking Nordquist when they might see their loan repaid. Nordquist was stalling them."

Vaughan said, "So he planned the ultimate stall, and killed them both?"

Kulpa opened the top drawer of the desk, revealing a small laser pistol. "A Kulatov MkII blaser. The same type which killed Kormier and Travers."

Kapinsky said, "I want a copy of the diary, and the SoC report."

Kulpa smiled. "I thought you might." He passed her a pin. "This is a download of the diary. I'll get you the SoC report as soon as they've made it." He hesitated, then said, "I was talking to my superior. This was your case, and you were on your usual rate of commission if you cracked it."

"Looks like Nordquist did us out of it," Kapinsky said.

Kulpa shook his head. "My boss thinks you did enough to earn the commission. He suspects Nordquist knew you were after him. It might've been one of the things that pushed him over the edge."

A member of the SoC team looked in through the viewscreen and called Kulpa.

"Excuse me," the cop said, leaving Vaughan and Kapinsky in the lounge.

"Well, what do you know," Kapinsky said, "we get the twenty thousand without getting our hands dirty."

Vaughan stared at her. "You don't believe a word of this, do you?"

She looked at him. "Come again, Vaughan?"

"This?" He indicated the desk. "The diary entry. The supposed loan. The pix. It's too neat. You know what I think?"

"I've a feeling you're going to tell me."

"It's a set up, a buy out. The cops have been conned, either knowingly or not. Kulpa probably believes all this—but his superior's in on it. Why else do you think he's given us the commission? To shut us up, for Chrissake."

"And who do you think's behind the cover-up?"

"Come on. Who else? Scheering-fucking-Lassiter, that's who."

"And Nordquist?"

"Some poor schmuck chosen as the decoy by the real assassin. And this," he said, snatching up the pix of the three men, "you'll probably find is a very clever fake."

"The case is closed, Vaughan. We've been paid."

"Paid off," Vaughan said. He stared at her. "You're not going to sit back, take their money, and forget about who killed Kormier and Travers, are you?"

Kapinsky sighed. "We're dealing with a professional, Vaughan. And, what's more, a pro with multicolonial backing."

"Christ, and not one hour ago you were all for slicing this Denning exec and seeing what he knew about Mallory. Listen, it's all the more important that we do that, now."

"You've changed your tune, Vaughan."

"Too right I have. Back then we were going on a hunch."

"And we aren't now?" Kapinsky said. "Seems to me your conspiracy theory is just so much guesswork, Vaughan."

He thought about it. "Okay, let's not jump into anything. I'll do some investigating. If I find something that points to Nordquist being an innocent party in all this, then we see what Denning and Scheering are hiding, okay?"

.

Kapinsky held his gaze. "For what, Vaughan? We've been paid. So we find out that Scheering's behind the killings, what do we gain?"

Vaughan shook his head. "Call me naïve, but we gain the satisfaction of bringing criminals to justice, of righting a wrong."

"You sound like some kid's superhero," Kapinsky said. "So we find out that Scheering hired an assassin, that he's covering up something on some far away colony planet. It's not our ballpark, Vaughan. Get real. We're bit-part players. We do what we're paid for, keep our noses clean with those in power, and get on with our little lives."

"You don't know how fucking cynical that sounds, Kapinsky."

She stared at him. "It sounds," she said, "like the Vaughan I knew, once upon a time."

"Yeah, well, that Vaughan's dead and gone," he said. He let a silence stretch. "So... there's nothing I can do to persuade you to look a bit further into this?"

Kapinsky sighed. "Vaughan, we're beat. Let's give up before we find ourselves in deep shit, okay?"

Kulpa looked into the room. "If you've a minute..."

As they joined him on the patio, Vaughan activated his handset and scanned Kulpa. The sergeant was on the level—he was merely taking orders to close the case from his divisional commander.

He killed his implant and stared up into the blue sky. A private air-car was banking over the edge of the Station, a sleek silver coupé with a grin like a shark. An insect-wing door hinged open and a tall woman hauled herself out of the low-slung driver's seat.

Kapinsky said, "Who's this?"

"Indira Javinder," Kulpa replied. "She's another of your lot working on the case."

"Our lot?" Kapinsky echoed, eyeing him.

"A telepath."

Vaughan watched the woman as she strode around the shimmering pool, and he wondered where he'd heard the name before.

She was, he had to admit, striking: so tall as to appear attenuated, as thin as an off-worlder from some low-grav planet, and dressed to maximise the effect in a one-piece jet black bodysuit and a tricorne perched on the back of her shaven skull.

She was Indian, flat chested and stooped, with a hawk-like beak of a nose and pockmarked cheeks.

The impression she gave, Vaughan thought, was that of the Grim Reaper customised for the late twenty-first century, scythe replaced by a laser strapped to her anorexic waist.

Javinder... Vaughan knew, then, where he'd heard the name before.

"Kulpa?" the woman said, ignoring both Kapinsky and Vaughan.

"Javinder... My boss told me you were on your way." The big Sikh seemed deferential, as if overawed in the presence of the telepath. He indicated the corpse and escorted Javinder across the patio.

Vaughan turned to Kapinsky. "Javinder. Ring a bell?"

She shook her head. "Should it?"

"Think back to the interview with Shelenko. She said she was questioned by a private investigator."

"Javinder," Kapinsky said.

"So Javinder's linked Mulraney's killing and this one."

"Not necessarily. It might just be coincidence." Kapinsky stopped, then said, "What the hell's she doing?"

As Vaughan watched, the Indian telepath stood beside the lounger containing the corpse, then knelt. She reached out with long, black-nailed fingers and laid her hand across the dead man's brow.

The she closed her eyes as if in concentration.

Something turned cold within Vaughan's stomach.

"What the fuck's she doing?" Kapinsky hissed at him.

He knew very well what she was doing—and at the same time he knew that what she was doing was impossible, this long after the subject's death.

Not looking at Kapinsky, but staring at the attenuated Indian as she bowed her head as if in pain, he said, "She's a necropath."

"Come again?"

"A necropath. She can read the minds of the dead."

Kapinsky stared at him. "How the hell do you know that?"

"Seen them on the movies," he wisecracked. He almost told her that, years ago, back in Canada, he'd been implanted with the hardware to read dead minds, and had done so for the Toronto homicide division before he'd burned out.

She said, "I've read about them, of course. Knew they were around. Never thought I'd see one in action."

You're not, Vaughan thought. He knew that what they were witnessing here was nothing more than an elaborate charade.

He looked at Kapinsky. "How long's Nordquist been dead?"

She glanced at her handset. "Nearly three hours."

Indira was putting on an act. He knew he was right, knew that he was onto something.

The woman was genuflecting before the corpse, her fingers spanning its head like some psychic healer. She let out a low moan, then a sob, and broke the connection.

She remained kneeling, motionless, her head hanging, for perhaps a minute.

Around her, Kulpa and the SoC team watched in silence like the chorus in a Greek tragedy.

At length, Javinder rose to her feet, towering over Kulpa, and took a long, deep breath. The two conferred for a while, the sergeant nodding from time to time. The expression on his face comprised awe with supreme gratitude.

"Wonder what the hell she read," Kapinsky murmured.

"I wonder," Vaughan echoed, sarcastic.

A minute later the tall Indian turned on her heel and strode off towards the air-car, something imperious in her disregard of the onlookers.

Kulpa joined them. "I thought you might like to see that," he said, as if he had personally stage-managed the private performance of a world-famous diva.

Kapinsky said, "She was a necropath, right?" Across the patio, the air-car fired up and rose into the air, banking away over the ocean

Kulpa nodded. "Right. Quite something, ah-cha?"

Aware of his pulse, Vaughan said, "What did she tell you?"

"She said she accessed his dying thoughts. They were weak, but readable. As we knew, Nordquist was in financial difficulties. He owed a lot of people a lot of money. He was the guy who killed Kormier and Travers—but his other debtors were queuing up... he couldn't think of another way out, except for..." He gestured towards the suicide and fell silent.

Vaughan chose his next question carefully. "And do you know who she was working for, sergeant?"

Kulpa nodded. "She was hired by the multicolonial, Scheering-Lassiter. The murder victims Kormier and Travers were employed by S-L. They wanted it cleared up."

And they've got it cleared up, very neatly, Vaughan thought. But they'd staged this little display of duplicity without reckoning that one of the audience might know something about how necropaths worked.

He walked away from Kulpa and Kapinsky, around the pool, and came to the balcony rail. He gripped it, leaning over and staring at the scintillating expanse of the Bay of Bengal.

He felt good, secure in the knowledge that he was right, that he knew now, for sure, who was responsible for the deaths of Kormier, Travers, Nordquist, and before them Dana Mulraney.

Kapinsky joined him. "Vaughan? What is it?"

His answering smile turned to laughter.

Kapinsky said, "You okay?"

"I'm fine. Never felt better."

"You going to explain yourself?"

He nodded. "Sure. She, Javinder, was faking it."

"What?"

"She didn't read Nordquist's dead mind."

She looked dubious. "And you'd know, would you?"

He held her gaze. "Too damned right I'd know, Kapinsky."

She sneered. "The holo-movies, right? You've seen necros work on the movies?"

He ignored the jibe. "She didn't read Nordquist," he said. "What she told Kulpa was bullshit. She's working for Scheering, right? So of course she'd tell him that Nordquist was in deep shit financially."

"Vaughan, for Chrissake." She shook her head, exasperated. "What makes you think—"

He interrupted, reaching out suddenly and gripped her upper arm. She winced as he pulled her to him and hissed, "She was bullshitting. That performance, kneeling and pretending to read Nordquist, it was a fake—"

"How the hell do you know, Vaughan?"

"Because you can't read dead minds after three fucking hours, Kapinsky. One hour, maybe you can pick up weak signals, the odd deep memory, but even then you'd be lucky. Three hours... forget it. The brain's so much dead meat. Stone cold. There's nothing firing in there, the synapses have long since given up the ghost."

"Like I said, Vaughan. How the hell do you know this?"

He hesitated, looking at her. Even if he told her, she wouldn't believe him. There was only one way to prove that Javinder had faked the reading.

"Okay, listen." He looked around. Kulpa and the SoC team were clearing up around the corpse. "Years ago, before I came to the Station, I worked for the Toronto Homicide Department. I was a necropath."

She stared at him, her expression combining revulsion and respect. "Straight up?"

"We got to the scene an hour after the crime, and we might be lucky. Any later and we were chasing shadows. Two hours and the investigating officer wouldn't even call us in."

Kapinsky was watching him, doubt in her eyes.

Vaughan said, "There's one way I can prove it," he said.

He lifted his handset. "I'll switch my shield off, okay? You can go in, access my memories. You can read for yourself that necropaths are fucked if the corpse is two hours cold."

She held his gaze. "I think I believe you," she said, her expression indicating that she'd rather not access his memories of reading dead minds.

"Like hell you do," he said, and swiftly tapped in the code to kill his shield.

He thought back to his Toronto days, to the last corpse he'd scanned, then opened up to her his knowledge of a working necropath.

Seconds later she reeled away, holding her temple. "Christ, Vaughan," she said, gripping the rail for support.

He activated his shield, staring at her.

She took a breath and straightened up. "Okay, okay... So Scheering is hiding something."

He smiled. "It isn't just a hunch any more. Now we know. Javinder was hired to put us off the trail."

He paused, then said, "We've got to scan Denning, Kapinsky. We've got to find out what the bastards are up to on Mallory."

FIFTEEN

I AM HORTAVAN

Pham sat in the gnarled root system of an old banyan tree on the edge of Gandhi Park, Level Three, and stared out across the flat lawns and paths. It was a smaller park than Ketsuwan, and not so busy—the perfect place for Pham to hide from the killer. She had spent the past two nights not on a bench, which was too open and obvious, but in the cover of the banyan.

Yesterday, Khar had helped her win more money. A card sharp in a nearby corridor had set up a small table, taking money from gullible passers-by who thought they could guess which card came next in a certain sequence. Pham, guided by Khar, had guessed right three times running, and won over two hundred baht, before the angry card sharp had refused to allow her to play any more.

She had celebrated with a big Thai meal in a proper restaurant overlooking the park. Afterwards, in the shade of the banyan, she had tried to question Khar, but the thing in her head had remained stubbornly silent.

This morning, she tried again.

"Khar," she said. "Please talk to me."

She waited. There was no answering voice in her head.

She said, "Do you realise that it's rude not to reply when you're spoken to, Khar? There you are, living in my head, enjoying yourself thanks to me, and you don't even have the good manners to be polite. What would your mother say, if you had a mother?"

Silence. Pham grew angry. "Khar! Why won't you talk to me?"

Just when she thought Khar was not going to reply, the voice sounded in her head. *Because it's safer if I don't*, it said.

"Safer?" she asked, glad that it had spoken, but puzzled by what it said.

The less you know, the less there is for the killer to read.

She thought about that. "The killer's a telepath?"

Correct.

The silence stretched. That was bad. It was bad enough that the killer was trying to find her, but even worse that the killer was a mind-reader too.

"Khar," she asked at last, knowing that the thing in her head would not answer her question. "Just what are you?"

Evidently Khar was considering whether to tell her. At last it said, *As the telepath knows this already, there is no danger in telling you. I am a Hortavan, a being from another world.*

Pham shook her head in wonder. "Am I going mad, or do I have an alien in my head?"

You are quite sane, Pham.

She laughed, but it was a nervous laugh. "Why did the telepath kill the man in the park?"

Because he, the telepath, wanted me dead.

Pham thought about that. "Which is why the killer is trying to find me, ah-cha? He read my mind when you got into my head, and now he wants to kill me—and you."

That is correct. I am sorry.

Pham shrugged. "I don't know what to say. I've never had an alien in my head before—and I've never been chased by a killer. You said that soon you'll move on?"

That is correct. In time, I will leave you. You will be safe, then.

She thought about her next question, then said, "Why does the telepath want to kill you, Khar?"

Silence. "Khar? Please answer me."

At last the voice came again. *Because I am opposed to what the telepath's employers are doing on my planet.*

Pham frowned, thinking through Khar's words. "What are they doing?" she asked at last.

It will be best, and safer for you, if you do not know that.

"Ah-cha," she said, nodding. "But can you tell me what you are doing on Earth?"

I... I am trying to locate someone, Khar said.

"Who?" she asked.

Again, it would be dangerous to tell you that.

"But it could only be dangerous," she said, frowning in concentration, "if a telepath read what I know."

Correct.

"Well—" she made a spread-fingered gesture of frustration. "Why wouldn't it be dangerous if a telepath read *your* thoughts?"

That is impossible. My thoughts cannot be read by humans. My mind is too alien.

Pham shrugged. "So how come I can communicate with you?"

She felt, then, what might have been a smile in her head. *Because I have studied your mind*, Khar replied, *and I am communicating with you in your own language. I am reading your thoughts—you are not reading mine.*

That made a kind of sense. She asked, "How long will you stay in my head, Khar?"

Until I have found who I am looking for.

"Any idea how long that might be?"

No, Khar responded, and then fell silent.

Pham sat in the roots of the banyan tree and watched life go on around her. All these people were leading their own very important lives, going about their business, and not one of them knew about her and the alien in her head. It made her feel proud and important... and also a little scared.

She was about to ask Khar which planet it came from, when its voice sounded in her head. It was the first time that Khar had asked her something.

Pham, do you trust me?

It was odd, but she had never thought about that before. She felt no fear of the thing in her head—never had—and Khar had helped her win money, after all.

She shrugged. "Ah-cha. I think so, yes."

Will you help me find who I am looking for?

She thought about that. "Will it be dangerous?"

A few seconds elapsed, and then Khar replied, *I will attempt to make it as safe as possible.*

"So it *will* be dangerous."

It might be.

Pham thought about it. "Thing is, you can control me, right? So even if I said I didn't want to help me, you could make me do it."

I would not force you to do anything, Pham. If you refuse, which is entirely reasonable, then I will move on, find someone else.

It was Pham's turn to be silent for a time, now. She considered what Khar had said. How would she feel, not having the special alien in her head? She would miss him, his conversation and his help. Khar had become a kind of friend.

Of course, if she agreed to help him, then she would be in danger, no matter what Khar said.

She smiled to herself. Until now, she had always thought of Khar as an "it". Now she realised that she thought of Khar as "him".

She said, "This person you're looking for... I know you can't tell me who it is, but can you tell me if he's bad?"

Khar replied, *Yes, he is bad.*

She considered this, then said, "Then I'll help you, Khar." She paused. "I bet you knew that—I bet you read my thoughts—even before I answered, ah-cha?"

Pham felt the smile in her head again.

She said, "So... how do we find this person you're looking for?"

She took a 'chute up to Level One, then walked to a train station and caught a northbound express to

Kandalay. At first, leaving the safety of Gandhi Park, she felt afraid, vulnerable. She thought that everyone was looking at her, that everyone knew she had an alien riding in her head. She also thought that at any minute the telepathic killer would find her again, and this time he wouldn't just call out her name, but shoot her dead.

But as the train carried her rapidly north, and no one in the carriage paid her the slightest attention, she realised that she was safe. She was one small girl among millions of people, and even if the killer could read her mind, he would have to find her first.

When the train pulled into Kandalay station, she left the carriage with the rest of the passengers and found herself on a wide, quiet street lined with grand houses and flashy air-cars. Pham had never seen such a quiet, unpopulated area before—it was even quieter than Gandhi Park. She tried to imagine living in one of the big houses along this street—they were bigger even than Mr Prakesh's factory. Twenty people could live in one of these houses quite comfortably. She thought of her bunk on Level Twenty. In these houses she would have a room to herself.

Khar interrupted her thoughts. *Turn left and walk along the street towards the open area bordering the edge of the Station.*

She turned and strolled along the street, hitching her teddy-bear backpack onto her shoulders. Khar had suggested she have a shower at a communal washing block before she set off, and then buy a new set of clothes. She was dressed now in a brand-new pair of blue trousers, a white blouse, and real leather sandals instead of her old, worn flip-flops.

She said, "Does the person you're trying to find know that you're coming, Khar?"

No.

"So it'll be a surprise?"

Khar did not reply immediately. It was a while before he said, *The man is an enemy of my people. I need to find him, watch him, before we approach.*

"And then?" Pham felt her heart beating fast.

And then I must consider the best, and safest, course of action.

"Khar," Pham said after a while, "the man you're trying to find, he has something to do with what is happening to the people on your planet, right?"

The mind-smile from Khar, again. *Pham, for a seven-year-old orphan with no formal education, you are perspicacious.*

Pham laughed. "And what does that mean?"

He told her.

She smiled. "Thanks—so, I'm right, ah-cha?"

Ah-cha.

She paced on, along the deserted sidewalk, staring towards the end of the street and the gates of what looked like a park. She said. "So... this person is working with the telepath?"

Yes.

She fell silent. She was thinking that, as Khar could read her thoughts, he would know what she was thinking: that the situation was more danger-ous than Khar had told her it might be.

She smiled to herself as he responded to that. *Pham, I will be careful, okay? You might find this hard to believe, but I have become close to you over the past two days.*

"Close? You're sitting in my head!" She laughed. "But thanks anyway."

They came to the gates. She stopped and stared through the bars. The green area beyond the gates and the perimeter fence was a kind of park. She saw men riding around in little buggies. From time to time they climbed out, took sticks from the buggy, and stroked the grass with them. Then they climbed back into the buggies and drove off, stopped, climbed out again and stroked the grass.

"What are they doing?" she asked.

It is a very popular game with the rich of Earth. It is called golf.

She watched more closely, and this time saw that the men were hitting tiny white balls across the grass.

"It isn't as exciting as skyball," she said. "So what now?"

You will not be allowed through the gates. Turn left and walk along the fence.

She did as instructed. Trees grew inside the green area and obscured the view of the players. From time to time she could glimpse buggies going back and forth, and men hitting the small white balls towards poles with flags on top. It looked like a crazy game to Pham.

Now, Khar said, *climb over the fence.*

She looked over her shoulder. The golf area was next to a parking lot full of big shiny air-cars and ground-effect vehicles. She could see no one looking her way.

Quickly she dug her fingers through the diamond-mesh fencing, crammed her toes into the gaps, and hauled herself up. Seconds later she swung over the top and jumped down into the grass, ducking behind a bush and breathing hard.

"Now what?"

Move to the edge of the fairway.

"What's the fairway?" she asked.

The mown area where the buggies and the players are. Make sure you aren't seen.

"Ah-cha." She crept forward and ducked behind a bush next to the fairway. One part of her was excited. The other part, the little kid just up from the depths of the Station, wondered if all this was real. Was she really sneaking through the open grass on Level One, with an alien in her head?

She peered through the leaves of the bush at a passing buggy.

"How do you know this guy will be here?"

Khar said, *Every Sunday at eleven, he plays a round of golf, alone. It's the only time his bodyguards leave his side.*

"How do you know all this?"

A hesitation, then the voice in her head said, *Kormier, the man killed in the amusement park. I obtained the information from his mind.*

Pham thought about this, then said, "Were you hiding inside Kormier's mind, before he was shot?"

Khar replied, *That is correct.*

Pham nodded, and then said, "And if the man comes along today?"

We just watch. Later, when we find the safest location in which to apprehend him.

"And then what?"

Silence. Then Khar said, *There! Stop...*

"What is it?" Pham felt her pulse quicken.

The buggy to your left, coming into view from the ninth hole...

"That's him?"

That is him.

Pham stared. The driver of the buggy was a big Westerner with a big face and wavy silver hair. He looked rich and overfed, and Pham didn't like the look of his thick lips.

Despite what Khar had said, the man was not alone. In the seat beside him was another Westerner, not as big as the first man.

"Khar, I thought—"

I'm sorry.

"What?" Pham said in panic.

The buggy had stopped. The dark Westerner jumped out. He swung around madly, as if looking for something, someone. He pulled a laser from his jacket and cried out to the silver-haired Westerner in a language Pham didn't understand.

The big white man ducked down in the buggy, wrapping his head in his arms,

He knows you're here! Khar said. *Very well. Get back to the fence and climb over. Run through the car park. There's a 'chute station on the next street. I'll guide you. Now run!*

The Westerner—the telepathic killer, Pham wondered?—was still turning, laser sweeping the fairway. He focused on the rough grass where Pham was cowering.

Pham took off. Putting the bush between her and the Westerner, she ran like the wind, dodging trees and bushes and arriving at the fence in seconds. She had no memory of climbing over—but a second later she was on the other side and sprinting through the car park.

The first laser shot smashed the windshield of a flier about a metre from Pham—the second hit the tank of a ground effect vehicle, and the resulting explosion almost knocked her off her feet. She kept running, glancing over her shoulder to see a great blooming cloud of oily black smoke obscuring the golf course. There was no sign of the killer, who would have to take a detour around the fire to get to her.

She had gained a few seconds.

Left, Khar ordered as she sprinted from the parking lot. She streaked down the street. The advantage of being in a rich area like this was that there was no one on the streets to get in her way, or to try to stop her.

Seconds later she came to a 'chute station.

The cage was open. Pham was about to launch herself into it when Khar said, *No! He will expect you to take the 'chute. There's an air-taxi rank across the road. Take a taxi south.*

Pham looked around madly. Sure enough, a dozen shiny fliers lined the far side of the street.

Pham ran across to the first one and hauled open the door. She climbed into the back seat just as the Westerner emerged from the car park and sprinted towards the closing gate of the downchute cage.

"Central Station," Pham said.

The Westerner collided with the gate, gripped it, and stared down at the descending cage.

The flier lifted with a roar, turning on its axis and presenting Pham with a grandstand view of her pursuer, who was shouting crazily now and kicking the gate.

Pham found herself almost crying with relief as the flier banked and screamed south towards safety.

I'm sorry, Pham, Khar said.

This time it was Pham's turn to give *him* the silent treatment, even though she knew that Khar would be able to read the anger in her mind, as well as the irrepressible surge of excitement.

SIXTEEN

DENNING

Vaughan hired a beat-up Benz air-car and for the next three mornings parked it on a tree-lined street in the select Mizrabad district of Level One. All the residences along the street were set in extravagant acreages of garden and lawn, and boasted a variety of architectural styles, from ultra modern dome-dwellings as low-slung as watch glasses to retro Twentieth Century ranches. Denning's residence was relatively modest, a split-level Mediterranean villa set at the back of a sloping lawn.

His air-taxi arrived at 9:44am. The vehicle swooped down to the street, parked at the kerb and sounded its horn, once. Seconds later Denning hurried out, a tall figure in a high-collared business suit, carrying a softscreen scroll and a slim briefcase. Vaughan took an instant dislike to the man, something cloned and corporate in his immaculate appearance. He watched the air-taxi power up and climb, heading north towards the Scheering-Lassiter headquarters. The thought of abducting Denning sent his pulse racing.

On the second day, the air-taxi arrived at 9:43. This time Denning emerged accompanied by a short, blonde European woman that Vaughan knew, from Kapinsky's records, was his wife. They slipped into the back of the vehicle and set off.

On the third morning, Denning emerged from the villa alone and set off to work.

At nine the following morning Vaughan was in Kapinsky's office, going over the details of the abduction. "So you're happy driving?" she asked him.

Last night Kapinsky had hired a Tata limousine, identical to the taxi that picked Denning up every day. She'd given false ID to the company and had worn a chu.

"I'm fine," Vaughan said. "I'll get there at three minutes before quarter to ten."

"I've arranged for his regular limo to be delayed for a while." She smiled at his enquiring glance. "A contact of mine—he'll stage a small crash before take-off."

"And you'll be waiting on the landing pad of the Mitsubishi building?"

"Ready and waiting with my scalpel and synthi-flesh. Denning won't suspect a thing. We'll take his wallet and softscreen and he'll assume he's been rolled."

She indicated the chu case on the desk. "Its default program is a European male in his early thirties. This is the spray." She tossed him the canister. "A two second blast straight into his face'll be enough to keep him under for at least thirty minutes. You'll need these, too." She passed him a pair of surgical gloves.

"Anything else?"

Kapinsky was staring at him, shaking her head. "You do realise we've been paid, and paid well, for this case already? We're effectively working for nothing here—absolutely no reward—and running the risk of landing ourselves in big trouble?"

"Two things, Kapinsky. We'll get to the bottom of what Scheering's covering up on Mallory, and it's my guess that it isn't anything nice. And if we find out the identity of the assassin and stop him, we'll be saving a few lives into the bargain."

Kapinsky grunted. "Get real. Some other assassin'll be more than willing to take on the workload."

"Okay, so we'll be saving one life in particular."

The Australian squinted. "And who's that?"

"The kid, yeah? Pham, the girl who saw the killing in the amusement park. The assassin wants her dead, and the sooner we can nail the assassin..."

She was smiling. "You're a regular white knight, Vaughan. She's a street-kid. The assassin would be doing her a favour."

"Christ, you're a heartless bastard, Kapinsky."

She shrugged. "You still think the killer wants her dead for something he read in her head?" She said this with what he chose to interpret as a patronising smile.

"Well, I don't think Pham saw him that night. So yeah, I think he wants her dead for some other reason."

When he thought of Pham, the danger she was in, he realised how powerless he was to find her and save her from the assassin. She was one tiny street-kid among millions on the Station. The only heartening factor was that the assassin would find her difficult to trace, too.

"Okay, Vaughan," Kapinsky said. "You ready for this?"

"See you in thirty minutes." He quit the office and rode the upchute to the parking lot on Level One.

The Tata limousine stood alone, its silver carapace resplendent in the tropical sun. Vaughan slipped into the driver's seat and wedged the canister of anaesthetic between his thighs. He slipped on the surgical gloves and opened the chu case.

He turned on the chu and held it before him. A hollowed face, as if the skull had been sucked from it, stared back at him with dark holes where the eyes should have been.

Carefully he pulled the chu over his head and arranged its features, taking time to align the eyes and lips to his own.

Then he checked himself in the rear-view mirror, and the transformation was little short of miraculous. A stranger stared back at him, fair where he was dark, pale-skinned compared to his swarthiness and permanent five o'clock shadow. He smiled, and the expression on the face was nothing like his own, even though the holographic capillaries of the chu covered his own musculature. Feeling confident in the disguise, he checked his handset. It was approaching 9:30—time he was setting off.

He powered up the air-car and hauled it into the air. It was a quiet time of day, and the air traffic above the Station was minimal. He inserted the vehicle into a eastward air-lane, a great curving

swathe of pale blue light beamed from aerial bea-
cons, the thrust of the turbos pressing him back into
the padded seat. He slowed and peeled the vehicle
into a southbound air-lane, heading for Mizrabad.

The odd thing was, he felt less apprehensive than
he had yesterday, watching Denning and looking
ahead to today. If he kept his nerve and thought
through each situation as it came up, nothing could
go wrong. He'd gone through the scheme again and
again with Kapinsky, and he was backed by the best
devices money could buy. It was only a matter of
time before Denning was in the back of the car, his
mind laid bare to their probes.

At 9:40 he overflew the spacious gardens and
seemingly toy houses of the Mizrabad district and
came in to land at the end of Denning's street. He
waited two and a half minutes, counting off the seconds on his handset, then gunned the turbos and
crawled along the kerb until he was sitting outside
the villa.

At precisely 9:43 he sounded the horn once, and
waited, fingering the canister of anaesthetic and
looking through the side window towards the side
entrance of the villa.

A minute elapsed without any sign of Denning.
Another minute ticked by, and Vaughan considered
what he might do if Kapinsky's man failed to delay
the bona fide limousine much longer. He glanced in
the rear-view mirror: if he saw an air-taxi
approaching, he would power up and get out of
here, pick up Kapinsky and begin planning again
from scratch.

He sounded the horn again, for longer this time.
Seconds later the side door of the villa opened,

and Vaughan let out a breath.

Then he saw who was approaching the car down the drive, and he cursed out loud.

It was Denning's wife. He could always start up and head off, but some instinct counselled him to go through with the charade.

The woman pulled open the passenger door and ducked to stare in at him. "My husband's working at home today—he did call to cancel the car."

Vaughan smiled. "Word never got back to me. No worries—"

"But I'm heading north. If you'd give me a minute...?"

"No problem," Vaughan said, cursing his luck.

As she hurried into the villa, he sat back and went through all the options. When she emerged again, carrying a bag, he knew exactly what he was going to do.

"Where to?" he asked as she slipped into the back seat.

"New Mumbai. The Hindustan roof-park will be fine."

He nodded and powered up, easing the car into the air and slipping into a blue northbound lane. The Hindustan building was only a kilometre from where he'd arranged to meet Kapinsky. He'd drop the woman off then make the short hop to the Mitsubishi building and tell Kapinsky what he'd planned.

Three minutes later he eased the limo onto the landing deck of the Hindustan building and cut the turbos.

The woman said, "Great. What do I owe?"

"This one's on the company, okay?"

"Say, thanks." She dazzled a smile, slipped from the car and ran across the apron.

Vaughan lifted the Benz into the air and headed across the Station, towards the imposing monolith of the Mitsubishi pile. He wondered how Kapinsky might react when he turned up without the golden goose.

He saw her as he banked sharply and came in to land on the marked rank, a small figure in a white suit.

She yanked open the passenger door, her face a picture of dismay. "Where the fuck is he, Vaughan?"

"Change of plan, Kapinsky." He told her what had happened.

"So what now? We delay a day, go through with it tomorrow?"

"I've got a better idea," he said as he took off again, heading south through a canyon of sun-reflecting skyscrapers.

"Go on."

"We go to Denning's place. I get out; you take the limo to the end of the street and wait. I ring his bell, wait till he answers, then hit him with this." He lifted the canister. "After that I just drag him inside and cut the shield."

"I'm not sure..."

"What?" Vaughan glanced at her. "Look, if anything, it'll work better than our original plan. I'll get inside his pad, take a look around—"

"I wanted to read him too, Vaughan."

He shrugged. "Tell you what, when I'm through and you pick me up, you can read what I read, yeah?"

"After what I read in there yesterday?" she asked.

She stared at him. "You sure this'll work?"

"For Chrissake, what can go wrong?"

She nodded. "Okay, let's do it."

He smiled, adrenalin pumping through him as he eased the flier down towards Mizrabad.

He landed in the street. "I'll be ten, maybe fifteen minutes, okay?"

"Any trouble and you call me, got that?"

He took the carry-case containing the scalpel, the synthi-flesh spray, and a deactivated mind-shield and climbed from the flier. As Kapinsky shuffled into the driver's seat and powered up, he turned and looked towards the house, set atop a long, sloping lawn. He took a breath and walked up the drive.

He slipped the case under his arm and the canister of anaesthetic into his jacket pocket.

He stopped before the side door, found the bell and rang.

The seconds ticked by, demarcated by the thump of his heart. His face sweated, but the chu allowed the perspiration to bead naturally on its surface. He mopped the sweat and rang the bell again.

What if Denning was so immersed in his work that he decided to ignore the bell?

He was looking for a way to break into the house when he heard a sound beyond the door and it opened quickly, as if Denning was intent on showing his annoyance at being disturbed.

"Yes?" the exec snapped, staring at Vaughan.

He acted, pulling the canister from his pocket and letting Denning have a blast in the face at close range.

The exec didn't even have time to register surprise

before he crumpled. Vaughan stepped over Denning and hauled him into the villa.

He left him slumped in the hall, did a quick reconnaissance of the place, then dragged the unconscious body into the kitchen. The room was marble-floored, and any spilled blood would be easy to clean up.

He laid the carry-case beside the body, opened the lid, and took out the scalpel. Next he carefully unfastened the executive's shirt. The mind-shield was located just below his left clavicle, raised like an old-fashioned pacemaker. He took a wad of tissues from the carry-case and held them below Denning's implant as he made a quick, lateral slice through the skin and squeezed out the silver oval of the mind-shield. He mopped the blood, cleaned the shield, and slipped it into the carry-case.

He took out the deactivated shield and, surprised at how easily it slipped into place, inserted it into the slit on the exec's chest and sealed the incision with a strip of synthi-flesh spray. Seconds later there was not the slightest sign of a wound to indicate the operation.

Then, taking a breath to prepare himself for the onslaught of the executive's mind, he activated his implant.

Denning's recent memories hit him in a dizzying rush: breakfast with his wife, Celia, dinner with her last night, and their lovemaking hours later. Vaughan experienced the heady wonder of Denning's love for his wife, the underlying regret that they could never have children. He also read the man's overwhelming ambition to succeed at his job, his ruthlessness in pursuit of that goal.

He dived deeper, pushing past emotions—love

and hate and petty jealousies—and looking for thoughts and recollections of Mallory.

He found them, in abundance. As head of the Mallory department, Anton Denning's mind was like a massive com file packed with information about the colony world, from the arcane minutiae of governmental legislation to reports from scientists in the field.

Vaughan sifted through tangled memories of meetings with government officials, scientists, colony workers, and members of Denning's own department here on Earth. The exec visited the planet half a dozen times a year and reported back to Gustave Scheering after every trip.

Most of Denning's dealings with the colonists were mind-numbingly routine; he was responsible for trade quotas, the industrial development on the planet, the facilitation of business links between Earth and the colony. Vaughan searched for any trace of a Scheering-Lassiter cover-up concerning matters ecological, but found none.

He did come across a series of interesting memories, however. On Denning's last trip to Mallory, some three months ago, he had been taken by a group of archaeological engineers to visit the crash site of an extraterrestrial starship.

Vaughan accessed the memories, vicariously sharing in Denning's wonder at the sight of the beached leviathan.

It had come down on a remote upland plain between a range of mountains in the south of the colony's main continent. The area was uninhabited, and largely inaccessible, and the scientists had flown Denning to the site by air-car.

Not a lot of the kilometre-long alien starship remained, other than its gothic superstructure and its nose-cone, which had ploughed up a tumulus, long since grassed over, of the alpine meadow's rich soil. The ship was vast and otherworldly, its becalming made all the more poignant by the state of its once magnificent tegument: much of its outer shell had disintegrated, leaving only spars and struts like the skeleton of some ancient, burned-out cathedral.

Denning recalled certain facts relayed to him by the scientists.

It had crash-landed on Mallory in the region of a hundred thousand years ago; no trace of survivors had been discovered, either in the immediate vicinity of the ship, or in the extant life forms of the planet. Also, no record of the appearance of the extraterrestrial beings had been discovered: nothing remained within the ship to suggest the creatures' shape, height, much less their physical appearance.

The scientists told Denning that they assumed the aliens had died shortly after arriving on Mallory, perhaps due to what they termed as the "non-sustainable living conditions" of the planet.

Fascinating though the scenic tour of the crashed alien starship was, Vaughan forced himself away from these recollections, sifting Denning's thoughts for any sign of discord between his employers and the environmental watchdog organisation Eco-Col.

Here, he found something of interest. Denning, in the normal course of his duties, had little to do with the ecological side of Mallory's development—this was handled by another executive of the Scheering-

Lassiter organisation.

However, Vaughan learned that in two days Denning was due to leave for Mallory. Denning knew nothing about what was expected of him on the colony world—but he was soon to find out.

Vaughan placed his knuckles against the marble floor to steady himself, like a sprinter in the starting blocks, as he pushed aside the din of Denning's emotional life and concentrated on a call Denning had received yesterday.

The call had been from the head of the organisation, none other than Gustave Scheering himself, to inform Denning that he would leave for Mallory in three days on a mission vital for the security of not only the organisation but the planet itself.

Scheering would call again, giving more information about the trip: Denning's duties while on Mallory, the team he would take, and the contacts he would make on arrival.

The time Scheering had arranged to call Denning was today, at 11am precisely.

Vaughan quickly swept through Denning's more recent dealings with Scheering, his last committee meeting, but found nothing of interest.

He withdrew his probe, discovered that he was sweating—and then realised why. He had been submerged in Denning's psyche for almost twenty minutes.

He looked at his watch. It was ten minutes to eleven.

Scheering was due to call Denning at eleven, by which time Denning would be conscious, but groggy, recovering from the effects of the assault and assessing the extent of the break in.

He thought through the options. Scheering was in the habit of calling Denning on a secure line, which could be neither intercepted, recorded, nor traced. Denning was in the habit of deleting all record of his calls from Scheering, retaining pertinent details only in his memory.

Vaughan stood. With only minutes to go before Denning regained consciousness, he had to act fast.

He moved to the bedroom and ripped open drawers and cupboards, strewing their contents in a passable imitation of the work of a desperate burglar. Behind him, in the kitchen, Denning's mind was a glow set against the concerted mind-noise of other nearby citizens.

Vaughan found a holdall in one cupboard and a hoard of expensive-looking jewellery in another, and tipped the jewellery into the bag. He moved to the lounge, opening wall-units, then found Denning's study. He would have liked more time to go through his com files, but that was impossible now.

The com, he noted, was against the far wall—an outer wall. He tipped a plastic filing unit, messed up the desk, and left the study.

He tapped Kapinsky's code into his handset. "Vaughan, what the hell's going on? You okay?"

"I think I'm onto something, but don't wait for me. I might be another five, ten minutes. It might look suspicious if you're seen hanging around in the vicinity of a break-in, okay?"

"Check. I'm outta here."

"See you back at the office in an hour," he said, and cut the connection.

He returned to the kitchen, found a washcloth

and cleaned the blood from the marble floor, then looked around to ensure he'd left no telltale traces of his presence.

Then he fastened Denning's shirt and hauled the unconscious body from the kitchen, through the hall and into the study.

It was 10:55. Scheering would be calling in five minutes.

He dropped the executive into a genuine leather recliner. The guy was moaning, struggling against the effects of the anaesthetic. He would be awake in less than a minute.

Vaughan hurried into the hall with the holdall containing the jewellery, picked up the carry-case from where he'd left it, then slipped from the villa.

He moved around the building, towards where the study was situated. Out of sight of passers-by, and hidden from neighbours by a stand of bougainvillea, he squatted down and leaned against the wall, sending out a probe towards Denning.

He glanced at his watch.

It was one minute to eleven.

He hoped Scheering was a punctual man.

He hoped, also, that Denning did not decide to call in the cops before he was distracted by Scheering's communiqué.

He scanned. Denning came around groggily, reliving the sudden flare of panic at the sight of the blonde stranger raising the canister of...

Then Vaughan experienced a vicarious surge of rage that the sanctity of Denning's personal safety, his very home, had been abused.

He was oblivious of the fact that his mind-shield

had been removed.

Denning staggered to his feet, gripping the desk for support. He looked around at the mess Vaughan had left, then through the hall to the bedroom and the strewn possessions there. Denning assumed that he'd been the victim of an opportunist thief, no more.

Then Denning moved to call in the cops. He was reaching towards the com on the desk when it chimed with an incoming.

Instantly, Denning recalled Scheering's promise to call him.

Conflicting emotions chased themselves through his mind. He wanted to call in the law, catch the bastard who did this, but at the same time he knew he had to access this call, and present a calm, unruffled exterior to his boss. The last thing he wanted was to let Scheering know that he'd allowed himself to be knocked out and burgled like some dumb pleb.

Sixty per cent of his job was all about performance. The rest was appearance.

He tapped the accept key and slipped into the swivel chair, arranging a smile of greeting.

Vaughan, perhaps two metres from where Denning sat, held himself in a tight, foetal ball and concentrated.

Denning watched Scheering materialise on his screen, his big face florid with good living and excess. Vaughan recognised the man from the flattering portrait he'd seen in the S-L headquarters the other day. His ego, Vaughan read now in Denning's mind, was as vast as his colonial empire.

"Denning," Scheering said with his accustomed

gruffness. "You all set for Mallory?"

Denning expanded his smile. "All set, sir."

"Good man. This is a big job, Denning. I won't accept anything other than success."

"You can rely on me."

"I know this link is secure, but take the usual precaution, understood?"

"I'll delete all record of the call, sir."

Vaughan screwed his eyes shut, something about Denning's obsequiousness turning his stomach.

Scheering was saying, "You're going to Mallory on *The Queen of Kandalay*, the day after tomorrow, and you're taking with you a crack team of investigators. You're also taking Indira Javinder, the necropath."

Curiosity flared in Denning's mind. "Yes, sir."

"Your mission, Denning, is to flush out a cell of environmental radicals, though to grace them with the term 'cell' is perhaps overdoing it. They are dangerous to the security of Scheering-Lassiter and to Mallory."

"Understood, sir."

"I want them," Scheering went on, "alive or dead. That is why the necropath is going along with you. The radicals have information, and I want that information."

"Sir."

Scheering smiled. "Intelligence on Mallory has pinpointed the exact whereabouts of the radicals, Jenna Larsen and Johan Weiss." He paused. "Are you ready, Denning—I'm sending this information through a scrambler. Use the usual program to decode it, and then destroy all trace of this communication."

"Understood, sir."

Denning downloaded the coded information, routed it through a decoding program, and immediately ran a scouring program to erase all record of it from his com system.

He committed the information to memory, and nodded to his superior.

Vaughan read that Larsen and Weiss were, according to Scheering's intelligence sources, holed up in a mountain retreat twenty kilometres from the alien starship, in a deserted settlement known as Campbell's End.

Scheering had the radicals under observation: a security team had made itself at home in a shack on the approach road to the settlement, awaiting Denning.

"Very good, Denning," Scheering smiled. "I'll see you on your return."

Denning felt a surge of smug pride, like a pupil commended by his headmaster. "Thank you, sir."

Scheering cut the connection, and Denning thought twice about calling in the cops for a simple case of burglary: if word of his lapse got back to Scheering...

By this time Vaughan was hurrying down the drive, the carry-case in one hand and the holdall in another. He killed his implant, and the ensuing mind-silence was like a balm.

He paused at the end of the street, accessed his handset and called up the schedule of voidliner flights from Bengal Station to Mallory. The next direct link lifted off at eight in the morning.

He made his way to the nearest 'chute station and dropped to the second level, then took the northbound shuttle ten stops. When he had the carriage to himself, he reached into his pocket and altered the controls of the chu. From the window beside him, a blonde Scandinavian stared back with an expression of ill-concealed triumph.

He alighted at the 'chute station beneath Chandi Road, then caught the upchute to Level One and found a public lavatory. In a cubicle he removed the chu, slung his jacket over his arm, then made his way to Nazruddin's. He felt he deserved a beer or two.

On the way, he stopped at a stall and ordered a plate of pakora, surrounded by a noisy gaggle of street-kids. As he left, he forgot to pick up the holdall. When he glanced back, the kids had found the bag and were retreating in delight to divide the spoils. Vaughan smiled. They'd get a fraction of the cost of the jewels when they sold them on to a fence, but they'd still be able to keep themselves in dhal and rice for a year.

He reached Nazruddin's and ordered a Blue Mountain beer, and only then thought about how to tell Sukara that he would be away from Earth for almost a week.

SEVENTEEN

PREMONITIONS

Sukara routed the scan from her handset to the screen in the lounge and sat, fascinated, watching her baby.

What amazed her was the fact of its perfection. From next to nothing, or rather from microscopically small seeds, the girl had evolved into this—a pink, almost translucent, miniature human being floating in its amniotic universe, knees drawn up, hands waving about its head. Without Jeff, she thought, this wouldn't have been possible. She tried to think of life without the man she loved, and the thought, like the thought of death, terrified her. He was so vast a part of her existence that she would be nothing without him. Everything she did, her every action and thought, was in some way influenced by Jeff Vaughan, and far from being restricted by this, she felt liberated. For so many years she had been alone, with no one dependant on her; now Jeff loved her, and told her so in so many ways, and he filled her thoughts with happiness.

And lately, thanks to Jeff, she had had Li to think of too. It was amazing, but the child was not yet born and she was already planning the future—or rather not so much planning, but daydreaming of Li at one year old, at three, and then five. The other day, over coffee, she had even found herself thinking ahead to when Li would be sixteen, and going off to study at university.

With such pleasant notions, however, came the reverse: the nagging worry every parent was beset by when thinking of the future. Fear for her child's welfare, its health, its well-being in a world full of cynical and grasping people.

For the past few days Sukara had been visited by vague feelings of despair, indefinable but real. It was as if some terrible event in her future was reaching back to inform her, to warn her to be mentally prepared. She could not tell if this terrible event would befall her—if she were to die in some awful way: and even then, she was not fearful for herself, but could only think of Jeff, without her. Or whether something was going to happen to Li, or to Jeff. She had never had such feelings in the past, which made these ones all the more disturbing. Everything in her life was so good, too good: how could someone be so lucky and not suffer the consequences?

The door that gave straight onto the outer corridor sighed open, sliding into the wall, and Jeff stood in the opening, smiling tiredly at her. He stepped inside and she launched herself into his arms. "Hey," he laughed.

And she found herself weeping against his chest. "I'm so happy," she said.

He stroked her hair. "Watching Li again?"

She laughed. They had sat in the sunken sofa last night, with a bottle of wine, running the scan of their daughter over and over. She had found something different to be fascinated with on each run through, some particular movement, expression, the utter perfection of the unborn child.

She looked up at him. "How are you?"

"Tired. It's been a long day."

"Tell me about it." She sniffed him. "Heh. You're sweaty!"

He hesitated. "I'll get a shower, then we'll go for a meal, okay?"

She beamed. "What's the occasion?"

He hesitated again, and in that fraction of a second pause, Sukara knew that something was wrong.

He smiled. "No occasion. I just thought it might be nice... I'll be back in five minutes."

She slipped into the sunken bunker and killed the scan, sitting and staring at the blank screen and wondering what Jeff was going to tell her.

Something about the case he was working on, no doubt. Something had gone wrong. The killer had threatened Jeff and Kapinsky, or had even tried to kill him. Was that why he was so sweaty, because he'd been trying to evade the killer?

She told herself she was being paranoid.

She moved to the bedroom and changed into a pair of baggy maternity trousers and a loose-fitting shirt, then returned to the lounge to put her flip-flops on as Jeff stepped from the shower and changed.

He was his old self as he came into the lounge and kissed her. "Where would you like to eat?"

"Silly question, Jeff!"

"Ruen Thai it is, then."

They took the upchute to Level One and walked through Himachal Park. The sun was going down, and the heat of the day was dying. Couples and families were taking advantage of the cool early evening to stroll through the park, and Sukara found it almost impossible to believe that soon she too would be a mother, with a little girl as beautiful as these children to look after and to love.

"How's the case going, Jeff?" she asked.

"We made a big breakthrough today," he replied.

"Tell me about it."

"Over dinner, okay?" he said, and something in his tone alarmed her.

They left Himachal Park and crossed the busy Chandi Road, moving down a tree-lined street to the three-storey building that housed the Ruen Thai.

It was early, and they selected a window table overlooking the quiet street.

"Jeff, is everything okay?"

He reached across the table and smiled. "You're amazing, you know that? I couldn't keep a secret from you."

"I knew something was wrong," she whispered.

"You sure you're not telepathic?"

She smiled. "What is it?"

They were interrupted by the waitress. They ordered, Sukara her usual extra hot gaeng panang and Jeff a green Thai curry with rice and noodles.

Jeff said, "You've got the mind-shield on you?"

"Of course." She tapped her shirt pocket. "You were saying?"

"The case was officially closed today."

She stared, wide-eyed. "You solved it? You got the killer?"

"If only. No, the police think they got the killer, think he killed himself. But it's a cover-up. Someone high up in the force has been bribed to look the other way, close the case and pay off Kapinsky and me."

Sukara slowly shook her head.

Jeff went on, "The Scheering-Lassiter people are behind the killings. They're trying to cover up something that's happening on one of their colony worlds."

"Do you know what?"

"If we knew that, Su, we'd be close to closing the case."

Sukara shrugged. "So that's it. You've been paid off. What now? You work on another case?" She hoped so, fervently she hoped that would be the end of trying to track down the laser killer.

Jeff was watching her. He shook his head. "We're not going to let it lie. We're not going to be bought off."

His words sank like weights in her gut. She felt sick. "But..." she managed at last, "isn't that dangerous? I mean, if someone high up in the Scheering company wants the case closed, and if you ignore that and try to find out the real killer..." She shrugged. "Won't that be dangerous, Jeff?" Now she knew the reason for his earlier hesitation, his reluctance to talk about the case until now.

He nodded. "Yes, it's dangerous."

Their food arrived. It looked great, but Sukara had never felt less like eating.

"So..." she said in a small voice, "so why can't you just ignore this one, work on something else?"

"You sound just like Kapinsky," he said. He reached across the table and took her hands. "Su, two years ago, you remember Osborne?"

"How could I forget the bastard?"

"Well, the laser killer working for Scheering is probably even more dangerous than him. He's a hired killer. He'll go on killing, taking life after innocent life, as long as Scheering pays him."

She looked into his eyes. "So it's Jeff Vaughan's job to stop him?" she said, and then wished she hadn't sounded so mocking.

He squeezed her fingers. "Su, not only is it my job to nail the killer, I've got to find out what Scheering's trying to cover up on the colony world."

The lead weight in her stomach turned to ice. She wanted to shout at Vaughan, hit him, ask him how he could be so cruel. She wanted to tell him to think of her, to think of their unborn daughter. How could he go off to another planet, venture into enemy territory, and leave her behind to worry herself sick about him?

She shook her head. "What do you mean?"

"Su, I'm taking a voidship to Mallory tomorrow. It's the only way. I'll be gone about six days."

She was weeping. She couldn't help it. "Six days? Six fucking days? Jeff, we've never had a day apart—and now you're going off for nearly a week!"

"I won't exactly be enjoying myself."

She slammed down her knife and fork. "That's not the point! You'll be in danger! I'll be worried sick!"

"Su, Su. Listen. I can look after myself. I'll be fine. And someone has to stop what's going on there."

"What is going on?" she asked through her tears.

"I... I don't know. It's something big enough to have Scheering hire killers to silence people working for his organisation."

"And silence investigators trying to get at the truth!"

He was silent for a time, shaking his head. "I've got to go, Su. I couldn't live with myself if I just sat back and let Scheering get on with it. Look at it this way, if I crack the case, no more innocent people will be lasered to death."

She nearly said, "And if you don't crack the case, you'll be lasered to death." But she held her tongue. Jeff was determined, and she told herself that she was being selfish. She hated her husband for what he was putting her though, but at the same time a small, odd part of her felt a certain pride that he would risk himself to save the lives of others.

She nodded, wordlessly, returning the pressure of his fingers. "I love you so much, Jeff, I just can't imagine life without out you."

Pain passed across his eyes. "I'm sorry, Su," he said.

They finished the meal in silence, Sukara unable to appreciate her dish. They left the restaurant as the sun was sinking into the sea, and they lingered a while in Himachal Park to watch the last pink filaments of cirrus fade over India.

They made love that night, slowly, on their sides, Jeff holding her to his stomach, cupping her swollen belly in his right arm, and afterwards they clung to each other in silence like the survivors of some natural catastrophe.

In the morning she helped him pack, and then went with him by flier to the spaceport.

He held back passing through the boarding check until the last call, and then hugged Sukara to him. She found his lips. "Be careful, Jeff," she whispered, steeling herself against the tears she wanted to shed.

"Love you," he said, turned and strode through the barrier and disappeared from sight.

A vast cold weight of depression settled over her. She had never felt as alone as she did now, not even when Tiger had left her in Bangkok all those years ago.

She made her way to the observation lounge and stood by the rail, staring through the great viewscreen across the apron of the spaceport to the mammoth, streamlined shape of the voidship, connected to the terminal building by boarding umbilicals.

It was strange to think of her husband taking his place aboard the ship, strange to think that in less than two days he would set foot on an alien planet, nearly seventy light years away.

Thirty minutes later the connecting corridors and tubes retracted, and the voidliner powered up with a deafening crescendo of engines. It rose, ever so slowly, and despite herself Sukara felt a strange thrilling sensation in her chest as the colossal vessel inched slowly across the spaceport, out over the sea, beautiful in its vastness and power.

When the voidship was beyond the edge of the Station, hanging over the ocean like some vast fish surreally translated into the air, it began to phase from this reality. It shimmered, losing substance, then flickered in and out of existence briefly before vanishing in an instant.

Sukara found herself crying, wondering where Jeff was now.

Slowly, rubbing at her tears with her fingertips, she left the spaceport and made her way home. She knew now the reason for the premonitions of tragedy she had experienced for the past few days.

She knew, with a terrible and inevitable certainty, that she would never see her husband again.

EIGHTEEN

WELCOME TO MALLORY

"Welcome to Mallory, Mr Lacey," the customs officer said, handing back the ID card. "Here on business?"

"Pleasure," Vaughan said. "Sightseeing in the southern mountains."

"Have a great stay."

Vaughan stepped through the customs barrier and collected his luggage, a single holdall, then made his way out into the arrival lounge. The slightly lighter gravity of the colony planet gave his gait an odd buoyancy.

Kapinsky had issued him with a false ID card and, should he need to use it, a chu which he'd concealed inside his musiCom. He was unarmed—weapons of all types were not allowed to be brought into Mallory—but with luck he would neither need to defend himself, nor to attack.

The spaceport at Mackintyre, Mallory's capital city, was smaller than many international airports on Earth, and a tenth of the size of the 'port on

Bengal Station. Just three ships a week arrived on Mallory from Earth, plus a couple from other nearby colony worlds. The place had a quaint backwater feel about it, and this impression was heightened when he stepped through the sliding glass doors and looked out over Mackintyre.

The 'port was situated on a rise of land above a plain across which the large town sprawled, a series of timber buildings built on a grid-pattern of streets. Vaughan felt an immediate wave of nostalgia: the capital had the look and feel of a remote settlement in his native Canada, the same type of weatherboard dwellings in spacious gardens pressed flat by a seemingly limitless expanse of blue sky.

Only the presence of three large moons, tumbling visibly overhead as if tossed by a celestial juggler, told him that he was off-world.

His first task was to hire a vehicle, and then buy a decent map-pin for his handset. He found a car-hire place next to the terminal building, staffed by two women in light blue uniforms like air-hostesses. His request to hire a flier for six days was met with surprise, then a bright smile. "I'm sorry, sir. Air-traffic, other than that authorised for government use, is prohibited on Mallory. We have a range of the latest ground-effect vehicles for hire, though."

He bought a map-pin from the counter, and after inserting it into his handset and studying the screen, he asked if they had a sturdy four-wheel drive for hire.

The woman took him into an enclosed lot and gave him the choice of a Bison all-terrain jeep or a beat-up mountain truck. He selected the Bison.

Ten minutes later he drove from the compound and headed into town, surprised at the physicality of driving a road vehicle after the smooth handling of air-cars. It was a long time, over ten years, since he'd last driven a vehicle whose wheels were in contact with the ground.

He found a general store and bought provisions to last him a few days: half a dozen two-litre canisters of water, a dozen foil-wrapped self-heating meals, and a bag of local fruit not dissimilar to bananas. He had a long drive ahead of him, and much of it would be through sparsely populated terrain.

He put the Bison on a southward course and headed out of town—an operation that took all of five minutes.

With the town behind him, he pulled off the road and consulted the map on his handset. He was on the larger of Mallory's two Africa-sized continents; Mackintyre was situated on the western coast, close to the planet's equator. His destination, Campbell's End, was located in the southern mountains some five hundred kilometres south of the capital.

He started the engine and set off again. The road, here at least, was good: a wide, straight blacktop. If it remained in a similar state all the way, then he should reach his destination in five or six hours. He planned to spend the night in the town of Lincolnville, ten kilometres from Campbell's End, and then consider his next move in the morning.

The day on Mallory was longer than that of Earth: twenty-six hours divided, now that it was late Autumn, into days of twelve hours, and long fourteen hour nights. Eta Ophiuchi, a blue-white main sequence star, burned with a distinctly orange cast. The ambient light, combined with fields of blue grass, created a definite alien atmosphere. Vaughan found the experience somewhat disconcerting, his senses confused by the contrast between the familiarity of man-made roads, cars, farmsteads, and the otherworldly combination of triple moons, sallow light, and the spiked, blue grass.

As he drove, he passed through the region of farmed land around Mackintyre and came to an area of old upland meadow, scattered with polychromatic wildflowers and bizarre, spiral-trunked trees. The horizon in three directions was crenellated by distant, snow-capped mountain ranges, their peaks tinted tangerine in the afternoon light. He was to notice this geographical effect during his long drive south: the road cut through range after range of low mountains, crossed high pastures, and always the horizon presented ever more mountain ranges. He had read, on the voyage here, that Mallory had once boasted six continents, but over the course of millions of years tectonic drift had brought them together to form two vast land-masses: where they joined, like the pieces of a jigsaw puzzle, mountain ranges were pushed up from the fertile grassland.

He passed through great areas of cultivated land. At points, the road swept around bluffs to give an elevated view of oceans of wheat, with lone timber farmsteads lost in the vastness like becalmed galleons.

At one point, perhaps halfway through his journey, he pulled into the side of the road and climbed out. The view was no less than a visual assault of beauty. He had been climbing the foothills of a mountain range for an hour, and he looked down on a cascade of blue grassland, chivvied by the wind so that it presented alternate shades of silver and indigo, like caressed velvet. Beyond, in stark contrast, was the bright golden expanse of wheat, stretching to the far horizon and the enclosing palisade of peaks.

He ate a meal here and pored over the map on his handset. Lincolnville was another two hundred kilometres distant, beyond the next mountain range and across the plain.

He had discussed tactics with Kapinsky in the little time they had to prepare before he caught the voidliner. It was imperative that he reach the environmentalists and warn them that Denning and his team were coming for them, and that Gustave Scheering's order was to bring them in dead or alive. They possessed, according to Scheering, information dangerous to the corporation and to Mallory—though as the business concern and the planet were one and the same thing, Vaughan knew that Scheering's claim for the safety of Mallory was nothing more than a rhetorical flourish with which to impress his underlings.

In an ideal world he would find the radicals, warn them, learn what their big secret was, and get out again. With luck, the information might lead him to the apprehension of the assassin on Earth, even the salvation of the street-kid Pham. Or was he being too optimistic? Did his sanguine take on existence, since meeting Sukara, blind him to the dangers involved in messing with a ruthless multicolonial like Scheering-Lassiter?

The difficulty would be in locating the radicals at Campbell's End without alerting their watchers to the fact of his presence. As there was nothing he could do to foresee how he might go about avoiding this, he decided to worry about it tomorrow, after he had reached Lincolnville.

He finished the pre-packed meal of broiled fish and greens—bland almost to the point of tastelessness after a diet of Indian and Thai cuisine back home—and strolled away from the Bison. He stood on the edge of the road and stared out over the wind-ruffled blue plain. Experimentally, he tapped the start-up code into his handset and activated his implant.

He scanned, but was unable to detect the transition between his implant being turned off and its functioning. All was silent. He turned, pushing out his mind-probe towards the last farmstead he had passed, perhaps fifty kilometres away.

Did he detect the faintest hint of mind-noise, or was he deluding himself?

Smiling, he climbed back into the Bison. He decided to leave his implant active, as an experiment to see how deserted this landscape really was.

Gunning the engine, he drove into the mountains.

He braked on a high mountain pass and stared down across the plain, a fertile expanse of farmland nursed in the lap of the enclosing peaks. As he started up and took the winding road down into the valley, he looked out over a sea of golden wheat and, beyond, vast squares of cultivated land bearing another crop entirely, this one dark green but anonymous at this distance.

He left the mountain pass in his wake and raced along the high straight road between fields of wheat. Kilometres ahead and to his right, he made out another farmstead set back from the road. Remembering that his implant was activated, he scanned ahead. He came across no mind-signatures—the silence continued. He wondered idly if the farm were deserted, or its owners away.

Only when he was a kilometre from the farm did he make out the tiny shape of a beetling harvester, a red bug against the golden field. He assumed, quite naturally, that the machine must be automated, as he still could detect no human mind-presence. Then he drew closer, and saw upon the back of the harvester the dark shape of the farmer, turned in his seat to monitor the threshing.

He pushed out a mind-probe, directly towards the farmer. Even at this distance he should have picked up something, some sub-stratum of emotion, if not articulated thoughts. But the silence suggested that the man did not exist... or was shielded.

He drew alongside the farmstead and slowed, so that he was a matter of only a hundred metres from the harvester when it reached the end of the field and turned. The farmer in the driving seat gave a friendly wave as Vaughan passed.

He scanned again, and his probe slipped off and around a mind-shield, the faint white noise of static in the place of vibrant thoughts.

He drove on, wondering why a farmer this far from civilisation and the possibility of telepaths should wish to shield his mind.

The mountains ahead, which an hour ago had been an apparent hand's width above the level of the plain, now reared to fill the windscreen. The plain rose, and the road with it, hugging the contours of the foothills and turning in long loops through undulating countryside patched with strange trees and shrubs like explosions of crimson flame. Squat-bodied birds, with long beaks like chopsticks, darted from bush to bush imbibing nectar from blooms as long as clarinets.

He wound down the side-screen and the Bison was flooded with a sweet heady scent. The sun was setting behind the mountains, turning the air a combustible tangerine hue, and he suddenly wished that Sukara was with him to appreciate the alien beauty of the colony world.

Then his regret was replaced by curiosity, again, as his vehicle passed a truck that had pulled into the side of the road. A dozen men in uniforms stood at the side of the road, smoking and chatting. He was moving at speed, and was unable to tell if the men were militia, though he suspected so. He could tell, however, that to a single individual they were shielded. His transit, so close, should have brought their minds flaring into his like so many burning torches, but again all he detected was the slippery blitz of static, and then nothing as he raced on by.

Even if they had been militia, it was strange that every one of the troop had worn a shield. Vaughan could understand, perhaps, a commanding officer choosing to keep his thoughts a secret... but even that was decidedly odd in such a sequestered backwater.

Then he saw the second truck, and the lasercordon barring the way. Half a dozen men and women in camouflage fatigues hung around the vehicle, their interest stirring as he approached. They pushed themselves from where they had been lounging, unslung weapons, and moved into the road.

He scanned, and read nothing.

The officer in charge strolled along the centre of the road as Vaughan approached, a palm raised nonchalantly to halt him.

Vaughan slowed, opening the side-screen as he drew alongside the officer.

The woman had the crew cut and overfed face of a career soldier, and the intimidating gaze of one backed by the authority of superior firepower.

She rested an arm on the roof of the Bison and pushed her face close, inspecting both Vaughan and the interior of the vehicle with one quick sliding glance.

"ID."

Sweating despite himself, Vaughan produced his card. He waited, staring through the windscreen at the blue laser cordon, as the officer processed his ID through a com on her hip.

He wondered if the sweat standing out on his face would be seen by the soldier as a sign of his fear, and therefore his guilt. To get so far, only to be picked up by a random road-block...

But the card passed muster. She handed it back, and Vaughan gave silent praise to Lin Kapinsky.

"What're you doing this far south, Mr Lacey?" The woman spoke with a colonial twang, high and nasal.

"I'm on holiday," he said. "Someone suggested I take a look at the southern ranges. I thought I'd check them out."

"Think again, Mr Lacey. The road's closed."

He thought fast. "Is there any other way I can get to Preston?" he asked, naming the town a hundred kilometres beyond his destination. If he managed to reach Lincolnville some other way, he didn't want the military to know he was there.

"All the roads are closed hereabouts, Mr Lacey."

He stared at her. "And when will they be reopened?"

"That," she said, "I can't say. Military operation, Mr Lacey. And who can say how long military operations might last?"

Vaughan gave a theatrical sigh. "And I was told the southern range was one of the best."

"Well, why don't you take my advice, turn yourself around, and check out MacArthur's Range away back. That's almost as pretty, take it from me."

"You know," Vaughan said, "I might just do that."

The woman nodded. "Safe journey, Mr Lacey."

He reversed, giving the officer a salute, turned the Bison and accelerated back along the road.

A military operation. He wondered if it might be linked to Denning's imminent arrival? If so, Scheering was leaving nothing to chance.

He felt a cold dread in the pit of his stomach. Perhaps he'd been a fool to think he would be able to waltz in here, warn the radicals, and skip back out again with their secret in his possession.

It was going to be a tad trickier than that.

He travelled five kilometres north, then pulled into the side of the road. From his earlier examination of the area on his handset, he recalled secondary roads branching off the main highway at intervals and twisting further into the foothills.

He consulted the map and charted three narrower roads, which left this one and climbed south. One of them, a particularly tortuous track, looped around a low peak and approached Lincolnville from the south-east. It would put another hundred kilometres on his journey, maybe delay his arrival until after sunset, but the track looked insignificant enough not to warrant an army blockade.

And if the militia had barred this track, then he would test the Bison's off-road capabilities and head for Lincolnville over the hills.

He set off again and ten kilometres further along the highway turned right up a pot-holed minor road, heading into the mountains.

He travelled for an hour. The track was rough and unfinished, and at one point a landslide had slurred the track ten metres down the hill, but the Bison was equal to the challenge. He passed a couple of farms, clearly occupied, but again detected not the slightest mind-noise from within. He wondered if it were mandatory for the citizens of Mallory to wear shields, and if so then why the government had passed such a Draconian law. What might the average citizens of the colony world know that their government did not want the rest of the universe to find out?

The fiery orange sun was a hand's breadth above the mountain peaks high to his left when he came around a great loop in the road and was presented with a spectacular panorama: the hillside shelved away to form a long, broad valley, its blue grass scintillating in the twilight.

The track edged along the margin of the valley, and Vaughan made out, perhaps two kilometres distant, the telltale glow of a laser cordon. Beside it, reduced to the size of a child's toy, was a militia truck.

Vaughan braked, heart thudding, and considered his options.

According to the map, he was still a hundred kilometres from Lincolnville. There were no roads branching from this one that would take him anywhere near his destination.

He supposed he could always conceal the truck, wait until nightfall, and see then if the military checkpoint remained—the laser cordon presented an obvious indication of their presence. But if the militia were aiding Denning's mission, then they would remain *in situ* until the exec and his teams arrived.

He scanned the surrounding land. The valley was wide, and easily navigable by the Bison, but not so wide that his passage would go unnoticed by the military. To his left the hillside climbed acutely, graduating to rocky outcrops and minor peaks. Hardy though the Bison was, he doubted it could negotiate such precipitous terrain.

He was startled by a noise coming from behind him. He turned in his seat and made out, perhaps a couple of hundred metres further up the valley, the first of a herd of... animals, obviously, but animals the like of which Vaughan had never seen before.

Only when visually aware of the creatures did he sense their presence in his mind: an inchoate, tuneless music, totally alien and unsettling. He turned off his implant.

The leading beast was huge—that was the first thing that struck him—perhaps four metres high. It was brown-skinned, and wore its tegument in what looked like sections of armour.

There, its resemblance to anything Earth-like finished. Its four legs were thick and long, its head huge. It had a thick trunk perhaps a metre long, on either side of which sprouted a lethal array of tusks like tines. Above huge black eyes, arranged on each side of the head, was another set of tines. It looked ferocious, and the thunderous sound of its bellow echoed like a war cry.

It approached the Bison and slowed. The others, behind it, slowed too. Vaughan counted over twenty in the herd, many of them the size of their leader.

The others halted, as one, and seemed to be watching their leader as it slowed and took small, cautious steps towards the vehicle.

Two metres away, the great beast halted.

Vaughan stared, and the creature stared back at him. He felt suddenly, profoundly, moved. After his initial alarm, it came to him that he had nothing at all to fear from these animals, and only then realised that the side-screen was still wound down.

The beast blinked, regarding him, and though Vaughan knew that Mallory possessed no intelligent life forms, he felt as if he were communicating on some level with a creature wise beyond its classification.

Then the beast surprised him.

It moved forward, a single step bringing it right up to the flank of the Bison. Then, before Vaughan could react, it raised its short, thick trunk and reached out towards his head.

His first instinct was to draw away, his second to sit tight.

The trunk, its nostril panting a warm, fetid breath, came in through the window and caressed his head, pressing itself against his skin, inhaling like a vacuum cleaner, sniffing, then settled on his forehead. There it remained for perhaps ten seconds. Vaughan, his pulse racing, looked up, along the length of its trunk, into the dark discus of its left eye.

The eye blinked, gently.

Then the animal broke contact, swung around and harrumphed to the rest of the herd. They began moving around the Bison, trundling across the track and heading into the high foothills. Their leader was the last to move off. Watching it back off, then move around the vehicle after the others, Vaughan felt impelled to call out some kind of farewell, or lift a hand in a valedictory gesture. Instead, he just watched them go in silence, aware that he had participated in a once-in-a-lifetime experience.

In single file the herd passed through a cutting in the rocks above. When it came to the leader's turn to ease itself between the slabs of rock, it paused, turned, and stared at Vaughan. It lifted its truck and issued a low, bassoon-like note, and Vaughan received the crazy impression that it was telling him to follow them.

Convinced that he was deluding himself, but curious nevertheless, he climbed from the Bison and crossed the track, climbing through blue grass and tumbled scree towards where the khaki rump of the creature was shuffling on up the cutting.

The gap was wider than he first thought, easily wide enough to admit the Bison. He followed the beast, though its strides had taken it far up the cutting, and found that the pass opened out into a greensward—or rather bluesward—which ran aslant between a tumble of boulders below and the flanks of rocks above.

By now the leader of the herd had crossed the clearing and was moving through another cutting, though this time it did not turn to encourage his pursuit... if indeed it had originally.

Vaughan paused and considered his options. He was no doubt anthropomorphising the creature's actions, but what did he have to lose?

He returned to the Bison, started it up and left the track. It bucked over the uneven ground, rocking him in his seat, as he approached the cutting. He slowed, and the truck scraped through with centimetres to spare on either side. Minutes later he emerged on the bluesward and accelerated across the sloping ground towards the far rocks. The next five minutes would determine whether he had deluded himself.

This pass was wider than the last, and longer, and when it ended the Bison emerged into a dazzling wash of dying sunlight and Vaughan was amazed to find himself on what was obviously a man-made track, rougher than the one he had left but a track nevertheless... which meant that, at some point in the past, it must have led somewhere.

He followed it, the Bison pitching back and forth. The track climbed, then levelled out and paralleled the lie of the valley to his right, hidden though it was by a fold in the hills.

Of the creatures—his unwitting helpers?—there was no sign.

He travelled for two hours through the gradually dimming light, and at one point came to a high crest in the track that afforded a vantage point over the hills to the valley. He stopped the Bison and stared out. Far below, and behind him now, was the dazzling line of light that was the laser cordon.

He continued on his way, and the track fell away down the hillside. At last, in darkness now and the vehicle's powerful headlamps lighting the way, the track joined the original road. Vaughan accelerated, hardly daring to believe that he had bypassed the military checkpoint, and an hour later he came to the highway leading to his destination. A couple of kilometres further on a sign declared that Lincolnville was just fifty kilometres distant.

The highway climbed, wound through the foothills, and less than an hour later Vaughan came to a collection of weatherboard dwellings, strung out along a single main road, and a sign welcoming him to Lincolnville, population five hundred. There was no sign, he was relieved to see, of any military presence.

Half a dozen four-wheel drives were pulled up outside the town's only hotel-cum-bar. Vaughan parked the Bison beside them, shouldered his holdall, and made for the plinth of steps to the hotel's veranda.

He was about to push through the double doors when he stopped. He dropped his bag and considered his handset. So far on his journey south, he had yet to come across an unshielded mind. He wondered if the citizens of Lincolnville likewise had something to hide.

He activated his implant, and instantly knew the answer.

Mind-silence, except for the confused emotions of a newborn baby on the second floor of the hotel.

Vaughan entered and found himself in timber-panelled lobby. The place had the appearance of something from a Wild West holo-movie set.

To the right was a door leading to a small bar, occupied by half a dozen men and women.

A Nordic blonde girl in her teens, obviously surprised to see him, appeared behind the reception counter.

He asked for a room for tonight, and if he could buy a meal. He was in luck as far as accommodation went, but the kitchen was closed. He took a small room on the second floor, fetched a meal from the Bison, and ate it while staring out of the window at the darkened main street and the looming shape of the mountains to the south. They were shadowed and dark against the starscape, and gave Vaughan the impression of dour hostility. Tomorrow, first thing, he would be heading further south, towards Campbell's End. He pushed the thought to the back of his mind.

Melancholy, he went down to the bar and ordered a local beer—thin and insipid compared to his regular Blue Mountain. It was late, and he was the only customer.

He took his beer to a table near the window and stared out.

Minutes later, snow began to fall, reminding him of Canada.

The girl's question startled him.

"I said," she repeated, "are you with the military?"

"Excuse me?"

She was wiping the table next to his, camouflaging her shyness with a truculent stare.

"You a soldier?"

He smiled. "No. A tourist?"

She shook her head. "A tourist? Then how you get through the roadblocks?"

He considered his reply. "I've been in Preston for a few days. Last night I camped in the hills."

She seemed reluctant to believe him. "So you're nothing to do with what's going on in the valley? You're not with the S-L forces?"

He smiled again, trying to reassure her. "What is going on?" he asked.

She resumed her polishing with renewed vigour. "You're a tourist, so you don't need to know, do you?"

"Still, I'd like to know."

She stopped and looked at him. "How do I know you're not an S-L spy?"

He showed her his ID. "See. Earth citizen."

She peered at it, then looked at him dubiously. "But then a S-L spy would have cover, wouldn't he?"

He took a sip of beer, considering his next words. "Someone told me that everyone around here carries mind-shields? Is that right?"

She moved to the next table, and Vaughan thought she was refusing to reply. Then she said, "Carry them? We're implanted, mister. Everyone on Mallory."

Vaughan nodded. "Is that a government edict?"

"Huh?" Incomprehension showed in her Scandinavian eyes.

"Is it a law that everyone on Mallory should be implanted?"

"Everyone over the age of ten, yes," she said. She thought about it, then went on, "S-L don't want telepaths from Earth learning all about them, do they?"

"All about them?"

The girl decided she'd said enough, wished Vaughan good night and told him that the bar was closed now. If he wanted another beer he could help himself.

He did just that, and sat in the darkened barroom considering the events of the day. High above the mountains was a spread of stars in an alien arrangement, and he wondered where Sol might be.

He realised he was seventy light years away from Earth, and Sukara.

NINETEEN

THE TELEPATH

Pham spent the night under the banyan tree in Gandhi Park, and in the morning sat on her blanket and wondered what to do next.

Since being chased by the laser killer yesterday, she had been unable to rouse Khar. At first she thought that he might be sulking, or that he was so ashamed of nearly getting her killed that he couldn't bring himself to speak to her.

Now she wondered if he had left her in the night, flown from her head and lodged in someone else's.

If he had done that, then she was both upset that he had left without saying goodbye, and a little afraid now that she was alone. Khar had helped her since she had arrived on the upper decks. Okay, he'd got her into trouble yesterday, but he had won her money and kept her company and filled her head with interesting thoughts. And, to be truthful, there was something exciting about being chased by a killer. It was like something from her favourite holo-movies.

"Khar," she said now. "Why aren't you talking?"

The silence stretched, then the familiar voice sounded in her head. *I am communing.*

She smiled to herself, relieved that he was still there. "Communing? Who with?"

It would be better if you did not know that.

"Ah-cha," she said. She was quiet for a while, then said, "I've decided I'm going to look for Abdul today."

Do you know where to find him?

"He told me he begged on Chandi Road. I'll look there."

Very well, Pham.

"Okay, so I'll leave you to your communing, Khar."

He did not reply.

She stuffed her blanket into her teddy-bear backpack, hitched it onto her back and left the park.

She had missed Abdul since hurrying away from the starship a couple of days ago. She wanted to explain why she had left so quickly, and apologise. She was sure Abdul would understand. It was strange, but she'd only met him two or three times, and then only for a few hours each time, but she felt as if she had known him for years. She thought of his smile, his big staring eyes... He was like the brother she had never had.

She took the upchute two levels to the upper deck, then caught the train to Chandi Road.

The long, wide road that ran parallel to the spaceport was solid with a noisy, colourful river of humanity. It was as if a skyball stadium was constantly emptying spectators out into the street. Pham wondered where each citizen was heading.

All of them were going about their own private business, spending perhaps minutes on the road before leaving it, their places taken by other pedestrians.

Pham pushed through the crowd, heading for Patel's Sweet Centre where she had first met Abdul. He'd told her that his begging patch was between Patel's and a restaurant called Nazruddin's. She was sure to find him somewhere along the street.

She had to cut across the crowd flowing along the length of the road, and it was like swimming against a great surging torrent of water. She was carried way past Patel's by the time she emerged from the press and jumped out onto the sidewalk, catching her breath in the quiet space between the stall of a chai vendor and a paan kiosk.

She looked up and down the sidewalk, scrutinising the kids hurrying along its length, their hands outstretched towards the well-dressed citizens promenading before the expensive shop-fronts. Most of the time the kids were ignored, but now and then a man or woman tossed a small denomination note their way, to keep them quiet. Sometimes fights broke out among the street-kids as they fought for notes that fluttered to the ground.

Pham watched them and thought of Abdul living like this, and the idea made her unhappy.

She walked towards Patel's. She was still wearing the smart clothes she had bought yesterday, and she earned hostile glances from the street-kids who thought she was a little rich kid out shopping.

The odd thing was, while part of her hated the life these kids were living, relying on baht from fat, bored rich people, another part envied the fact that the children existed in one big family. It might not always be a happy family, but at least they had each other to talk to, to play with, to share their problems with.

She would like to be part of that family, but not if it meant living on the spaceship and working for Dr Rao.

The double shop-front of Patel's was an Aladdin's cave full of a hundred different kinds of Indian sweets, piled in pyramids and ziggurats and cones like exotic multicoloured temples.

Pham slipped into the shop and bought a selection of barfi in a big bag, then stepped out onto the sidewalk and looked for Abdul.

He was not among the kids rushing up and down outside Patel's and neighbouring shops. She wanted to ask them if they knew where he was, but shyness stopped her approaching the scruffy, ragged urchins. She hurried along the sidewalk towards Nazruddin's, hoping that Abdul had not decided to take a holiday today.

He was not outside Nazruddin's, so she walked further along the road, and then back again. She consoled herself by stuffing delicious barfi into her mouth, and washing it down with a cup of spiced ginger chai from a roadside stall.

There was no sign of Abdul along his usual patch, so the only thing left to do was to ask one of the street-kids if they knew where he was.

She stood beside the chai stall, watching the kids. Some of them looked rough, as if they'd rather punch her in the face than answer her questions. But one young girl caught her eye and smiled shyly.

Pham smiled in return and offered her the bag of barfi. The girl, a Tamil by the shape and colour of her small, dark face, nodded and dipped a hand into the bag.

"I wonder if you can help me," Pham asked the girl.

The Indian nibbled the barfi like a mouse, jogging her head from side to side.

Pham went on, "I'm looking for a boy called Abdul. I don't know his last name. He works around here."

The girl's eyes widened, as if in alarm. "Abdul? Abdul Mohammed?"

"I don't know—he has only one arm."

"Ah-cha! That is Abdul Mohammed. You haven't heard?"

Pham's stomach heaved. She felt sick. "Heard what?" she asked in a whisper.

"Someone beat him up. Many broken bones. Almost killed him."

Pham felt dizzy. "Who? Who did this?"

"A Westerner. He asked Abdul questions."

"Where is Abdul now?"

"Dr Rao treated him, but he was injured very badly. Dr Rao took him to hospital." The girl considered for a second, then took Pham's hand. "Come. I will take you."

Her heart beating wildly, Pham gripped the kid's sticky hand and followed her along the sidewalk and down a side street. They passed through crowded alleys, deafened by the cries of street traders and the jet engines of passing air-cars.

Five minutes later they came to a small Ayurvedic clinic with a big red cross flashing on and off outside. The girl pointed across the road. "Abdul is in there, ward three."

Pham hesitated, part of her oddly reluctant to face Abdul now that she knew where he was. She turned to the girl, slipped a ten baht note into her hand, then hurried across the road and into the hospital before she changed her mind.

A Thai nurse in a brilliant white uniform smiled at her from behind the reception desk.

"I have come to see Abdul Mohammed," Pham said. "Ward three."

The nurse pointed through swing doors and along a corridor. "Through there, and it's the first door on your right."

Pham moved slowly towards the door and pushed it open. The thing was, if the Westerner who had beaten up Abdul was the laser killer looking for Pham, then why had he assaulted Abdul and asked questions? He was telepathic, after all: why hadn't he simply read Abdul's mind?

She felt a sudden wave of relief. Perhaps the man who beat him up had nothing to do with the laser killings.

Perhaps Abdul would be glad to see her.

She approached the door on the right and eased it open timorously, peering in at the beds.

Only one of the four beds on the small ward was occupied, but Pham did not recognise the boy stretched out on the white sheets, his legs encased in silver machines. His face was bruised and swollen, his eyes closed.

Pham felt tears sting her eyes and trickle down her cheeks. She backhanded them away and stepped towards the bed.

Abdul heard her and opened his eyes.

"Pham!" he said in a small voice. "You shouldn't... you're in danger!"

Pham ran forward and gripped the boy's right hand. "Abdul, I'm sorry!"

He grinned, and despite the bruises that made him look like a different person, she recognised him from the grin. "Not your fault. I took you to the amusement park, after all."

She smiled through her tears. "What happened?"

"Yesterday, Dr Rao came to me in the spaceship. He said someone was looking for you—he said that this person would be looking for me, also."

Pham opened her eyes wide. "The laser killer," she said in a small voice.

"Ah-cha. Anyway, Dr Rao gave me a small metal disc. He called it a mind-shield. He said I should keep it on me at all times, and that it would stop a telepath from reading my mind—stop a telepath from reading where you might be."

"But what happened?"

Abdul shrugged, smiling sadly. "He found me. He must have read other kids' minds, and found out where I was. Last night, I was begging near the spaceport when I saw this guy... The way he was looking at me. I knew something was wrong. So I ran."

"But the killer caught you, ah-cha?"

"But I almost got away! I ran across the Pindi Bridge, but he chased me and kicked me. I fell off the bridge, breaking my legs. Even then, Pham, I tried to get away."

Pham reached out and squeezed his hand, tears dribbling down her cheeks.

"The killer, he jumped down and kicked me, then searched for the mind-shield and threw it away. He was evil. He said he was going to kill you."

Pham just shook her head, fear like a fist gripping her heart.

"Then he read everything, Pham. He read what we did that night in Kandalay amusement park, what we saw, where you were planning to spend the night."

Pham nodded. "He nearly found me in Ketsuwan Park. I ran before he could shoot!"

"He saw you, and didn't shoot?"

Pham nodded. "Ah-cha. He ran after me, called my name."

Abdul frowned, then winced as the gesture pained him. "But he told me he was going to kill you... Why did he call your name, when he could've simply lasered you dead?" He thought about it. "What did this guy look like?"

Pham considered. "Tall, dark haired. He needed a shave. He was wearing a leather jacket."

Abdul was smiling. "That wasn't the killer," he said. "That was Vaughan, the detective. Dr Rao said he's a good man. He's trying to find the killer, so he needs to question you. He was at Nazruddin's a couple of days ago, with Dr Rao. Vaughan questioned me, asked all about you." Abdul squeezed her fingers. "But you're in danger, Pham. What if the killer is watching the hospital?"

Pham felt a cold hand grip her spine. She shook her head, wordlessly. "Okay, I should go."

"Don't go back to Ketsuwan Park!" Abdul warned. "Keep away from Chandi Road and everywhere else you've been lately!"

Pham smiled. "Do I look like a complete idiot? I haven't been back to Ketsuwan Park since Vaughan saw me."

They sat in silence for a time. Abdul smiled bravely, and indicated the machines on his legs. "Expensive healers," he said proudly. "Dr Rao is paying for it all. He is a good man, Dr Rao."

Pham thought about the last time she had seen Abdul, on the spaceship with Dr Rao. She said, "I'm sorry I ran away the other day. I didn't want to stay on the ship. Something about it, about Dr Rao…"

Abdul reached up and touched her cheek with gentle fingers. "It's okay, I understand."

In a tiny voice, she asked, "Abdul, how did you lose your arm? Tell me, honestly?"

He smiled, and said, "Dr Rao removed it so that I could make a living, begging on the streets. Don't hate Dr Rao, Pham. I agreed to the operation. I wanted it to happen."

Pham nodded silently, too overwhelmed by the course of events to criticise an action she had no way of comprehending.

Abdul said, "You aren't safe here, Pham. You should go."

"I'll see you again."

"Don't come back here. I'll find you, ah-cha?"

"I'll be—"

"Shh! Don't tell me. If the telepath comes back and reads me…"

Pham shook her head. "I *am* a complete idiot!" A thought occurred to her. "If this Vaughan man is good, and trying to find the killer, I should try to find him and tell him everything I know." Tell him, she thought, about the voice called Khar in her head.

Abdul nodded. "Perhaps that would be best."

"But how would I find him?"

Abdul thought about it, then said, "Dr Rao will know where Vaughan lives. I'll give you Dr Rao's com number, ah-cha?"

She found a pen and some paper in her backpack and wrote down Dr Rao's number.

She stood and smiled at Abdul, then leaned forward and kissed his face, attempting to find an area that wasn't bruised and swollen.

She hurried from the hospital, half expecting the killer to emerge and laser her down. She ran along the street, found a com kiosk and hauled open the door.

She had difficulty reaching the receiver, and then entering the code, but at last she heard the dial tone purring in the handset.

It seemed an age before an impatient voice snapped, "Yes, who is it? This is my private line and I am a very busy man."

"Dr Rao, you've got to help me. This is Pham. I met you the other day."

"Pham?" he said, uncertain. Then: "Kali strike me dead! Pham, the epicentre of the typhoon of chaos and destruction!"

"Dr Rao, you must help me. I need to find a man called Vaughan. He is a detective. He is working on the case of the laser killer."

"Vaughan is attempting to locate you," Rao said. "Where are you, girl?"

"I'm in the street near the hospital."

"Where exactly, girl?"

She looked up and down the street, saw a sign, and said, "I am on the corner of Tagore Street—"

"One moment, please. Hold the line and I will attempt to locate Vaughan and tell him where you are."

"Ah-cha!" Pham said, relief sweeping through her. She fed another ten baht note into the phone-machine and waited what seemed like five minutes while Dr Rao tried to contact the detective.

At last he said, "Pham, are you still there?"

"I'm here."

"Unfortunately, for some unknown reason I am unable to contact Mr Vaughan."

"But I need to find him..."

A long silence followed, broken by Dr Rao's, "Ah-cha. Very well, I will give you his address. When you find Mr Vaughan, tell him that Dr Rao sent you, ah-cha?"

"Ah-cha. I'll do that."

"Mr Vaughan has recently moved from Level Ten and now has a big place on Level Two, 12 Nehru Boulevard, Chittapuram. Have you got that?"

"Thank you Dr Rao!" Pham called, and slammed down the receiver.

She left the kiosk and hurried along the street, losing herself in the crowd and heading for the train station on Chandi Road. When she reached the station she took her map-book from her backpack and looked for Nehru Boulevard on Level Two.

A minute later she found it. It was not far from here, a couple of kilometres south of the spaceport. She boarded a southbound train and five minutes later alighted at Jaggernath station, then dropped to Level Two and followed the map towards the exclusive outer edge.

Nehru Boulevard was a wide street with occasional viewscreened recesses, which overlooked the ocean. Between these viewing points were luxury apartments. Pham found number ten and stood across the boulevard, nervous now that the time had come to approach the detective.

"Khar," she said under her breath, "am I doing the right thing?"

Seconds later, the voice in her head responded. *There are certain dangers inherent in approaching Vaughan, especially if the killer is aware that Vaughan is working on the case.*

"So you think—"

However, it is also true that Vaughan might be of use to us.

Pham nodded. That was that, then.

She was about to cross to the double doors of number twelve when a small Thai woman approached the doors, loaded with shopping. She was heavily pregnant and beautiful, even though her face was divided in two by a big scar.

Resting the bag of shopping on one knee, the woman fumbled with a key-card and let herself into number ten.

Pham smiled to herself. She liked the look of the woman. Could she be Vaughan's wife or lover, she wondered.

Feeling oddly confident, Pham crossed the boulevard and knocked on the door.

TWENTY

RADICALS

Vaughan woke early on his first full day on Mallory. Intense sunlight filled the room with gold and, outside, burned up last night's fall of snow.

He breakfasted at the same table he'd occupied the night before, served this time by a middle-aged woman who showed no inclination to chat. Over a bowl of local fruit salad and good coffee, he consulted the map and charted a route to Campbell's End.

The highway passed ten kilometres from the small township. Two minor roads branched off it and headed for the settlement, one direct and the other taking a circuitous route and coming into the town from the rear. Vaughan recalled that Scheering had told Denning about a shack on the outskirts of the town, being used by the S-L agents. The question was: on which road was the shack situated? Vaughan sipped his coffee and considered his options.

The only other customers were two men in their fifties, who Vaughan had watched draw up in a small truck. Bales of blue grass stacked on the flat-bed suggested they were farmers.

They sat at the next table over steaming mugs of coffee and cooked breakfasts, and when they nodded good-morning Vaughan returned the pleasantry. "I'm heading for Campbell's End," he said. "I was wondering what the roads were like?"

"Campbell's End?" one of the farmers said around a mouthful of egg. "Why the interest, all of a sudden?"

Vaughan assumed ignorance. "Interest?"

"Campbell's been deserted ever since the drought, twenty years back. It's a ghost town—or was. Then a month back a couple move in, fix a house up on the main street. Last week two guys move into a shack out of town a-ways." He shrugged. "Place is awful pretty in summer, but come winter..." He smiled at his partner, who laughed.

Vaughan nodded. "I'm just passing through, on my way to do a little hiking in the mountains." He hesitated. "I was thinking of stopping in Campbell's for a night. I don't suppose one of the couples would put me up?"

The farmer shrugged. "That'd be for them to say. We Mallorians are a pretty hospitable people, so you might be in luck."

Vaughan leaned towards the farmers' table, indicating the map on his handset. "The shack on the outskirts, do you know which road it's on?"

The farmer looked at the screen, then jabbed a weathered forefinger at the lower road. "This one. Around here, about a kay out of town. The roads should be fine at this time of year."

"And roadblocks?" he asked, confident now he knew where the S-L agents were holed-up.

The farmer shook his head. "The military finished what they were doing last night."

Curious, Vaughan considered his next question. "What were they doing?" he asked with all the innocence of a wide-eyed off-worlder.

This time the second farmer replied. "The annual cull," he said, casting a glance at his partner.

Vaughan sensed an uneasiness about the pair. "The cull?"

"The military are taking out a few tuskers," the second man said, and fell to finishing his breakfast.

Vaughan nodded his thanks and returned to his coffee. The tuskers...? He wondered if they could be the gentle pachyderms he'd encountered on his way here.

He set off south again immediately after breakfast, the side-screen of his Bison wound down to combat the increasing heat of the day.

He turned on to the highway and headed towards the silver mountains, rising ahead of him like a thicket of scimitar blades. The highway bypassed Campbell's End and cut through the mountains a hundred kilometres south.

An hour after setting off, Vaughan came to the first of two turnings to the settlement. The first looped around the town, while the second, five kilometres further south, headed directly into Campbell's End.

The S-L agents occupied a shack on the second road, a kilometre out of town.

Vaughan turned left along the first turning, leaving the metalled highway and bucking over another neglected track, climbing through a spectacular landscape of undulating hills, the blue grass catching the light of the sun like a billion blades.

To his right was a broad valley, with the highway he had left bisecting it as straight as a laser. He made out the direct track, which left the highway and meandered towards the town. Ahead, the hills crumpled before the massifs and Vaughan saw, nestling picturesquely on ridges high above the valley, a series of tiny, white-painted dwellings. He slowed the Bison and looked back along the direct track: there, perhaps a kilometre out of town, were three or four tumbledown buildings.

He accelerated, considering the best course of action. The obvious thing would be to locate the so-called radicals and warn them of the danger they faced, without alerting the surveillance team to the fact. He would leave the Bison on this side of town and make his way in on foot. He was beginning to wish that Kapinsky had come up with some way of smuggling a weapon onto the planet, but they had decided it would be safer not to attempt the subterfuge.

Vaughan hauled the Bison over a rutted crest of track, rounded a outcropping of grey rock, and braked suddenly. He sat at the wheel, staring through the windshield with a mixture of shock and revulsion.

Slowly, he eased open the door and climbed down. He stepped off the track, onto the sward of blue grass, which shelved steeply towards the broad valley.

He was not mistaken—the shapes dotting the valley were not boulders, but beasts identical to those he had encountered the previous evening. The tuskers, as the farmers had called them.

There were nine of the creatures, a couple of families, perhaps. He counted four full-sized animals, as big as the leader of the herd he had encountered, and five smaller creatures, including two no larger than small ponies.

He stood before the slaughtered beasts and was overcome by a wave of anger.

They had been lasered through the head, though two tuskers had obviously survived the first strike, as they bore macabre lacerations to their necks and bodies.

They had died where they fell, crumpled with legs splayed or bent beneath their bodies, as undignified in death as they had been full of dignity and ponderous grace in life.

Vaughan examined the wounds. He was no expert, but he guessed that the slaughter had occurred a matter of hours ago, perhaps last night as he'd followed the other herd through the cutting in the rocks.

The culling of various types of animals on settled worlds was not proscribed—some beasts were considered vermin, or a danger to settlers—but Vaughan could see no way that the tuskers might fit into either category.

As he walked away from the scene of carnage, he began to wonder if this had something to do with the deaths of Kormier, Travers, and Mulraney, and perhaps why members of Eco-Col were being targeted by Denning's team.

But surely the culling of the tuskers was being carried out legally, with the permission of and supervision by the colonial council? Why, otherwise, would Scheering risk the illegal slaughter of innocent creatures?

Troubled, and wondering where the killings might fit into his investigations to date, Vaughan gunned the Bison's engine and accelerated towards the distant township.

He braked on a ridge a few hundred metres above the scattered buildings of Campbell's End, climbed down and stared out across the ghost-town.

The fifty-odd buildings were in a state of disrepair, ravaged by both the forces of summer and winter: paintwork seared by the sun, the wood beneath warped by rain and frost.

More importantly, there was no sign of life. He activated his implant and scanned, but sensed nothing. He looked for the radicals' vehicle—assuming they had one, which was likely—but in vain. When he walked into the village, he would check the garages and other places of possible concealment. None of the dwellings looked lived in, and many of them appeared uninhabitable. If the radicals knew of the likelihood that they would be either watched or followed, then they would have selected the least likely building in which to conceal themselves. Which begged the question, what were they doing up here anyway?

Perhaps, he thought as he returned to the Bison and backed it behind a concealing outcropping, they were here to monitor the cull.

He left the vehicle and made his way down the incline and into the township.

An eerie silence hung about the place, though he realised that the town was no more silent than any of the other places where he had stopped on his way south. It was the presence of buildings and the absence of people—of the everyday commerce of such communities, the noise of cars and music and conversation—that seemed so unnatural, lending the settlement the melancholy atmosphere of somewhere evacuated in haste, the focus of some tragic happening.

There were fewer than fifty buildings strung out along the main street, and Vaughan entered them one by one and scanned for telltale signs of recent habitation.

All the houses were empty, rotting inside and taken over by animals, the Mallorian equivalent of rats and mice and larger rodents.

He trod carefully over the planks of dilapidated verandas, pushing open screen-doors to reveal front rooms and kitchens devoid of human life. There was something mausoleum-like about many of the houses, with items of furniture, pictures and personal possessions still *in situ*.

When emerging from each dwelling, he made sure that the street was empty, that Scheering's men had not seen his arrival and decided to investigate. He moved slowly from house to house and then, with perhaps only another half dozen dwellings to check, he came across signs of recent occupation.

From the outside the house was no different to any of the others: a tumbledown weatherboard frontage, smashed windows, a door hanging awry on one hinge...

But inside, in a room at the back of the house overlooking the valley, he found a portable heater and two armchairs arranged either side of a small table bearing the foil remains of self-heating meals.

In another room he found a mattress, and beside it a couple of old books, and another heater. This, then, was where the radicals had holed up—but where were they now?

He emerged into the lambent noon sunlight and looked up and down the main street. The surface of the road was metalled—or rather had been at one point. Now it was crumbled at the edges, and in places worn down to the underlying aggregate.

He was about to go back into the house, and search it more thoroughly, when he saw track marks in the gravel drive beside the house. They were the unmistakable, churned prints of a big off-road vehicle. He stepped from the drive, onto the road. It was possible to follow the progress of the vehicle across the patched tarmac road—its weight had crumbled the edges like broken biscuit—and up a track into the hills. Here, the surface of the unmade track bore the perfect, ribbed prints of the off-roader. He walked up the track, shielding his eyes and gazing up the incline. The track left the settlement, crossed the road on which he had come in, and wound further into the hills.

Vaughan followed the incline to the crossroads. The track-marks were continued on the other side of the road, imprinting themselves on the shale of the cutting. The off-roader had turned neither right nor left, but had continued on into the mountains.

He was tempted to return to the Bison and give chase, but before that decided to see if the Scheering-Lassiter men had been aware of the radicals' departure. It would make his job much easier if they were still encamped in their shack on the edge of town, oblivious of the radicals' escape.

He made his way back down the track and crossed the main street, passing between two buildings and looking down over the valley. He found the winding thread of the road that left the highway and approached the settlement, and the two shacks, which according to the farmers had been recently occupied.

He sat on the back veranda and, for the next hour, studiously watched the shacks for the slightest sign of life.

All was still, silent—and it was only after he'd been gazing at the dwellings for over an hour that he noticed the twin circular burn marks outside the nearest shack.

He stood, staring, and knew instantly what they were.

He hurried back to where he'd concealed the Bison, gunned the engine and slewed the vehicle on the road into the settlement, accelerating along the main street and out of town towards the highway.

Five minutes later he came to the first shack and drew to a halt.

He climbed from the cab and approached the burn marks on the gravel outside the shack. He knelt, examining the perfect circles of carbonised ash.

They were the landing and take-off marks of a twin-engined flier, and they looked as if they had been made very recently.

So the radicals had taken to the hills and Scheering's men had given chase?

He returned to the Bison. There was only one course of action now: he would attempt to follow the track-marks of the off-roader to wherever they might lead.

He turned the Bison and made his way back into Campbell's End, then turned off up the track and crossed the secondary road, the track becoming uneven, dangerous, as he climbed ever higher.

Soon it ceased to be a track altogether and petered out into blue grassland rising between jagged spurs of rock, terrain that would pose no trouble for an off-roader, but which even his Bison found hard going.

The off-roader's parallel track-marks patterned the grassland like an extended equation sign, leading him onwards.

Perhaps a kilometre further on, the track-marks veered left, seemingly into the very flank of a sheer rock face, and Vaughan made out a cutting between rearing grey slabs. He manhandled the Bison left, moving from bright sunlight to inky shadow, and peered ahead. At least, here, the going was easier, as if the surface of the cutting had been levelled to form a passable track at some point in the past.

The track between the rocks climbed, widening out so that sunlight was once more admitted and shone down from beyond the snow-capped peaks like shafted searchlights.

Then the track became a definite road, though unmetalled and crude. It levelled out and hugged the side of the mountain, with a precipitous, sick-making drop to the right. He peered over once, which was enough. The side of the mountain continued sheer for perhaps a hundred metres.

The track continued along the side of the cliff face for perhaps two kilometres, then climbed and passed between two jutting shoulders of gunmetal grey rock. He passed into cold shadow again, not for the first time wondering where the radicals had headed.

Ahead, the track climbed seemingly without end: the vanishing point was so distant that the flanks of the rock on either side seemed to come together and close off the track completely. As he climbed, so the temperature dropped, and he turned on the Bison's heater. Snow began to fall, a talcum drift so fine it obscured the view ahead until stray gusts of wind ripped it aside to reveal the endless, narrowing vista of grey rock.

It seemed a primitive form of travel, this bucking over unmade roads in a ground-effect vehicle, when there were such inventions as fliers, which would have made the journey a breeze.

He wondered how he might evade being seen by Scheering's men, who had the double advantage of elevation and speed.

He would worry about that, he decided, when the time arrived.

Suddenly, without warning, the cutting levelled out, the grey rock faces on either side pulled back like a stage effect and Vaughan found himself on a rise overlooking a precipitous track which led down to a narrow cutting between boulders the size of buildings. He wondered if he had actually passed through the mountain range and was emerging on the far side.

He examined the map on his handset and attempted to trace his course so far. He found

Campbell's End, and the two tracks that led from the highway. The track he had taken into the mountains was not marked, but he estimated his course by charting a probable route using contour lines as his guide.

If he was where he thought he was, then he had indeed passed through the range: the cutting ahead should lead him into a vast, flat valley cupped between this mountain range and the one to the south. He wondered if this was the radicals' destination.

He set off again, his satisfaction of making good progress tempered by the uncertainty of what might lie ahead.

He dropped, easing the Bison into the cutting between the boulders, and considered the irony of getting so far only to be stopped by the narrowness of the defile ahead. He reassured himself with the thought that, going by the track-marks of the off-roader, that vehicle was altogether larger than the Bison.

His fears proved unfounded. The Bison squeezed through the cutting with a metre to spare, and thirty minutes later emerged from between the rocks onto a narrow track overlooking the high valley.

He braked, climbed from the Bison and stared down into the sunlit valley. The starship was just under two kilometres away, but its size—a kilometre from its blunt nose-cone to its flaring tail-fins—made it seem much closer.

He stared at the wrecked vessel, experiencing an odd sensation of déjà vu as he recalled the alien starship from Denning's memories.

It was similar in shape to other ships he'd seen over the years, but also strangely *other* in the baroque sweep of its lateral sponsons and bulging, galleon-like mid-section. It struck him as magnificent but also tragic, like some neglected epitaph to the extinct beings which had piloted it across the light years: great sections of the ship's panelling were missing, showing its interior framework like bones, and much of the vessel was embroidered with growths of vegetation, hung with vines and creepers like the ruins of some ancient cathedral.

Only then, still basking in the visual wonder of the starship and what it represented, did Vaughan make out the shape of the off-roader, made minuscule as it sat in the shadow of the alien vessel.

He scanned the sky, but there was no sign of the flier.

He hurried back to the Bison and rummaged among his luggage for the binoculars.

He turned them on the starship and powered up the magnification. The vessel leaped towards him, becoming even vaster, and he made out the beetle shape of the off-roader and, beside it, the stick-like figures of a man and a woman: the radicals, Jenna Larsen and Johan Weiss.

They were discussing something, gesturing towards the ship—specifically at a rent in the skin of the vessel.

As he watched, the couple turned, and for a stomach-churning second he believed that, somehow, they were aware of him watching them.

But they were looking up, into the air.

Weiss grabbed Larsen's arm, gestured towards the starship. In seconds they had ducked through the rent and concealed themselves.

Vaughan lowered the binoculars and made out the shape of a flier, high above the valley, as it banked through the air towards the starship. He lifted the binoculars, sighted the flier, and watched with mounting apprehension.

The flier came in low, flowing a metre above the grassland. There were two dark figures in the flier, both men, and armed with laser rifles. The flier slowed as it approached the radicals' off-roader.

Perhaps a hundred metres from the starship, the flier cut its turbos and settled onto the grassland. Scheering's men jumped out, rifles at the ready, and walked slowly towards the off-roader.

Vaughan magnified the image. The two men wore regular clothing, thermal leggings and padded jackets. The bulky rifles they carried seemed incongruous in the hands of people dressed so casually, and therefore even more sinister. He watched, at a remove of kilometres, helpless to intervene in the drama about to be enacted in the shadow of the alien starship.

Scheering's agents paused twenty metres from the off-roader. One of the men cupped a hand to his mouth, obviously calling out.

They looked at each other, nodded, and the first man called out again.

The second man gestured. They made for the cover of the off-roader, knelt and released a volley of laser fire into the rent where the radicals had concealed themselves.

Their fire was returned, but from further along the starship's flank. A single, searingly blue vector hit the off-roader.

Vaughan lowered the binoculars, dazzled—but even from kilometres away the detonation of the vehicle was blinding. Seconds later he heard the muffled crump of the explosion, as flame erupted from its petrol tank and debris showered down across the plain in seeming slow motion.

He raised his binoculars again, and made out two blackened, twisted figures, still writhing, beside the wreckage of the off-roader.

Heart thudding, he watched for what seemed like minutes before the small figure of a radical—Johan Weiss—emerged from the starship and approached the off-roader.

Of the second radical, Jenna Larsen, there was no sign.

Weiss stood before the twisted wreckage of his vehicle, staring down at the carbonised remains of his pursuers, then dropped into a sitting position and held his head in his hands.

Vaughan slipped the binoculars into his pocket. For the time being, the danger from Scheering's men was annulled—but soon, perhaps in a matter of hours, Denning's team would arrive from Earth. He considered his options and decided to conceal the Bison in the cutting and walk the rest of the way to the starship.

He climbed back into the truck, backed it between the rocks, and then set off.

Twenty minutes later he was perhaps half a kilometre from the starship. The radical was still seated on the grass, head bowed. As Vaughan approached, the man looked up and stared across the plain.

He rose to his feet and lifted his laser warily, aiming at Vaughan.

Sunlight illuminated the scene, the great derelict length of the alien vessel, the smouldering debris of the off-roader. It looked like a shot from an epic holo-movie.

Raising his arms above his head, Vaughan made his slow way through the grass towards the radical.

TWENTY-ONE

GHOST

Jeff had been away for just one day and already Sukara was missing him like crazy.

She found herself looking up at a sound from the next room, thinking it was him, or anticipating the evening meal when she would be able to tell him...

But their next evening meal together would be days away, and until then Sukara faced the prospect of one long, lonely day after another.

As the hours passed, so her conviction that something terrible was about to happen became stronger and stronger. She was convinced that if something didn't happen to Jeff on Mallory, then tragedy would befall herself or Li here on Earth. She could feel it, an edgy premonition that fluttered in her chest and made her hands shake.

On the second full day of his departure Sukara took the upchute to Level One, strolled through the park and had coffee at the café overlooking the sea. She normally enjoyed these occasions, but at the prospect of returning to an empty, Jeff-less apartment, she felt miserable.

She wondered—even if Jeff survived this mission—if this would be the first of many cases that would take him away from her. She might have a great Level Two apartment, and more money to spend than she had ever dreamed of, but all that would mean nothing if much of the time Jeff was not with her to share their new life.

She bought a comic from a stall in the coffee shop, returned to her table, and flicked through the garish pages. She hadn't read a comic for nearly two years, and at one time she had been addicted to their colourful, action adventure stories: they had allowed her to escape from the hardship of her life in Bangkok. Now she had no reason to escape, and she saw that the stories were melodramatic and trashy. Last year Jeff had bought her real books to read, and despite her initial reluctance she had soon found herself enjoying the complex stories of everyday human drama. She decided, as she left the coffee shop and crossed the park, that she would lose herself in a book when she got back. It might take her mind off Jeff's absence for a while.

She stopped by the market on the way back and bought a few vegetables and a mango, Jeff's favourite fruit. She would eat it tonight and think of him, out there on alien soil beneath a strange sun.

She had just deposited the bag in the kitchen when a knock sounded at the door.

Her first impulse was to ignore it. She'd been pestered by beggars recently, and people trying to sell her things she didn't want. Then she thought that it might be her friend, Lara.

She hurried through the lounge and hit the control. The door slid aside, revealing a diminutive Thai girl who looked about five years old.

Sukara took a breath. The girl wore her hair in a bob, with a straight-cut fringe, and she was wearing a white Tigers' T-shirt. For a second, she knew that the apparition before her was the ghost of her sister, come to accompany her through a difficult time.

Then the notion passed. The girl standing shyly before her was real, her smile uncertain as she looked up at Sukara and rehearsed her words.

Sukara was about to say, "I'm sorry. I'm busy at the moment. Not today—"

But the child said in quick Thai, "I'm looking for a man called Vaughan. Dr Rao said that he lived here."

Sukara nodded warily. "That's right. But he's away at the moment."

The kid's face seemed to crumple. She looked desperate. "Away? But when will he be back? I've got to see him!"

Sukara recalled what Jeff had told her about the case he was working on. "Who are you?"

"My name is Pham," the girl said.

Sukara's heart kicked. She looked up and down the corridor, but no one was in sight. "I'm Sukara," she said, then took the girl by the shoulder and almost dragged her inside.

Pham's reaction to the apartment would have been almost comical, if it hadn't been so sad. She stared around her, goggling at the size of the lounge. For a second, her quest to find Jeff seemed to be forgotten as she took in the luxury in which other people lived.

Her big eyes returned to Sukara, who smiled and sat the girl in a sunken bunker and brought her a glass of Vitamilk.

Pham drank it down quickly, leaving a thin white moustache across her top lip.

Sukara reached out and touched the girl's shoulder. "Pham, Jeff told me about you."

"Jeff is Vaughan? What did he say?"

"About what you saw in the amusement park, and that the killer is trying to find you."

Pham sat, her legs hanging over the side of the sofa, her feet not touching the floor, and pulled a face so comical in its exaggerated despair that Sukara had to smile.

"Where have you been sleeping until now?" she asked.

The girl shrugged. "In a park. The killer has been looking for me. He beat up a friend of mine, a boy called Abdul. He nearly killed him. Abdul told me about Vaughan—I thought he might be able to help me."

It was strange, but as she stared at the tiny girl on the sofa, the child's calm Thai features overlaid any memory of Tiger's appearance that Sukara might have retained. It was as if Pham had become Tiger, and the transformation twisted something deep in Sukara's chest.

She reached out and took the girl's hand. "It's okay. Don't worry. Jeff would help you, if he were here. But he's gone to Mallory, working on the case of the laser killer. He won't be back for a few days."

"But..." Pham began.

"It's okay," Sukara said, watching the child's expression as she went on, "you don't think I'd send you back out there, do you?"

"You mean…?" Pham looked around the lounge as if it were Aladdin's cave. "I can stay here, with you?"

Sukara smiled. "Would you like that?"

Pham appealed to her with sudden, pathetic eagerness. "I'd be no trouble! I'd cook and clean and shop for you. And I could sleep here—" she thumped the cushion beside her with the ham of her small fist. "I'd be very clean and quiet."

Sukara laughed. She wanted to take the girl in her arms and hug her. She wondered if her daughter would be as pretty as Pham.

"There's a spare room, with a nice bed. You can have that until Jeff gets back and sorts things out."

The girl stared at her, open-mouthed.

Sukara said, "Jeff told me that you left the factory where you worked, came up here all alone." The parallels between Pham's story and Tiger's brought a sudden pain to Sukara's chest; it was as if she were reliving her own desperate loneliness in the days and weeks when Tiger left her. "You were very brave."

Pham shrugged. "I always wanted to see the upper levels," she said. "I wanted to see the sky."

"You never saw it before now?"

Pham shook her head, and Sukara said, "So what do you think?"

Pham grinned. "It goes on for ever and it's so big!"

Sukara laughed. "And then you found yourself chased by a killer!"

Pham turned down her bottom lip in a pantomime gesture of fear. She looked around the lounge, then back to Sukara, and said, "What is Jeff doing on Mallory?"

"He said he had a lead. The Scheering people are doing something on the colony world, and they don't want anyone finding out what it is. Jeff's gone to find out what the big secret is."

"Does he have any contacts on Mallory?"

Sukara looked at the kid. That was a sophisticated question for a child of her age. She nodded. "He has a couple of names, people he'll try to find."

Pham nodded.

Sukara said, "Jeff said that you were orphaned…?"

Matter-of-factly, Pham nodded and said, "My parents were killed in a dropchute accident three years ago. I've been working in the factory since I was four."

Sukara stared at the tiny parcel of skin and bone before her. "You're seven?"

Pham nodded proudly. "Nearly eight," she said.

She looked about five, or less, with her skinny brown legs sticking out from her baggy shorts, and the T-shirt drooping from her shoulders as if on a hanger.

Sukara frowned. "What did you hope to find up here, Pham?"

The girl shrugged. "I wanted to see the sky," she said. "Then I wanted to find work. I can work hard. After that I could find a small place to live. But most of all I…" She stopped, as if embarrassed, and shook her head avoiding Sukara's enquiring gaze.

"But most of all, what?" Sukara prompted.

After a hesitation, Pham said, "I wanted to see the Tigers play in their new stadium."

Sukara nodded. "That sounds like a good thing to do. I'll tell you what, why don't we go to a game later in the week, okay? They play on Sunday, don't they?"

Pham nodded and smiled, and Sukara felt a sudden kick in her stomach that had nothing to do with her own, biological child.

"Okay, let's show you your new room, Pham," Sukara said, smiling as she pictured Jeff's face when he came back to find Pham living with them.

Perhaps the little girl would bring good luck with her, Sukara thought as she led Pham to her room.

TWENTY-TWO

STARSHIP CARNAGE

Under the light of an alien sun, with three moons sailing high overhead, Vaughan stood on the blue grass of the mountain plain, arms raised above his head.

The radical, Weiss, levelled his laser pistol. "Who the hell are you?" he said, "And what the fuck are you doing here?"

Vaughan glanced at the carbonised remains of the two men on the blue grass, contorted like melted plastic.

"I'm on your side, Weiss. I'm an investigator, working for the widow of Robert Kormier—"

"Kormier's dead?"

"Along with a colleague of his, Travers."

"Travers too? Christ." Weiss was in his forties, thin faced and bald headed. His eyes looked haunted, harried, and he hadn't shaved for a few days. He wore a threadbare one-piece thermal suit, ripped at the knees.

Vaughan took a step forward, but Weiss twitched his laser level again. "Stay there! How the hell do I know you're not working for Scheering?"

Vaughan nodded. "That's reasonable. You don't. I'd be as wary, in your situation." He paused, then went on, "Kormier and Travers were murdered by an assassin on Earth a little under a week ago. Around nine months ago, a woman called Dana Mulraney was killed—we think by the same hired assassin. I suspect Scheering-Lassiter were behind the murders."

Weiss was watching him, his face pulled tight with suspicion. "I knew about Dana. We were close. I worked with her up north. The bastards are picking us off, one by one."

Vaughan said, "Why did Scheering want Kormier dead?"

Weiss hesitated. "Kormier worked for Scheering, but he didn't like what was happening here. He contacted Eco-Col, told them what he suspected."

"The tusker cull, right? Scheering's men were going over quota?"

Weiss sneered, a facial tic drawing his right eye into an involuntary flutter. "Going over quota? Listen, they're intent on eradicating every last Grayson's Pachyderm on the planet." He stared at Vaughan, then said, "We don't call them tuskers— that's what the farmers call them. They were discovered by one of the original explorers—Douglas Grayson."

Vaughan lowered his arms, and to his relief Weiss was amenable. "Let's get this right. It isn't a cull? Scheering's ordered the elimination of the entire population?"

Weiss gave the slightest nod. "You got it."

"Christ, but if word got out..."

Weiss stared at him, something almost like contempt in his gaze. "What do you think we've been trying to do, for the past few months? As well as saving the creatures, we've been trying to get Eco-Col to believe us."

Vaughan said, "You don't work for Eco-Col?"

"I did. So did Jenna and a dozen others. When we found out that Scheering was not only going over quota, but eradicating every last herd of Grayson's... well, we went to our superiors and reported the situation."

Vaughan shook his head. "There should have been an outcry."

"Too right. But it was a big claim, and Eco-Col were wary of accusing a respected figure like Scheering of such a crime. They sent someone to investigate."

"Don't tell me—Travis, right?"

Weiss laughed, bitterly. "Right. He came here, closely guarded, of course. He monitored the cull, checked figures—all doctored by Scheering's lackeys. Then we got to him. Kormier told Travers, proved to him that Scheering wanted every last pachyderm dead. When Travers confronted Scheering, told him that he was returning to Earth to make his report... well, he effectively signed his own death warrant."

Vaughan asked the obvious question, "So okay, but why the hell does Scheering want to eradicate the animals?"

"Ostensibly, because the pachyderms destroy crops every spring season, do millions of dollars worth of damage. They got a culling quota from the colonial authorities, permission to take out a hundred bulls every year. They began the slaughter last year—only they didn't limit themselves just to bulls, or to the agreed figure."

Vaughan thought of the herd of slaughtered animals he'd seen that morning. "So that's the ostensible reason." He paused. "What's the real reason Scheering wants them out of the way?"

Weiss drew his thin lips into a smile that suggested not the slightest trace of humour. "Mallory's rich. The Scheering organisation mine ten per cent of all the gold produced in the colonies, and twenty percent of all the uranium."

Vaughan shrugged. "So... how do the pachyderms stop them doing that?"

"Hear me out. Mallory is Scheering's richest planet. It makes his fortune, keeps all his fat shareholders in luxury. But if the truth got out, then the colonial authorities would close the whole place down, order an immediate evacuation." He finished with a smile, watching Vaughan's slowly dawning comprehension.

"The authorities would only do that if..." The idea was too much to take in all at once.

Weiss was nodding. "If any of the indigenous life forms were classified on the Baumann scale as sentient."

Vaughan said, "And the pachyderms qualify?"

"Well, that's the odd thing. You see, not all of them do—that's why the original explorers, and the xeno-zoological teams who followed them, classified them as non-sentient."

"Wait a minute—that's not possible. Some of the pachyderms are intelligent, but some aren't?"

Weiss shrugged. "I know. Crazy, but it's true. Look, who's to say that intelligence evolves in the same way all over the galaxy? Here, only certain creatures develop what we term as sentience, for whatever reasons that might be. Fact remains, even if one in a hundred pachyderms were registered as A1 sentient, that'd be enough to close the planet down. And Scheering wouldn't be happy about that."

Vaughan thought back to yesterday, when the leader of the herd he'd encountered on the way south had seemed to lead him from the track towards the cutting, as if it had intuited his need to avoid the militia.

Vaughan looked up, past Weiss to the flank of the starship. "Larsen's covering me, right?"

Something hardened in the radical's eyes. "Jenna's dead." He gestured to the twisted remains of Scheering's men. "They got her with their first shot." He stared at Vaughan. "You haven't answered my question—what are you doing here?"

"My investigations on Earth led me to one of Scheering's executives, guy called Denning. He was ordered to lead a team here, link up with these two—" he nodded towards the bodies, "and bring you in, dead or alive."

"So you thought you'd get here before them, warn me?"

"That's about it. I knew where you were holed up, but when I got to Campbell's you'd headed out, followed by Scheering's men."

"We knew they were watching us, but we figured they wouldn't make a move till we headed for the starship."

"They were ordered to keep you under surveillance, and only apprehend you if you tried to reach the ship."

"You know a hell of a lot about their operations," Weiss snapped, "for someone not involved with Scheering."

Slowly, so as not to arouse suspicion, Vaughan reached into his jacket pocket and produced his real ID card and his investigator's licence. He tossed them across to Weiss.

The radical held the cards in one hand, the pistol in the other, still aimed at Vaughan's chest.

Weiss looked up. "You're telepathic?"

"That's how I know so much about what Denning's up to," he said.

Weiss narrowed his eyes. "How come? All Scheering's operatives are shielded."

"Yeah, they are until you cut their shields out with a scalpel," Vaughan said. "Then they're not."

Weiss returned the cards. "When's Denning due on Mallory?"

"This morning. His ship landed at ten. How long would it take for him and his team to fly down here from Mackintyre?"

"Say two hours, three maximum."

"And another hour to trace you this far." Vaughan looked at his watch. "I reckon they'll be showing up any time now." He activated his implant and sent out a scan. The man before him, like every other adult on the planet, was shielded—and there was no distant mind-noise from the approaching Denning.

Weiss said, "What's that?"

Vaughan told him.

"Early warning system," the radical said, "or are you signalling to him my whereabouts?"

Vaughan sighed. "I understand your suspicion, Weiss. I'd feel the same way." He thought about it. "Look, do you think I'd've walked in here unarmed, risking my life when you've just shot dead two of Scheering's men?"

"How do I know you're not armed?"

Vaughan raised his arms. "Search me."

Warily, one-handed, Weiss did so—keeping his laser on Vaughan at all times.

Weiss nodded. "You're clean."

Vaughan smiled. "Believe me, I'm on your side." He paused, then said, "Look, with Denning on his way, I don't think we should be hanging about."

Weiss nodded and looked at the starship, then back at Vaughan, as if wondering how much to tell the stranger.

Vaughan said, "Scheering seems to think that you're pretty important. He told Denning you had vital information. Scheering wants it so desperately he's sent a necropath along, so if you were killed in the confrontation she'd be able to read you."

Weiss said, "And you expect me to tell you what that information might be?"

Vaughan said, "Like I said, I'm on your side."

Weiss nodded, slowly, watching Vaughan. "I know the whereabouts of Breitenbach, Vaughan," he said at last.

Vaughan blinked. "Who?"

Weiss smiled. "Know something, either you're a damned fine actor, or you're on the level. Breitenbach is how it all began—the guy who discovered that certain of the pachyderms were intelligent. Then he vanished, around five years ago. We thought Scheering had got him. But word got out—

he contacted Travers, told him to tell Jenna what he needed. What Breitenbach needed, that is."

"Which is?"

Weiss took a few seconds to reply, looking at Vaughan and then towards the starship. "We've got to take something from the ship, ferry it to Breitenbach. It's important. Vitally important."

Vaughan nodded. "Look, I won't ask where Breitenbach is, okay? That way you might trust me."

"Thing is, I'll need your help with this stuff, now that Jenna..." He stopped, then went on, "We were going to take the off-roader, but seeing as how the bastards have left their flier, we'll take that."

They crossed to the flier and climbed aboard. Weiss checked the controls, then eased the vehicle into the air and through a fracture in the ship's panelling.

"What are we looking for?" Vaughan asked.

"Breitenbach calls them alien crystals, and before you ask, no, I have no idea why he wants them. We work in cells of two and three. We're told as much as we need to know. It's safer that way, in case Scheering captures us."

Weiss settled the flier and Vaughan climbed out.

After the sunlight, it was dim within the belly of the ship. After a few seconds his eyes adjusted, and for the first time he became aware of the ship's true dimensions. From the outside, he had seen only the bulging flank, unaware of the vessel's width.

It was as if he were standing on the grass of a sport's stadium. The decking underfoot was missing, presumably ripped up on impact, and the vegetation grew unhindered. Higher decks had collapsed, so that it was possible to look up and see, overhead, great rents in the panelling where patches of daylight showed through.

He looked right and left along the length of the ship, where corrosion and stress fractures from the impact had removed bulkheads. Pillars and fallen panels and twisted wreckage had become supports for vines and various grasses.

Weiss gestured towards a hunched figure beside a hole in the side of the ship. "I'd like to give Jenna a decent burial. Help me with the body—in the trunk."

A single laser strike had caught her in the sternum, and as Vaughan took her beneath the arms and lifted, he avoided the stare of her glazed eyes.

They laid the body as gently as possible in the flier's trunk, and Weiss closed the lid and gestured. "This way."

Vaughan followed the radical across the grass, passing through columns of sunlight, two small figures dwarfed by the dimensions of the derelict alien architecture.

They walked the length of the ruptured starship for perhaps half a kilometre, arriving at a section relatively undamaged in the crash-landing. Here they passed down buckled, tubular corridors, obviously designed for beings smaller than themselves. Weiss and Vaughan were forced to duck as they hurried along, sometimes encountering lengths of corridor crushed like children's drinking straws along which they had to crawl. Some sections were in darkness, others lit by sunlight slanting in from slashes and fractures in the walls.

At last the corridor opened out into a circular chamber, the silver, curving walls marked with hieroglyphs. Vaughan stared around him, then looked up at a transparent dome.

"This was some kind of observatory," Weiss said. He indicated the lettering etched into the metal walls. "Breitenbach says those are a kind of star-chart."

"How does he know?"

Weiss looked at Vaughan. "Breitenbach knows a lot about the aliens, according to what Travers told Jenna. Don't ask me how. Perhaps when we meet him..." He shrugged. "Okay, this way."

They passed down another corridor, this one undamaged. Vaughan had never before been aboard an extraterrestrial starship, and he was surprised at how similar this one was to Terran vessels in general layout and design, and at the same time how alien it was in the specifics, the small-scale details of hand-holds and press-select panels: they seemed designed for small, childlike hands.

"What did the aliens look like?" he asked Weiss at one point.

"I heard this third hand, from Jenna, who got it from Breitenbach. They were humanoid, two arms, two legs, but small—like kids, only covered in short, wiry hair. And red."

"So scientists found remains?"

Weiss looked back at him over his shoulder. "That's the odd thing. They didn't. None were ever discovered."

"So how come Breitenbach—?"

"I'm as curious as you, Vaughan. Down here. We're nearly there."

A recess, let into the wall of the corridor, dropped to the deck below by means of staple-shaped rungs, clearly meant for small feet. Weiss went first, gripping the flashlight in his teeth, and Vaughan followed, his feet slipping off the rungs as he descended.

They found themselves in a small chamber, its corners curiously rounded off. The only illumination was the dancing beam of Weiss's light.

He found what he was looking for: at the far end of the room was a circular plug like the door of a bank vault.

Weiss paused before it, studying a press-select panel in the wall. Vaughan squinted at the hieroglyphs on each tiny keypad. Quickly Weiss tapped in a code, then stepped back quickly as, with a sudden hiss, the great metal plug ejected itself and swung open.

He grinned at Vaughan.

"This hasn't been opened for thousands of years, Vaughan. We're the first humans to enter here."

Vaughan gestured. "After you."

Weiss stepped inside, and as he did so a light came on overhead. The chamber was small, two by two metres, and surprisingly cold, as if refrigerated.

Three racks stood against the walls, and stacked on each one were what looked like faceted, blood-red gemstones the size of a fist, scintillating in the light. Vaughan counted eighteen individual stones, six to a single rack.

Vaughan gestured towards the glittering, bloody stones, and found himself whispering, "What are they?"

"Nobody knows," Weiss said, then grunted a humourless laugh. "Well, no one but Breitenbach.

The scientists didn't have a clue. They guessed at some form of propulsion device, or even fuel."

"What does Breitenbach want them for?" Vaughan murmured to himself. He reached out and touched one of the stones, expecting a cold surface. To his surprise, it was warm.

Weiss said, "Let's get them back to the flier."

He lifted a rack from the wall and carried it from the chamber, and Vaughan took a second. One was as much as he could carry in comfort. "We'll come back for the other," Weiss said, propping the rack against the wall as he climbed from the room. Vaughan passed him the crystals, and then his own rack, and followed the radical up the narrow ladder.

Slowly, carrying the racks with care, dragging them through crushed corridors, they made their way along the length of the ship to the open area where they had left the flier.

They stowed the gemstones on the back seat of the flier and were about to return for the third rack when Vaughan raised a hand to his temple.

The sudden, faint signal of a distant mind impinged upon his consciousness.

"What is it?" Weiss looked alarmed.

"Denning. They're on their way."

Weiss nodded. "Where are they?"

Vaughan scanned, sending out a probe. He could not make out, at this remove, individual thoughts—merely a miasma of mind-noise, fragments of emotion, like faint music heard briefly on a weak radio frequency.

"Hard to tell. I'd guess they're about five kilometres away, maybe less."

"We got time to fetch the third rack and get out of here?"

Vaughan calculated. "It's not worth the risk. If I'm wrong, and they're closer…"

"We could always leave them in the flier, come back later."

"And what if the bastards are at the other side of the valley," Vaughan said, "and have the ship under surveillance?"

"So what do we do?"

"If we conceal the flier somewhere in the ship, then lie low…"

Weiss nodded. "They'll find the wreckage of the off-roader, and the bodies. Thing is, will they realise the bodies are their own men… or will they assume they're mine and Jenna's? They're beside our off-roader, after all."

"Christ," Vaughan said, remembering Indira Javinder. "They've got a necropath with them."

Weiss was staring at him, his thin face slick with sweat. "Will he be able to read the bastards' minds? They're burnt pretty bad."

Vaughan calculated. "They died less than an hour ago—but as you say, they're badly burned. It's touch and go. There might be a lingering cerebral signature, enough for Javinder to identify them…" He shook his head, aware of the adrenalin slamming through his system. "We'll just have to hide…" He was about to suggest that Weiss should fry the bodies' heads with his laser when he caught the faint beacon of Denning's mind-signal.

"What?" Weiss said, alerted by something in Vaughan's expression.

"They're entering the valley. We have about three minutes, maybe less."

Weiss looked up, scanning the ship. "Okay. We'll take the flier up there, conceal it on the gallery, and lie low."

They jumped aboard the flier and Weiss lofted it into the air. Vaughan held tight as they rose with a dizzying rush. Weiss banked the flier and they slipped over the crumpled lip of an upper deck, which overlooked the belly of the ship like a gallery.

He eased the flier down, out of sight from below, then jumped out and opened the trunk of the flier. He took something from Jenna Larsen's belt and tossed it to Vaughan. "Do you know how to use it?"

It was a standard automatic laser pistol. He nodded.

Weiss made for a rip in the flank of the ship. Vaughan followed, heart thudding, aware of a cold sweat clamping his torso.

It was a long time since he'd last endangered himself like this and, despite the adrenalin thrill, he had the crystal clear desire to be back home with Sukara, drinking coffee in some top level café bar.

He crouched beside Weiss, pressing himself against the curving skin of the ship and peering through the gap that cut through the metal like a slash in a Chinese lantern.

He concentrated. Denning's mind was closer now, individual thoughts discernible against the background music of his emotions.

Denning was in a flier with Javinder and two other Scheering men. They were entering the valley, and Denning could make out the starship and the wreckage of the off-roader. The exec felt relief that at last the chase was over, then a stabbing resentment that the surveillance team had got there before him.

Denning raised binoculars, focused on the off-roader, and made out the two twisted corpses.

>>>*Hope to hell Javinder can read something in there...* Vaughan read, along with apprehension as to what Scheering might say if the radicals had died without divulging their information.

Then Denning wondered where the hell the surveillance team was, and he looked around the bowl of the valley for any sign of their flier. Seconds later he made out Vaughan's concealed Bison, and a thought niggled at him: why had the surveillance team bothered with a ground-effect vehicle?

Then he said to the pilot, "Let's get down there, fast!"

Vaughan peered through the rent. At the far side of the valley, against the grey slabs of the mountainside, he made out the flash of silver that was Denning's flier, banking and heading towards the starship.

Beside him, Weiss fingered his laser. "They'll stop by the off-roader," he whispered. "Check the bodies. If they realise they aren't who they thought they were, they'll come looking... might even enter the ship."

Vaughan shook his head. "They'll come looking even if they think the bodies are yours," he pointed out. "They'll wonder where their colleagues are. The first place they'll look is in here."

Weiss grimaced, his nervous tic pulling at his left eyelid. "I can't risk not getting to Breitenbach with the crystals," he said. "If there's any chance of them finding the flier, then I start shooting. You okay with that?"

Vaughan hesitated, then nodded. The thought of killing, even if it meant the success of Weiss's mission, filled him with dread.

He turned back to the slit in the metal, hoping the corpses out there were too dead and fried to offer up their true identities.

The flier was slowing and coming in to land beside the off-roader. The two heavies jumped out before it settled and stood at the ready, big laser rifles on their hips, looking ridiculous in such confrontational postures before imaginary foe.

Denning climbed out slowly, staring at the blackened, shrivelled bodies beside the off-roader. Vaughan read his squeamish revulsion before he averted his eyes and nodded to Javinder. Denning's heart rate had increased, and he was sweating, overcome with apprehension and fear. Below his strata of fear, an aggrieved voice was telling himself that he was an executive, not a combat marine. He gripped a laser pistol in a palm wet with sweat.

Vaughan looked down on the tableau, his vicarious experience of Denning's heightened emotion feeding back and increasing his own tension. He wondered, for a second, if he should deactivate his implant, save himself the torture of sharing this unpleasant man's craven thoughts.

But that would be a tactical error. Denning was in charge down there. Whatever he ordered, the team did. If Vaughan continued to monitor his thoughts, he could pre-empt any actions they might take.

Javinder, dressed in her trademark black body-suit, knelt beside the first body and closed her eyes. This time there were none of the theatricals she had used to impress the cops back on Bengal Station. She merely concentrated for a second, then moved towards the second corpse and knelt again.

Vaughan looked down, watching Denning, and at the same time had a mental image of what Denning was seeing, along with running commentary of his thoughts.

Denning was staring at the Indian necropath, anxious. The executive was no fool. He knew that something was wrong. If the bodies were those of the radicals, then where was the surveillance team? If this was the team, horribly mutilated before him, then their killers, the radicals, were at large some-where.

At that second the executive looked up, his gaze running over the length of the ship.

Vaughan felt a stab of alarm—then realised that the sweep of Denning's gaze had passed the rent where he was crouching.

He felt a hand on his arm, squeezing. "You read-ing him?" Weiss whispered.

Vaughan nodded. "He's suspicious. Wait—"

Down below, Javinder looked up, shaking her head. At first, Vaughan took the gesture to mean that she was beaten, that there was no hope she could read the dying thoughts of bodies so badly burned...

Then she said to Denning, "It's Rasmussen and Zijac."

A flare of fear bloomed in Denning's mind, oblit-erating all other thought and emotion for several seconds. Then the executive wondered where his colleague's flier might be. If the radicals had taken it, he thought...

Vaughan pulled back his probe, startled by the degree of the exec's fear as he scanned the sky for his enemy. At the same time, he was heartened that Denning should be so frightened of what might lie ahead.

Perhaps Denning would order that they leave the area immediately, not bother to search the ship.

Denning said to Javinder, "This is the radicals' vehicle. It looks like they took the flier."

"They might be anywhere by now," Javinder replied.

Denning nodded. Self-preservation vied in his mind with the desire to do Scheering's bidding successfully: Denning hoped that the radicals had fled in the flier, but he knew that he had to search the ship.

Vaughan turned to Weiss, who was peering through the rent, trying to discern visually what Vaughan was able to read.

Even then, even though Vaughan knew what he should do, something in him was reluctant to tell Weiss that they were about to enter the ship.

But what was the alternative? Scheering's team would shoot first, ask questions later. Denning had been ordered to take the radicals dead or alive... and the fact that Vaughan was not a radical was a technicality Denning's team were hardly likely to consider in the heat of battle.

He said to Weiss, "They're coming in."

Seconds later Denning ordered, "Okay. We'll search the ship. Javinder, we'll go in this way," he indicated a gaping hole in the ship, perhaps a hundred metres away. "You go in there," he said to the heavies, gesturing towards the rent that gave admission to the great chamber above which Vaughan and Weiss were crouching.

Even as Denning gave the order, Vaughan felt the executive's fear combined with the ego-kick of being in command.

He watched Denning and Javinder hurry along the side of the ship, Denning's thoughts slackening off. Then he turned his attention to the heavies.

He stood, so he could watch them as they ran from the grass and into the ship. They passed from sight. He heard them below. "Okay, we take the front end first, section by section. I'll go in first."

Weiss was on his feet. He crept towards the lip of the gallery, gesturing for Vaughan to follow. "I'll take them out. Cover me, okay?"

Vaughan nodded, his gut tight. They split. Weiss fell to his knees and aimed over the edge. Vaughan stretched himself out, flat on his belly, and hauled himself to the edge of the sheared metal.

He peered over.

The heavies were moving away from where he and Weiss lay, which made what happened next so sickening.

Weiss fired, a single quick pulse of blinding blue light accounted for the first Scheering man, drilling a neat hole the diameter of a coin between his shoulder blades and killing him instantly.

The second heavy, alerted, turned and raised his rifle. Weiss's second shot hit him in the chest, sending him sprawling backwards across the grass. Vaughan closed his eyes, grateful that the men's dying thoughts were shielded. Then he considered Denning, whose thoughts he would read as he died—if he failed to kill his implant in time.

Weiss stood, staring down at the dead men with distaste. "What now? We wait for the others to investigate, or go after them?"

Vaughan scanned. He was aware of the beacon of Denning's thoughts, half the length of the ship away.

Javinder had stopped him. "I'm sure I heard something," she told him.

Denning's chest contracted with fear. "What?"

"Get onto Dean and Hernandez—"

But Denning was already lifting his handset and tapping in the heavies' code.

He said, "Nothing. Maybe the signal's blocked by a bulkhead?"

The necropath gave him a withering look, and Denning realised that the woman was one of the few individuals he feared, besides Gustave Scheering.

"What do we do?" Denning found himself saying, and hating himself for delegating command so easily.

"Back to where they entered the ship. I'll go in first."

Denning was swamped with relief as they ran back up the outside of the ship. Javinder knew how to handle such situations, he told himself. She'll pull us through.

Vaughan told Weiss, "They're coming back. The woman will enter first."

Weiss nodded and crouched, laser aimed over the edge of the gallery as he awaited Javinder's arrival.

What possible alternative to this killing was there, Vaughan asked himself as he watched Weiss. There could be no half-measures.

Denning and Javinder were five metres from the entrance, and he turned to Weiss and hissed, "Three metres, two, one..."

On cue, crouching, Javinder leapt through the gap, plastered herself against the outer skin of the ship and scuttled, like the spider she so resembled, along the wall and below the shelf of the gallery. Weiss cursed as she passed out of sight.

Denning was still outside, laser gripped ready, but fearful of following.

Weiss whispered, "Follow me," and ran lightly towards the back of the gallery. A fracture in the decking revealed the level below. Weiss crouched, pistol aimed, waiting for Javinder to show herself.

Vaughan made the edge, peered down with mounting apprehension, his own pistol levelled.

Seconds later, Javinder came into view. How she had worked out—or guessed—that he and Weiss were above her, he never would know: but as she stepped into view she was staring up at them, rifle lofted.

She fired a fraction of a second after Weiss.

Vaughan watched, immobilised by horror, as Weiss's pulse sliced through the Indian's lower face, opening a gaping hole into which her brain dropped and slopped down over her chest, hanging between her breasts as she slumped into a sitting position against a bulkhead.

Reeling, Vaughan turned and saw with incredulity that Javinder's shot had punched a hole in the radical's stomach. Weiss fell to his knees, hands pressed to the smouldering wound, his expression comprising disbelief and appeal to Vaughan to help him.

He caught Weiss, eased him down on the deck.

"In here," Weiss gasped, scrabbling futilely at a pocket on the chest of his thermal suit.

Vaughan ripped the pocket open, pulled out a palmCom.

Weiss whispered, "Password: Salvation. Code: 4884. Don't get it wrong, or the file will self-corrupt. Take the crystals to…"

Vaughan was aware then of two things simultaneously. Before him, Weiss had died, and outside the ship Denning had heard the laser fire and his thoughts blazed with resolve.

The exec's first thought was to run—his second, fuelled as much by rage as by the desire not to fail, was to fight.

Vaughan slipped the palmCom into his jacket.

Denning had entered the ship and pressed himself against the wall, slipping under the gallery and out of sight. He had seen the direction of Weiss's last shot, and knew where the enemy was situated. He realised he was fighting for his life: it was kill or be killed, and fear sluiced through his system, alongside hatred for the radicals.

Vaughan smiled. Perhaps it would make killing Denning that bit easier, knowing what the man intended.

But he thought not. No man was purely evil. Denning was fighting for his life, following orders he thought perfectly legitimate. He didn't know the full story; as far as he was concerned, the radicals were merciless killers.

Vaughan considered boarding the flier, leaving Denning with his life, and taking the crystals... But there was still one rack left in the ship. How vital was it to Breitenbach's plans?

He probed. Denning was below him, staring up at the underside of the gallery's deck, pistol aimed.

Vaughan looked across the gallery. A recess in the fallen wall revealed rungs leading down the shaft. He hurried across to it, careful to make no sound, and peered. The rungs dropped to a tubular corridor, not visible from where Denning was.

He lowered himself into the corridor, moving with exaggerated care, then found another set of rungs descending to the corridor he and Weiss had followed earlier.

He probed. Denning was perhaps ten metres from him, still in the belly of the ship, still looking up fearfully at the gallery deck.

Vaughan hurried along the corridor. He'd get the last rack, return to the flier, and leave while Denning was occupied elsewhere in the ship.

He came to the section of crushed corridor and fell to his hands and knees. Minutes later he arrived at the astrodome, and stopped. A quick probe told him that Denning had heard something, was aware that Vaughan was no longer on the gallery.

Denning's first thought was to secure the high ground, and he looked around for a way to achieve this.

What chance had Vaughan now of getting away in the flier, if Denning climbed to the gallery?

Pushing the thought to the back of his mind, he hurried through the astrodome along another corridor, and at last dropped into the chamber. He crossed to the open vault, paused on the threshold to stare in at the scintillating crystals, and wondered if their safe delivery had been worth the lives of the six people so far.

He hauled the last rack from the wall and made his way back along the length of the ship, slowed by the weight of the crystals, all the time scanning for the exec.

Denning made his move, running towards a section of the second deck, which had sheared and fallen, creating a ramp which led to the gallery where the flier was situated. Denning saw the flier, and seconds later came across Weiss. Elation flooded him at the sight of the dead radical, followed by fear at the thought that at any second he might slam into a lethal laser pulse.

Vaughan hauled the rack along the crushed corridor, then climbed a level and approached the rungs which climbed to the gallery.

He laid the rack on the deck and considered what to do now.

He probed. Denning approached the flier cautiously, facing away from the recess in the wall where Vaughan would emerge.

Vaughan climbed, holding his breath. He could see across the gallery, to where Denning was peering into the flier, pistol ready.

Vaughan eased himself onto the deck and raised the pistol.

Denning was moving around the flier, heart pumping. He planned to use the vehicle as cover and lie low for a while, allowing the enemy to make the next move.

The executive presented the perfect target. One shot now would send him to his death.

Vaughan stepped forward, raised the pistol, and aimed at Denning's back.

He hesitated, then called out. "Move and you're dead!"

He felt utter dread and panic surge through the executive, a despair and fear and regret which combined to rock Vaughan.

"Drop your pistol and raise your arms," Vaughan called. "If you do as I say, you'll live."

Vaughan read in Denning's frantic mind a hopeless disbelief, the sure knowledge that he was dead, and this prompted him to turn and raise the laser and fire in a great actinic sweep.

But thought preceded action, and Vaughan dived across the deck, below the arc of laser fire, aimed his own pistol and fired.

The shot blasted Denning in the chest, sending him sprawling across the deck. He lay on his back, staring up at the ribbed architrave of the alien starship, and his last thoughts as he lay dying were how beautiful the ribbing was, followed by sudden images of his wife, and his mind was sluiced by his love for her.

Vaughan cried out and killed his implant, and blessed silence sealed over him, sparing him the agony of the executive's passing.

He took deep breaths, forcing himself to his feet and towards the recess, not once looking towards the dying executive. He climbed down and retrieved the rack, hauling it back to the gallery and across to the flier.

He placed it beside the others on the back seat, then moved to the trunk and opened it. He would rather not fly with Larsen's corpse as company. He would be making his way to Mackintyre, eventually, and any random check by the military on the way... He lifted the body out and lay it on the deck.

He recalled what Weiss had said about giving Jenna a decent burial, and he wished he could give both the radicals a fitting send off. Success in delivering the crystals to Breitenbach would have to stand as their epitaph.

He climbed into the flier and pulled Weiss's palm-Com from his jacket.

He turned it on and said, "Salvation. 4884."

The screen flared. Vaughan stared at the map, the flashing point denoting his present position and the marked route through the mountains towards, he presumed, wherever Breitenbach was concealed.

He started the flier and lifted it from the deck. He averted his eyes from Denning's corpse as he flew over the lip and dropped the flier into the belly of the ship.

He eased it through the rent, out into the startling sunlight of the valley. He half expected to encounter opposition, something in him wondering that his escape could be so easy. He was leaving behind him a scene of carnage, and he felt a sour, corroding sense of guilt as he fled.

Consulting the palmCom, he followed the route towards the southern mountains, passing between low, snow-covered peaks. He thought of the woman back on Bengal Station, who would in time be informed of Denning's brave death in the line of duty.

He realised he still had the laser in the pocket of his jacket. He lowered the side-screen, took the pistol, and tossed it out into the biting wind, watching it spin end over end against the cold grey slab of the mountainside.

He looked ahead, at the layered summits of the southern mountains as they stretched towards the horizon, and thoughts of Denning's widow turned his mind to Sukara.

TWENTY-THREE

THE KILLER

Sukara watched Pham as she dried two cups at the sink. She was so short that she had to stand on a fruit box to reach the blower.

For the past few days, Pham had been her constant companion. Their days had soon fallen into a routine. After breakfast, taken in the kitchen while watching the boats far below, they would leave for a stroll through Himachal Park, stop for a coffee, and then go on to the market to do the day's shopping. Occasionally, Sukara took Pham to see the sights of the Station—the voidship spaceport, the vast monotrain terminal at New Madurai, the open market on Level Two at which everything made on Earth could be bought, as well as many things from the colony worlds.

Out with Pham, the little girl's hand in hers, Sukara experienced an odd feeling of pride. It was as if this were a foretaste of what it would be like as a mother—this feeling of not being one person, but two, as your cares were not wholly centred on

yourself but on one someone else even more important.

She was getting close to Pham, she realised, and if
this was what it was like to be a mother, then she
awaited *real* motherhood with even more than her
original eager anticipation.

Sukara taught Pham to cook, the basics first, then
working up to Thai, Indian, and Burmese curries,
the subtle distinction of spices between the cuisines
and their respective cooking methods.

Pham was a keen pupil. She was intelligent—once
told, she never forgot—and she was intuitive. Often
she sensed Sukara's sadness at Jeff's absence, and her
worry also. More than once, after an evening meal
as they sat on the balcony, drinking wine and Vitamilk and staring up at the stars, Pham had said to
her, "Don't worry, Sukara, Jeff will soon be back."

"I can't help worrying, Pham. I sometimes wish
he'd never taken the job. I sometimes think I'd be
happier on Level Ten, if I knew Jeff was safe."

Pham smiled, and came out with another of her
observations that seemed wise beyond her years.
"Jeff is a good person, and the world needs good
people. Scheering is evil." She shrugged. "If Jeff
didn't go to Mallory to investigate what's happening there, who would?"

Sukara looked at the kid. "Do you know what is
happening on Mallory, Pham?"

The child looked away quickly, and said non-
committally, "Evil is happening there. That is why
Scheering hired an assassin to kill people here."

Sukara nodded, and not for the first time wondered if Pham was telling her everything she knew
about the case.

On the day Sukara was due to take Pham to see the Tigers play the Sydney Seahawks, Pham told her that first she had to go and see a friend.

They were sitting on the balcony after breakfast, Pham absorbed in a comic book, Sukara watching a voidship phase in and slowly approach the spaceport. She was dreaming of Jeff's return. She would go to the spaceport to welcome him back, launch herself into his arms, and never let him go away again.

Pham lowered her comic book. "Sukara, is it okay if I go out alone this morning?"

"What for?" Pham had never asked to go out alone before, and Sukara was both concerned and curious.

"I need to see a friend. Abdul. He was in hospital. I need to see how he is."

Sukara nodded. "Are you sure you'll be okay?"

Pham grinned. "I'll be fine. The killer didn't catch me, did he?"

There's always a first time, Sukara found herself thinking. "You've got my code? Make sure you ring every hour to tell me you're okay, okay?"

Pham nodded. "I'll be back by one o'clock."

"And at four we go to see the Tigers," Sukara said, looking forward to the match. She wondered if her own daughter would be a Tigers fan.

Sukara watched the girl slip from the apartment, wondering if this was what a mother felt like when her daughter left home unsupervised.

For the next couple of hours she cooked an Indian meal for after the game tonight, then thought about Jeff's return in a few days. She wondered how he might react to find that they had a lodger, and then wondered what he might think best for Pham's long-term care.

The odd thing was, since Pham's arrival here, Sukara's premonitions of doom and tragedy had vanished. She was no longer visited by the conviction that something would soon happen to spoil her happiness. She told herself that her earlier fear had been the result of hormones. She lodged her hands on the jut of her belly and smiled.

Her thoughts of Jeff and the baby were interrupted by the chime of the door.

It was too early for Pham to get back, she thought as she crossed to the door and touched the control. But perhaps Jeff had arrived home early... Her heart leaped at the thought.

The door slid open to reveal a tall Westerner, dressed in a smart suit, standing on the threshold and smiling pleasantly at her.

"Sukara Vaughan?"

She was hesitant. "Yes?"

He hung an ID before her eyes for a second, then flipped the wallet shut before she had time to examine the card.

"I would like a word with your husband, Ms Vaughan."

"Jeff's away at the moment. He'll be back in a few days."

"Can you tell me where your husband is?" he said. He had a slow, patronising way of speaking as if he thought Sukara might not understand him otherwise.

She shook her head. "Just away. On business."

"Ah," the man said, and nodded. "But you see, it's a business matter that I need to see Mr Vaughan about—the case he is working on at the moment."

There was something creepy and not-to-be-trusted about the Westerner, with his pale skin and golden hair and red-rimmed eyes. Sukara said, "Then you could go and see his business partner about it. She's Lin Kapinsky—"

"I've tried to contact Kapinsky. She's away, working on another case."

Sukara shrugged. "Then I don't think I can help," she said. She made to hit the close control.

The Westerner stopped the door with his foot, and the casual way in which he did this frightened Sukara. "When might your husband be back?"

"A few days. Two or three. I really don't know."

The man smiled. "I don't think you're telling me all that you know, Sukara."

She felt suddenly sick. She shook her head, wordlessly, and knew that she was powerless to get rid of her interrogator.

"Where has Vaughan gone?" he snapped.

Her stomach flipped. "Away. Off-planet."

"Off-planet?" he repeated, smiling. "Where precisely off-planet?"

She shook her head. She looked past the Westerner, in the hope that she might by lucky enough to see a passing cop and call for help.

The corridor was deserted.

The Westerner reached up, his hand striking cobra-fast, and clutched Sukara's throat. He exerted pressure and pushed her at the same time. She staggered backwards, tripped, and fell into a sunken bunker.

By the time she righted herself, fear coursing through her along with the desire to shout for Jeff to help her, the Westerner had entered the apartment and closed the door behind him.

She cowered on the sofa, curling herself into a tight ball, not wanting to admit to herself who this man might be.

"What do you want?"

"I told you. I need to see Vaughan." He looked around the apartment, smiling to himself. She recalled a word that Jeff had taught her. The man was *arrogant*.

He looked at her as she scrunched into a tight, defensive ball, and said, "You see, Vaughan is working on a case that was officially closed. The cops found the killer and paid off Kapinsky and your husband. I just called around to remind him about this."

Sukara shook her head. "How did you find out where he lives?"

"An old acquaintance of his, one Dr Rao."

Jeff had mentioned Rao in the past. She wondered how the Westerner had obtained the information. An awful thought occurred to her. Could it be that this man was the laser killer?

The Westerner smiled, and what he said next confirmed Sukara's worst fears. "Is your shield portable, Sukara, or sub-dermal?"

Her stomach turned, and she knew then that this was the event that her premonitions had been warning her about. She was in her apartment with the telepathic killer who would stop at nothing to get what he wanted.

He was staring at the screen of his handset. "Portable, I see. That's good. Otherwise I would be forced to cut it from your flesh, and that would be terribly messy."

Sukara fought her tears, and the panic rising through her. He would make her get rid of the shield and then read her mind…

And he would find that Pham would be returning here soon…

He pulled something from inside his jacket and levelled it at Sukara.

She had never seen a laser before, except in the movies, and she was surprised now at how small and insignificant it looked. It was hard to imagine that a single pulse could end her life.

"Take your shield," the man was saying, "and throw it across the room."

Now Sukara could not stop her tears. They trickled over her cheeks—but she was determined not to sob. She shook her head.

The blinding lance of white light burned a hole in the seat beside Sukara, and she screamed.

"The next shot will amputate your right hand," the Westerner said. "Get rid of the shield!"

Now she was sobbing, uncontrollably, as she fumbled in the pocket of her shirt and found the silver oval of the mind-shield.

She pulled it out, fingers trembling, and could only think of Pham.

"Good girl," the man smiled. "Now, over there."

She could do nothing, she told herself, nothing at all but obey him. Even so, as she tossed the shield across the carpet she could not but help feel that she had betrayed both Pham and Jeff.

The man stared at her, eyes wide in concentration. He flung back his head and brayed with laughter.

"I don't believe it," he said to himself in a whisper. "I trawl the fucking length and breadth of the

Station, and all the while..." He stared at her. "When will she be back?"

She knew that her every thought was open to him, that she could withhold nothing.

The Westerner smiled. "So... I think I'll just make myself comfortable and wait for Pham to get back," he said. "And then I might as well wait for Vaughan to return."

Sukara was slowly shaking her head, wondering how it had come to this. Life had been so good; she had been so happy, and all that was about to end at the hands of this evil man.

Now she knew that she had been right to fear her forebodings.

The Westerner said, "There is no such thing as good and evil, merely those who are powerful, and those who are weak."

She watched him raise the pistol and aim at her, and she could only think of Jeff and Pham, and of her unborn baby.

Then he fired his laser and shot Sukara through the head.

TWENTY-FOUR

BREITENBACH

Vaughan thought back to the laser fight in the starship, overcome now with an odd retrospective dread; he had felt fear at the time, but fear only for himself. Now he realised that, had he died back there, Sukara would have borne the brunt of his passing, alone on Bengal Station, bringing up their daughter. The idea filled him with horror, and he told himself that no more would he put himself in a situation where his life was at risk.

Which was a fine sentiment, but he wondered if the combined forces of Scheering-Lassiter would bear that in mind if they apprehended him.

He flew a convoluted course south, through the snow-clad massifs of the southern range, following the route marked on the screen of Weiss's palm-Com. He had completed around half the journey so far, which had taken him a couple of hours. He hoped to reach Breitenbach well before sunset.

He was perpetually on the lookout for pursuers. He turned in his seat, attempting to scan three hundred and sixty degrees for any sign of fliers, like an old-fashioned fighter pilot. He wondered how long it might be before Denning's team was missed. No doubt Denning had had orders to report his progress at intervals, and after a while without word from him a search party would be sent out. How long, after that, would it be before an alert was broadcast for S-L forces to be on the lookout for a stolen flier?

Not that there seemed to be much sign of life in this region of Mallory. This range of mountains was the longest on the planet, stretching the thousand-kilometre length of the southern coastline and extending inland, in places, for a hundred kilometres. It was bitterly cold and inhospitable down there, and Vaughan wondered what kind of bolt-hole Breitenbach had fashioned for himself.

Ten minutes later he made out the first sign of a road far below, though on further inspection it was less a road than a precarious track carved into the side of the mountain. It wended its way around the cliff face and over a saddle-like ridge. He slowed and consulted his map. A faint track was marked, leading to the coast. Breitenbach's position was marked as a circle on the screen of the palmCom, a hundred kilometres west of the road.

For the next twenty kilometres Vaughan's route would follow the track below, before he peeled off west and began the last leg of the journey.

As he came over the crest of the track, between the mountain peaks, he saw with a sudden jolt of shock that there was a vehicle far below. Then he saw the others—four military troop carriers strung out in convoy along the narrow track. He throttled back, slowing, so as not to overtake the convoy and show himself. He took the flier up, beyond the peaks of the nearby mountains, then pulled the binoculars from his jacket and focused on the vehicles.

The trucks, splotched with blue and white camouflage markings, leapt into silent life in the viewfinder as they trundled south. Each vehicle carried perhaps thirty soldiers, sitting in rows under glassed-in canopies, gripping laser rifles.

His first thought was that they were looking for him; his second, that he was being paranoid. They were doing what the rest of the military was doing in this part of the planet: slaughtering the pachyderms.

He took a great loop around the mountain peak and rejoined the track ten kilometres further on. Five minutes later, looking down at the narrow grey track slung around the mountainside like a contour line, he saw the object of the military exercise.

Perhaps twenty Grayson's pachyderms were strung out along the track, plodding slowly south, their long articulated legs taking what seemed like great, slow motion strides. Compared to the progress of the following troop carriers, the herd was moving at a snail's pace. It could only be a matter of minutes before the military caught up, and then it would be a bloody rout, with nowhere for the animals to run: a precipitous drop of a thousand metres to the left, and lasers burning mercilessly from the rear.

Vaughan, hanging five hundred metres above the pachyderms, had never felt as powerless in his life. The carnage was inevitable. The only imponderable was whether he should remain to witness it.

Any intervention on his part would be futile, he knew, and would only alert the military's attention to his presence. He had a duty to Weiss, Larsen, and the other radicals, to deliver the crystals to Breitenbach.

He was about to bank right, away from the track, when he noticed that the file of animals down below was slowing and coming to a stop. Then he saw why: the leader of the herd, a great bull with a daunting array of facial tusks, had come to a halt and was easing his way up a defile in the rock face. It disappeared, and was followed by the second in line. Slowly, as the minutes ticked by, one by one the pachyderms inserted themselves into the fissure and continued on their journey up the narrow cutting. The last animal slipped into the cliff face perhaps a minute before the first troop carrier hove into view around a bend in the mountain.

Hardly able to believe that the creatures had managed to save themselves, Vaughan watched as the carriers approached the cutting. Had they tracked the pachyderms so far, perhaps with heat-seeking devices, and would they easily detect their sudden turn?

The first troop carrier approached the fissure and showed no sign of slowing down. The other vehicles raced by, and when the last carrier passed the cutting Vaughan punched the dashboard in jubilation.

He banked, slowed, and eased the flier into the cutting, ascending so as not to startle the creatures. A minute later he overflew the slowly plodding file, pressing his face against the side-screen to look down at their leader.

At that second, the great bull looked up, as if sighting the flier, and raised its abbreviated trunk as if both in greeting and in acknowledgement of its herd's close escape.

It struck Vaughan, then, that the bull was the same one that had led him towards the detour on his first day on Mallory. He smiled at the romantic notion and accelerated away from the herd, following the route on the palmCom south-west.

Fifteen minutes later the southern ocean came into view, a stretch of silver lamé coruscating on the horizon beyond the last of the mountain peaks. According to the palmCom, Breitenbach was in hiding in the mountains overlooking the sea.

The more he thought about the lone radical, the more questions he realised there were to be answered. Breitenbach, if Weiss were to be believed, was privy to the secrets of the crash-landed extra-terrestrials—though how this might be so, when the ship had arrived on Mallory many thousands of years ago, and no aliens had survived to this day, was a mystery. According to Weiss, Breitenbach had described to Travers the aliens' appearance, which seemed an impossibility. Could it be, Vaughan speculated as the mountain peaks flicked by outside, that the aliens had survived the crash-landing and lived on in the mountains of Mallory?

He smiled at the conceit.

And, disregarding the aliens, what was to be made of Breitenbach's claim that the pachyderms were sentient creatures—or that at least *some* of them were?

The thought that soon he would locate the radical, and have his questions answered, filled him with anticipation.

He glanced at the palmCom. He was perhaps ten kilometres from Breitenbach's position. He slowed, following the marked route as it took him over a broad valley cradled between soaring, scimitar peaks, and through a pass towards the coast.

Down below, on a path leading from the valley to the pass, he saw another dozen pachyderms ambling south in slow procession.

And then, once he'd seen the first herd, he made out many more: they were strung out across the valley, in single file, trundling with slow, ponderous footsteps on a journey which must have taken them over hundreds of kilometres through the mountains. And if Breitenbach was right, and the pachyderms were intelligent, then what might be signified by this mass exodus into the southern ranges?

He counted more than a hundred animals, then gave up and turned his attention to the palmCom.

Breitenbach was located some three kilometres away, beyond the pass. Vaughan banked the flier and skimmed across the valley, alongside the great caravanserai of alien beasts. Many of them turned their heads to regard his passage, but there was no sign of consternation or panic in their ranks. It came to Vaughan, fancifully, that they were aware he was on their side.

He hopped over the pass between the peaks and was confronted by the great shimmering expanse of the southern ocean. Above it to his right was the bloated orb of the late afternoon sun, and directly before him two of the three moons sailed in slow motion through the sky.

He glanced at the palmCom. The marked route veered right, hugging the mountains that paralleled the line of the shore. He banked and overflew a littoral of blue grassland, glancing inland at the sheer mountains in which Breitenbach evidently made his home.

He banked again, approaching the first range of grey peaks, and he understood then why the palm-Com had brought him in this way: before him, looming in the side of the mountain like a yawning mouth, was the opening to a great cave.

The marked route on the screen of the palmCom led directly into the cave.

He decelerated, eased the flier into the shadow of the opening, and came down on a shelf of rock as flat as a landing pad. The setting sun flung the shadow of the flier ahead of him, and illuminated a natural chamber without the slightest sign of habitation. When the turbos cut out, Vaughan sat for a while, then climbed from the vehicle and stared about him.

The first thing that struck him was the silence. It sealed around him like something solid and impermeable. When he took steps towards the back of the chamber, his boots rang on the rock, amplified and echoing. He felt as though he were trespassing on hallowed ground, the sound of his footsteps a profanity.

The second thing he noticed was an opening in the rock to his right, large enough to admit the flier. He looked around the chamber, but could see no other openings he might explore.

He was tempted to call Breitenbach's name, but something about the cathedral hush of the chamber prevented him.

He returned to the flier, turned on the headlights, and fired up the turbos. He eased the flier forward, its roar deafening in the confined space. In the cone of light flung before the vehicle, he made out the natural archway of the opening and steered the flier through it.

The corridor seemed, to Vaughan's untutored eye, to be a natural feature of the rock. It twisted and turned, narrowing and opening out by turns, but never closing to the point where the flier could not pass. He estimated he had been in the corridor for perhaps ten minutes when he made out, in the patch of darkness far ahead where the headlights of the flier did not reach, a glimmer of light.

He cut the turbos, and when the flier settled he turned off the headlights too. There, in the distance, was a hazy yellow glow: the light at the end of the tunnel.

He restarted the flier and flew along the remaining length of corridor. It opened out and the illumination grew brighter, and a minute later he could see through an arched opening—clearly not the work of nature—into an open area cradled in the mountain-tops.

The flier emerged into daylight and he cut the turbos, climbed out, and stared around him in amazement.

He was on a path that led down into a miniature valley, perhaps half a kilometre from end to end and almost as wide. Low peaks to his right admitted the day's last rays of sun, slicing the valley into two equal halves of light and darkness.

It was not the valley, however, that caused Vaughan's amazement, but rather what the valley contained.

At first he thought they were some kind of alien termite mounds, hundreds of them filling the valley in orderly rows. Then he made out, in each beehive-shaped construction, the unmistakable shapes of doors and slit windows.

From his perspective, looking down into the valley, he was unable to determine the size of each dwelling. Only when he saw the figure of the human being, standing beside a mound which barely reached to his shoulder, was he aware of their scale.

It was as if his eyes, momentarily tricked, had worked out the optical illusion. The dwellings were tiny and the human—it could only be the lone radical, Breitenbach—was like some giant guardian left on to monitor the safekeeping of the valley. The juxtaposition of the human and the mounds served also to highlight how alien the buildings were, with the fluted openings atop every mound, their triangular doorways and slit windows.

Breitenbach raised a hand in greeting.

TWENTY-FIVE

FINDING ABDUL

Pham paused on the steps of the train station and watched the press of humanity flowing down the street. The noise was intense, the babble of conversation never-ending. The occasional roar of fliers obliterated other sounds for brief seconds before the hubbub resumed.

She was jostled, carried down the steps and along the street. She fought her way through with bony elbows, came to the far side of the street, and looked for the turning that would take her to the hospital. She slipped onto the sidewalk and dashed through the less tightly packed pedestrians, then turned right.

She had a lot to tell Abdul. For the past four days she had been living in a plush Level Two apartment with a Thai woman who she had come to think of as the mother she didn't have. Sukara was patient and kind, and seemed to understand Pham, and their days had been full of fun and laughter.

She could not help but wonder what might happen when Sukara's husband, Vaughan, came back.

Khar had been silent since she had moved in with Sukara. Sometimes, at night, she had lain awake in her big bed in the spare room and tried to contact him, calling his name, asking if he were still there. Once, on the first day, he had reassured her that he was there, but had said nothing more. Every other time Pham had tried to summon him, Khar had remained silent.

Sometimes she wondered if she had dreamed of the voice in her head.

She turned down the side street to the hospital, looking forward to seeing her friend again. She hoped his leg had healed by now, and the bruising on his face.

As she entered the hospital and approached reception, she realised that she should have brought Abdul a gift, a comic or some sweets.

"I have come to see Abdul Mohammed," she told the woman behind the desk.

The receptionist consulted a screen and said, "Abdul Mohammed was discharged this morning."

Pham frowned. "Discharged?"

The woman smiled. "He left hospital. Went home."

Pham nodded, thanked the woman and left the building, disappointed. She recalled her last meeting with Abdul, and how he had warned her from going back to Chandi Road. He wondered where he might be, now. The chances were that he would be in none of his old haunts, for fear of the telepath finding him.

She wondered how she might begin to find him, and then had an idea.

She found a phone kiosk and dialled Dr Rao's personal number.

Seconds later he answered. "Speak. This is Dr Rao, and my time is a commodity in short supply."

"Dr Rao. Pham here. I'm trying to find Abdul. Is he at the starship?"

"Abdul is working—"

"But where?"

Rao sighed. "After his contretemps with the Westerner, he has moved his pitch. You will find him outside Allahabad station."

"Thanks, Dr Rao!"

"But tell me—did you locate Vaughan and inform him that it was through my good offices that…"

The phone began bleeping at her. "No money left, Dr Rao. Must go!"

Despite his squawked protests, she hung up and made her way to Chandi Road train station. She boarded an inbound train and alighted at Allahabad station, excited at the prospect of meeting her friend.

She pushed her way through the crowds that filled the street outside the station. Across the busy road she made out a row of expensive-looking restaurants. She thought Abdul might be begging there, and ran across the road dodging motorbikes and auto-rickshaws.

She found a gaggle of street-kids playing kabadi, but Abdul wasn't among them. "Has anyone seen Abdul Mohammed?" she asked.

A boy stopped playing long enough to say, "Abdul was beaten up bad by a suit. Almost killed."

Pham's heart lurched. Could Abdul have been beaten up again? "When was this?" she asked.

"Oh, last week. His leg was broken."

Pham breathed a sigh of relief, thanked the boy and hurried on. She stopped outside an Indian sweet shop, staring in at the piled barfi. She would buy some as a gift for Sukara. She jumped when a familiar voice called her name.

She turned. "Abdul!"

She took his hand, stared at his beaming face.

"No bruises," she said.

"And look. The leg is as good as new!"

She looked back at the window. "Would you like some chai and barfi?"

"Here? It's expensive."

She laughed and pulled him into the old-fashioned, air-conditioned shop. Wooden stalls were set around the tiled floor, and Brahmin customers sipped chai from small china cups and picked at plates of barfi.

They found a booth at the back of the shop and ordered chai and a selection of sweets from a uniformed waiter.

"You'll never guess where I'm living," Pham said around a mouthful of gulab jamon.

"The Ritz? The Ashok-Hilton?"

"Even better! A big apartment in Chittapuram, Level Two!"

Abdul goggled, and Pham laughed at his expression and told him all about going to Vaughan's apartment and meeting Sukara, and staying with her while Vaughan was away. "And that was thanks to you, Abdul."

"It was?"

"You told me about Vaughan, after all," she said. "You told me he was a good man."

Abdul took a big gulp of chai. "But what will you do when Vaughan gets back?"

Pham frowned. She knew what she would like to happen—but that was impossible. Sukara was having a little girl in two months; she would not want the bother of looking after Pham as well.

She shook her head. "I don't know. Maybe Vaughan can find me a job, and I can rent an apartment somewhere."

Abdul smiled. "I hope that happens, Pham."

She told him about the skyball match Sukara was taking her to see later that day. "We might be going next week, too. If you like, I'll ask if you can come too, ah-cha?"

"Really? I'd love to see the Tigers play!"

For the next hour she told him all about life on Level Two, the size of the rooms in the apartment, all the luxuries like a bathroom with a real bath, the kitchen with dozens of strange appliances. Most of all she wanted to tell him how happy she was to have someone who liked her, but she didn't want to brag about this to Abdul, or remind herself that one day soon it would end.

The big clock on the wall read two o'clock, and Pham drained her glass of chai. "I'd better be going, Abdul. I'll ask Sukara about the next Tigers' match, ah-cha?"

"Will I see you before then?"

"I'll meet you outside here tomorrow."

"I'll be here from eight till six, Pham."

They slipped from the shop, and Pham turned and waved before squeezing herself back into the scrimmage of pedestrians moving towards the station.

She caught a train back to Chandi Road, then walked to Chittapuram. It was only a kilometre, and she was feeling great. In fact, she could not remember a time in her life when she felt better. In Abdul she had a good friend, and she was sure that whatever happened in the future, she and Sukara would remain friends. Pham could even baby-sit for her when she wanted to go out with Vaughan.

She took the dropchute and strolled along the quiet corridor to Chittapuram. From time to time she stopped at an observation gallery and stared through the viewscreen at the vast ocean and the voidships approaching the Station.

She looked ahead to the rest of the day, the Tigers' game with Sukara, and the Indian meal afterwards.

She came round the slight bend and approached the door to Sukara's apartment.

The voice in her head commanded: *Stop!*

"Khar! So you're still there?"

Stop, Pham! Do not enter the apartment!

She laughed. "Why not? I don't understand. I'm going to—"

She tried to take a step, move towards the door, but it was as if she were frozen to the spot.

Pham, you are in grave danger if you enter the apartment!

"But what about Sukara?" Pham cried.

Khar was silent for a second, then said, *Do as I say, do you understand? Do exactly as I say, and all will be well.*

She nodded. "Ah-cha."

Pham, go to the spaceport. Vaughan will return soon. If you go to terminal two, Colonial Arrivals, you can sleep on the loungers until he gets back. Look out for ships from Mallory, understood?

"Ah-cha, but why—?"

Just do it! Khar commanded with such urgency that Pham set off at a run towards the 'chute station.

This is what Vaughan looks like, Khar said, and a sudden image of the detective appeared in her head.

"Ah-cha," she said.

Tell him, when he gets back, that I will do everything I can to help him.

She felt a sudden heat in her head, and a quick dizziness followed by a strange sensation of absence. "Khar?" she asked as she ran. "*Khar?*"

But there was no answering voice in her head as she sprinted along the corridor towards the 'chute station and the spaceport.

TWENTY-SIX

THE HORTAVANS

Vaughan stood beside his flier and stared down at the radical.

Breitenbach was tall and thin, as if years of privation in this mountain redoubt had taken its toll; he wore a tattered thermal suit and scuffed boots. From this distance, perhaps fifty metres, he would have passed for a beggar on any street corner on Earth.

Vaughan raised a hand in greeting, then slipped back into the flier. He gunned the turbos, then activated his implant. As he'd expected, Breitenbach was shielded. The mind-silence continued.

He eased the flier from the mouth of the opening and hopped it down into the valley, coming to rest on an avenue of the miniature mounds ten metres from where Breitenbach stood, watching him.

He climbed out and stepped forward. Something stopped him perhaps halfway towards the hermit radical: the sense that he was in the presence of someone whose appearance indicated nothing at all about his true being. Vaughan felt disconcerted, and at the same time overawed.

Breitenbach's face was thin and pale, his eyes watery and lips down-turned, and yet there was something scholarly in the lineaments, the ghost of the man he had once been.

Vaughan found himself saying, "I have the crystals."

Breitenbach smiled, the gesture patrician, bestowing beneficence on a minion.

"I'm—" he began, but a gesture from Breitenbach stopped him.

"No names, my friend. The less we know about each other…" It was said with a smile, in an accent Vaughan thought English.

He was about to tell Breitenbach that he was not part of the radical network on Mallory, but the man gestured and said, "If you could help me get them into position, that would be most kind. Then, perhaps, you might care to join me in a meal?"

Vaughan smiled. "That would be good."

"I'm afraid I can't offer you anything but a selection of vegetables and pulses—but they're home-grown," Breitenbach said with a smile, gesturing towards a long vegetable patch beyond the dwellings. "I manage to grow enough to sustain me, despite the inclement climate."

Vaughan stared around. "How long have you lived here?" he asked.

"A little over five years," Breitenbach said. "I am a wanted man on Mallory. I'd done as much as I could, and it was only a matter of time before Scheering apprehended me. Then," he paused, his eyes brightening as he remembered something, "then events conspired to bring me here." He gestured around the valley, as if showing off Shangri-La. "And what more fitting venue for the role I now find myself playing?"

Vaughan gestured towards the mounds. "You didn't build these yourself?"

Breitenbach smiled. "They are the work of the Hortavans," he said, then gestured towards the flier. "But come, we have work to do, and the light fades."

The Hortavans, Vaughan repeated to himself as he opened the rear door of the flier and hauled out the crystals. Were they the extraterrestrials?

He set the racks on the grass, and Breitenbach knelt and caressed the elongated stones with reverence.

When he looked up, Vaughan saw tears in the old man's eyes.

Breitenbach stood and pointed to a path that wound up the side of the valley, to an opening in the rock opposite that through which Vaughan had entered. "We will carry them up there," the radical instructed.

He picked up one rack and, with difficulty, Vaughan carried two. He followed Breitenbach along the path, up the hillside and into a narrow cutting in the rock. This one, unlike the wider corridor down which he'd arrived, had the appearance of being hewn from the rock: the corridor was squared off, finished, though obviously built for the passage of beings smaller than themselves. They were forced to stoop as they struggled with the weight of the racks.

The light from the valley soon gave out, but the period of darkness lasted only a few minutes. From up ahead came the wan glow of twilight.

They emerged on a wide ledge cut into the side of the mountain, which afforded a spectacular view of peak after snow-clad peak as they receded into the interior.

The ledge, Vaughan saw, was merely part of a long winding track, which followed the side of the mountain, disappearing inland between distant rock faces. Vaughan could only assume that this track, too, had been constructed by the Hortavans. It was the inland access to the hidden valley, though the narrowness of the corridor had precluded the flier's entry.

A cold wind blew along the ledge, cooling Vaughan's sweat-soaked face.

They stopped, laying the racks on the ground and resting.

"What now?" Vaughan asked, staring along the track.

"Now," Breitenbach said, "we place them." He indicated recesses chiselled into the face of the rock above the ledge. Each recess was a metre from the next, and they receded along the side of the track for perhaps twenty metres.

Breitenbach eased a stone from the rack and approached the closest recess, holding the gem before him with something like awe.

He paused before the chiselled niche, then reached up and inserted the stone. To Vaughan's amazement it slid home as if precision cut to fit the inlet.

Vaughan took a stone and slid it into the next inlet, ignorant as to what he was doing and yet, at the same time, aware that he was taking part in something vitally important. The perfection with which the hollowed rock accepted the stones seemed natural and right, and each insertion filled him with a certain inexplicable satisfaction.

Ten minutes later the racks were empty, and the row of ruby gems set into the mountainside caught the last of the day's light.

"And now?" Vaughan asked.

"Now we eat," Breitenbach answered, and then, with a smile as if aware of what Vaughan had meant, he went on, "And in the morning, at first light, they arrive... If you wish, you may stay and watch the ceremony at sunrise."

And with that he turned and entered the corridor through the mountain. Vaughan followed, a little dazed.

Could it be, then, that the Hortavans had survived? Would he witness an extraterrestrial ceremony involving the stones as the sun came up on an alien world seventy light years from Earth? The idea was too great for his imagination to grasp. He wished suddenly that Sukara could be with him to witness whatever was about to happen.

He followed the radical through the mountain and back into the valley, and they sat outside one of the small dwellings. Breitenbach gathered wood and built a fire, igniting it with a lighter, and in a primitive cooking pot boiled a broth of pulses, vegetables, and herbs.

A single moon rode high, casting opal light across the valley.

Vaughan ate the stew, surprised at how good it was, and fetched the canisters of water from the flier, along with the remaining pre-packed meals as a gift for the radical.

Vaughan opened the whisky he'd bought in Mackintyre and offered Breitenbach a shot. The oldster's eyes lighted. "Perhaps just one," he said. "It would be sacrilege to greet such a momentous day with a hangover."

Vaughan poured a generous measure into Breitenbach's scratched plastic mug, and a smaller quantity into his own.

He took a mouthful. It was rough, but warming. He wondered if he had brought out the alcohol with the express purpose of loosening the old man's tongue.

He said, "I'm not who you think I am," and watched Breitenbach's reaction.

To his credit, the oldster kept his calm.

"And who," he said, "did you think I thought you were?"

Vaughan smiled. "One of the radical cell, working against Scheering-Lassiter, working on behalf of Grayson's pachyderms."

Breitenbach inclined his head. "I assumed so, yes. But, then again, you don't have the air about you of a government agent."

"I'm on your side, Breitenbach. Rest assured on that score. I'm as opposed to the ruling regime here as you are. But... well, it's a long story."

The old man smiled and raised his mug. "Well, I like long stories, sir, and we do have all night, after all."

Vaughan smiled. He refilled his glass, offered Breitenbach another. He accepted a shot.

As the firelight flickered around the valley, illuminating Breitenbach's long face, his eyes which seemed to have experienced so much, Vaughan told the radical that he was a telepathic detective investigating three killings on Bengal Station.

Breitenbach leaned forward. "And these killings?"

"Kormier, Travers, and a few months ago a woman called Mulraney."

The radical nodded. "I knew they'd got Mulraney," he said. "I was hoping Travers would finish his report, before..." His expression bleak, he looked at Vaughan. "You know who is responsible, of course?"

"Well, there's no doubt in my mind that Scheering hired the assassin. I'd like to implicate the bastard, but..." He smiled and shook his head. "But that'd be impossible. The best I can hope for is to get the assassin." He looked up. "It would help if I knew exactly why Scheering wanted these people dead. Weiss—my contact on Mallory—told me about the pachyderms. He claimed they were sentient, or at least some of them were."

Breitenbach stared into the flames. "Travers was an independent xeno-biologist. Eco-Col brought him in to monitor the cull. We got to him, told him what we knew, proved to him that certain of the Grayson's pachyderms could be classed on the Baumann scale as sentient. That of course had massive implications for the colonisation, the exploitation, of the planet. He presented his findings to Scheering when he returned to Earth—we advised him against this course of action, by the way." The radical shrugged. "Travers was an academic, and like so many academics he lived in his ivory tower, blind to the machinations of the outside world. I think he was oblivious to the lengths someone like Scheering would go to in order to safeguard his interests."

"He learned the hard way," Vaughan said. "And Kormier? He was a friend of Travers—he knew the truth about the pachyderms, right?"

Breitenbach smiled. "Oh, he knew the truth, very well."

Vaughan stared at the radical, puzzled by something in his tone. "What do you mean by that?"

Breitenbach said, "I mean, Mr Vaughan, that Kormier found out in the very same way that I did, all those years ago." He fell silent, staring at the fire but seeing something else, long ago.

"What happened?" Vaughan murmured.

Still staring at the flames, Breitenbach said, "I came to Mallory as an independent naturalist almost fifteen years ago. Not much was known about Grayson's pachyderms back then. I'd made a study of the African elephant, shortly before its extinction, and the elephant analogue of Charybdis. When I read up about Grayson's, I knew I had to come here and study them. Of course, at that point there was no cull. Scheering had no idea how dangerous the pachyderms would be to his plans for the planet."

Vaughan finished his whisky. He refilled his mug while Breitenbach contemplated the past, then offered the radical another shot. The old man nodded, lost in reverie.

"And?" Vaughan prompted.

"Oh, I bought a cheap flier—they weren't proscribed then—and toured the southern continent. I observed the animals. I grew very close to them. I came to understand them, respect them. And then I came to suspect that they were more intelligent than I or anyone else had assumed. At least, some of them were. Even then, though, I was reluctant to fully believe that I had stumbled upon a sentient race. At first I ascribed my suspicion of sentience to my becoming too close to the animals, identifying too personally with individuals."

"What made you suspect intelligence?"

Breitenbach smiled. "It was a cumulative effect—not just one incident. I'd been living among a herd of three families for six months—they are peaceable creatures, Vaughan. They accepted me. I became..." He shook his head, as if in retrospective wonder. "I became very close to a particular cow. She seemed... well, I thought I was taking leave of my senses at the time, but she seemed able to empathise with my emotions."

Nursing his whisky, Vaughan smiled and shook his head.

"While I was living with the herd, I had news from Earth that my father had died. That evening, as I sat alone outside my tent, the cow—I called her Lucy, for some reason—came up to me and quite simply laid her trunk on my shoulder. I know it sounds ridiculous—anthropomorphising random actions of alien creatures—but it was as if Lucy were communicating to me, commiserating with my loss."

Vaughan frowned. "That's hardly evidence of sentience," he began.

Breitenbach went on, "That was the first incident, the gesture that made me wonder. A few days later I left my camp and trekked into the nearby mountains. I walked for a few days, making notes on local fauna. On the way back I slipped and fell down a ravine, breaking my leg." He looked up at Vaughan. "I knew I was dead. I had sufficient food and water for a couple of days, the break was bad, and I'd left my com back at camp, sixty kilometres away."

"And?"

"And the following morning I heard a noise further down the ravine, the clatter of rocks. The mountains are home of some predatory lion-analogues." He smiled. "The irony wasn't lost on me: the naturalist, devoured by native fauna."

"But it wasn't a lion."

"It wasn't. A couple of pachyderms plodded into sight down the ravine. Imagine my amazement when I realised that one of them was Lucy. She approached, inspected my leg with her trunk. Between them they managed to get me onto Lucy's back and carry me back to camp."

"Some story," Vaughan said.

"Lucy knew," Breitenbach said. "She knew I was in distress and came to me."

"Are you saying the pachyderms are telepathic?" Vaughan tried to keep the scepticism from his voice.

"Telepathic, empathetic—the terminology doesn't matter. She knew. She saved my life."

Vaughan stared into the fire. He shrugged. "I don't want to come over as the sceptic, Breitenbach. But her saving your life doesn't prove sentience. You could claim that some animals on Earth, certain dogs, are empathetic."

Breitenbach nodded. "I could. Of course, you're right. However, by that time, I was certain in my mind that the pachyderms were sentient, and then I found out for certain that they were."

He excused himself, climbed slowly to his feet and made his way around the back of an alien dwelling. As the old man relieved himself, Vaughan wondered about his story. Could it be that the old man was deluded, that the pachyderms were no more than merely clever? But, then, why the cull, and why had Scheering ordered the murders of people convinced of the pachyderms' sentience?

There had to be something to Breitenbach's story, bizarre though it was.

The old man returned, lowering himself with creaking bones into a cross-legged position before the fire. He took up his whisky and contemplated the liquid, then sipped.

"A few months later I left the herd," Breitenbach said in a soft voice. "I wanted to study others. I was curious as to why one individual in a herd should evince signs of intelligence, when the members of the same herd showed no such indications. I found another herd, just north of where we are now, and a couple of days later it happened."

He finished his whisky and held out the mug for Vaughan to refill. Replenished, he continued, "I was following the herd south—the pachyderms migrate from the central plains to the edge of the southern continent around this time every year. The way through the mountains is treacherous, and a number of the creatures perish with every migration. On this occasion I saw an old bull stumble and fall down a steep drop. He must have fallen fifty metres. I was in the flier—I descended to the foot of the cliff, though I knew there was nothing I could do but be with the bull as it died. I... I approached him, knelt beside the animal. It was horribly injured, its skull stove in, back broken. It was still alive. Its massive eyes regarded me..." Breitenbach paused, reliving the event. Tears filmed his eyes. Vaughan looked into his drink, waiting for the old radical to resume, and at the same time wondering quite what proof the dying bull vouchsafed Breitenbach as to its sentience.

He continued, "Before it died, Vaughan, the bull communicated with me. It showed me that it was an intelligent, conscious, morally aware creature, worthy of equal status with all other sentient beings the galaxy over."

Vaughan leaned forward. "How did it do this?"

The radical took a long drink of whisky, pursing his lips around the mouthful. He nodded, staring at Vaughan as if wondering how to go about telling him what had happened next.

At last he said, changing the subject, "What did your contact—Weiss, was it?—tell you about the Hortavans, the alien race which crash-landed here thousands of years ago?"

Vaughan blinked, put out by the sudden change of tack. "Not much, only what he'd heard from Jenna Larsen, who'd heard it from you."

"But what did he say?"

Vaughan shrugged. "He claimed you knew about the aliens—he didn't even know what they were called. He said you knew about the star charts, the crystals."

"And how do you think I know about the Horta-vans?" Breitenbach said.

"I don't know. But I guess you're going to tell me, right?"

Breitenbach smiled. "Over a hundred thousand years ago," he said, "the race known as the

Hortavans came to Mallory. They were fleeing their home planet, which had been engulfed in a supernova. They'd had plenty of time to prepare their exodus—their ship contained all their population."

Vaughan was about to say something—along the lines that the ship had hardly seemed *that* big—but Breitenbach went on. "It wasn't their intention to remain on Mallory: it was supposed to be merely an exploratory stop-over. The ship encountered difficulties when coming down, and crash-landed in the valley north of here. The majority of the Hortavans were killed in the accident. Only a few hundred thousand survived."

"The experts claimed they were extinct," Vaughan said, "that Mallory wasn't habitable." Breitenbach inclined his head. "That is so. The corporeal Hortavans, those charged with guardianship of the crystals, succumbed to the malign viruses of Mallory—but not before partially discharging their duties."

"Which were?"

"The corporeal Hortavans took from the ship the crystals and distributed them around the southern continent. They almost accomplished this task, but succumbed to disease before they could unload the last chamber."

"The last chamber?" Vaughan said. "The crystals I brought here?"

The radical nodded. "The last of the stored Hortavans," he said.

Vaughan laughed, a nervous reaction to his inability to comprehend what Breitenbach was telling him, to piece together the disparate clues. "I don't understand. What are the crystals?"

The radical raised his mug. "Each faceted crystal, Vaughan, contains the identities of Hortavan individuals."

Vaughan sat back and raised his head to the stars. "The identities? I don't—"

"Perhaps 'identities' is the wrong term. They contain the very essences of Hortavan individuals. They are an extremely ancient and advanced race. They had long since discovered how to record themselves, their very essences. When the supernova came, they were ready. Millions of individuals were stored in the matrix of the crystals for the long voyage to a new, safer world. Some remained corporeal, to crew the ship and facilitate the recorded Hortavans' eventual rebirth."

"Jesus Christ," Vaughan whispered.

"Millions perished in the crash-landing, when the crystals were destroyed. A few thousand survived in the crystals. The corporeal Hortavans did their best to disseminate their fellows, before death overcame them."

Vaughan interrupted, "The pachyderms? The Hortavans are the pachyderms, right? Or rather, some of the pachyderms are?"

Breitenbach smiled. "The Hortavans are not an evil race, Vaughan. They would not take over a species and obliterate their identities. They live in the minds of the pachyderms as separate entities, content to experience existence but, more importantly, to contemplate the eternal verities of life."

Vaughan thought back to what the radical had said. "The dying bull—you said it communicated with you?"

Breitenbach fixed Vaughan with a suddenly intense gaze. "It communicated with me—it also did more than that. The Hortavan that existed within the pachyderm's dying sensorium... *transferred* itself into mine. I knew instantly that something had happened. I felt euphoric, though I was ignorant as to the reason why. That knowledge came only days later, when the Hortavan had mastered my thoughts, ideas, and language, and was able to communicate... I thought at first I was going mad—but the Hortavan was compassionate. He communicated only briefly, and reassured me that I was not mad, that its intent was not evil, that it was alive in me, but would not reveal itself if that was what I wished. I overcame my fear, and over the years came to understand the alien, or rather the xenopath, as I called it, and its race."

Vaughan sat back, staring at Breitenbach. "And when Sheering found out about the pachyderms?"

"He had scientists studying the animals, of course. They came upon the truth of the Hortavan mind-transference and mind-reading abilities. They discovered that the transfer could not be effected if the potential subject was mind-shielded, which was why the Scheering's governing council legislated that every citizen of the planet should be shielded, ostensibly to safeguard against telepaths from Earth intent on stealing vital Mallorian trade secrets. By that time I'd acquired a mind-shield, in case a Scheering telepath read of my secret."

Vaughan said, "And then Scheering instituted the cull, to get rid of the evidence before Eco-Col learned the truth and the colonial authorities closed the planet down?"

Breitenbach nodded. "I tried to warn Eco-Col. A Mallorian informer told Scheering, and from that date I have been a wanted man. I co-ordinate resistance from various locations in the mountains, relying on cells of so-called radicals to spread the word."

Vaughan considered Breitenbach's story, then said, "You said Kormier found out the same way as you did?"

Breitenbach nodded. "He was monitoring a cull two hundred kilometres north of here, when he came upon a dying pachyderm. It communicated with him, and he cut out his mind-shield and allowed the Hortavan to transfer itself into his mind." Breitenbach paused, then went on, "Then he made a big mistake. He informed his superior here on Mallory that the cull should cease, little realising that the authorities already knew about the Hortavans and the pachyderms. He became a liability to Scheering, and when he returned to Earth…"

Vaughan closed his eyes. "And the slaughter continues."

"The Hortavans are becoming adept at evading the militia," Breitenbach said, "thanks to their mind-guests." He paused and smiled, finishing his whisky. "It is late. We have an early start in the morning."

Vaughan said, "The crystals?"

"Did you notice the pachyderms heading this way? They were being led by their mind-guests. In the morning we will witness the transference."

Vaughan drained the alcohol, his senses numbed by its effect, and by what Breitenbach had told him.

The radical showed him to a beehive mound, equipped with a sleeping mat and a thermal cover.

Breitenbach bade him goodnight, and Vaughan lay in the confined space, staring up at a patch of stars which showed through the overhead flue. He was awake for a long time, his head awash with dizzying images, before the alcohol eased him into sleep.

TWENTY-SEVEN

TRANSFERENCE

Vaughan was awoken by bright sunlight and he sat upright suddenly, wondering if the dialogue with Breitenbach the night before had been nothing but a dream.

He struggled through the narrow aperture of the mound. Breitenbach was standing across the avenue, as large as life, shrugging himself into his tattered thermal jacket.

"I trust you slept well?"

Vaughan laughed. "I think the whisky helped."

They breakfasted on local fruit and water, sitting around the dead embers of the fire as the sun rose over the peaks and warmed the valley.

Later, Breitenbach led the way through the corridor to the ledge where the night before they had positioned the Hortavan gemstones. Vaughan emerged blinking into the sudden wash of sunlight, staring along the winding track to where it vanished between distant peaks and wondering what exactly to expect.

"When are they due?" he asked. He leaned against the cold bulk of the mountainside and inclined his face towards the warmth of Eta Ophiuchi. "They'll be here shortly," Breitenbach said with certainty.

Vaughan stared at the old man. "I was wondering last night... but I didn't want to ask—"

"Go on."

Vaughan looked into the oldster's eyes. "Are you aware of the Hortavan in your head?" he asked. "I mean, what is it like, sharing... *yourself* with a wholly alien being?"

Breitenbach smiled. "Most of the time I am unaware of the Hortavan's presence. It's content to abide in my consciousness, contemplating its own thoughts without my knowledge. Occasionally it will communicate with me—it learned our language very quickly—and I with it."

"That must be strange."

Breitenbach smiled again. "Voices in the head, Mr Vaughan. No stranger than being a telepath, privy to the thoughts of others. Except, in my case, those thoughts can reciprocate. The alien in here—" he touched his temple, "has eased the loneliness of my existence these past five years."

"If it wished," Vaughan began tentatively, "it could assume control of you, dictate your thoughts?"

"I assume that that would be entirely possible," Breitenbach said. "There have been times, when I have been ill or injured, when the Hortavan has assumed control and eased me through, but in the normal course of events, the alien is content merely to exist."

Vaughan thought about it, then gestured at the crystals lodged in the cliff face. "Then why don't they remain in the stones?" he asked. "Why do they risk becoming the mind-parasites of creatures whose lives are under threat?"

"Think of the crystals as cold sleep facilities," Breitenbach replied. "The stored Hortavans are not conscious, but are suspended between life and death. The crystals are perishable, or rather they can sustain the identity matrices of the Hortavans for only so long. That period is coming to an end. Already, many of the crystals have corrupted; many lives have been lost. Of course there is a danger in transferring the remaining Hortavans to the pachyderms, but my guest—" again he gestured to his temple, "thought it the lesser of the two evils to effect the transfer. The southern range is riddled with subterranean caves where the Hortavans can take refuge in times of crisis."

Vaughan looked along the track to the snow-clad peaks scintillating in the morning sun. He thought of the military patrol he had seen yesterday, and the procession of pachyderms crossing the last valley. What if the militia had happened upon them?

"There must be a way to stop the slaughter," he said.

Breitenbach smiled. "We have tried, and we are trying, and we will try, my friend. We have informed Eco-Col, but they're conservative and take our claims lightly. We had hoped that Professor Travers's report might persuade them."

"Have you gone to the authorities on Earth?"

"We've tried everything. What you fail to realise is how powerful Gustave Scheering is, how much control he has of governments and colonial representatives. He is a ruthless multi-millionaire and controls many top politicians and colonial representatives."

Vaughan considered. "If Scheering himself could be persuaded... If he could become the unwitting host of a Hortavan, then surely—"

Breitenbach laid a hand on Vaughan's shoulder. "Do you think we haven't thought of that, my friend? Kormier tried to get to Scheering, with the express intent of transferring his Hortavan guest. He was not the first to try." Breitenbach made a gesture of hopelessness. "Scheering is aware of the danger. He is paranoid about security. He keeps himself surrounded by bodyguards at all times." He stopped and looked along the length of the track. His sudden smile was as radiant as the sun. "At last," he murmured.

Vaughan turned.

In the distance he saw the giant form of a Grayson's pachyderm round the bend in the track, pause and raise its trunk in what could have been interpreted as a bellow of triumph. It advanced, taking great, slow loping strides as if wading through quicksand. Behind it, in procession, came other pachyderms. Soon the length of the track was filled with the creatures, trunk to tail.

The leading bull paused fifty metres before where Vaughan and Breitenbach stood. It raised its trunk and caressed the cliff face—and Vaughan realised that it had touched not the rock but the first of the inset crystals.

Breitenbach said, "The bull is already host to a Hortavan. It is greeting its people."

"And the other pachyderms?" Vaughan began.

"Watch," Breitenbach said.

The second pachyderm in line drew level with the first crystal, and something happened so swift and fleeting that Vaughan thought it a trick of his eyes, and then wondered if anything had happened at all.

He watched, more closely, as the third animal drew alongside the crystal.

An instantaneous while light pulsed from the embedded stone, hit the pachyderm's massive brow and dissipated. It was over in a fraction of a second; had he blinked, he would have missed the miraculous event of the transference.

As each animal drew alongside the recess, the crystal discharged an alien consciousness and the pachyderms proceeded, plodding stoically after their leader, as if nothing at all had occurred.

"How many alien minds does one crystal contain?" Vaughan asked.

"Perhaps a hundred," Breitenbach replied. "Though some crystals have corrupted over time, and lost many of their stored identities."

Vaughan wanted to laugh aloud at the improbability of what he was witnessing, the sheer miracle of the transfer, and at the same time the wonder of the racial salvation it represented.

By now the first bull had reached the mouth of the corridor. It paused, reached out its short trunk to Breitenbach and touched the old man on the forehead. Breitenbach closed his eyes briefly, then opened them and smiled in delight.

As the bull loped past, easing its way into the corridor, Breitenbach said, "It thanks you for risking your life to ensure the renewed existence of its fellows."

Vaughan could only smile and shake his head as he turned and watched the procession of pachyderms take on board their cargo of extraterrestrial intelligence.

The animals passed by one by one, their wrinkled hides pungent, something statuesque and graceful in the colossal gravity of their tread as they followed their leader into the corridor.

Vaughan said, "Where are they headed now?"

"From my valley, a cutting leads to a vast underground chamber, where the pachyderms usually spend six months before heading north again. This time, however, they will avoid the northern valleys and Scheering's militia, and remain in hiding."

Vaughan looked along the track. The last animal of perhaps fifty was passing the crystals. "There will be others?" he asked.

"Until the last of the crystals are empty," Breitenbach said. "They will come in their individual herds over the course of the next few weeks."

Vaughan watched the last pachyderm pass the recess. A white light sprang forth, hit the creature, and vanished.

He stared. There was something about the light...

It reminded him of something he had seen, and recently: the reflection of a laser, he had thought at the time.

On the surveillance film of Robert Kormier's murder...

The laser had struck Kormier, and only later, on watching the killing in slow motion, had Vaughan noticed the white light lance from Kormier and hit the watching girl full in the face...

Kormier's Hortavan, making the transfer as he died.

Making the transfer to its new host, the Thai girl, Pham...

Breitenbach was turning and following the last of the pachyderms down the corridor, gesturing Vaughan to follow.

He did so, as if in a daze.

Now he knew why the killer had been so intent on tracing Pham—not because he feared she had witnessed the killing, but because he had read the girl's mind and was aware of the transfer. The assassin had killed Kormier because he was playing host to the alien—and he would stop at nothing to trace and eradicate the alien's new host, Pham.

They came to the valley, the sunlight blinding after the shadows of the corridor. Already, the last of the pachyderms were making their way through a narrow fissure in the rock at the far end of the valley.

Breitenbach said, "You will stay a while longer?"

"I must get back to Mackintyre. I have a return flight to Earth."

Breitenbach inclined his head. "I wish you a safe journey, and thank you for what you have done for the Hortavans."

Vaughan said, "I intend to do more. I have... I have an idea, a way I might be able to stop the slaughter."

Breitenbach smiled. "You would earn the eternal gratitude of the Hortavan race, if you succeeded, my friend." Even as Breitenbach said this, Vaughan detected scepticism in his tone.

He hesitated, wondering whether to tell the radical his plan.

Breitenbach gestured. "It is best if I do not know," he said. "If Scheering's henchmen found me..."

They shook hands, and Vaughan crossed to the flier and eased himself in behind the controls. He hoisted the vehicle into the air and looked down at Breitenbach.

The old radical was a tiny, tattered figure, his right arm lifted in farewell.

Vaughan waved, then lifted the flier from the valley and accelerated over the enclosing peaks.

He followed the jagged line of the coast, keeping on the seaward side of the mountains in order to avoid the military patrols, and then turned inland towards Mackintyre.

He discovered he was thinking ahead—to trying to find Pham among the teeming millions on Bengal Station.

TWENTY-EIGHT

THE VOICE IN HER HEAD

The last thing Sukara recalled was the Westerner, smiling as he raised his laser and shot her in the head. And now this... Was she going mad?

The voice in her head said: *Be calm. Do not be alarmed. I am with you, and I will help.*

She recalled only vague memories of what had happened. The Westerner wanting Vaughan, making her discard her mind-shield. He had read that Pham was due back soon.

Oh, God—Pham!

Be calm, said the voice. *Pham is safe. She will not return here immediately.*

He shot me, Sukara thought. I knew that I was dead, that I'd never again see Jeff.

You are not dead, Sukara.

My baby! she thought, cradling the swell of her stomach. Is Li okay?

Your child is unaffected, said the voice.

Sukara felt the panic subside. Who... what are you? she thought.

*I will explain later. All that matters now is that I
will help you. But you must do as I say. We are still
in danger.*

He lasered me through the head, Sukara thought.
How can I be alive?

*I entered your mind, made certain repairs, eased
you through the trauma of your death and brought
you back to life.*

The idea was beyond Sukara's comprehension.
All she knew was that she was indeed still alive. She
would see Jeff again!

We are still in danger, said the voice. *You must do
as I say.*

Okay, Sukara thought.

She felt the cover of the sofa beneath her body.
She was lying where the Westerner had shot her, in
the sunken bunker in the middle of the lounge.

Pain? She considered this, and found that, mirac-
ulously, she felt nothing. The killer had lasered a
hole in her head, killed her, and now she did not
even have a headache.

Where do you come from? She thought.

I am from the planet of Mallory, said the voice.

Mallory, Sukara thought. But that's where Jeff is!

Then she remembered the killer. He must still be
here.

*That is correct. He is waiting for Pham, and then
for Vaughan. He is in the kitchen now, eating.*

Later, she knew that her reaction was ridiculous,
but at the time she experienced a sudden indignation that the killer was helping himself to her
food.

She thought: But if Jeff comes back, walks right
into...

Calm yourself. I will have dealt with the assassin before Vaughan's return.

How? She thought.

I will tell you that in a little while, when you are fully recovered.

Fully recovered, Sukara laughed to herself. The killer lasered me dead, and now I am recovering... She wondered if she were dreaming.

This is no dream, Sukara. This is reality. Open your eyes.

Cautiously she did so. She was lying on her back on the sofa. She reached up, touched her forehead where the laser had struck her. Her fingers touched a sticky crust of blood.

She pulled her hand away, horrified.

The voice in her head explained: *I had to leave the external wound, Sukara, so as not to alert the killer to your resurrection.*

Then she thought: But he's a telepath! He'll read my mind and know I'm still alive!

That is my immediate concern, the voice said. *At the moment his implant is deactivated. I surmise that he will activate it soon, before Pham returns.*

Then he *will* read my mind! Sukara thought in panic.

We must retrieve your mind-shield.

She had tossed it across the room, she remembered.

She tried to move, but the voice said: *Careful. Move your legs first, and then your body. I am monitoring the assassin. Freeze when I tell you, do you understand?*

I understand.

She moved her legs, wincing as they fizzed with painful pins and needles. Then she shifted her body to a more comfortable position on the sofa. Now she was able to look over the edge of the sunken bunker, across the lounge and into the kitchen.

She saw the killer as he crossed the kitchen, fixing himself a sandwich, and the sight of him filled Sukara with dread.

Be calm. I am with you, the voice soothed.

The killer passed from sight. She heard the cooler door open and shut, and a hiss as the cap was removed from a bottle of Blue Mountain beer.

It was irrational, but what incensed her was not so much that he had shot her through the head, but that he was helping himself now to Jeff's beer.

She shifted her gaze to where she had thrown her mind-shield, and there it was. It sat on the pile of the carpet, winking silver in the light of the afternoon sun that cascaded through the window.

It was perhaps three metres from where she lay, midway between the bunker and the kitchen door.

I could get it! Sukara thought.

But the voice in her head counselled caution. *Not yet. I am monitoring the assassin. I will tell you when to move.*

You can read his thoughts?

Not so much read his thoughts, as interpret his intentions. I am aware of his emotions, through the barrier of his shield. Be prepared...

Okay, Sukara thought.

But even then, she thought, even when I have the shield and he can't read my mind, how will we overcome the killer before Pham and Jeff get back?

I told you, the voice said patiently, *Pham will not return when she planned to, and by the time Vaughan returns we will have dealt with the assassin.*

How?

Leave that to me, Sukara. For the time being, be calm, and await my instructions.

The odd thing was, even though there was an armed killer in the next room, who had killed her once and would have no qualms about killing her again, she felt curiously calm. She wondered if the voice in her head, which had healed her wound and brought her back from the dead, was responsible for her mental state now, as she lay in the bunker and stared through the door of the kitchen.

He is staring through the window at the void-ships, the voice reported. *He is drinking beer and waiting for his sandwich to toast. When he crosses the kitchen again, and busies himself with extracting the sandwich from the machine, then that is the time to move. Retrieve the shield in silence and return to the sofa when I tell you to do so.*

Sukara nodded. Okay.

He is about to move, the voice said, and Sukara saw him pass across the kitchen and out of sight again. She heard him open the toaster, and then the voice in her head said: *Now!*

She moved. She sprang from the bunker and dashed across the room, heart pounding. She grabbed the shield, flooded with elation, then froze at the sound of footsteps from the kitchen.

The killer's shadow, cast by the light from the window, appeared at the door.

It was as if, then, Sukara lost control of her own movements. She froze, but a fraction of a second later she was moving again, rolling across the carpet towards the bunker and over the edge. She hit the cushion, closed her eyes and lay very still, breathing hard.

She knew that the voice in her head had taken control of her, and she felt at once alarmed and relieved.

He heard you, the voice said. *He came to the door to listen again, but he did not notice that the shield was no longer on the carpet. It is okay, Sukara. He has returned to the kitchen.*

She slipped the mind-shield into her pocket and arranged herself on the cushions so that she could see across the lounge to the kitchen door.

Will he notice that I've moved a little? she wondered.

As far as he is concerned, the voice said, *you are dead. He will not notice that you have moved.*

Reassured, Sukara lay and waited for the killer to appear.

And then, she thought, what do we do when he comes back in here?

We lie very still. We wait. At some point he will put down his pistol—then, we make our move.

Does he have the pistol on him now?

He placed it on the worktop while he prepared his food.

Sukara nodded. She considered what the voice had told her, then thought: How did you enter my head?

A hesitation, then: *I came from Pham, and before Pham another human, one who had visited Mallory.*

And why did you come to Earth?

In a bid to help my people, who are being killed by the government of Mallory.

And you can move from head to head at will?

Most of the time, yes.

Sukara considered that. So... she thought, why don't you just enter the killer's head now and make him stop what he's doing?

She felt what might have been a smile in her mind. *Because the assassin is shielded, Sukara. We cannot enter shielded minds.*

She nodded. Tough, she thought.

But do not worry. We will prevail.

She thought of Jeff. She wanted him in her arms. When she had him back, she told herself, she would never let him go again.

She heard movement, footsteps in the kitchen. The killer appeared in the doorway, then stepped into the lounge carrying a sandwich in one hand and the pistol in the other. Sukara half shut her eyes and watched the blurred shape of the killer as he crossed the lounge.

He pulled a chair into position to the left of the sliding door, sat down, and began eating his sandwich. Holding the pistol on his lap. He hadn't even given Sukara a single glance.

She opened her eyes fully and watched him.

He was sitting between Sukara and the door with his back to her. She could easily leave the bunker, sneak up on him and... She looked around for a handy, heavy object with which to crack his skull.

The only thing to hand was a flower arrangement beside the bunker, which would hardly double as a cosh.

Be patient, Sukara.

But he has a pistol and we have nothing! How will we stop him!

Leave the logistics to me, the voice said. *Be ready, that is all I ask of you.*

Sukara smiled. I'm ready, she thought.

The killer lounged in the chair and finished the sandwich. She wondered what kind of person would calmly kill someone, then fix themselves a meal and sit patiently waiting to kill someone else. And he had killed others, too, taking the lives of whoever he was paid to kill... She thought back two years to when she'd shot Osborne. She had had to do that then, in order to save Jeff's life, but even so she had felt inescapable waves of guilt in the aftermath. But how could this man kill and keep on killing people and live with the knowledge that he had extinguished so many innocent lives?

The thought made her so angry that, if she were able to, then, she would have shot the bastard dead without a second thought.

The irony was not lost on her, and she smiled.

He is preparing to move to the bathroom, the voice said. *We must be ready*.

Sukara nodded, her pulse racing.

The killer stood and stretched, the pistol in his extended right hand. He turned and headed for the bathroom door. Sukara watched him through half-closed eyes.

He stepped from the lounge, closing the door behind him.

Get up, commanded the voice.

Sukara moved from the bunker, amazed at how well she felt, considering that fifteen minutes ago she had been dead. She crossed the room towards the bathroom door and paused, looking around.

There, said the voice.

In a wall recess stood a metal statuette, an elephant with its trunk raised. She grabbed the animal by the trunk, surprised at how heavy it was. All the better, she thought.

She moved to the bathroom door, beside which stood a tall unit holding glasses and drinks. Sukara positioned herself on the other side of the unit, so that it was between herself and the bathroom door.

She should, she realised, be more frightened than she felt. She was curiously calm. Are you helping me? she asked.

I am doing what is necessary to prevent further deaths, said the voice.

She wondered if it said this to lessen her guilt at what she was about to do, and then she wondered if she would feel any remorse at bludgeoning the killer.

The bathroom door opened and the killer stepped into the lounge.

Sukara moved from behind the unit.

She raised the statuette above her head, conscious of its heft, the damage it would do.

At that second, just as she was about to propel the elephant on its downward swing towards the blonde head of the killer, he turned, suddenly aware.

She cried out and swung the statuette.

The blow caught the side of his forehead. The killer dropped to his knees.

For a fraction of a second, Sukara hesitated.

Then the thing in her head took control.

As if watching the actions of her body from a remove, she was aware of launching herself towards the killer, striking him again across the side of the head and then stamping down hard on his wrist as he fell to the floor.

She wrested the pistol from his grip and staggered away across the lounge.

She felt the control of her body return to her as she stood, shaking, facing the killer as he pulled himself upright.

She levelled the pistol.

The killer stared, and understanding came to him. Blood trickled down his face, and Sukara could not bring herself to feel the slightest compassion. He reached out, smiling, almost placatory—as if seeking exoneration for his deeds to date.

Sukara found herself wanting to ask him how he could take innocent lives and live with himself, but at the same time all she wanted to do was to pull the trigger and kill the bastard.

Tell him, the voice said, *to deactivate his implant.*

Faltering, Sukara said, "Deactivate your implant!"

The killer smiled. "What? And let the alien into my head? I'd rather die."

He advanced at step, a hand outstretched. "I know I can't appeal to the alien, but you, Sukara, do you know what it is to take a life?"

Sukara managed a smile. "You tried to kill me, and my baby. You are... *evil*. Don't you think you deserve to die?"

"There is no such thing as evil," the man said. "Merely those who are weak, and those who are strong."

Sukara stared at him through sudden tears. "And I am strong," she said.

The killer moved, dived towards her, and at that precise second Sukara blacked out.

TWENTY-NINE

HOMECOMING

Vaughan stood in the observation nacelle as *The Spirit of Olympus* materialised over the Bay of Bengal.

His relief at having escaped Mallory in one piece had soon turned to frustration. For two days he had slept, stared out into the grey of voidspace, or read in a bid to occupy his thoughts.

As soon as he reached the Station he would contact Kapinsky, bring her up to date on events on Mallory, and together they would attempt to locate the street-kid, Pham.

The ship stuttered from voidspace. Ahead, rising from the calm blue waters of the ocean, as solid as an anvil, was Bengal Station. Vaughan felt an odd sense of homecoming.

As the ship approached, he looked along the sheer, kilometre-high western façade of the Station, trying to pinpoint the long viewscreen of his apartment. He thought he saw it—a tiny silver lozenge among thousands of others, and wondered what Sukara would be doing there. It was seven in the morning, Indian time, and Su would be getting up and fixing breakfast. He smiled as he considered the look on her face in an hour or so when he walked through the door.

The ship slowed and came in over the edge of the Station. Down below he made out Himachal Park, reduced to the size of an architect's model, with early risers out for a morning stroll. The spaceport was as busy as ever, with ships arriving and departing in a constant flow. *The Spirit of Olympus* decelerated, inching towards a docking ring and finally connecting with a peal that reverberated throughout the length of the ship.

Vaughan shouldered his holdall and made for the exit. As he shuffled from the vessel, a 'port security team boarded, the telepaths amongst them scanning the minds of the alighting passengers.

At customs he made for the Station Nationals channel, showed his ID to a tired officer, and stepped out onto the vast floor of the arrivals terminal. He paused to tap Kapinsky's code into his handset.

Her sharp face appeared after a long delay. She looked tired. "Vaughan. I was trying to get some sleep."

"It's eight in the morning, Kapinsky."

"I just got back from India. I'm beat."

"Okay, but we need to meet. I've learned a lot. I'm seeing Sukara for an hour or two, but I'll be at the office around midday, okay?"

Kapinsky nodded. "I need my beauty sleep, Vaughan. But okay, I'll see you then."

He decided to walk home. It would take about ten minutes. The alternative, a train to the nearest 'chute station, would take longer at this time of day.

He shouldered his holdall and set off for the exit. Later he'd try to work out with Kapinsky how to go about locating the street-kid, Pham. Of course, there was always the possibility that the killer had found her while he'd been away, in which case they would face the almost impossible task of trying to work out where the Hortavan might have transmitted itself to—always supposing that there had been an unshielded mind in the vicinity when its host was killed.

Vaughan tried not to think about that.

He was about to step through the exit when he heard a small voice behind him.

"Mr Vaughan! Mr Vaughan!"

He turned.

A skinny Thai waif in a Tigers' T-shirt and baggy red shorts smiled timorously at him. "Mr Vaughan! Khar said that I had to find you. He said that he would help you."

"Pham?" he said, incredulous.

She nodded, her big eyes wide beneath her jet fringe. "Khar said I shouldn't go back to your apartment. He said I'd be in danger. I had to come here, find you."

Vaughan shook his head, trying to take in her words. "Khar is...?" he began, then tapped the code into his handset and activated his implant.

Her small mind flared, along with the background mind-noise of a thousand other citizens, and Vaughan concentrated. The Hortavan xenopath, Khar, had ridden her mind until a day ago. After that, she'd had no contact with it.

Yesterday the Hortavan had warned her against entering the apartment, where for the past five days she'd lived with Sukara.

Alarm hit him with a sickening rush. He took her hand. "Come with me!"

"Ah-cha."

He hurried from the 'port, the little girl running at his side in order to keep up. The contents of her mind filled his, her thoughts and emotions, dreams and desires. Dominant in her mind was how wonderful the past few days had been, living in the plush apartment with Sukara. Vaughan found himself holding back tears. He scanned for the alien in her mind, but found nothing.

He shut down his implant as they headed for the nearest 'chute station.

"The alien in your mind, Pham—has it left?"

She looked up at him as she jogged along. "Khar has gone?"

"You didn't know?"

"I thought he was being quiet."

"Do you know *when* it might have left you?" he asked as they boarded a downchute cage with a couple of businessmen and dropped to Level Two.

She shook her head.

But why had Khar warned her against entering the apartment, Vaughan thought as they exited the 'chute cage and hurried along the boulevard towards Chittapuram. What if the killer had traced Pham there, had forced entry and...

Sukara!

Fear exploded through him. He ran, then remembered Pham. She was stumbling after him. He scooped her up, slung her onto his back and jogged along the corridor towards his apartment.

It seemed farther away than he recalled from his leisurely strolls with Sukara, and for some reason the corridors were crowded this morning. The journey seemed to take an age.

Five minutes later he approached the last observation viewscreen before their door, and paused. He lowered Pham to the floor and stood her against the viewscreen. "Stay there until I call you, okay?"

She nodded, once. "Ah-cha," she said obediently.

He took a deep breath, trying to control his heartbeat as he hurried along the corridor. He stopped outside the sliding door to his apartment, wishing that he had never given Sukara the mind-shield so that he might read her now, reassure himself that she was okay.

His hand shaking uncontrollably, he fumbled with his key-card and swiped the door open.

He stepped inside, a solid block of incipient grief frozen in his chest.

He saw the dead Westerner first. He lay on the floor on his back, a hole the size of a fist in his chest.

And then he saw Sukara. She lay in the sunken sofa, her eyes closed. In the middle of her forehead was the small, round entry point of a laser. Grief ripped painfully through him—followed, instantly, by a voice in his head.

Do not worry, Vaughan. Sukara is well. The assassin killed her, but I healed her.

Groggily, Sukara opened her eyes, stared up at him, and smiled. She reached into her pocket, pulled something from it, and tossed it across the room.

"Activate your implant, Jeff, for me."

He almost fell into the bunker and pulled her into his arms.

He had sworn he would never read her mind, but now he activated his handset. The alien in her head withdrew, as if curling itself up, and instantly her mind flared, and Vaughan was rocked by the force of her emotions. He read her love for him as she wrapped her arms around his neck and sobbed.

Later he fetched a blanket from the bedroom and draped it over the killer's corpse, then stepped from the apartment and looked along the corridor. He called Pham's name, and her head peeped around the corner of the observation gallery. He signalled for her to join him.

She ran along the corridor. "Is Sukara...?" she began.

Vaughan smiled and gestured through the door, and Pham sped in and launched herself at Sukara. Vaughan followed her and closed the door behind him.

He held Sukara and the street-kid while they cried tears of relief and Vaughan marvelled at the purity of his wife's mind.

"He killed me, Jeff! The killer killed me, but the alien brought me back to life. And then..." She shook her head. "I have no memory of how the killer died."

Vaughan experienced, through her memories, the events of the previous day.

Khar spoke in her mind: *I took control, Sukara. You were weakening, and anyway I did not want you to live with the memory of what I did then.*

"*You* shot the killer?"

I took control of you and did the only thing possible, to save you. I have kept you unconscious until now, to aid the healing process.

He said to the alien, "I've been to Mallory, and experienced what Scheering is doing to your race. I've returned to Earth to help you."

The alien said to him, *There is only one way our salvation might be achieved, Vaughan. If you will allow me into your mind, I will tell you...*

"Please," Vaughan murmured, and wondered what it might feel like to share his head with an alien being.

He deactivated his mind-shield.

"Goodbye, Khar," Sukara said.

Seconds later he felt a moment of dizziness, a quick heat in his head, and then a voice, *There. I am one with you.*

To Vaughan's surprise, it was not dissimilar to reading a human mind. He was not physically aware of the presence in his head, but could detect its thoughts and emotions, alien and largely unreadable as they were.

Vaughan said, "I'll contact Kapinsky, get her to bring her cam and chu over, okay?"

You are one step ahead of me, my friend, said the voice in his head.

Vaughan entered Kapinsky's code into his handset. She appeared on the screen, scowling at having been pulled from sleep. "Vaughan? What now?"

"I have the killer, Kapinsky," he said. "He's dead."

"What?"

"I'm at my apartment. Get over here and bring your chu and the digiCam, okay? I'll explain when you get here." He cut the connection.

Sukara and Pham were holding each other and staring at him. "Jeff," Sukara said, "will you please tell me what's happening?"

He took Sukara's hand and led her into the sunken sofa. She sat down next to him, Pham perched beyond her, staring at Vaughan with big eyes as he ordered his thoughts and explained what had happened to him on Mallory.

THIRTY

SCHEERING

While Sukara and Pham were in the kitchen, fixing coffee, Kapinsky knelt beside the killer's corpse and peeled off his chu to reveal a balding European in his forties. She photographed the man's true face and downloaded the image into the memory of her own chu.

Vaughan went through the killer's jacket, found his ID card, and slipped it into his pocket.

Two minutes later Kapinsky held up the mesh mask of the chu and conjured the dead man's face.

"How's that, Vaughan?" The killer's head hung from Kapinsky's right hand, as if she'd beheaded the guy and was parading the trophy in triumph.

"It looks good enough to convince Scheering," he said.

"What does the alien in your head think about it?" Kapinsky asked.

Khar said, *The likeness is perfect. Your build, Vaughan, is superficially similar to the assassin's. If*

*you wear the man's jacket, then Scheering will have
no intimation of our deception, until too late.*

Vaughan said to Kapinsky, "Khar's satisfied."

"And you say the alien knows where Scheering'll
be?"

He nodded. "When Khar was in Kormier's head,
he tried to access Scheering. Kormier knew Scheering, his itinerary."

"So where's Scheering now?" Kapinsky asked.

Khar said, *He is in his villa until twelve every day,
when he heads by air-car to the Scheering-Lassiter
headquarters. I will direct you to the villa. Though
security is tight, you will have no trouble entering
his residence with the killer's ID.*

Vaughan reported this to Kapinsky. She indicated
the killer. "What about the stiff?"

"We'll wait till we've got Scheering, then call in
the cops." He looked at his watch. It was ten.
"We've plenty of time to get to Scheering's place
before midday."

They had coffee in the kitchen while Vaughan
explained to Sukara what they were doing.

She looked alarmed. "I don't want you to go,
Jeff!"

"Su, I'll be fine. There's nothing to worry about,
okay?"

"I'll look after him, kid," Kapinsky said.

Vaughan kissed Sukara and pulled the chu over
his head, the elastic nexus clamping his face. She
winced. "Jeff!" She shook her head. "You don't
know how much that looks like him."

"Stay here until I get back." He chucked Pham
under the chin. "See you later, Pham."

Sukara followed him to the door, her eyes avoiding the covered corpse, and embraced him.

He pulled on the killer's jacket, waved at Sukara, and stepped into the corridor. It was midday, and the corridors were crowded with citizens going about their business. Vaughan felt a tightness in his chest, an apprehension. At the same time he was aware of Khar in his head, soothing him.

Five minutes later they took the upchute to Level One and boarded an air-taxi to Scheering's villa on the north side of the Station.

As the flier screamed over the sunlit Station, Khar said, *You experienced the slaughter of my kind on Mallory. Your memories are painful.*

It is painful, he thought in reply, to witness what my fellow humans are capable of in the name of exploration, colonisation—in the name of making money.

I have experienced much goodness in your race, Khar said. *Kormier, Pham, Sukara, and yourself.*

Vaughan smiled. Bit-part players, he thought back at the alien.

A human, many years ago, said that power corrupts.

That's a frightening thought, Khar—the idea that we are all potential evildoers given the attainment of power.

Khar smiled in his head. *There is a flaw in your argument, Vaughan. In my experience, truly good humans do not crave power.*

Is it not power I crave now to end Scheering's genocide of your race? Vaughan thought.

Not so much power, the alien told him, *as the temporary ability to right a wrong.*

I just hope it works, Vaughan thought.

It will, my friend. Thanks to you, my people will survive.

Vaughan thought about that. The fact was overwhelming, so much so that he could not take it in. Through the simple actions he was taking now, he would ensure the continued existence of an alien race on a planet light years from Earth.

He glanced through the side window. They were banking over the edge of the 'port, coming down in a wide area of designer grassland dotted with expensive villas. Scheering's residence overlooked the ocean, a sprawling split-level mansion surrounded by a high fence and accessed through a wrought iron gate.

The taxi settled on an adjacent landing pad and Kapinsky instructed the driver to wait. "I'll stay here," she said to Vaughan. She passed him a small automatic, along with the anaesthetic spray, synthiflesh, and a scalpel. He concealed them in his jacket.

Kapinsky punched his shoulder. "Good luck, Vaughan."

"Back in ten minutes," he said confidently and slipped from the flier.

He took a breath, aware of Khar in his head, steadying his nerves, and walked across the landing pad to the gate in the high perimeter fence. He activated his implant and scanned the mansion. As he suspected, there was not the slightest sign of mental activity from the building: Scheering and his employees were shielded.

He thumbed the intercom and hung the killer's ID card before a staring camera lens. "I've come to see Scheering. Priority."

A voice spoke from the grille. "Where you been, Keilor? The Old Man's been waiting. Okay, get yourself in here."

The gate swung slowly open and Vaughan slipped through and approached the mansion through a garden arrayed with miniature palms and bougainvillaea, the sunlight bringing him out in an uncomfortable sweat. Guards strolled along the crazy-paved pathways, armed with laser carbines. Around the perimeter fence, more guards patrolled with snarling dogs.

Vaughan paused before the front door, wondering whether protocol dictated he should enter or ring the bell. No sooner had he had the thought, than he felt a stirring in his head. Khar, dictating his actions...

He rang the bell, and a second later a silver-suited heavy pulled open the door and ushered him in. "The Old Man's in his study, Keilor. Go on through." The bodyguard indicated a door at the end of a long, timber-floored corridor. Vaughan nodded and made his way towards it, Khar subliminally easing his nerves.

The first hurdle over, he thought. The chu fooled the heavy, at least.

Be calm, Khar said. *You will succeed.*

He paused before the door, took a deep breath and knocked. Of course, if Scheering were not alone...

"Come in, Keilor."

He opened the door and stepped inside. The first thing that struck him was the size of the room. He had expected a medium-sized study, not this great open space of timber flooring and white walls, backed by a vast window that looked out over the dazzling azure sea.

The second thing Vaughan noted, with relief, was that Scheering was alone.

The head of the Scheering-Lassiter organisation, the biggest multicolonial concern in the galaxy, one of the wealthiest men on this or any other planet, sat behind a big wooden desk at the far end of the room, leaning forward and staring at his visitor. He was silver-haired and heavy-jowled. Even seated, there was something imposing, almost regal, in his bearing. He was like an enthroned monarch, imperiously aware of his power.

"The girl? You said you'd bring her in by midday."

Vaughan knew he should approach the desk and spray Scheering in the face with the anaesthetic, take no risks and get the job done as quickly and efficiently as possible.

Instead, something made him deviate from the script. He walked across the room until he was a couple of metres from the desk, staring down at Scheering.

Then he slipped the pistol from his jacket and levelled it. "Raise your hands. Stand up and back away from the desk."

Scheering's big face formed a faltering smile. "Keilor, this is some kind of stunt, right? A joke?"

"Stand up!" Vaughan snapped, stepping forward and aiming the pistol at Scheering's forehead.

Scheering stood quickly, toppling his chair and backing towards the picture window.

"Hands up!"

Obediently, Scheering raised his fat paws. "Keilor?" he peered at Vaughan, doubtfully.

Be careful, Khar warned.

Vaughan reached up and removed the chu.

The colour drained from Scheering's face. He shook his head and said in a croak, "What do you want? If it's money, that can be arranged."

Vaughan could not help but smile. "Is that how you get out of every problem, Scheering? Throw money at it? Or are some problems too difficult to buy your way out of? What do you do then?"

"I don't know what you're talking about."

"If you can't buy what you want, you employ violence, right? You either hire assassins like Keilor, or send your armies in to kill innocents."

"What do you want?" Scheering tried to imbue the question with authority, but his voice wavered.

"I want to bring an end to the slaughter of aliens on Mallory," Vaughan said, and delighted at the look of alarm that briefly filled Scheering's eyes.

He walked around the desk, keeping the pistol aimed at Scheering. "Sit down. On the floor!"

The big man looked at the polished timber flooring as if the indignity of sitting upon it was beyond him. Vaughan stepped forward, brandishing the weapon, and Scheering clumsily fell to his knees, then manoeuvred his bulk into a sitting position against the glass.

Vaughan swivelled the chair Scheering had just vacated and sat down, leaning forward. "Tell me something, do you manage to sleep with the thought that you're personally responsible for the deaths of hundreds, thousands, of aliens?"

Scheering managed a smile. He seemed to have overcome his initial shock, taken stock of the situation. He rallied, perhaps buying time. "It was a choice between the continued prosperity of six million colonists on Mallory and the lives of a few thousand aliens." He shrugged. "It was no choice, my friend. I look after my people."

"You look after yourself," Vaughan said. "You look after your investors, your shareholders. You do evil and call it good."

"As I am fond of telling the man you impersonated," Scheering smiled, "there is no such thing as good and evil, only—"

"Only those who are strong, and those who are weak," Vaughan finished.

Scheering stared at him. "And Keilor?" he said. "What did you do—?"

"He's dead," Vaughan replied. "He wasn't strong enough, in the end."

Fear showed in Scheering's eyes. "What do you want?"

"Personally," Vaughan said, "I want to kill you. The animal in me wants recompense for all the misery and suffering you and your company have caused, to aliens and humans alike."

Scheering was sweating, and it had nothing to do with the sunlight streaming in through the window at his back. A trickle ran from his brow and tracked down the side of his nose. For a second, Vaughan mistook it for a tear.

Scheering said, "You do realise, don't you, that this office is monitored? You don't think I'd overlook such a security risk?"

Vaughan smiled. "Monitored? Then your security team must be looking the other way. I don't see anyone rushing to your aid."

Scheering moved, then. For a man of his bulk, he leapt up with surprising agility. He flung himself towards the wall, reaching out for a security alarm.

Vaughan stood and kicked out, connecting with the man's padded gut. Scheering grunted and slumped to the floor. Vaughan stood over him and kicked out again, this time turning Scheering onto his back.

The millionaire stared up at him, something quailing and defeated in his eyes. Vaughan smiled. Revenge was sweet.

"How would you like to die, Scheering? A quick laser pulse to the head, killing you instantly? Or should I strangle you, slowly? Give you time to think about all the people you ordered Keilor to murder, all the Hortavans you massacred?"

"Don't kill me!" Scheering pleaded.

Vaughan laughed. "Kill you? I'd like to, but death's too good for you. I came here with not the slightest intention of killing you."

Scheering blinked up at him. "Then what?" he said, a pitiful note of desperation in his voice.

"I want you to live to regret your actions on Mallory," Vaughan said. "I want you to see the error of your policy there, and overturn it."

Scheering blinked. "I... I understand. My life, for promises—"

Vaughan cut in. "As if I'd trust you to keep promises!"

The millionaire stammered, "Then how?"

Vaughan smiled. "Think about it. How can I let you live, and be assured that things will change on

Mallory? You're a greedy man, Scheering. You have vested interests. Nothing comes between you and profits. Not even a race of innocent aliens."

"I don't understand."

"I said think about it. I'm going to let you live, and you're going to change your policy on Mallory."

Sudden understanding flared in Scheering's eyes. "No!"

Vaughan smiled. "Yes. I have a Hortavan xenopath riding in my head."

He was rewarded, then, by an expression of total fear on Scheering's overweight face. "No! You can't!"

Vaughan moved. He knelt on Scheering's chest, ensuring he hurt the millionaire. "This is for all those innocent whose lives you've destroyed, Scheering."

He pulled the spray from his pocket and gave Scheering a short blast, just enough to subdue him without knocking him out entirely. He wanted the bastard awake while he did what he had to do next.

He ripped open the front of Scheering's silk shirt and located the discreet bulge of his implanted mind-shield just below the right clavicle. Scheering stared up at him, terror in his eyes. He looked, Vaughan thought, like a rat confronted by a cobra about to strike.

The millionaire slurred, "No, please…"

Vaughan sliced with the scalpel, making a bloody incision through the man's chest. Scheering made a low moan of pain and protest, and when Vaughan looked up he saw that the millionaire was weeping.

He pressed down on the rectangular bulge beneath Scheering's flabby pectoral, and the bloody mind-shield slipped out. He tossed it across the room.

His implant still activated, Vaughan was swamped by a maelstrom of rage and ego, fear and dread. The millionaire knew what was about to happen, and Vaughan read a terrible sense of loss as Scheering began to understand that everything he had worked and schemed for, the power he had accrued over the decades, was quickly coming to an end.

The ego of the man sickened him, and he deactivated his implant. The ensuing mind-silence was an instant relief.

"No," Scheering moaned. "You can't do this."

"Think again, pal."

Khar stirred in Vaughan's head. *There are no words to thank you enough, my friend. I will be in touch. Goodbye, Vaughan.*

Farewell, Vaughan thought, and felt a dizzying heat pass through his head as Khar vacated his mind and lodged itself in Scheering's consciousness.

Vaughan retrieved the shield and slipped it back under the sliced flesh of Scheering's chest, then sealed the wound with synthi-flesh. The millionaire struggled, too enfeebled to get to his feet.

"Vaughan..."

It was Scheering's voice, but modulated, softened.

"Khar?"

"I am in control, Vaughan. If you would assist me..."

Vaughan helped the millionaire to his feet, then eased him onto the chair behind the desk.

Scheering stared at him, and Vaughan told himself that he could detect, somewhere behind the man's eyes, the tempering sensibility of the alien.

Scheering gestured. "I... I am in full control of Scheering, though to inhabit the mind responsible for such atrocities..." He fell silent, then smiled. "To have such power at one's fingertips," he said, "such means to effect good in the galaxy..."

Vaughan said, "What will the world think when Scheering becomes an altruist?"

Khar-in-Scheering smiled. "That," he said, "will be very interesting."

Vaughan moved around the desk, found the chu where he'd dropped it and pulled the mask over his head.

He reached out and shook the man's hand. "Goodbye, Khar," he said.

"I will be in contact, Vaughan. Perhaps you and your family would like to visit Mallory, one day?"

Vaughan nodded. "I'd like that," he said.

"The blessings of my kind go with you, my friend."

Vaughan turned and left the study. He walked along the corridor, towards the front door. The heavy appeared, grinning. "The Old Man give you a roasting, huh?"

Vaughan smiled. "Too right, bud," he said, and stepped through the front door.

The sunlight dazzled, warming him. He crossed the garden, affecting nonchalance as he passed the guards, hurried through the wrought iron gates to the landing pad.

He slipped into the back seat of the air-taxi.

Kapinsky peered at him. "You took your time. I was getting worried."

He pulled off the chu and passed it to Kapinsky, along with the pistol. "It's done," he said, and sat back as the flier lifted, turned and carried him south, towards home.

He felt, suddenly, very light-headed. He thought ahead, to life with Sukara and their daughter. He would throw himself with pleasure into such small-scale domesticity, while on a distant colony world an alien race enjoyed a secure future. It was a dichotomy too wondrous to comprehend.

He stared out through the side window at the Station passing far below, and something in him wanted to laugh out loud in delight.

FAMILY LIFE

Pham couldn't stop herself from crying when Sukara passed her the baby.

They were sitting in the sofa bunker in the Level Two apartment. Sukara had arrived home from hospital just an hour earlier.

"Like to hold her, Pham?" Sukara asked.

Pham stared at the tiny, scrunched up baby in the crook of Sukara's arm. She looked up at Jeff, as if asking his permission. He smiled and gestured for her to go ahead.

Sukara eased the tiny bundle into her arms, and Pham stared at little Li's tiny face, touched her minuscule fingers, and she wept. Sukara leaned over and kissed the top of her head.

"So beautiful," Pham murmured.

Jeff's handset chimed and he accessed the call.

The screen showed the thin face of Lin Kapinsky, Jeff's business partner. "Hey, Jeff—you heard the news?"

"What?"

"Switch on to Channel Ten."

Sukara grabbed the controls and zapped the wallscreen across the room. The screen flared, showing an overweight Westerner in a silver-grey suit. He was standing at a dais, flanked by other important-looking men and women, and reading from a softscreen.

"Hey," Jeff said. "That's Scheering."

He looked at Pham and smiled. Scheering was the man who Khar now lived in, she knew. She watched the screen as the man made his speech.

"And therefore the scaled withdrawal of the human population on the former colony world of Mallory will begin at midnight tonight, and from today forward the rights of the sentient beings known as the Hortavans will be recognised as sovereign..." He went on, detailing the exodus.

On Jeff's screen, Lin Kapinsky said, "Scheering contacted me an hour ago, Jeff. He's finalised payment for the work you did on Mallory. How does fifty thousand baht sound?"

Jeff smiled. "Should keep the wolf from the door for a while."

"Of course, I'll be taking my cut."

"And me with my growing family," Jeff smiled.

Lin said, "Oh, I almost forgot about that—congratulations, Jeff. What does it feel like to have a daughter?"

Jeff reached out and stroked Li's cheek. Then he lifted Pham onto his knee. "Two daughters, Lin. We officially adopted Pham a couple of days ago."

"Hell, Jeff, you'll be so busy housekeeping you won't have time to work for me. Speaking of which..."

"I'm on holiday, Lin."

The face on the screen smiled. "Sure you are, Jeff. But back next week, okay? We have work to do!"

Jeff laughed and cut the connection.

Pham looked up at him and stroked his unshaven chin. "Fifty thousand baht, Jeff? Ice creams all round?"

Sukara laughed and ruffled Pham's hair.

"Hey," Jeff said. "Why not? Let's find an expensive café up top and celebrate, okay?"

His handset chimed again. Pham made out a small, wrinkled face staring out of the screen.

She looked up at Jeff. He seemed amazed. "Breitenbach? Christ, where the hell are you?"

The old man laughed. "Where else?" he said. "Bengal Station."

"When did you get in?"

"This morning," Breitenbach said. "It appears I've been evicted from Mallory."

"I've just heard the news."

"You know something? I think I'll miss those mountains." The old man laughed. "Anyway, I was hoping we might meet. I want to hear all about what happened."

"That'll be great."

Breitenbach smiled, then said, "I have a lot to thank you for, Mr Vaughan."

Jeff arranged to meet the old man later that day, and cut the connection.

"Who's Breitenbach, Jeff?" Pham asked.

"Tell you all about him over ice cream," he said. He reached out and stroked Sukara's cheek.

Pham looked down at the tiny baby in her lap. My little sister, she thought. And it came to her with amazement, not for the first time, that she was part of a real and loving family.

The girl who, three months ago, had left Level Twenty would never have believed it possible.

Later, with Li swaddled in a papoose on Sukara's chest and Pham riding on Jeff's shoulders, they left the apartment and rose into the sunlight.

ABOUT THE AUTHOR

Eric Brown's first short story was published in *Interzone* in 1987, and he sold his first novel, *Meridian Days*, in 1992. He has won the British Science Fiction Award twice for his short stories and has published thirty books: SF novels, collections, books for teenagers and younger children, and he writes a monthly SF review column for *The Guardian*. His latest books include the novella, *Starship Summer*, and the novel *Kéthani*. He is married to the writer and mediaevalist Finn Sinclair and they have a daughter, Freya.

His website can be found at:
www.ericbrown.co.uk

NECROPATH

A BENGAL STATION NOVEL

ERIC BROWN

www.solarisbooks.com ISBN: 978-1-84416-649-7

Bengal Station: an exotic spaceport that dominates the ocean between India and Burma. Jaded telepath, Jeff Vaughan, is employed by the authorities to monitor incoming craft. When he discovers a sinister cult, he's drawn into a deadly investigation. Not only must he solve a series of murders, but he has to save himself from the psychopath out to kill him.

◗ SOLARIS SCIENCE FICTION